Introducing Discworld . . .

The Discworld is a world not totally unlike our own, except that it is flat, and magic is as integral as gravity to the way it works. Though some of its inhabitants are witches, dwarfs, wizards and even policemen, their stories are fundamentally about people being people.

The Discworld novels can be read in any order, but the Death series is a good place to start.

Discworld novels starring Death

Mort
Reaper Man
Soul Music
Hogfather
Thief of Time

A full list of the Discworld novels in order can be found at the end of this book

Terry Pratchett was the acclaimed creator of the global bestselling Discworld series, the first of which, *The Colour of Magic*, was published in 1983. In all, he was the author of over fifty bestselling books which have sold over 100 million copies worldwide. His novels have been widely adapted for stage and screen, and he was the winner of multiple prizes, including the Carnegie Medal. He was awarded a knighthood for services to literature in 2009, although he always wryly maintained that his greatest service to literature was to avoid writing any.

SOUL MUSIC

Discworld™: A Death Novel

TERRY PRATCHETT

PENGUIN BOOKS

TRANSWORLD PUBLISHERS
Penguin Random House, One Embassy Gardens,
8 Viaduct Gardens, London SW11 7BW
www.penguin.co.uk

Transworld is part of the Penguin Random House group of companies
whose addresses can be found at global.penguinrandomhouse.com

First published in Great Britain in 1994 by Victor Gollancz Ltd
Corgi edition published 1995
Corgi edition reissued 2005
Corgi edition reissued 2013
Penguin paperback edition published 2022

A CIP catalogue record for this book
is available from the British Library.

ISBN
9781804990377 (B format)

Typeset in Minion by Jouve (UK), Milton Keynes.
Printed and bound in Great Britain by Clays Ltd, Elcograf S.p.A.

The authorized representative in the EEA is Penguin Random House Ireland,
Morrison Chambers, 32 Nassau Street, Dublin D02 YH68.

Penguin Random House is committed to a sustainable
future for our business, our readers and our planet. This book
is made from Forest Stewardship Council® certified paper.

SOUL MUSIC

THE HISTORY

This is a story about memory. And this much can be remembered . . .

. . . that the Death of the Discworld, for reasons of his own, once rescued a baby girl and took her to his home between the dimensions. He let her grow to become sixteen because he believed that older children were easier to deal with than younger children, and this shows that you can be an immortal anthropomorphic personification and still get things, as it were, dead wrong . . .

. . . that he later hired an apprentice called Mortimer, or Mort for short. Between Mort and Ysabell there was an instant dislike and everyone knows what that means in the long term. As a substitute for the Grim Reaper Mort was a spectacular failure, causing problems that led to a wobbling of Reality and a fight between him and Death which Mort lost . . .

. . . and that, for reasons of his own, Death spared his life and sent him and Ysabell back into the world.

No one knows why Death started to take a practical interest in the human beings he had worked with for so long. It was probably just curiosity. Even the most efficient rat-catcher will sooner or later take an interest in rats. They might watch rats live and die, and record every detail of rat existence, although they may never themselves actually know what it is like to run the maze.

But if it is true that the act of observing changes the thing which is observed,* it's even more true that it changes the observer.

Mort and Ysabell got married.

They had a child.

This is also a story about sex and drugs and Music With Rocks In.

Well . . .

. . . one out of three ain't bad.

Actually, it's only thirty-three per cent, but it could be worse.

*Because of quantum.

WHERE TO FINISH?

A dark, stormy night. A coach, horses gone, plunging through the rickety, useless fence and dropping, tumbling into the gorge below. It doesn't even strike an outcrop of rock before it hits the dried river-bed far below, and erupts into fragments.

Miss Butts shuffled the paperwork nervously.

Here was one from the gel aged six:

What We Did On our Holidys: What I did On my holidys I staid with grandad he has a big White hors and a garden it is al Black. We had Eg and chips.

Then the oil from the coach-lamps ignites and there is a second explosion, out of which rolls – because there are certain conventions, even in tragedy – a burning wheel.

And another paper, a drawing done at age seven. All in black. Miss Butts sniffed. It wasn't as though the gel had only a black crayon. It was a fact that the Quirm College for Young Ladies had quite expensive crayons of all colours.

* * *

And then, after the last of the ember spits and crackles, there is silence.

And the watcher.

Who turns, and says to someone in the darkness:

YES. I COULD HAVE DONE SOMETHING.

And rides away.

Miss Butts shuffled paper again. She was feeling distracted and nervous, a feeling common to anyone who had much to do with the gel. Paper usually made her feel better. It was more dependable.

Then there had been the matter of . . . the accident.

Miss Butts had broken such news before. It was an occasional hazard when you ran a large boarding school. The parents of many of the gels were often abroad on business of one sort or another, and it was sometimes the kind of business where the chances of rich reward go hand in hand with the risks of meeting unsympathetic men.

Miss Butts knew how to handle these occasions. It was painful, but the thing ran its course. There was shock and tears, and then, eventually, it was all over. People had ways of dealing with it. There was a sort of script built into the human mind. Life went on.

But the child had just sat there. It was the *politeness* that scared the daylights out of Miss Butts. She was not an unkind woman, despite a lifetime of being gently dried out on the stove of education, but she was conscientious and a stickler for propriety and thought she knew how this sort of thing should go and was vaguely annoyed that it wasn't going.

'Er . . . if you would like to be alone, to have a cry—' she'd prompted, in an effort to get things moving on the right track.

'Would that help?' Susan had said.

It would have helped Miss Butts.

All she'd been able to manage was: 'I wonder if, perhaps, you fully understood what I have told you?'

The child had stared at the ceiling as though trying to work out a difficult problem in algebra and then said, 'I expect I will.'

It was as if she'd already known, and had dealt with it in some way. Miss Butts had asked the teachers to watch Susan carefully. They'd said that was hard, because . . .

There was a tentative knock on Miss Butts's study door, as if it was being made by someone who'd really prefer not to be heard. She returned to the present.

'Come,' she said.

The door swung open.

Susan always made no sound. The teachers had all remarked upon it. It was uncanny, they said. She was always in front of you when you least expected it.

'Ah, Susan,' said Miss Butts, a tight smile scuttling across her face like a nervous tick over a worried sheep. 'Please sit down.'

'Of course, Miss Butts.'

Miss Butts shuffled the papers.

'Susan . . .'

'Yes, Miss Butts?'

'I'm sorry to say that it appears you have been missed in lessons again.'

'I don't understand, Miss Butts.'

The headmistress leaned forward. She felt vaguely annoyed with herself, but . . . there was something frankly unlovable about the child. Academically brilliant at the things she liked doing, of course, but that was just it; she was brilliant in the same way that a diamond is brilliant, all edges and chilliness.

'Have you been . . . doing it?' she said. 'You promised you were going to stop this silliness.'

'Miss Butts?'

'You've been making yourself invisible again, haven't you?'

Susan blushed. So, rather less pinkly, did Miss Butts. I mean, she thought, it's *ridiculous.* It's against all reason. It's— oh, no . . .

She turned her head and shut her eyes.

'Yes, Miss Butts?' said Susan, just before Miss Butts said, 'Susan?'

Miss Butts shuddered. This was something else the teachers had mentioned. Sometimes Susan answered questions just before you asked them . . .

She steadied herself.

'You're still sitting there, are you?'

'Of course, Miss Butts.'

Ridiculous.

It wasn't invisibility, she told herself. She just makes herself inconspicuous. She . . . who . . .

She concentrated. She'd written a little memo to herself against this very eventuality, and it was pinned to the file.

She read:

You are interviewing Susan Sto Helit. Try not to forget it.

'Susan?' she ventured.

'Yes, Miss Butts?'

If Miss Butts concentrated, Susan was sitting in front of her. If she made an effort, she could hear the gel's voice. She just had to fight against a pressing tendency to believe that she was alone.

'I'm afraid Miss Cumber and Miss Greggs have complained,' she managed.

'I'm always in class, Miss Butts.'

'I dare say you are. Miss Traitor and Miss Stamp say they see you all the time.' There'd been quite a staffroom argument about that.

'Is it because you *like* Logic and Maths and don't like Language and History?'

Miss Butts concentrated. There was no way the child could have left the room. If she really stressed her mind, she could catch a suggestion of a voice saying, 'Don't know, Miss Butts.'

'Susan, it is really *most* upsetting when—'

Miss Butts paused. She looked around the study, and then glanced at a note pinned to the papers in front of her. She appeared to read it, looked puzzled for a moment, and then rolled it up and dropped it into the wastepaper basket. She picked up a pen and, after staring into space for a moment, turned her attention to the school accounts.

Susan waited politely for a while, and then got up and left as quietly as possible.

Certain things have to happen before other things. Gods play games with the fates of men. But first they have to get all the pieces on the board, and look all over the place for the dice.

It was raining in the small, mountainous country of Llamedos. It was always raining in Llamedos. Rain was the country's main export. It had rain mines.

Imp the bard sat under the evergreen, more out of habit than any real hope that it would keep the rain off. Water just dribbled through the spiky leaves and formed rivulets down the twigs, so that it was really a sort of rain concentrator. Occasional *lumps* of rain would splat on to his head.

He was eighteen, extremely talented and, currently, not at ease with his life.

He tuned his harp, his beautiful new harp, and watched the rain, tears running down his face and mingling with the drops.

Gods *like* people like this.

It is said that whosoever the gods wish to destroy, they first make mad. In fact, whosoever the gods wish to destroy, they first hand the equivalent of a stick with a fizzing fuse and Acme Dynamite Company written on the side. It's more interesting, and doesn't take so long.

Susan mooched along the disinfectant-smelling corridors. She wasn't particularly worried about what Miss Butts was going to think. She didn't usually worry about what anyone thought. She didn't know why people forgot about her when she wanted them to, but afterwards they seemed a bit embarrassed about raising the subject.

Sometimes, some teachers had trouble seeing her. This was fine. She'd generally take a book into the classroom and read it peacefully, while all around her The Principal Exports of Klatch happened to other people.

It was, undoubtedly, a beautiful harp. Very rarely a craftsman gets something so right that it is impossible to imagine an improvement. He hadn't bothered with ornamentation. That would have been some kind of sacrilege.

And it was new, which was very unusual in Llamedos. Most of the harps were old. It wasn't as if they wore out. Sometimes they needed a new frame, or a neck, or new strings – but the *harp* went on. The old bards said they got better as they got older, although old men tend to say this sort of thing regardless of daily experience.

Imp plucked a string. The note hung in the air, and faded. The harp was fresh and bright and already it sang out like a bell. What it might be like in a hundred years' time was unimaginable.

His father had said it was rubbish, that the future was written in stones, not notes. That had only been the start of the row.

And then he'd said things, and *he'd* said things, and suddenly the world was a new and unpleasant place, because things can't be unsaid.

He'd said, 'You don't know anything! You're just

a stupid old man! But I'm giving my life to music! One day soon *everyone* will say I was the greatest musician in the world!'

Stupid words. As if any bard cared for any opinions except those of other bards, who'd spent a lifetime learning how to listen to music.

But said, nevertheless. And, if they're said with the right passion and the gods are feeling bored, sometimes the universe will reform itself around words like that. Words have always had the power to change the world.

Be careful what you wish for. You never know who will be listening.

Or what, for that matter.

Because, perhaps, something could be drifting through the universes, and a few words by the wrong person at the right moment may just cause it to veer in its course . . .

Far away in the bustling metropolis of Ankh-Morpork there was a brief crawling of sparks across an otherwise bare wall and then . . .

. . . there was a shop. An old musical instrument shop. No one remarked on its arrival. As soon as it appeared, it had always been there.

Death sat staring at nothing, chinbone resting on his hands.

Albert approached very carefully.

It had continually puzzled Death in his more introspective moments, and this was one of them, why his servant always walked the same path across the floor.

I MEAN, he thought, CONSIDER THE SIZE OF THE ROOM . . .

. . . which went on to infinity, or as near infinity as makes no difference. In fact it was about a mile. That's big for a room, whereas infinity you can hardly see.

Death had got rather flustered when he'd created the house. Time and space were things to be manipulated, not obeyed. The internal dimensions had been a little too generous. He'd forgotten to make the outside bigger than the inside. It was the same with the garden. When he'd begun to take a little more interest in these things, he'd realized the role people seemed to think that *colour* played in concepts like, for example, roses. But he'd made them black. He liked black. It went with anything. It went with everything, sooner or later.

The humans he'd known – and there had been a few – had responded to the impossible size of the rooms in a strange way, by simply ignoring them.

Take Albert, now. The big door had opened, Albert had stepped through, carefully balancing a cup and saucer . . .

. . . and a moment later had been well inside the room, on the edge of the relatively small square of carpet that surrounded Death's desk. Death gave up wondering how Albert covered the intervening space when it dawned on him that, to his servant, there was *no* intervening space . . .

'I've brought you some camomile tea, sir,' said Albert.

HMM?

'Sir?'

SORRY. I WAS THINKING. WHAT WAS IT YOU SAID?

'Camomile tea?'

I THOUGHT THAT WAS A KIND OF SOAP.

'You can put it in soap *or* tea, sir,' said Albert. He was worried. He was always worried when Death started to think about things. It was the wrong job for thinking about things. And he thought about them in the wrong way.

HOW VERY USEFUL. CLEAN INSIDE AND OUT.

Death put his chin on his hands again.

'Sir?' said Albert, after a while.

HMM?

'It'll get cold if you leave it.'

ALBERT . . .

'Yessir?'

I HAVE BEEN WONDERING . . .

'Sir?'

WHAT'S IT ALL ABOUT? SERIOUSLY? WHEN YOU GET RIGHT DOWN TO IT?

'Oh. Er. Couldn't really say, sir.'

I DIDN'T WANT TO DO IT, ALBERT. YOU KNOW THAT. NOW I KNOW WHAT SHE MEANT. NOT JUST ABOUT THE KNEES.

'Who, sir?'

There was no reply.

Albert looked back when he'd reached the door. Death was staring into space again. No one could stare quite like him.

Not being seen wasn't a big problem. It was the things that *she* kept seeing that were more of a worry.

There were the dreams. They were only dreams, of course. Susan knew that modern theory said that dreams were only images thrown up while the brain was filing the day's events. She would have been more reassured if the day's events had *ever* included flying white horses, huge dark rooms and lots of skulls.

At least they were only dreams. She'd seen other things. For example, she'd never mentioned the strange woman in the dormitory the night Rebecca Snell put a tooth under the pillow. Susan had watched her come through the open window and stand by the bed. She looked a bit like a milkmaid and not at all frightening, even though she had walked *through* the furniture. There had been the jingle of coins. Next morning the tooth had gone and Rebecca was richer by one 50-pence coin.

Susan hated that sort of thing. She knew that mentally unstable people told children about the Tooth Fairy, but that was no reason for one to exist. It suggested woolly thinking. She disliked woolly thinking, which in any case was a major misdemeanour under the regime of Miss Butts.

It was not, otherwise, a particularly bad one. Miss Eulalie Butts and her colleague, Miss Delcross, had founded the college on the astonishing idea that, since gels had nothing much to do until someone married them, they may as well occupy themselves with learning things.

There were plenty of schools in the world, but they were all run either by the various churches or by the Guilds. Miss Butts objected to churches on logical grounds and deplored the fact that the only Guilds that considered girls worth educating were the Thieves and the Seamstresses. But it was a big and dangerous world out there, and a gel could do worse than face it with a sound knowledge of geometry and astronomy under her bodice. For Miss Butts sincerely believed that there were no basic differences between boys and gels.

At least, none worth talking about.

None that Miss Butts would talk about, anyway.

And therefore she believed in encouraging logical thought and a healthy enquiring mind among the nascent young women in her care, a course of action which is, as far as wisdom is concerned, on a par with going alligator-hunting in a cardboard boat during the sinking season.

For example, when she lectured to the school, pointed chin trembling, on the perils to be found outside in the town, three hundred healthy enquiring minds decided that 1) they should be sampled at the earliest opportunity, and logical thought wondered 2) exactly how Miss Butts *knew* about them. And the high, spike-topped walls around the college grounds looked simple enough to anyone with a fresh mind full of trigonometry and a body honed by healthy fencing, calisthenics and cold baths. Miss Butts could make peril seem really *interesting.*

Anyway, that was the incident of the midnight visitor. After a while, Susan considered that she must have imagined it. That was the only logical explanation. And Susan was good at those.

* * *

Everyone, they say, is looking for something.

Imp was looking for somewhere to go.

The farm cart that had brought him the last stretch of the way was rumbling off across the fields.

He looked at the signpost. One arm pointed to Quirm, the other to Ankh-Morpork. He knew just enough to know that Ankh-Morpork was a big city, but built on loam and therefore of no interest to the druids in his family. He had three Ankh-Morpork dollars and some change. It probably wasn't very much in Ankh-Morpork.

He didn't know anything about Quirm, except that it was on the coast. The road to Quirm didn't look very worn, while the one to Ankh-Morpork was heavily rutted.

It'd be sensible to go to Quirm to get the feel of city life. It'd be sensible to learn a bit about how city people thought before heading for Ankh-Morpork, which they said was the largest city in the world. It'd be sensible to get some kind of job in Quirm and raise a bit of extra cash. It'd be sensible to learn to walk before he started to run.

Common sense told Imp all these things, so he marched off firmly towards Ankh-Morpork.

As far as looks were concerned, Susan had always put people in mind of a dandelion on the point of telling the time. The college dressed its gels in a loose navy-blue woollen smock that stretched from neck to just above the ankle – practical, healthy and as attractive as a plank. The waistline was somewhere around knee level. Susan was beginning to fill it out, however, in accordance with the ancient rules hesitantly and erratically alluded to by Miss Delcross in Biology and Hygiene. Gels left her class with the vague feeling that they were supposed to marry a rabbit. (Susan had left with the feeling that the cardboard skeleton on the hook in the corner looked like someone she'd known . . .)

It was her hair that made people stop and turn to watch her. It was pure white, except for a black streak. School regulations required that it be in two plaits, but it had an uncanny tendency to unravel itself and spring back into its preferred shape, like Medusa's snakes.*

And then there was the birthmark, if that's what it was. It only showed up if she blushed, when three faint pale lines appeared across her cheek and made it look exactly as though she'd been slapped. On the occasions when she was angry – and she was quite often angry, at the sheer stupidity of the world – they glowed.

In theory it was, around now, Literature. Susan hated Literature. She'd much prefer to read a good book. Currently she had Wold's *Logic and Paradox* open on her desk and was reading it with her chin in her hands.

She listened with half an ear to what the rest of the class was doing.

It was a poem about daffodils.

*The question seldom addressed is *where* Medusa had snakes. Underarm hair is an even more embarrassing problem when it keeps biting the top of the deodorant bottle.

Apparently the poet had liked them very much.

Susan was quite stoical about this. It was a free country. People could like daffodils if they wanted to. They just should not, in Susan's very definite and precise opinion, be allowed to take up more than a page to say so.

She got on with her education. In her opinion, school kept on trying to interfere with it.

Around her, the poet's vision was taken apart with inexpert tools.

The kitchen was built on the same gargantuan lines as the rest of the house. An army of cooks could get lost in it. The far walls were hidden in the shadows and the stovepipe, supported at intervals by soot-covered chains and bits of greasy rope, disappeared into the gloom somewhere a quarter of a mile above the floor. At least, it did to the eye of the outsider.

Albert spent his time in a small tiled patch big enough to contain the dresser, the table and the stove. And a rocking chair.

'When a man says "What's it all about then, seriously, when you get right down to it?" he's in a bad way,' he said, rolling a cigarette. 'So I don't know what it means when *he* says it. It's one of his fancies again.'

The room's only other occupant nodded. His mouth was full.

'All that business with his daughter,' said Albert. 'I mean . . . daughter? And then he heard about apprentices. Nothing would do but he had to go and get one! Hah! Nothing but trouble, that was. And you, too, come to think of it . . . you're one of his fancies. No offence meant,' he added, aware of who he was talking to. 'You worked out all right. You do a good job.'

Another nod.

'He always gets it wrong,' said Albert. 'That's the trouble. Like when he heard about Hogswatchnight? Remember that? We had to do the whole thing, the oak tree in a pot, the paper sausages, the pork dinner, him sitting there with a paper hat on saying IS THIS JOLLY? I made him a little desk ornament thing and he gave me a brick.'

Albert put the cigarette to his lips. It had been expertly rolled. Only an expert could get a rollup so thin and yet so soggy.

'It was a good brick, mind. I've still got it somewhere.'

SQUEAK, said the Death of Rats.

'You put your finger on it, right enough,' said Albert. 'At least, you would have done if you had a proper one. He always misses the point. You see, he can't get over things. He can't forget.'

He sucked on the wretched homemade until his eyes watered.

'"What's it all about, seriously, when you get right down to it?"' said Albert. 'Oh, dear.'

He glanced up at the kitchen clock, out of a special human kind of habit. It had never worked since Albert had bought it.

'He's normally in by this time,' he said. 'I'd better do his tray. Can't think what's keeping him.'

* * *

The holy man sat under a holy tree, legs crossed, hands on knees. He kept his eyes shut in order to focus better on the Infinite, and wore nothing but a loincloth in order to show his disdain of discly things.

There was a wooden bowl in front of him.

He was aware, after a while, that he was being watched. He opened one eye.

There was an indistinct figure sitting a few feet away. Later on, he was sure that the figure had been of . . . someone. He couldn't quite remember the description, but the person must certainly have had one. He was about . . . this tall, and sort of . . . definitely . . .

EXCUSE ME.

'Yes, my son?' His brow wrinkled. 'You are male, aren't you?' he added.

YOU TOOK A LOT OF FINDING. BUT I AM GOOD AT IT.

'Yes?'

I AM TOLD YOU KNOW EVERYTHING.

The holy man opened the other eye.

'The secret of existence is to disdain earthly ties, shun the chimera of material worth, and seek oneness with the Infinite,' he said. 'And keep your thieving hands off my begging bowl.'

The sight of the supplicant was giving him trouble.

I'VE SEEN THE INFINITE, said the stranger, IT'S NOTHING SPECIAL.

The holy man glanced around.

'Don't be daft,' he said. 'You can't *see* the Infinite. 'cos it's *infinite*.'

I HAVE.

'All right, what did it look like?'

IT'S BLUE.

The holy man shifted uneasily. This wasn't how it was supposed to go. A quick burst of the Infinite and a meaningful nudge in the direction of the begging bowl was how it was supposed to go.

''S black,' he muttered.

NOT, said the stranger, WHEN SEEN FROM THE OUTSIDE. THE NIGHT SKY IS BLACK. BUT THAT IS JUST SPACE. INFINITY, HOWEVER, IS BLUE.

'And I suppose you know what sound is made by one hand clapping, do you?' said the holy man nastily.

YES. *CL*. THE OTHER HAND MAKES THE *AP*.

'Ah-ha, no, you're wrong there,' said the holy man, back on firmer ground. He waved a skinny hand. 'No sound, see?'

THAT WASN'T A CLAP. THAT WAS JUST A WAVE.

'It *was* a clap. I just wasn't using both hands. What kind of blue, anyway?'

YOU JUST WAVED. I DON'T CALL THAT VERY PHILOSOPHICAL. DUCK EGG.

The holy man glanced down the mountain. Several people were approaching. They had flowers in their hair and were carrying what looked very much like a bowl of rice.

OR POSSIBLY EAU-DE-NIL.

'Look, my son,' the holy man said hurriedly, 'what exactly is it you want? I haven't got all day.'

YES, YOU HAVE. TAKE IT FROM ME.

'What do you *want*?'

WHY DO THINGS HAVE TO BE THE WAY THEY ARE?

'Well—'

YOU DON'T KNOW, DO YOU?

'Not *exactly.* The whole thing is meant to be a mystery, see?'

The stranger stared at the holy man for some time, causing the man to feel that his head had become transparent.

THEN I WILL ASK YOU A SIMPLER QUESTION. HOW DO HUMANS FORGET?

'Forget what?'

FORGET ANYTHING. EVERYTHING.

'It . . . er . . . it happens automatically.' The prospective acolytes had turned the bend on the mountain path. The holy man hastily picked up his begging bowl.

'Let's say this bowl is your memory,' he said, waving it vaguely. 'It can only hold so much, see? New things come in, so old things must overflow—'

NO. I REMEMBER EVERYTHING. EVERYTHING. DOORKNOBS. THE PLAY OF SUNLIGHT ON HAIR. THE SOUND OF LAUGHTER. FOOTSTEPS. EVERY LITTLE DETAIL. AS IF IT HAPPENED ONLY YESTERDAY. AS IF IT HAPPENED ONLY TOMORROW. *EVERYTHING.* DO YOU UNDERSTAND?

The holy man scratched his gleaming bald head.

'Traditionally,' he said, 'the ways of forgetting include joining the Klatchian Foreign Legion, drinking the waters of some magical river, no one knows where it is, and imbibing vast amounts of alcohol.'

AH, YES.

'But alcohol debilitates the body and is a poison to the soul.'

SOUNDS GOOD TO ME.

'Master?'

The holy man looked around irritably. The acolytes had arrived.

'Just a minute, I'm talking to—'

The stranger had gone.

'Oh, master, we have travelled for many miles over—' said the acolyte.

'Shut up a minute, will you?'

The holy man put out his hand, palm turned vertical, and waved it a few times. He muttered under his breath.

The acolytes exchanged glances. They hadn't expected this. Finally, their leader found a drop of courage.

'Master—'

The holy man turned and caught him across the ear. The sound this made was definitely a *clap.*

'Ah! Got it!' said the holy man. 'Now, what can I do for—'

He stopped as his brain caught up with his ears.

'What did he mean, *humans*?'

Death walked thoughtfully across the hill to the place where a large white horse was placidly watching the view.

He said, GO AWAY.

The horse watched him warily. It was considerably more intelligent than most horses, although this was not a difficult achievement. It seemed aware that things weren't right with its master.

I MAY BE SOME TIME, said Death.

And he set out.

It wasn't raining in Ankh-Morpork. This had come as a big surprise to Imp.

What had also come as a surprise was how fast money went. So far he'd lost three dollars and twenty-seven pence.

He'd lost it because he'd put it in a bowl in front of him while he played, in the same way that a hunter puts out decoys to get ducks. The next time he'd looked down, it had gone.

People came to Ankh-Morpork to seek their fortune. Unfortunately, other people sought it too.

And people didn't seem to want bards, even ones who'd won the mistletoe award and centennial harp in the big Eisteddfod in Llamedos.

He'd found a place in one of the main squares, tuned up and played. No one had taken any notice, except sometimes to push him out of the way as they hurried past and, apparently, to nick his bowl. Eventually, just when he was beginning to doubt that he'd made the right decision in coming here at all, a couple of watchmen had wandered up.

'That's a harp he's playing, Nobby,' said one of them, after watching Imp for a while.

'Lyre.'

'No, it's the honest truth, I'm—' The fat guard frowned and looked down.

'You've just been waiting all your life to say

that, ain't you, Nobby,' he said. 'I bet you was *born* hoping that one day someone'd say "That's a harp" so you could say "lyre", on account of it being a pun or play on words. Well, har har.'

Imp stopped playing. It was impossible to continue, in the circumstances.

'It *is* a harp, actualllly,' he said. 'I won it in—'

'Ah, you're from Llamedos, right?' said the fat guard. 'I can tell by your accent. Very musical people, the Llamedese.'

'Sounds like garglin' with gravel to *me*,' said the one identified as Nobby. 'You got a licence, mate?'

'Llicence?' said Imp.

'Very hot on licences, the Guild of Musicians,' said Nobby. 'They catch you playing music without a licence, they take your instrument and they shove—'

'Now, now,' said the other watchman. 'Don't go scaring the boy.'

'Let's just say it's not much fun if you're a piccolo player,' said Nobby.

'But surelly music is as free as the air and the sky, see,' said Imp.

'Not round here it's not. Just a word to the wise, friend,' said Nobby.

'I never ever heard of a Guilld of Musicians,' said Imp.

'It's in Tin Lid Alley,' said Nobby. 'You want to be a musician, you got to join the Guild.'

Imp had been brought up to obey the rules. The Llamedese were very law-abiding.

'I shallll go there directlly,' he said.

The guards watched him go.

'He's wearing a nightdress,' said Corporal Nobbs.

'Bardic robe, Nobby,' said Sergeant Colon. The guards strolled onwards. 'Very bardic, the Llamedese.'

'How long d'you give him, sarge?'

Colon waved a hand in the flat rocking motion of someone hazarding an informed guess.

'Two, three days,' he said.

They rounded the bulk of Unseen University and ambled along The Backs, a dusty little street that saw little traffic or passing trade and was therefore much favoured by the Watch as a place to lurk and have a smoke and explore the realms of the mind.

'You know salmon, sarge,' said Nobby.

'It is a fish of which I am aware, yes.'

'You know they sell kind of slices of it in tins . . .'

'So I am given to understand, yes.'

'Weell . . . how come all the tins are the same size? Salmon gets thinner at both ends.'

'Interesting point, Nobby. I think—'

The watchman stopped, and stared across the street. Corporal Nobbs followed his gaze.

'That shop,' said Sergeant Colon. 'That shop there . . . was it there yesterday?'

Nobby looked at the peeling paint, the little grime-encrusted window, the rickety door.

''Course,' he said. 'It's *always* been there. Been there *years*.'

Colon crossed the street and rubbed at the grime. There were dark shapes vaguely visible in the gloom.

'Yeah, right,' he mumbled. 'It's just that . . . I mean . . . was it there for years *yesterday*?'

'You all right, sarge?'

'Let's go, Nobby,' said the sergeant, walking away as fast as he could.

'Where, sarge?'

'Anywhere not here.'

In the dark mounds of merchandise, something felt their departure.

Imp had already admired the Guild buildings – the majestic frontage of the Assassins' Guild, the splendid columns of the Thieves' Guild, the smoking yet still impressive hole where the Alchemists' Guild had been up until yesterday. And it was therefore disappointing to find that the Guild of Musicians, when he eventually located it, wasn't even a building. It was just a couple of poky rooms above a barber shop.

He sat in the brown-walled waiting room, and waited. There was a sign on the wall opposite. It said 'For Your Comforte And Convenience YOU WILL NOT SMOKE'. Imp had never smoked in his life. Everything in Llamedos was too soggy to smoke. But he suddenly felt inclined to try.

The room's only other occupants were a troll and a dwarf. He was not at ease in their company. They kept looking at him.

Finally the dwarf said, 'Are you elvish?'

'Me? No!'

'You look a bit elvish around the hair.'

'Not ellvish at allll. Honestlly.'

'Where you from?' said the troll.

'Llamedos,' said Imp. He shut his eyes. He knew

what trolls and dwarfs traditionally did to people suspected of being elves. The Guild of Musicians could take lessons.

'What dat you got dere?' said the troll. It had two large squares of darkish glass in front of its eyes, supported by wire frames hooked around its ears.

'It's a harp, see.'

'Dat what you play?'

'Yes.'

'You a druid, den?'

'No!'

There was silence again as the troll marshalled its thoughts.

'You *look* like a druid in dat nightie,' it rumbled, after a while.

The dwarf on the other side of Imp began to snigger.

Trolls disliked druids, too. Any sapient species which spends a lot of time in a stationary, rock-like pose objects to any other species which drags it sixty miles on rollers and buries it up to its knees in a circle. It tends to feel it has cause for disgruntlement.

'Everyone dresses like this in Llamedos, see,' said Imp. 'But I'm a bard! I'm not a druid. I hate rocks!'

'Whoops,' said the dwarf quietly.

The troll looked Imp up and down, slowly and deliberately. Then it said, without any particular trace of menace, 'You not long in dis town?'

'Just arrived,' said Imp. I won't even reach the door, he thought. I'm going to be mashed into a pulp.

'Here is some free advice what you should know.

It is free advice I am giving you gratis for nothing. In dis town, "rock" is a word for troll. A bad word for troll used by stupid humans. You call a troll a rock, you got to be prepared to spend some time looking for your head. Especially if you looks a bit elvish around de ears. Dis is free advice 'cos you are a bard and maker of music, like me.'

'Right! Thank you! Yes!' said Imp, awash with relief.

He grabbed his harp and played a few notes. That seemed to lighten the atmosphere a bit. Everyone knew elves had never been able to play music.

'Lias Bluestone,' said the troll, extending something massive with fingers on it.

'Imp y Celyn,' said Imp. 'Nothing to do with moving rocks around at allll in any way!'

A smaller, more knobbly hand was thrust at Imp from another direction. His gaze travelled up its associated arm, which was the property of the dwarf. He was small, even for a dwarf. A large bronze horn lay across his knees.

'Glod Glodsson,' said the dwarf. 'You just play the harp?'

'Anything with strings on it,' said Imp. 'But the harp is the queen of instruments, see.'

'I can blow anything,' said Glod.

'Realllly?' said Imp. He sought for some polite comment. 'That must make you very popullar.'

The troll heaved a big leather sack off the floor.

'*Dis* is what I play,' he said. A number of large round rocks tumbled out on to the floor. Lias picked one up and flicked it with a finger. It went *bam*.

'Music made from rocks?' said Imp. 'What do you callll it?'

'We call it *Ggroohauga*,' said Lias, 'which means, music made from rocks.'

The rocks were all of different sizes, carefully tuned here and there by small nicks carved out of the stone.

'May I?' said Imp.

'Be my guest.'

Imp selected a small rock and flicked it with his finger. It went *bop. A* smaller one went *bing.*

'What do you do with them?' he said.

'I bang them together.'

'And then what?'

'What do you mean, "And then what?"'

'What do you do after you've banged them together?'

'I bang them together again,' said Lias, one of nature's drummers.

The door to the inner room opened and a man with a pointed nose peered around it.

'You lot together?' he snapped.

There was indeed a river, according to legend, one drop of which would rob a man of his memory.

Many people assumed that this was the river Ankh, whose waters can be drunk or even cut up and chewed. A drink from the Ankh would quite probably rob a man of his memory, or at least cause things to happen to him that he would on no account wish to recall.

In fact there was another river that would do the

trick. There was, of course, a snag. No one knows where it is, because they're always pretty thirsty when they find it.

Death turned his attention elsewhere.

'Seventy-five dollllars?' said Imp. 'Just to pllay music?'

'That's twenty-five dollars registration fee, twenty per cent of fees, and fifteen dollars voluntary compulsory annual subscription to the Pension Fund,' said Mr Clete, secretary of the Guild.

'But we haven't got that much money!'

The man gave a shrug which indicated that, although the world did indeed have many problems, this was one of them that was not his.

'But maybe we shallll be ablle to pay when we've earned some,' said Imp weakly. 'If you could just, you know, llet us have a week or two—'

'Can't let you play anywhere without you being members of the Guild,' said Mr Clete.

'But we can't be members of the Guild until we've played,' said Glod.

'That's right,' said Mr Clete cheerfully. 'Hat. Hat. Hat.'

It was a strange laugh, totally mirthless and vaguely birdlike. It was very much like its owner, who was what you would get if you extracted fossilized genetic material from something in amber and then gave it a suit.

Lord Vetinari had encouraged the growth of the Guilds. They were the big wheels on which the clockwork of a well-regulated city ran. A drop of oil here . . . a spoke inserted there, of course . . . and by and large it all *worked.*

And gave rise, in the same way that compost gives rise to worms, to Mr Clete. He was not, by the standard definitions, a bad man; in the same way a plague-bearing rat is not, from a dispassionate point of view, a bad animal.

Mr Clete worked hard for the benefit of his fellow men. He devoted his life to it. For there are many things in the world that need doing that people don't want to do and were grateful to Mr Clete for doing for them. Keeping minutes, for example. Making sure the membership roll was quite up to date. Filing. *Organizing.*

He'd worked hard on behalf of the Thieves' Guild, although he hadn't been a thief, at least in the sense normally meant. Then there'd been a rather more senior vacancy in the Fools' Guild, and Mr Clete was no fool. And finally there had been the secretaryship of the Musicians.

Technically, he should have been a musician. So he bought a comb and paper. Since up until that time the Guild had been run by real musicians, and therefore the membership roll was unrolled and hardly anyone had paid any dues lately and the organization owed several thousand dollars to Chrysoprase the troll at punitive interest, he didn't even have to audition.

When Mr Clete had opened the first of the unkempt ledgers and looked at the unorganized mess, he had felt a deep and wonderful feeling. Since then, he'd never looked back. He had spent a long time looking down. And although the Guild had a president and council, it also had Mr Clete, who took the minutes and made sure things ran smoothly and smiled very quietly to himself. It is a strange but reliable fact that whenever men throw off the yoke of tyrants and set out to rule themselves there emerges, like a mushroom after rain, Mr Clete.

Hat. Hat. Hat. Mr Clete laughed at things in inverse proportion to the actual humour of the situation.

'But that's nonsense!'

'Welcome to the wonderful world of the Guild economy,' said Mr Clete. 'Hat. Hat. Hat.'

'What happens if we pllay without belonging to the Guilld, then?' said Imp. 'Do you confiscate our instruments?'

'To start with,' said the president. 'And then we sort of give them back to you. Hat. Hat. Hat. Incidentally . . . you're not elvish, are you?'

'Seventy-five dollars is *criminall*,' said Imp, as they plodded along the evening streets.

'Worse than criminal,' said Glod. 'I hear the Thieves' Guild just charges a percentage.'

'And dey give you a proper Guild membership and everything,' Lias rumbled. 'Even a pension. And dey have a day trip to Quirm and a picnic every year.'

'Music *should* be free,' said Imp.

'So what we going to do now?' said Lias.

'Anyone got any money?' said Glod.

'Got a dollar,' said Lias.

'Got some pennies,' said Imp.

'Then we're going to have a decent meal,' said Glod. 'Right here.'

He pointed up at a sign.

'Gimlet's Hole Food?' said Lias. 'Gimlet? Sounds dwarfish. Vermincelli and stuff?'

'Now he's doing troll food too,' said Glod. 'Decided to put aside ethnic differences in the cause of making more money. Five types of coal, seven types of coke and ash, sediments to make you dribble. You'll like it.'

'Dwarf bread too?' said Imp.

'*You* like dwarf bread?' said Glod.

'Llove it,' said Imp.

'What, *proper* dwarf bread?' said Glod. 'You *sure*?'

'Yes. It's nice and crunchy, see.'

Glod shrugged.

'That proves it,' he said. 'No one who likes dwarf bread can be elvish.'

The place was almost empty. A dwarf in an apron that came up to its armpits watched them over the top of the counter.

'You do fried rat?' said Glod.

'Best damn fried rat in the city,' said Gimlet.

'Okay. Give me four fried rats.'

'And some dwarf bread,' said Imp.

'And some coke,' said Lias patiently.

'You mean rat heads or rat legs?'

'No. Four fried rats.'

'And some coke.'

'You want ketchup on those rats?'

'No.'

'You *sure*?'

'No ketchup.'

'And some coke.'

'And two hard-boilled eggs,' said Imp.

The others gave him an odd look.

'Wellll? I just llike hard-boilled eggs,' he said.

'And some coke.'

'And two hard-boiled eggs.'

'And some coke.'

'Seventy-five dollars,' said Glod, as they sat down. 'What's three times seventy-five dollars?'

'Many dollars,' said Lias.

'More than two hundred dollllars,' said Imp.

'I don't think I've even *seen* two hundred dollars,' said Glod. 'Not while I've been awake.'

'We raise money?' said Lias.

'We can't raise money by being musicians,' said Imp. 'It's the Guilld llaw. If they catch you, they take your instrument and shove—' He stopped. 'Llet's just say it's not much fun for the piccollo pllayer,' he added from memory.

'I shouldn't think the trombonist is very happy either,' said Glod, putting some pepper on his rat.

'I can't go back home now,' said Imp. 'I said I'd . . . I can't go back home yet. Even if I *could*, I'd have to raise monolliths llike my brothers. Allll they care about is stone circlles.'

'If *I* go back home now,' said Lias, 'I'll be clubbing druids.'

They both, very carefully, sidled a little further away from each other.

'Then we play somewhere where the Guild won't

find us,' said Glod cheerfully. 'We find a club somewhere—'

'Got a club,' said Lias, proudly. 'Got a *nail* in it.'

'I mean a night club,' said Glod.

'Still got a nail in it at night.'

'I happen to know,' said Glod, abandoning that line of conversation, 'that there's a lot of places in the city that don't like paying Guild rates. We could do a few gigs and raise the money with *no* trouble.'

'Allll three of us together?' said Imp.

'Sure.'

'But we pllay dwarf music and human music and trollll music,' said Imp. 'I'm not sure they'llll go together. I mean, dwarfs llisten to dwarf music, humans llisten to human music, trolllls llisten to trollll music. What do we get if we mix it allll together? It'd be dreadfull.'

'We're getting along okay,' said Lias, getting up and fetching the salt from the counter.

'We're musicians,' said Glod. 'It's not the same with real people.'

'Yeah, right,' said the troll.

Lias sat down.

There was a cracking noise.

Lias stood up.

'Oh,' he said.

Imp reached over. Slowly and with great care he picked the remains of his harp off the bench.

'Oh,' said Lias.

A string curled back with a sad little sound.

It was like watching the death of a kitten.

'I won that at the Eisteddfod,' said Imp.

'Could you glue it back together?' said Glod, eventually.

Imp shook his head.

'There's no one left in Llamedos who knows how, see.'

'Yes, but in the Street of Cunning Artificers—'

'I'm real sorry. I mean real sorry, I don't know how it got dere.'

'It wasn't your faullt.'

Imp tried, ineffectually, to fit a couple of pieces together. But you couldn't repair a musical instrument. He remembered the old bards saying that. They had a soul. All instruments had a soul. If they were broken, the soul of them escaped, flew away like a bird. What was put together again was just a thing, a mere assemblage of wood and wire. It would play, it might even deceive the casual listener, but . . . You might as well push someone over a cliff and then stitch them together and expect them to come alive.

'Um . . . maybe we could get you another one, then?' said Glod. 'There's . . . a nice little music shop in The Backs—'

He stopped. Of *course* there was a nice little music shop in The Backs. It had *always* been there.

'In The Backs,' he repeated, just to make sure. 'Bound to get one there. In The Backs. Yes. Been there *years*.'

'Not one of these,' said Imp. 'Before a craftsman even touches the wood he has to spend two weeks sitting wrapped in a bullllock hide in a cave behind a waterfallll.'

'Why?'

'I don't know. It's traditionall. He has to get his mind pure of allll distractions.'

'There's bound to be something else, though,' said Glod. 'We'll buy something. You can't be a musician without an instrument.'

'I haven't got any money,' said Imp.

Glod slapped him on the back. 'That doesn't matter,' he said. 'You've got friends! We'll help you! Least we can do.'

'But we allll spent everything we had on this meall. There's no more money,' said Imp.

'That's a negative way of looking at it,' said Glod.

'Wellll, yes. We haven't got any, see?'

'I'll sort out something,' said Glod. 'I'm a dwarf. We know about money. Knowing about money is practically my middle name.'

'That's a *long* middle name.'

It was almost dark when they reached the shop, which was right opposite the high walls of Unseen University. It looked the kind of musical instrument emporium which doubles as a pawnshop, since every musician has at some time in his life to hand over his instrument if he wants to eat and sleep indoors.

'You ever bought anything in here?' said Lias.

'No . . . not that I remember,' said Glod.

'It shut,' said Lias.

Glod hammered on the door. After a while it opened a crack, just enough to reveal a thin slice of face belonging to an old woman.

'We want to buy an instrument, ma'am,' said Imp.

One eye and a slice of mouth looked him up and down.

'You human?'

'Yes, ma'am.'

'All right, then.'

The shop was lit by a couple of candles. The old woman retired to the safety of the counter, where she watched them very carefully for any signs of murdering her in her bed.

The trio moved carefully amongst the merchandise. It seemed that the shop had accumulated its stock from unclaimed pledges over the centuries. Musicians were often short of money; it was one definition of a musician. There were battle horns. There were lutes. There were drums.

'This is junk,' said Imp under his breath.

Glod blew the dust off a crumhorn and put it to his lips, achieving a sound like the ghost of a refried bean.

'I reckon there's a dead mouse in here,' he said, peering into the depths.

'It was all right before you blew it,' snapped the old woman.

There was an avalanche of cymbals from the other end of the shop.

'Sorry,' Lias called out.

Glod opened the lid of an instrument that was entirely unfamiliar to Imp. It revealed a row of keys; Glod ran his stumpy fingers over them, producing a sequence of sad, tinny notes.

'What is it?' whispered Imp.

'A virginal,' said the dwarf.

'Any good to us?'

'Shouldn't think so.'

Imp straightened up. He felt that he was being watched. The old lady *was* watching, but there was something else . . .

'It's no use. There's nothing here,' he said loudly.

'Hey, what was that?' said Glod.

'I said there's—'

'I heard something.'

'What?'

'There it is again.'

There was a series of crashes and thumps behind them as Lias liberated a double-bass from a drift of old music-stands and tried to blow down the sharp bit.

'There was a funny sound when you spoke,' said Glod. 'Say something.'

Imp hesitated, as people do when, after having used a language all their lives, they're told to 'say something'.

'Imp?' he said.

WHUM-Whum-whum.

'It came from—'

WHAA-Whaa-whaa.

Glod lifted aside a pile of ancient sheet-music. There was a musical graveyard behind it, including a skinless drum, a set of Lancre bagpipes without the pipes and a single maraca, possibly for use by a Zen flamenco dancer.

And something else.

The dwarf pulled it out. It looked, vaguely, like a guitar carved out of a piece of ancient wood by a blunt stone chisel. Although dwarfs did not, as a rule, play stringed instruments, Glod knew a guitar when he saw one. They were supposed to be shaped like a woman, but this was only the case if you thought women had no legs, a long neck and too many ears.

'Imp?' he said.

'Yes?'

Whauauaum. The sound had a saw-edged, urgent fringe to it. There were twelve strings, but the body of the instrument was solid wood, not at all hollow – it was more or less just a shape to hold the strings.

'It resonated to your voice,' said Glod.

'How can—?'

Whaum-wha.

Glod clamped his hand over the strings, and beckoned the other two closer.

'We're right by the University here,' he whispered. 'Magic leaks out. It's a well-known fact. Or maybe some wizard pawned it. Don't look a gift rat in the mouth. Can you play a guitar?'

Imp went pale.

'You mean like . . . follk music?'

He took the instrument. Folk music was not approved of in Llamedos, and the singing of it was rigorously discouraged; it was felt that anyone espying a fair young maiden one morning in May was entitled to take whatever steps they considered appropriate without someone writing it down. Guitars were frowned upon as being, well . . . too easy.

Imp struck a chord. It created a sound quite unlike anything he'd heard before – there were resonances and odd echoes that seemed to run and hide among the instrumental debris and pick up additional harmonics and then bounce back again. It made his spine itch. But you couldn't be even the *worst* musician in the world without *some* kind of instrument . . .

'Right,' said Glod.

He turned to the old woman.

'You don't call this a music instrument, do you?' he demanded. 'Look at it, half of it's not even there.'

'Glod, I don't think—' Imp began. Under his hand the strings trembled.

The old woman looked at the thing.

'Ten dollars,' she said.

'Ten dollars? *Ten dollars*?' said Glod. 'It's not worth two dollars!'

'That's right,' said the old woman. She brightened up a bit in a nasty way, as if looking forward to a battle in which no expense would be spared.

'And it's ancient,' said Glod.

'Antique.'

'Would you listen to that tone? It's ruined.'

'Mellow. You don't get craftsmanship like that these days.'

'Only because we've learned from experience!'

Imp looked at the thing again. The strings resonated by themselves. They had a blue tint to them and a slightly fuzzy look, as though they never quite stopped vibrating.

He lifted it close to his mouth and whispered, 'Imp.' The strings hummed.

Now he noticed the chalk mark. It was almost faded. And all it was was a mark. Just a stroke of the chalk . . .

Glod was in full flow. Dwarfs were said to be the keenest of financial negotiators, second only in acumen and effrontery to little old ladies. Imp tried to pay attention to what was going on.

'Right, then,' Glod was saying, 'it's a deal, yes?'

'A deal,' said the little old lady. 'And don't go spitting on your hand before we shake, that sort of thing's unhygienic.'

Glod turned to Imp. 'I think I handled that pretty well,' he said.

'Good. Llisten, this is a very—'

'Got twelve dollars?'

'What?'

'Something of a bargain, I think.'

There was a thump behind them. Lias appeared, rolling a very large drum and carrying a couple of cymbals under his arm.

'I said I'd got no money!' Imp hissed.

'Yes, but . . . well, *everyone* says they've got no money. That's sense. You don't want to go around saying you've got money. You mean you've *really* got no money?'

'No!'

'Not even twelve dollars?'

'No!'

Lias dumped the drum, the cymbals and a pile of sheet-music on the counter.

'How much for everything?' he said.

'Fifteen dollars,' said the old woman.

Lias sighed and straightened up. There was a distant look in his eyes for a moment, and then he hit himself on the jaw. He fumbled around inside his mouth with a finger and then produced—

Imp stared.

'Here, let me have a look,' said Glod. He snatched the thing from Lias's unprotesting fingers and examined it carefully. 'Hey! Fifty carats at least!'

'I'm not taking *that*,' said the old woman. 'It's been in a troll's mouth!'

'You eat eggs, don't you?' said Glod. 'Anyway, everyone knows trolls' teeth are pure diamond.'

The old woman took the tooth and examined it by candlelight.

'If I took it along to one of those jewellers in Nonesuch Street they'd tell me it's worth two hundred dollars,' said Glod.

'Well, I'm telling you it's worth fifteen right here,' said the old lady. The diamond magically disappeared somewhere about her person. She gave them a bright, fresh smile.

'*Why* couldn't we just take it off her?' said Glod, when they were outside.

'Because she's a poor defencelless olld woman,' said Imp.

'Exactly! My point exactly!'

Glod looked up at Lias.

'You got a whole mouthful of them things?'

'Yup.'

'Only I owe my landlord two months' re—'

'Don't even fink about it,' said the troll levelly.

Behind them, the door slammed shut.

'Look, cheer up,' said Glod. 'Tomorrow I'll find us a gig. Don't worry. I know everyone in this city. Three of us . . . that's a *band*.'

'We haven't even practised together properlly,' said Imp.

'We'll practise as we go along,' said Glod. 'Welcome to the world of professional musicianship.'

Susan did not know much about history. It always seemed a particularly dull subject. The same stupid things were done over and over again by tedious people. What was the point? One king was pretty much like another.

The class was learning about some revolt in which some peasants had wanted to stop being peasants and, since the nobles had won, had stopped being peasants *really quickly*. Had they bothered to learn to read and acquire some history books they'd have learned about the uncertain merits of things like scythes and pitchforks when used in a battle against crossbows and broadswords.

She listened half-heartedly for a while, until boredom set in, and then took out a book and let herself fade from the notice of the world.

SQUEAK!

Susan glanced sideways.

There was a tiny figure on the floor by her desk. It looked very much like a rat skeleton in a black robe, holding a very small scythe.

Susan looked back at her book. Such things did not exist. She was quite certain about that.

SQUEAK!

Susan looked down again. The apparition was still there. There had been cheese on toast for supper the previous night. In books, at least, you were supposed to expect things after a late-night meal like that.

'You don't exist,' she said. 'You're just a piece of cheese.'

SQUEAK?

When the creature was sure it had got her full attention, it pulled out a tiny hourglass on a silver chain and pointed at it urgently.

Against all rational considerations, Susan reached down and opened her hand. The thing climbed on to it – its feet felt like pins – and looked at her expectantly.

Susan lifted it up to eye level. All right, perhaps it *was* a figment of her imagination. She ought to take it seriously.

'You're not going to say something like "Oh, my paws and whiskers", are you?' she said quietly. 'If you do, I shall go and drop you in the privy.'

The rat shook its skull.

'And you're real?'

SQUEAK. SQUEAKSQUEAKSQUEAK—

'Look, I don't understand,' said Susan patiently. 'I don't speak rodent. We only do Klatchian in Modern Languages and I only know how to say "My aunt's camel has fallen in the mirage". And if you are imaginary, you might try to be a bit more . . . lovable.'

A skeleton, even a small one, is not a naturally lovable object, even if it has got an open countenance and a grin. But the feeling . . . no, she realized . . . the *memory* was creeping over her from somewhere that this one was not only real but on her side. It was an unfamiliar concept. Her side had normally consisted of her.

The late rat regarded Susan for a moment and then, in one movement, gripped the tiny scythe between its teeth and sprang off Susan's hand, landed on the classroom floor, and scuttled away between the desks.

'It's not even as if you've *got* paws and whiskers,' said Susan. 'Not proper ones, anyway.'

The skeletal rat stepped through the wall.

Susan turned back to her book and ferociously read Noxeuse's Divisibility Paradox, which demonstrated the impossibility of falling off a log.

They practised that very night, in Glod's obsessively neat lodgings. These were behind a tannery in Phedre Road, and were probably safe from the wandering ears of the Musicians' Guild. They were also freshly painted and well scrubbed. The tiny room sparkled. You never got cockroaches or rats or any kind of vermin in a dwarf home. At least, not while the owner could still hold a frying-pan.

Glod and Imp sat and watched Lias the troll hit his rocks.

'What d'you fink?' he said, when he'd finished.

'Is that allll you do?' said Imp, after a while.

'They're rocks,' said the troll, patiently. 'That's all you can do. Bop, bop, bop.'

'Hmm. Can I have a go?' said Glod.

He sat behind the array of stones and looked at them for a while. Then he rearranged a few of them, took a couple of hammers out of his toolbox, and tapped a stone experimentally.

'Now, let's see . . .' he said.

Bambam-bamBAM.

Beside Imp, the guitar strings hummed.

'Without A Shirt,' said Glod.

'What?' said Imp.

'It's just a bit of musical nonsense,' said Glod. 'Like "Shave and a haircut, two pence"?'

'Sorry?'

Bam-bam-a-bambam, bam*BAM*.

'Shave and haircut good value for two pence,' said Lias.

Imp looked hard at the stones. Percussion wasn't approved of in Llamedos either. The bards said that anyone could hit a rock or a hollow log with a stick. That wasn't *music*. Besides, it was . . . and here they'd drop their voices . . . too *animal*.

The guitar hummed. It seemed to pick up sounds.

Imp suddenly had a nagging feeling that there was a lot you could do with percussion.

'Can I try?' he said.

He picked up the hammers. There was the faintest of tones from the guitar.

Forty-five seconds later, he put down the hammers. The echoes died away.

'Why did you hit me on the helmet at the end there?' said Glod, carefully.

'Sorry,' said Imp. 'I think I got carried away. I thought you were a cymball.'

'It was very . . . unusual,' said the troll.

'The music's . . . in the stones,' said Imp. 'You just have to llet it out. There's music in everything, if you know how to find it.'

'Can I try dat riff?' said Lias. He took the hammers and shuffled around behind the stones again.

A-bam-bop-a-re-bop-a-bim-bam-boom.

'*What* did you do to them?' he said. 'They sound . . . wild.'

'Sounded good to me,' said Glod. 'Sounded a whole lot better.'

Imp slept that night wedged between Glod's very small bed and the bulk of Lias. After a while, he snored.

Beside him, the strings hummed gently in harmony. Lulled by their almost imperceptible sound, he'd completely forgotten about the harp.

Susan awoke. Something was tugging at her ear. She opened her eyes.

SQUEAK?

'Oh, *nooo*—'

She sat up in bed. The rest of the girls were asleep. The window was open, because the school encouraged fresh air. It was available in large amounts for free.

The skeletal rat leapt on to the window-ledge and then, when it had made sure she was watching, jumped into the night.

As Susan saw it, the world offered two choices. She could go back to bed, or she could follow the rat.

Which would be a stupid thing to do. Soppy people in books did that sort of thing. They ended up in some idiot world with goblins and feeble-minded talking animals. And they were such sad, wet girls. They always let things *happen* to them, without making any *effort*. They just went around saying things like 'My goodness me', when it was obvious that any sensible human being could soon get the place properly organized.

Actually, when you thought of it like that, it was tempting . . . The world held too much fluffy thinking. She always told herself that it was the job of people like Susan, if there were any more like her, to sort it out.

She pulled on her dressing-gown and climbed over the sill, holding on until the last moment and dropping into a flower-bed.

The rat was a tiny shape scurrying across the moonlit lawn. She followed it around to the stables, where it vanished somewhere in the shadows.

As she stood feeling slightly chilly and more than slightly an idiot, it returned dragging an object rather bigger than itself. It looked like a bundle of old rags.

The skeletal rat walked around the side of it and gave the ragged bundle a good hard kick.

'All *right*, all *right*!'

The bundle opened one eye, which swivelled around wildly until it focused on Susan.

'I warn you,' said the bundle, 'I don't do the N word.'

'I'm sorry?' said Susan.

The bundle rolled over, staggered upright and extended two scruffy wings. The rat stopped kicking it.

'I'm a raven, aren't I?' it said. 'One of the few birds who speak. The first thing people say is, oh, you're a raven, go on, say the N word . . . If I had a penny every time that's happened, I'd—'

SQUEAK.

'All *right*, all *right.*' The raven ruffled its feathers. 'This thing here is the Death of Rats. Note the scythe and cowl, yes? Death of Rats. Very big in the rat world.'

The Death of Rats bowed.

'Tends to spend a lot of time under barns and anywhere people have put down a plate of bran laced with strychnine,' said the raven. 'Very conscientious.'

SQUEAK.

'All right. What does it – he want with me?' said Susan. 'I'm not a rat.'

'Very perspicacious of you,' said the raven. 'Look, I didn't ask to do this, you know. I was asleep on my skull, next minute he had a grip on my leg. Being a raven, as I said, I'm naturally an occult bird—'

'Sorry,' said Susan. 'I know this is all one of those dreams, so I want to make sure I understand it. You said . . . you were asleep on your *skull*?'

'Oh, not my *personal* skull,' said the raven. 'It's someone else's.'

'Whose?'

The raven's eyes spun wildly. It never managed to

have both eyes pointing in the same direction. Susan had to resist trying to move around to follow them.

'How do I know? They don't come with a label on them,' it said. 'It's just a skull. Look . . . I work for this wizard, right? Down in the town. I sit on this skull all day and go "caw" at people—'

'Why?'

'*Because* a raven sitting on a skull and going "caw" is as much part of your actual wizarding *modus operandi* as the big dribbling candles and the old stuffed alligator hanging from the ceiling. Don't you know anything? I should have thought anyone knows that who knows anything about anything. Why, a proper wizard might as well not even have bubbling green stuff in bottles as be without his raven sitting on a skull and going "caw"—'

SQUEAK!

'Look, you have to lead up to things with humans,' said the raven wearily. One eye focused on Susan again. 'He's not one for subtleties, him. Rats don't argue questions of a philosophical nature when they're dead. Anyway, I'm the only person round here he knows who can talk—'

'Humans can talk,' said Susan.

'Oh, indeed,' said the raven, 'but the key point about humans, a crucial distinction you might say, is that they're not prone to being woken up in the middle of the night by a skeletal rat who needs an interpreter in a hurry. Anyway, humans can't see him.'

'I can see him.'

'Ah. I think you've put your digit on the nub,

crux and gist of it all,' said the raven. 'The marrow, as you might say.'

'Look,' said Susan, 'I'd just like you to know that I don't believe any of this. I don't believe there's a Death of Rats in a cowl carrying a scythe.'

'He's standing in front of you.'

'That's no reason to believe it.'

'I can see you've certainly had a *proper* education,' said the raven sourly.

Susan stared down at the Death of Rats. There was a blue glow deep in its eye sockets.

SQUEAK.

'The thing is,' said the raven, 'that he's gone again.'

'Who?'

'Your . . . grandfather.'

'Grandad Lezek? How can he be gone again? He's dead!'

'Your . . . er . . . *other* grandfather . . . ?' said the raven.

'I haven't got—'

Images rose from the mud at the bottom of her mind. Something about a horse . . . and there was a room full of whispers. And a bathtub, that seemed to fit in somewhere. And fields of wheat came into it, too.

'This is what happens when people try to educate their children,' said the raven, 'instead of telling them things.'

'I thought my other grandad was also . . . dead,' said Susan.

SQUEAK.

'The rat says you've got to come with him. It's very important.'

The image of Miss Butts rose like a Valkyrie in Susan's mind. This was *silliness.*

'Oh, no,' said Susan. 'It must be midnight already. And we've got a geography exam tomorrow.'

The raven opened its beak in astonishment.

'You can't be saying that,' it said.

'You really expect me to take instructions from a . . . a bony rat and a talking raven? I'm going back!'

'No, you're not,' said the raven. 'No one with any blood in them'd go back now. You'd never find things out if you went back now. You'd just get educated.'

'But I haven't got *time*,' Susan wailed.

'Oh, *time*,' said the raven. 'Time's mainly habit. Time is not a particular feature of things for *you*.'

'How—'

'You'll have to find out, won't you?'

SQUEAK.

The raven jumped up and down excitedly.

'Can I tell her? Can I tell her?' it squawked. It swivelled its eyes towards Susan.

'Your grandfather,' it said, 'is . . . (dah dah dah *DAH*) . . . Dea—'

SQUEAK!

'She's got to know some time,' said the raven.

'Deaf? My grandfather is deaf?' said Susan. 'You've got me out here in the middle of the night to talk about *hearing difficulties*?'

'I didn't say deaf, I said your grandfather is . . . (dah dah dah *DAH*) . . . D—'

SQUEAK!

'All *right*! Have it your way!'

Susan backed away while the two of them argued.

Then she grasped the skirts of her nightdress and ran, out of the yard and across the damp lawns. The window was still open. She managed, by standing on the sill of the one below, to grab the ledge and heave herself up and into the dormitory. She got into bed and pulled the blankets over her head . . .

After a while she realized that this was an unintelligent reaction. But she left them where they were, anyway.

She dreamed of horses and coaches and a clock without hands.

'D'you think we could have handled that better?'

SQUEAK? 'Dah dah dah *DAH*' SQUEAK?

'How did you expect me to put it. "Your grandfather is Death?" Just like that? Where's the sense of occasion? Humans like drama.'

SQUEAK, the Death of Rats pointed out.

'Rats is different.'

SQUEAK.

'I reckon I ought to call it a night,' said the raven. 'Ravens are not generally nocturnal, you know.' It scratched at its bill with a foot. 'Do you just do rats, or mice and hamsters and weasels and stuff like that as well?'

SQUEAK.

'Gerbils? How about gerbils?'

SQUEAK.

'Fancy that. I never knew that. Death of Gerbils,

too? Amazing how you can catch up with them on those treadmills—'

SQUEAK.

'Please yourself.'

There are the people of the day, and the creatures of the night.

And it's important to remember that the creatures of the night aren't simply the people of the day staying up late because they think that makes them cool and interesting. It takes a lot more than heavy mascara and a pale complexion to cross the divide.

Heredity can help, of course.

The raven had grown up in the forever-crumbling, ivy-clad Tower of Art, overlooking Unseen University in far Ankh-Morpork. Ravens are naturally intelligent birds, and magical leakage, which has a tendency to exaggerate things, had done the rest.

It didn't have a name. Animals don't normally bother with them.

The wizard who thought he owned him called him Quoth, but that was only because he didn't have a sense of humour and, like most people without a sense of humour, prided himself on the sense of humour he hadn't, in fact, got.

The raven flew back to the wizard's house, skimmed in through the open window, and took up his roost on the skull.

'Poor kid,' he said.

'That's destiny for you,' said the skull.

'I don't blame her for trying to be normal. Considering.'

'Yes,' said the skull. 'Quit while you're a head, that's what I say.'

The owner of a grain silo in Ankh-Morpork was having a bit of a crackdown. The Death of Rats could hear the distant yapping of the terriers. It was going to be a busy night.

It would be too hard to describe the Death of Rats's thought-processes, or even be certain that he had any. He had a feeling that he shouldn't have involved the raven, but humans set a great store by words.

Rats don't think very far ahead, except in general terms. In general terms, he was very, very worried. He hadn't expected education.

Susan got through the next morning without having to go non-existent. Geography consisted of the flora of the Sto Plains,* chief exports of the Sto Plains,† and the fauna of the Sto Plains.‡ Once you mastered the common denominator, it was straightforward. The gels had to colour in a map. This involved a lot of green. Lunch was Dead Man's Fingers and Eyeball Pudding, a healthy ballast for the afternoon's occupation, which was Sport.

This was the province of Iron Lily, who was

*Cabbages.

†Cabbages.

‡Anything that ate cabbages and didn't mind not having any friends.

rumoured to shave and lift weights with her teeth, and whose shouts of encouragement as she thundered up and down the touchline tended towards the nature of 'Get some ball, you bunch of soft nellies!'

Miss Butts and Miss Delcross kept their windows closed on games afternoon. Miss Butts ferociously read logic and Miss Delcross, in her idea of a toga, practised eurhythmics in the gym.

Susan surprised people by being good at sport. Some sport, anyway. Hockey, lacrosse and rounders, certainly. Any game that involved putting a stick of some sort in her hands and asking her to swing it, definitely. The sight of Susan advancing towards goal with a calculating look made any goalie lose all faith in her protective padding and throw herself flat as the ball flashed past at waist height, making a humming noise.

It was only evidence of the general stupidity of the rest of humanity, Susan considered, that although she was manifestly one of the best players in the school she never got picked for teams. Even fat girls with spots got picked before her. It was so infuriatingly unreasonable, and she could never understand why.

She'd explained to other girls how good she was, and demonstrated her skill, and pointed out just how stupid they were in not picking her. For some exasperating reason it didn't seem to have any effect.

This afternoon she went for an official walk instead. This was an acceptable alternative, provided girls went in company. Usually they went into town and bought stale fish and chips from an unfragrant shop in Three Roses Alley; fried food was considered unhealthy by Miss Butts, and therefore bought out of school at every opportunity.

Girls had to walk in groups of three or more. Peril, in Miss Butts's conjectural experience, couldn't happen to units of more than two.

In any case it was certainly unlikely to happen to any group that contained Princess Jade and Gloria Thogsdaughter.

The school's owners had been a bit bothered about taking a troll, but Jade's father was king of an entire mountain and it always looked good to have royalty on the roll. And besides, Miss Butts had remarked to Miss Delcross, it's our *duty* to encourage them if they show any inclination to become *real* people and the King is actually quite *charming* and assures me he can't even *remember* when he last ate anyone. Jade had bad eyesight, a note excusing her from unnecessary sunshine, and knitting chain mail in handicraft class.

Whereas Gloria was banned from sport because of her tendency to use her axe in a threatening manner. Miss Butts had suggested that an axe wasn't a *ladylike* weapon, even for a dwarf, but Gloria had pointed out that, on the contrary, it had been left to her by her grandmother who had owned it all her life and polished it every Saturday, even if she hadn't used it at all that week. There was something about the way she gripped it that made even Miss Butts give in. To show willing, Gloria left off her iron helmet and, while not shaving off her beard – there was no actual *rule* about girls not having beards a foot long – at least plaited it. And tied it in ribbons in the school colours.

Susan felt strangely at home in their company, and this had earned guarded praise from Miss Butts. It was nice of her to be such a chum, she said. Susan had been surprised. It had never occurred to her that anyone actually *said* a word like chum.

The three of them trailed back along the beech drive by the playing field.

'I don't understand sport,' said Gloria, watching the gaggle of panting young women stampeding across the pitch.

'There's a troll game,' said Jade. 'It's called *aargrooha*.'

'How's it played?' said Susan.

'Er . . . you rip off a human's head and kick it around with special boots made of obsidian until you score a goal or it bursts. But it's not played any more, of course,' she added quickly.

'I should think not,' said Susan.

'No one knows how to make the boots, I expect,' said Gloria.

'I expect if it was played now, someone like Iron Lily would go running up and down the touchline shouting, "Get some head, you soft nellies",' said Jade.

They walked in silence for a while.

'I think,' said Gloria, cautiously, 'that she probably wouldn't, actually.'

'I say, you two haven't noticed anything . . . odd lately, have you?' said Susan.

'Odd like what?' said Gloria.

'Well, like . . . rats . . .' said Susan.

'Haven't seen any rats in the school,' said Gloria. 'And I've had a good look.'

'I mean . . . strange rats,' said Susan.

They were level with the stables. These were normally the home of the two horses that pulled the school coach, and the term-time residence of a few horses belonging to gels who couldn't be parted from them.

There is a type of girl who, while incapable of cleaning her bedroom even at knifepoint, will fight for the privilege of being allowed to spend the day shovelling manure in a stable. It was a magic that hadn't rubbed off on Susan. She had nothing against horses, but couldn't understand all the snaffles, bridles and fetlocks business. And she couldn't see why they had to be measured in 'hands' when there were perfectly sensible inches around to do the job. Having watched the jodhpured girls who bustled around the stables, she decided it was because they couldn't understand complicated machines like rulers. She'd said so, too.

'All right,' said Susan. 'How about ravens?'

Something blew in her ear.

She spun around.

The white horse stood in the middle of the yard like a bad special effect. He was too bright. He glowed. He seemed like the only real thing in a world of pale shapes. Compared to the bulbous ponies that normally occupied the loose-boxes, he was a giant.

A couple of the jodhpured girls were fussing

around him. Susan recognized Cassandra Fox and Lady Sara Grateful, almost identical in their love of anything on four legs that went 'neigh' and their disdain for anything else, their ability to apparently look at the world with their teeth, and their expertise in putting at least four vowels in the word 'oh'.

The white horse neighed gently at Susan, and began to nuzzle her hand.

You're Binky, she thought. *I know you. I've ridden on you. You're . . . mine. I think.*

'I say,' said Lady Sara, 'who does he belong to?'

Susan looked around.

'What? Me?' she said. 'Yes. Me . . . I suppose.'

'Oeuwa? He was in the loose-box next to Browny. I didn't knoeuwa you had a horse here. You have to get permission from Miss Butts, you knoeuwa.'

'He's a present,' said Susan. 'From . . . someone . . . ?'

The hippo of recollection stirred in the muddy waters of the mind. She wondered why she'd said that. She hadn't thought of her grandfather for years. Until last night.

I remember the stable, she thought. *So big you couldn't see the walls. And I was given a ride on you once. Someone held me so I wouldn't fall off. But you couldn't fall off this horse. Not if he didn't want you to.*

'Oeuwa. I didn't know you rode.'

'I . . . used to.'

'There's extra fees, you knoeuwa. For keeping a horse,' said Lady Sara.

Susan said nothing. She strongly suspected they'd be paid.

'And you've got noeuwa tack,' said Lady Sara.

And Susan rose to it.

'I don't need any,' she said.

'Oeuwa, *bareback* riding,' said Lady Sara. 'And you steer by the ears, ya?'

Cassandra Fox said: 'Probably can't afford them, out in the *sticks.* And stop that dwarf looking at my pony. She's *looking* at my pony!'

'I'm only looking,' said Gloria.

'You were . . . salivating,' said Cassandra.

There was a pattering across the cobbles and Susan swung herself up and on to the horse's back.

She looked down at the astonished girls, and then at the paddock beyond the stables. There were a few jumps there, just poles balanced on barrels.

Without her moving a muscle, the horse turned and trotted into the paddock and turned towards the highest jump. There was a sensation of bunched energy, a moment of acceleration, and the jump passed underneath . . .

Binky turned and halted, prancing from one hoof to the other.

The girls were watching. All four of them had an expression of total amazement.

'Should it do that?' said Jade.

'What's the matter?' said Susan. 'Have none of you seen a horse jump before?'

'Yes. The interesting point is . . .' Gloria began, in that slow, deliberate tone of voice people use when they don't want the universe to shatter, '. . . is that, usually, they come down again.'

Susan looked.

The horse was standing on the air.

What sort of command was necessary to make a horse resume contact with the ground? It was an instruction that the equestrian sorority had not hitherto required.

As if understanding her thoughts, the horse trotted forward and down. For a moment the hoofs dipped *below* the field, as if the surface were no more substantial than mist. Then Binky appeared to determine where the ground level should be, and decided to stand on it.

Lady Sara was the first one to find her voice.

'We'll tell Miss Butts of *youewa,*' she managed.

Susan was almost bewildered with unfamiliar fright, but the petty-mindedness in the tones slapped her back to something approaching sanity.

'Oh yes?' she said. 'And *what* will you tell her?'

'You made the horse jump up and . . .' The girl stopped, aware of what she was about to say.

'Quite so,' said Susan. 'I expect that seeing horses float in the air is silly, don't you?'

She slipped off the horse's back, and gave the watchers a bright smile.

'It's against school rules, anyway,' muttered Lady Sara.

Susan led the white horse back into the stables, rubbed him down, and put him in a spare loose-box.

There was a rustling in the hay-rack for a moment. Susan thought she caught a glimpse of ivory-white bone.

'Those *wretched* rats,' said Cassandra, struggling

back to reality. 'I heard Miss Butts tell the gardener to put poison down.'

'Shame,' said Gloria.

Lady Sara seemed to have something boiling in her mind.

'Look, that horse didn't really stand in mid-air, did it?' she demanded. 'Horses can't do that!'

'Then it couldn't have done it,' said Susan.

'Hang time,' said Gloria. 'That's all it was. Hang time. Like in basketball.* Bound to be something like that.'

'Yes.'

'That's all it was.'

'Yes.'

The human mind has a remarkable ability to heal. So have the trollish and dwarfish minds. Susan looked at them in frank amazement. They'd all seen a horse stand on the air. And now they had carefully pushed it somewhere in their memories and broken off the key in the lock.

'Just out of interest,' she said, still eyeing the hay-rack, 'I don't suppose any of you know where there's a wizard in this town, do you?'

'I've found us somewhere to play!' said Glod.

'Where?' said Lias.

Glod told them.

'*The Mended Drum?*' said Lias. 'They throw *axes*!'

*Until an unfortunate axe incident, Gloria had been captain of the school basketball team. Dwarfs don't have height but they *do* have acceleration, and many a visiting team member got a nasty shock when Gloria appeared rising vertically out of the depths.

'We'd be safe there. The Guild won't play in there,' said Glod.

'Well, yah, dey lose members in there. Their *members* lose members,' said Lias.

'We'll get five dollars,' said Glod.

The troll hesitated.

'I could use five dollars,' he conceded.

'One-third of five dollars,' said Glod.

Lias's brow creased.

'Is that more or less than five dollars?' he said.

'Look, it'll get us exposure,' said Glod.

'I don't want exposure in de Drum,' said Lias. 'Exposure's the last thing I want in de Drum. In de Drum, I want something to hide behind.'

'All we have to do is play something,' said Glod. 'Anything. The new landlord is dead keen on pub entertainment.'

'I thought they had a one-arm bandit.'

'Yes, but he got arrested.'

There's a floral clock in Quirm. It's quite a tourist attraction.

It turns out to be not what they expect.

Unimaginative municipal authorities throughout the multiverse had made floral clocks, which turn out to be a large clock mechanism buried in a civic flowerbed with the face and numbers picked out in bedding plants.*

*Or methane crystals. Or sea anemones. The principle is the same. In any case, it soon fills up with whatever is the local equivalent of fast-food boxes and derelict lager cans.

But the Quirm clock is simply a round flower-bed, filled with twenty-four different types of flower, carefully chosen for the regularity of the opening and closing of their petals . . .

As Susan ran past, the Purple Bindweed was opening and Love-in-a-Spin was closing. This meant that it was about half past ten.

The streets were deserted. Quirm wasn't a night town. People who came to Quirm looking for a good time went somewhere else. Quirm was so respectable that even dogs asked permission before going to the lavatory.

At least, the streets were *almost* deserted. Susan fancied she could hear something following her, fast and pattering, moving and dodging across the cobbles so quickly that it was never more than a suspicion of a shape.

Susan slowed down as she reached Three Roses Alley.

Somewhere in Three Roses near the fish shop, Gloria had said. The gels were not encouraged to know about wizards. They did not figure in Miss Butts's universe.

The alley looked alien in the darkness. A torch burned in a bracket at one end. It merely made the shadows darker.

And, halfway along in the gloom, there was a ladder leaning against the wall and a young woman just preparing to climb it. There was something familiar about her.

She looked around as Susan approached, and seemed quite pleased to see her.

'Hi,' she said. 'Got change of a dollar, miss?'

'Pardon?'

'Couple of half-dollars'd do. Half a dollar is the rate. Or I'll take copper. Anything, really.'

'Um. Sorry. No. I only get fifty pence a week allowance anyway.'

'Blast. Oh, well, nothing for it.'

In so far as Susan could see, the girl did not appear to be the usual sort of young woman who made her living in alleys. She had a kind of well-scrubbed beefiness about her; she looked like a nurse of the sort who assist doctors whose patients occasionally get a bit confused and declare they're a bedspread.

She looked familiar, too.

The girl took a pair of pliers from a pocket in her dress, shinned up the ladder and climbed in through an upper window.

Susan hesitated. The girl had seemed quite businesslike about it all, but in her limited experience people who climbed ladders to get into houses at night were Miscreants whom Plucky Gels should Apprehend. And she might at least have gone to look for a watchman, had it not been for the opening of a door further up the alley.

Two men staggered out, arm in arm, and zigzagged happily towards the main street. Susan stepped back. No one bothered her when she didn't want to be noticed.

The men walked through the ladder.

Either the men weren't exactly solid, and they certainly sounded solid enough, or there was something wrong with the ladder. But the girl had climbed it . . .

. . . and was now climbing down again, slipping something into her pocket.

'Never even woke up, the little cherub,' she said.

'Sorry?' said Susan.

'Didn't have 50p on me,' said the girl. She swung the ladder easily up on to her shoulder. 'Rules are rules. I had to take another tooth.'

'Pardon?'

'It's all audited, you see. I'd be in real trouble if the dollars and teeth didn't add up. *You* know how it is.'

'I do?'

'Still, can't stay here talking all night. Got sixty more to do.'

'*Why* should I know? Do *what*? *Whom* to?' said Susan.

'Children, of course. Can't disappoint them, can I? Imagine their little faces when they lift up their little pillows, bless them.'

Ladder. Pliers. Teeth. Money. Pillows . . .

'You don't expect me to believe you're the Tooth Fairy?' said Susan suspiciously.

She touched the ladder. It felt solid enough.

'Not *the*,' said the girl. '*A*. I'm surprised *you* don't know that.'

She'd sauntered around the corner before Susan asked, 'Why me?'

''cos she can tell,' said a voice behind her. 'Takes one to know one.'

She turned. The raven was sitting in a small open window.

'You'd better come in,' it said. 'You can meet all sorts, out in that alley.'

'I already have.'

There was a brass plate screwed on the wall beside the door. It said: 'C V Cheesewaller, DM (Unseen) B. Thau, B.F.'

It was the first time Susan had ever heard metal speak.

'Simple trick,' said the raven, dismissively. 'It senses you looking at it. Just give—'

'C V Cheesewaller, DM (Unseen) B. Thau, B.F.'

'. . . shut up . . . just give the door a push.'

'It's locked.'

The raven gave her a beady-eyed look with its head on one side. Then it said: 'That stops you? Oh, well. I'll fetch the key.'

It appeared a moment later and dropped a large metal key on to the cobbles.

'Isn't the wizard in?'

'In, yes. In bed. Snoring his head off.'

'I thought they stayed up all night!'

'Not this one. Cup of cocoa around nine, dead to the world at five past.'

'I can't just let myself into his house!'

'Why not? You've come to see me. Anyway, I'm the brains of the outfit. He just wears the funny hat and does the hand waving.'

Susan turned the key.

It was warm inside. There was the usual wizardly paraphernalia – a forge, a bench with bottles and bundles strewn over it, a bookcase with books rammed in anyhow, a stuffed alligator hanging from the ceiling, some very big candles that were just lava streams of wax, and a raven on a skull.

'They get it all out of a catalogue,' said the raven. 'Believe me. It all comes in a big box. You think candles get dribbly like that by themselves? That's three days' work for a skilled candle dribbler.'

'You're just making that up,' said Susan. 'Anyway, you can't just buy a skull.'

'You know best, I'm sure, being educated,' said the raven.

'What were you trying to tell me last night?'

'Tell you?' said the raven, with a guilty look on its beak.

'All that dah-dah-dah-DAH stuff.'

The raven scratched its head.

'He said I wasn't to tell you. I was just supposed to warn you about the horse. I got carried away. Turned up, has it?'

'Yes!'

'Ride it.'

'I did. It can't be real! Real horses know where the ground is.'

'Miss, there's no horse realer than that one.'

'I know his name! I've ridden him before!'

The raven sighed, or at least made a sort of whistling noise which is as close to a sigh as a beak can get.

'Ride the horse. He's decided you're the one.'

'Where to?'

'That's for me not to know and you to find out.'

'Just supposing I was stupid enough to do it . . . can you kind of hint about what will happen?'

'Well . . . you've read books, I can see. Have you ever read any about children who go to a magical faraway kingdom and have adventures with goblins and so on?'

'Yes, of course,' said Susan, grimly.

'It'd probably be best if you thought along those lines,' said the raven.

Susan picked up a bundle of herbs and played with them.

'I saw someone outside who said she was the Tooth Fairy,' she said.

'Nah, couldn't've been *the* Tooth Fairy,' said the raven. 'There's at least three of them.'

'There's no such person. I mean . . . I didn't know, I thought that's just a . . . a story. Like the Sandman or the Hogfather.'*

'Ah,' said the raven. 'Changing our tone, yes? Not so much of the emphatic declarative, yes? A bit less

*According to rural legend – at least in those areas where pigs are a vital part of the household economy – the Hogfather is a winter myth figure who, on Hogswatchnight, gallops from house to house on a crude sledge drawn by four tusked wild boars to deliver presents of sausages, black puddings, pork scratchings and ham to all children who have been good. He says 'Ho ho ho' a lot. Children who have been bad get a bag full of bloody bones (it's these little details which tell you it's a tale for the little folk). There is a song about him. It begins: *You'd Better Watch Out . . .*

The Hogfather is said to have originated in the legend of a local king who, one winter's night, happened to be passing, or so he said, the home of three young women and heard them sobbing because they had no food to celebrate the midwinter feast. He took pity on them and threw a packet of sausages through the window.†

†Badly concussing one of them, but there's no point in spoiling a good legend.

of the "There's no such thing" and a bit more of the "I didn't know", yes?'

'Everyone knows – I mean, it's not logical that there's an old man in a beard who gives everyone sausages and chitterlings on Hogswatchnight, is it?'

'I don't know about logic. Never learned about logic,' said the raven. 'Living on a skull ain't exactly logical, but that's what I do.'

'And there can't be a Sandman who goes around throwing sand in children's eyes,' said Susan, but in tones of uncertainty. 'You'd . . . never get enough sand in one bag.'

'Could be. Could be.'

'I'd better be going,' said Susan. 'Miss Butts always checks the dorms on the stroke of midnight.'

'How many dormitories are there?' said the raven.

'About thirty, I think.'

'You believe she checks them *all* at midnight and you don't believe in the Hogfather?'

'I'd better be going anyway,' said Susan. 'Um. Thank you.'

'Lock up behind you and chuck the key through the window,' said the raven.

The room was silent after she'd gone, except for the crackle as coals settled in the furnace.

Then the skull said: 'Kids today, eh?'

'I blame education,' said the raven.

'A lot of knowledge is a dangerous thing,' said the skull. 'A lot more dangerous than just a little. I always used to say that, when I was alive.'

'When was that, exactly?'

'Can't remember. I think I was pretty knowledgeable. Probably a teacher or philosopher, something of that kidney. And now I'm on a bench with a bird crapping on my head.'

'Very allegorical,' said the raven.

No one had taught Susan about the power of belief, or at least about the power of belief in a combination of high magical potential and low reality stability such as existed on the Discworld.

Belief makes a hollow place. Something has to roll in to fill it.

Which is not to say that belief denies logic. For example, it's fairly obvious that the Sandman needs only a small sack.

On the Discworld, he doesn't bother to take the sand out first.

It was almost midnight.

Susan crept into the stables. She was one of those people who will not leave a mystery unsolved.

The ponies were silent in the presence of Binky. The horse glowed in the darkness.

Susan heaved a saddle down from the rack, and then thought better of it. If she was going to fall off, a saddle wouldn't be any help. And reins would be about as much use as a rudder on a rock.

She opened the door to the loose-box. Most horses won't walk backwards voluntarily, because what they can't see doesn't exist. But Binky shuffled out by himself and walked over to the mounting block, where he turned and watched her expectantly.

Susan climbed on to his back. It was like sitting on a table.

'All right,' she whispered. 'I don't have to believe any of this, mind you.'

Binky lowered his head and whinnied. Then he trotted out into the yard and headed for the field. At the gate he broke into a canter, and turned towards the fence.

Susan shut her eyes.

She felt muscles bunch under the velvet skin and then the horse was rising, over the fence, over the field.

Behind it, in the turf, two fiery hoofprints burned for a second or two.

As she passed above the school she saw a light flicker in a window. Miss Butts was on her rounds.

There's going to be trouble over this, Susan told herself.

And then she thought: I'm on the back of a horse a hundred feet up in the air, being taken somewhere mysterious that's a bit like a magic land with goblins and talking animals. There's only so much more trouble I could *get* into . . .

Besides, *is* riding a flying horse against school rules? I bet it's not written down anywhere.

Quirm vanished behind her, and the world opened up in a pattern of darkness and moonlight silver. A chequer-board pattern of fields strobed by in the moonlight, with the occasional light of an isolated farm. Ragged clouds whipped past and away.

Away on her left the Ramtop Mountains were a

cold white wall. On her right, the Rim Ocean carried a pathway to the moon. There was no wind, or even a great sensation of speed – just the land flashing by, and the long slow strides of Binky.

And then someone spilled gold on the night. Clouds parted in front of her and there, spread below, was Ankh-Morpork – a city containing more Peril than even Miss Butts could imagine.

Torchlight outlined a pattern of streets in which Quirm would have not only been lost, but mugged and pushed into the river as well.

Binky cantered easily over the rooftops. Susan could hear the sounds of the streets, even individual voices, but there was also the great roar of the city, like some kind of insect hive. Upper windows drifted by, each one a glow of candlelight.

The horse dropped through the smoky air and landed neatly and at the trot in an alley which was otherwise empty except for a closed door and a sign with a torch over it.

Susan read:

CURRY GARDENS
Kitchren Entlance – Keep Out. Ris Means You.

Binky seemed to be waiting for something.

Susan had expected a more exotic destination.

She knew about curry. They had curry at school, under the name of Bogey and Rice. It was yellow. There were soggy raisins and peas in it.

Binky whinnied, and stamped a hoof.

A hatch in the door flew open. Susan got a brief

impression of a face against the fiery atmosphere of the kitchen.

'Ooorrh, nooorrrh! *Binkorrr!*'

The hatch slammed shut again.

Obviously something was meant to happen.

She stared at a menu nailed to the wall. It was misspelled, of course, because the menu of the folkier kind of restaurant always has to have misspellings in it, so that customers can be lured into a false sense of superiority. She couldn't recognize the names of most of the dishes, which included:

Curry with Vegetable 8p
Curry with Sweat, and Sore Balls of Pig 10p
Curry with Sweer and Sour, Ball of Fish 10p
Curry with Meat 10p
Curry with Named Meat 15p
Extra Curry 5p
Porn cracker 4p

Eat It Here Or,
Take It Away

The hatch snapped open again and a large brown bag of allegedly but not really waterproof paper was dumped on the little ledge in front of it. Then the hatch slammed shut again.

Susan reached out carefully. The smell rising from the bag had a sort of thermic lance quality that warned against metal cutlery. But tea had been a long time ago.

She realized she didn't have any money on her.

On the other hand, no-one had asked her for any. But the world would go to wrack and ruin if people didn't recognize their responsibilities.

She leaned forward and knocked on the door.

'Excuse me . . . don't you want anything—?'

There was shouting and a crash from inside, as if half a dozen people were fighting to get under the same table.

'Oh. How nice. Thank you. Thank you very much,' said Susan, politely.

Binky walked away, slowly. This time there was no bunched leap of muscle power – he trotted into the air carefully, as if some time in the past he'd been scolded for spilling something.

Susan tried the curry several hundred feet above the speeding landscape, and then threw it away as politely as possible.

'It was very . . . unusual,' she said. 'And that's it? You carried me all the way up here for takeaway food?'

The ground skimmed past faster, and it crept over her that the horse was going a lot faster now, a full gallop instead of the easy canter. A bunching of muscle . . .

. . . and then the sky ahead of her erupted blue for a moment.

Behind her, unseen because light was standing around red with embarrassment asking itself what had happened, a pair of hoofprints burned in the air for a moment.

* * *

It was a landscape, hanging in space.

There was a squat little house, with a garden around it. There were fields, and distant mountains. Susan stared at it as Binky slowed.

There was no depth. As the horse swung around for a landing, the landscape was revealed as a mere surface, a thin-shaped film of . . . existence . . . imposed on nothingness.

She expected it to tear when the horse landed, but there was only a faint crunch and a scatter of gravel.

Binky trotted around the house and into the stable-yard, where he stood and waited.

Susan got off, gingerly. The ground felt solid enough under her feet. She reached down and scratched at the gravel; there was more gravel underneath.

She'd heard that the Tooth Fairy collected teeth. Think about it logically . . . the only other people who collected any bits of bodies did so for very suspicious purposes, and usually to harm or control other people. The Tooth Fairies must have half the children in the world under their control. And this didn't look like the house of that sort of person.

The Hogfather apparently lived in some kind of horrible slaughterhouse in the mountains, festooned with sausages and black puddings and painted a terrible blood-red.

Which suggested *style.* A nasty style, but at least style of a sort. This place didn't have style of *any* sort.

The Soul Cake Tuesday Duck didn't apparently

have any kind of a home. Nor did Old Man Trouble or the Sandman, as far as she knew.

She walked around the house, which wasn't much larger than a cottage. Definitely. Whoever lived here had no taste at all.

She found the front door. It was black, with a knocker in the shape of an omega.

Susan reached for it, but the door opened by itself.

And the hall stretched away in front of her, far bigger than the outside of the house could possibly contain. She could distantly make out a stairway wide enough for the tap-dancing finale in a musical.

There was something else wrong with the perspective. There clearly was a wall a long way off but, at the same time, it looked as though it was painted in the air a mere fifteen feet or so away. It was as if distance was optional.

There was a large clock against one wall. Its slow tick filled the immense space.

There's a room, she thought. *I remember the room of whispers.*

Doors lined the hall at wide intervals. Or short intervals, if you looked at it another way.

She tried to walk towards the nearest one, and gave up after a few wildly teetering steps. Finally she managed to reach it by taking aim and then shutting her eyes.

The door was *at one and the same time* about normal human size and immensely big. There was a highly ornate frame around it, with a skulls-and-bones motif.

She pushed the door open.

This room could have housed a small town.

A small area of carpet occupied the middle distance, no more than a hectare in size. It took Susan several minutes to reach the edge.

It was a room within a room. There was a large, heavy-looking desk on a raised dais, with a leather swivel chair behind it. There was a large model of the Discworld, on a sort of ornament made of four elephants standing on the shell of a turtle. There were several bookshelves, the large volumes piled in the haphazard fashion of people who're far too busy using the books ever to arrange them properly. There was even a window, hanging in the air a few feet above the ground.

But there were no walls. There was nothing between the edge of the carpet and the walls of the greater room except floor, and even that was far too precise a word for it. It didn't look like rock and it certainly wasn't wood. It made no sound when Susan walked on it. It was simply surface, in the purely geometrical sense.

The carpet had a skull-and-bones pattern.

It was also black. Everything was black, or a shade of grey. Here and there a tint suggested a very deep purple or ocean-depth blue.

In the distance, towards the walls of the greater room, the metaroom or whatever it was, there was the suggestion of . . . something. Something was casting complicated shadows, too far away to be clearly seen.

Susan got up on to the dais.

There was something odd about the things around her. Of course, there was everything odd about the things around her, but it was a huge major oddness that was simply in their nature. She could ignore it. But there was an oddness on a human level. Everything was just slightly wrong, as if it had been made by someone who hadn't fully comprehended its purpose.

There was a blotter on the oversize desk but it was part of it, fused to the surface. The drawers were just raised areas of wood, impossible to open. Whoever had made the desk had *seen* desks, but hadn't understood deskishness.

There was even some sort of desk ornament. It was just a slab of lead, with a thread hanging down one side and a shiny round metal ball on the end of the thread. If you raised the ball it swung down and thumped into the lead, just once.

She didn't try to sit in the chair. There was a deep pit in the leather. Someone had spent a lot of time sitting there.

She glanced at the spines of the books. They were in a language she couldn't understand.

She trekked back to the distant door, went out into the hall, and tried the next door. A suspicion was beginning to form in her mind.

The door led to another huge room, but this one was full of shelves, floor to distant, cloud-hung ceiling. Every shelf was lined with hourglasses.

The sand pouring from the past to the future filled the room with a sound like surf, a noise made up of a billion small sounds.

Susan walked between the shelves. It was like being in a crowd.

Her eye was caught by a movement on a nearby shelf. In most of the hourglasses the falling sand was a solid silver line but in this one, just as she watched, the line vanished. The last grain of sand tumbled into the bottom bulb.

The hourglass vanished with a small 'pop'.

A moment later another one appeared in its place, with the faintest of 'pings'. In front of her eyes, sand began to fall . . .

And she was aware that this process was going on all over the room. Old hourglasses vanished, new ones took their place.

She knew about this, too.

She reached out and picked up a glass, bit her lip thoughtfully, and started to turn the thing upside down . . .

SQUEAK!

She spun around. The Death of Rats was on the shelf behind her. It raised an admonitory finger.

'All right,' said Susan. She put the glass back in its place.

SQUEAK.

'No. I haven't finished looking.'

Susan set off for the door, with the rat skittering across the floor after her.

The third room turned out to be . . .

. . . the bathroom.

Susan hesitated. You *expected* hourglasses in this place. You expected the skull-and-bones motif. But you didn't expect the very large white porcelain tub, on its own raised podium like a throne, with giant brass taps and – in faded blue letters just over the thing that held the plug chain – the words: C. H. Lavatory & Son, Mollymog St, Ankh-Morpork.

You didn't expect the rubber duck. It was yellow.

You didn't expect the soap. It was suitably bone-white, but looked as if it had never been used. Beside it was a bar of orange soap which certainly *had* been used – it was hardly more than a sliver. It smelled a lot like the vicious stuff used at school.

The bath, though big, was a human thing. There was brown-lined crazing around the plug-hole and a stain where the tap had dripped. But almost everything else had been designed by the person who hadn't understood deskishness, and now hadn't understood ablutionology either.

They had created a towel rail an entire athletics team could have used for training. The black towels on it were fused to it and were quite hard. Whoever actually *used* the bathroom probably dried themselves on the white-and-blue, very worn towel with the initials Y M R-C-I-G-B-S A, A-M on it.

There was even a lavatory, another fine example of C. H. Lavatory's porcelainic art, with an embossed frieze of green and blue flowers on the cistern. And again, like the bath and the soap, it suggested that this room had been built by someone . . . and then *someone else* had come along afterwards to add small details. Someone with a better knowledge of plumbing, for a start. And someone else who understood, really understood, that towels should be soft and capable of drying people, and soap should be capable of bubbles.

You didn't expect any of it until you saw it. And then it was like seeing it *again.*

The bald towel dropped off the rail and skipped across the floor, until it fell away to reveal the Death of Rats.

SQUEAK?

'Oh, all right,' said Susan. 'Where do you want me to go now?'

The rat scurried to the open door and disappeared into the hall.

Susan followed it to yet another door. She turned yet another handle.

Another room within a room lay beyond. There was a tiny area of lighted tiling in the darkness, containing the distant vision of a table, a few chairs, a kitchen dresser—

—and someone. A hunched figure was sitting at the table. As Susan cautiously approached she heard the rattle of cutlery on a plate.

An old man was eating his supper, very noisily. In between forkfuls, he was talking to himself with his mouth full. It was a kind of auto bad manners.

''S'not *my* fault! [spray] I was against it from the *start* but, oh no, he has to go and [recover piece of ballistic sausage from table] start gettin' involved, I told him, i's'not as if you're *not* involved [stab unidentified fried object], oh no, that's not his way [spray, jab fork at the air], once you get involved like that, I said, how're you getting out, tell me that [make temporary egg-and-ketchup sandwich] but, oh no—'

Susan walked around the patch of carpet. The man took no notice.

The Death of Rats shinned up the table leg and landed on a slice of fried bread.

'Oh. It's you.'

SQUEAK.

The old man looked around.

'Where? Where?'

Susan stepped onto the carpet. The man stood up so quickly that his chair fell over.

'Who the hells are *you?*'

'Could you stop pointing that sharp bacon at me?'

'I asked you a question, young woman!'

'I'm Susan.' This didn't sound enough. 'Duchess of Sto Helit,' she added.

The man's wrinkled face wrinkled still further as he strove to comprehend this. Then he turned away and threw his hands up in the air.

'Oh, yes!' he bawled, to the room in general. 'That just puts the entire tin lid on it, that does!'

He waved a finger at the Death of Rats, who leaned backwards.

'You cheating little rodent! Oh, yes! I smell a rat here!'

SQUEAK?

The shaking finger stopped suddenly. The man spun around.

'How did you manage to walk through the wall?'

'I'm sorry?' said Susan, backing away. 'I didn't know there was one.'

'What d'you call this, then, Klatchian mist?' The man slapped the air.

The hippo of memory wallowed . . .

'. . . Albert . . .' said Susan, 'right?'

Albert thumped his forehead with the palm of his hand.

'Worse and worse! What've you been telling her?'

'He didn't tell me anything except SQUEAK and I don't know what that means,' said Susan. 'But . . . look, there's no wall here, there's just . . .'

Albert wrenched open a drawer.

'Observe,' he said sharply. 'Hammer, right? Nail, right? Watch.'

He hammered the nail into the air about five feet up at the edge of the tiled area. It hung there.

'Wall,' said Albert.

Susan reached out gingerly and touched the nail. It had a sticky feel, a little like static electricity.

'Well, it doesn't feel like a wall to me,' she managed.

SQUEAK.

Albert dropped the hammer on the table.

He wasn't a small man, Susan realized. He was quite tall, but he walked with the kind of lopsided stoop normally associated with laboratory assistants of an Igor turn of mind.

'I give in,' he said, wagging his finger at Susan again. 'I *told* him no good'd come of it. He started meddlin', and next thing a mere chit of a girl— where'd you go?'

Susan walked over to the table while Albert waved his arms in the air, trying to find her.

There was a cheeseboard on the table, and a snuff box. And a string of sausages. No fresh vegetables at all. Miss Butts advocated avoiding fried foods and eating plenty of vegetables for what she referred to as Daily Health. She put a lot of troubles down to an absence of Daily Health. Albert looked like the embodiment of them all as he scuttled around the kitchen, grabbing at the air.

She sat in the chair as he danced past.

Albert stopped moving, and put his hand over one eye. Then he turned, very carefully. The one visible eye was screwed up in a frantic effort of concentration.

He squinted at the chair, his eye watering with effort.

'That's pretty good,' he said, quietly. 'All right. You're here. The rat and the horse brought you. Damn fool things. They think it's the right thing to do.'

'*What* right thing to do?' said Susan. 'And I'm not a . . . what you said.'

Albert stared at her.

'The Master could do that,' he said at last. 'It's part of the job. I 'spect you found you could do it a long time ago, eh? Not be noticed when you didn't want to be?'

SQUEAK, said the Death of Rats.

'What?' said Albert.

SQUEAK.

'He says to tell you,' said Albert wearily, 'that a chit of a girl means a small girl. He thinks you may have misheard me.'

Susan hunched up in the chair.

Albert pulled up another one and sat down.

'How old are you?'

'Sixteen.'

'Oh, my.' Albert rolled his eyes. 'How long have you been sixteen?'

'Since I was fifteen, of course. Are you stupid?'

'My, my, how the time does pass,' said Albert. 'Do you know why you're here?'

'No . . . but,' Susan hesitated, 'but it's got something to do with . . . it's something like . . . I'm seeing things that people don't see, and I've met someone who's just a story, and I *know* I've been here before . . . and all these skulls and bones on things . . .'

Albert's rangy, vulture-like shape loomed over her.

'Would you like a cocoa?' he said.

It was a lot different from the cocoa at the school, which was like hot brown water. Albert's cocoa had fat floating in it; if you turned the mug upside down, it would be a little while before anything fell out.

'Your mum and dad,' said Albert, when she had a chocolate moustache that was far too young for her, 'did they ever . . . explain anything to you?'

'Miss Delcross did that in Biology,' said Susan. 'She got it wrong,' she added.

'I mean about your grandfather,' said Albert.

'I remember things,' said Susan, 'but I can't remember them until I've seen them. Like the bathroom. Like you.'

'Your mum and dad thought it best if you forgot,' said Albert. 'Hah! It's in the bone! They was afraid it was going to happen and it has! You've *inherited*.'

'Oh, I know about that, too,' said Susan. 'It's all about mice and beans and things.'

Albert gave her a blank look.

'Look, I'll try to put it tactful,' he said.

Susan gave him a polite look.

'Your grandfather is Death,' said Albert. 'You know? The skeleton in the black robe? You rode in on his horse and this is his house. Only he's . . . gone away. To think things over, or something. What I reckon's happening is you're being sucked in. It's in the bone. You're old enough now. There's a hole and it thinks you're the right shape. I don't like it any more than you do.'

'Death,' said Susan, flatly. 'Well, I can't say I didn't have suspicions. Like the Hogfather and the Sandman and the Tooth Fairy?'

'Yes.'

SQUEAK.

'You expect me to believe that, do you?' said Susan, trying to summon up her most withering scorn.

Albert glared back like someone who'd done all his withering a long time ago.

'It's no skin off *my* nose what you believe, madam,' he said.

'You really mean the tall figure with the scythe and everything?'

'Yes.'

'Look, Albert,' said Susan, in the voice one uses to the simple-minded, 'even if there was a "Death" like that, and frankly it's quite ridiculous to go anthropomorphizing a simple natural function, no one can inherit *anything* from it. I know about heredity. It's all about having red hair and things. You get it from other people. You don't get it from . . . myths and legends. Um.'

The Death of Rats had gravitated to the cheese-board, where he was using his scythe to hack off a lump. Albert sat back.

'I remember when you got brought here,' he said. 'He'd kept on asking, you see. He was curious. He likes kids. Sees a lot of them really, but . . . not to get to know, if you see what I mean. Your mum and dad didn't want to, but they gave in and brought you all here for tea one day just to keep him quiet. They didn't like to do it because they thought you'd be scared and scream the place down. But *you* . . . you didn't scream. You laughed. Frightened the life out of your dad, that did. They brought you a couple more times when he asked, but then they got scared about what might happen and your dad put his foot down and that was the end of it. He was about the only one who could argue with the Master, your dad. You'd have been about four then, I think.'

Susan raised her hand thoughtfully and touched the pale lines on her cheek.

'The Master said they were raising you according to,' Albert sneered, 'modern methods. Logic. And thinking old stuff is silly. I dunno . . . I suppose they wanted to keep you away from . . . ideas like this . . .'

'I was given a ride on the horse,' said Susan, not listening to him. 'I had a bath in the big bathroom.'

'Soap all over the place,' said Albert. His face contorted into something approaching a smile. 'I could hear the Master laughing from here. And he made you a swing, too. Tried to, anyway. No magic or anything. With his actual hands.'

Susan sat while memories woke and yawned and unfolded in her head.

'I remember about that bathroom now,' she said. 'It's all coming back to me.'

'Nah, it never went away. It just got papered over.'

'He was no good at plumbing. What does Y M R-C-I-G-B-S A, A-M mean?'

'Young Men's Reformed-Cultists-of-the-Ichor-God-Bel-Shamharoth Association, Ankh-Morpork,' said Albert. 'It's where I stay if I have to go back down for anything. Soap and suchlike.'

'But you're not . . . a young man,' said Susan, unable to prevent herself.

'No one argues,' he snapped. And Susan thought that was probably true. There was some kind of wiry strength in Albert, as if his whole body was a knuckle.

'He can make just about anything,' she said, half to herself, 'but some things he just doesn't understand, and one of them's plumbing.'

'Right. We had to get a plumber from Ankh-Morpork, hah, he said he might be able to make it a week next Thursday, and you don't say that kind of thing to the Master,' said Albert. 'I've never seen a bugger work so fast. Then the Master just made him forget. He can make everyone forget, except—' Albert stopped, and frowned.

'Seems I've got to put up with it,' he said. 'Seems

you've a *right.* I expect you're tired. You can stay here. There's plenty of rooms.'

'No, I've got to get back! There'll be terrible trouble if I'm not at school in the morning.'

'There's no Time here except what people brings with 'em. Things just happen one after the other. Binky'll take you right back to the time you left, if you like. But you ought to stop here a while.'

'You said there's a hole and I'm being sucked in. I don't know what that means.'

'You'll feel better after a sleep,' said Albert.

There was no real day or night here. That had given Albert trouble at first. There was just the bright landscape and, above, a black sky with stars. Death had never got the hang of day and night. When the house had human inhabitants it tended to keep a 26-hour day. Humans, left to themselves, adopt a longer diurnal rhythm than the 24-hour day, so they can be reset like a lot of little clocks at sunset. Humans have to put up with Time, but days are a sort of personal option.

Albert went to bed whenever he remembered.

Now he sat up, with one candle alight, staring into space.

'She remembered about the bathroom,' he muttered. 'And she knows about things she couldn't have seen. She couldn't have been told. She's got his memory. She *inherited.*'

SQUEAK, said the Death of Rats. He tended to sit by the fire at nights.

'Last time he went off, people stopped dyin',' said

Albert. 'But they ain't stopped dyin' this time. And the horse went to her. *She's* fillin' the hole.'

Albert glared at the darkness. When he was agitated it showed by a sort of relentless chewing and sucking activity, as if he was trying to extract some forgotten morsel of teatime from the recesses of a tooth. Now he was making a noise like a hairdresser's U-bend.

He couldn't remember ever having been young. It must have happened thousands of years ago. He was seventy-nine, but Time in Death's house was a reusable resource.

He was vaguely aware that childhood was a tricky business, especially towards the end. There was all the business with pimples and bits of your body having a mind of their own. Running the executive arm of mortality was certainly an extra problem.

But the point was, the horrible, inescapable point was, that *someone* had to do it.

For, as has been said before, Death operated in general rather than particular terms, just like a monarchy.

If you are a subject in a monarchy, you are ruled by the monarch. All the time. Waking or sleeping. Whatever you – or they – happen to be doing.

It's part of the general conditions of the situation. The Queen doesn't actually have to come around to your actual house, hog the chair and the TV remote control, and issue actual commands about how one is parched and would enjoy a cup of tea. It all takes place automatically, like gravity. Except that, unlike gravity, it needs someone at the top. They don't necessarily have to do a great deal. They just have to be there. They just have to *be.*

'Her?' said Albert.

SQUEAK.

'She'll crack soon enough,' said Albert. 'Oh, yes. You can't be an immortal and a mortal at the same time, it'll tear you in half. I almost feels sorry for her.'

SQUEAK, agreed the Death of Rats.

'And that ain't the worst bit,' said Albert. 'You wait till her memory *really* starts working . . .'

SQUEAK.

'You listen to me,' said Albert. 'You'd better start looking for him *right away*.'

Susan awoke, and had no idea what time it was.

There was a clock by the bedside, because Death knew there should be things like bedside clocks. It had skulls and bones and the omega sign on it, and it didn't work. There were no working clocks in the house, except the special one in the hall. Any others got depressed and stopped, or unwound themselves all in one go.

Her room looked as though someone had moved out yesterday. There were hairbrushes on the dressing table, and a few odds and ends of make-up. There was even a dressing-gown on the back of the door. It had a rabbit on the pocket. The cosy effect would have been improved if it hadn't been a skeletal one.

She had a rummage through the drawers. This must have been her mother's room. There was a lot of pink. Susan had nothing against pink in moderation, but this wasn't it; she put on her old school dress.

The important thing, she decided, was to stay calm. There was always a logical explanation for everything, even if you had to make it up.

SQEAUFF.

The Death of Rats landed on the dressing table, claws scrabbling for a purchase. He removed the tiny scythe from his jaws.

'I think,' said Susan carefully, 'that I would like to go home now, thank you.'

The little rat nodded, and leapt.

It landed on the edge of the pink carpet and scurried away across the dark floor beyond.

When Susan stepped off the carpet the rat stopped and looked around in approval. Once again, she felt she'd passed some sort of test.

She followed it out into the hall and then into the smoky cavern of the kitchen. Albert was bent over the stove.

'Morning,' he said, out of habit rather than any acknowledgement of the time of day. 'You want fried bread with your sausages? There's porridge to follow.'

Susan looked at the mess sizzling in the huge frying-pan. It wasn't a sight to be seen on an empty stomach, although it could probably cause one. Albert could make an egg wish it had never been laid.

'Haven't you got any muesli?' she said.

'Is that some kind of sausage?' said Albert suspiciously.

'It's nuts and grains.'

'Any fat in it?'

'I don't think so.'

'How're you supposed to fry it, then?'

'You don't fry it.'

'You call that *breakfast*?'

'It doesn't have to be fried to be breakfast,' said Susan. 'I mean, you mentioned porridge, and you don't fry porridge—'

'Who says?'

'A boiled egg, then?'

'Hah, boiling's no good, it don't kill off all the germs.'

'BOIL ME AN EGG, ALBERT.'

As the echoes bounced across and died away, Susan wondered where the voice had come from.

Albert's ladle tinkled on the tiles.

'Please?' said Susan.

'You did the voice,' said Albert.

'Don't bother about the egg,' said Susan. The voice had made her jaw ache. It worried her even more than it worried Albert. After all, it was her mouth. 'I want to go home!'

'You are home,' said Albert.

'This place? This isn't my home!'

'Yeah? What's the inscription on the big clock?'

'"Too Late",' said Susan promptly.

'Where are the beehives?'

'In the orchard.'

'How many plates've we got?'

'Seven—' Susan shut her mouth firmly.

'See? It's home to part of you,' said Albert.

'Look . . . Albert,' said Susan, trying sweet reason in case it worked any better this time round, 'maybe there is . . . someone . . . sort of . . . in charge of things, but I'm really no one special . . . I mean . . .'

'Yeah? How come the horse knows you?'

'Yes, but I really *am* just a normal girl—'

'Normal girls didn't get a My Little Binky set on their third birthday!' snapped Albert. 'Your dad took it away. The Master was very upset about that. He was *trying*.'

'I mean I'm an ordinary kid!'

'Listen, ordinary kids get a xylophone. They don't just ask their grandad to take his shirt off!'

'I mean I can't help it! That's not my fault! It's not fair!'

'Really? Oh, why didn't you say?' said Albert sourly. 'That cuts a lot of thin ice, that does. I should just go out now, if I was you, and tell the universe that it's not fair. I bet it'll say, oh, all right then, sorry you've been troubled, you're let off.'

'That's sarcasm! You can't talk to me like that! You're just a servant!'

'That's right. And so are you. So I should get started, if I was you. The rat'll help. He mainly does rats, but the principle's the same.'

Susan sat with her mouth open.

'I'm going outside,' she snapped.

'I ain't stopping you.'

Susan stormed out through the back door, across the enormous expanses of the outer room, past the grindstone in the yard, and into the garden.

'Huh,' she said.

If someone had told Susan that Death had a house, she would have called them mad or, even worse, stupid. But if she'd had to imagine one, she'd have drawn, in sensible black crayon, some towering, battlemented, Gothic mansion. It would loom, and involve other words ending in 'oom', like gloom and doom. There would have been thousands of windows. She'd fill odd corners of the sky with bats. It would be impressive.

It wouldn't be a cottage. It wouldn't have a rather tasteless garden. It wouldn't have a mat in front of the door with 'Welcome' on it.

Susan had invincible walls of common sense. They were beginning to melt like salt in a wet wind, and that made her *angry*.

There was Grandfather Lezek, of course, on his little farm so poor that even the sparrows had to kneel down to eat. He'd been a nice old chap, so far as she could recall; a bit sheepish, now she came to think about it, especially when her father was around.

Her mother had told Susan that her own father had been . . .

Now she came to think about *that*, she wasn't sure what her mother had told her. Parents were quite clever at not telling people things, even when they used a lot of words. She'd just been left with the impression that he wasn't around.

Now it was being suggested that he was renowned for being around all the time.

It was like having a relative in trade.

A god, now . . . a god would be something. Lady Odile Flume, in the fifth form, was always boasting that her great-great-grandmother had once been seduced by the god Blind Io in the form of a vase of daisies, which apparently made her a demi-hemi-semi-goddess. She said her mother found it useful to get a table in restaurants. Saying you were a close relative of Death probably would not have the same effect. You probably wouldn't even manage a seat near the kitchen.

If it was all some kind of dream, she didn't seem at any risk of waking up. Anyway, she didn't believe that kind of thing. Dreams weren't like this.

A path led from the stable-yard past a vegetable garden and, descending slightly, into an orchard of black-leaved trees. Glossy black apples hung from them. Off to one side were some white beehives.

And she knew she'd seen it all before.

There was an apple tree that was quite, quite different from the others.

She stood and stared at it as memory flooded back.

She remembered being just old enough to see how logically stupid the whole idea was, and he'd been standing there, anxiously waiting to see what she'd do . . .

Old certainties drained away, to be replaced by new certainties.

Now she *understood* whose granddaughter she was.

* * *

The Mended Drum had traditionally gone in for, well, traditional pub games, such as dominoes, darts and Stabbing People In The Back And Taking All Their Money. The new owner had decided to go up-market. This was the only available direction.

There had been the Quizzing Device, a three-ton water-driven monstrosity based on a recently discovered design by Leonard of Quirm. It had been a bad idea. Captain Carrot of the Watch, who had a mind like a needle under his open smiling face, had surreptitiously substituted a new roll of questions like: *Were you nere Vortin's Diamond Warehouse on the Nite of the 15th?* and: *Who was the Third Man Who did the Blagging At Bearhugger's Distillery Larst week?* and had arrested three customers before they caught on.

The owner had promised another machine any day now. The Librarian, one of the tavern's regulars, had been collecting pennies in readiness.

There was a small stage at one end of the bar. The owner had tried a lunch-time stripper, but only once. At the sight of a large orang-utan in the front row with a big innocent grin, a big bag of penny pieces and a big banana the poor girl had fled. Yet another entertainment Guild had blacklisted the Drum.

The new owner's name was Hibiscus Dunelm. It wasn't his fault. He really wanted to make the Drum, he said, a fun place. For two pins he'd have put stripy umbrellas outside.

He looked down at Glod.

'Just three of you?' he said.

'Yes.'

'When I agreed to five dollars, you said you had a big band.'

'Say hello, Lias.'

'My word, that *is* a big band.' Dunelm backed away. 'I thought,' he said, 'just a few numbers that everyone knows? Just to provide some ambience.'

'Ambience,' said Imp, looking around the Drum. He was familiar with the word. But, in a place like this, it was all lost and alone. There were only three or four customers in at this early hour of the evening. They weren't paying any attention to the stage.

The wall behind the stage had clearly seen action. He stared at it as Lias patiently stacked up his stones.

'Oh, just a bit of fruit and old eggs,' said Glod. 'People probably get a bit boisterous. I shouldn't worry about that.'

'I'm not worried about it,' said Imp.

'I should think not.'

'It's the axe marks and arrow holles I'm worried about. Gllod, we haven't even practised! Not properlly!'

'You can play your guitar, can't you?'

'Wellll, yes, I suppose . . .'

He'd tried it out. It *was* easy to play. In fact, it was almost impossible to play badly. It didn't seem to matter how he touched the strings – they still rang out the tune he had in mind. It was, in solid form, the kind of instrument you dream about when you first start to play – the one you can play without learning. He remembered when he'd first picked up a harp and struck the strings, confidently expecting the kind of lambent tones the old men coaxed from them. He'd got a discord instead. But this was the instrument he'd dreamed of . . .

'We'll stick to numbers everyone knows,' said the dwarf. '"The Wizard's Staff" and "Gathering Rhubarb". Stuff like that. People like songs they can snigger along to.'

Imp looked down at the bar. It was filling up a bit now. But his attention was drawn to a large orang-utan, which had pulled up its chair right in front of the stage and was holding a bag of fruit.

'Gllod, there's an ape watching us.'

'Well?' said Glod, unfolding a string bag.

'It's an *ape*.'

'This is Ankh-Morpork. That's how things are here.' Glod removed his helmet and unfolded something from inside.

'Why've you got a string bag?' said Imp.

'Fruit's fruit. Waste not, want not. If they throw eggs, try to catch them.'

Imp slung the guitar's strap over his shoulder. He'd tried to tell the dwarf, but what could he say: this is too easy to play?

He hoped there was a god of musicians.

And there is. There are many, one for almost every type of music. *Almost* every type. But the only one due to watch over Imp that night was Reg, god of club musicians, who couldn't pay much attention because he'd also got three other gigs to do.

'We ready?' said Lias, picking his hammers.

The others nodded.

'Let's give 'em "The Wizard's Staff", then,' said Glod. 'That always breaks the ice.'

'Okay,' said the troll. He counted on his fingers. 'One, two . . . one, two, many, *lots*.'

The first apple was thrown seven seconds later. It was caught by Glod, who didn't miss a note. But the first banana curved viciously and grounded in his ear.

'Keep playing!' he hissed.

Imp obeyed, ducking a fusillade of oranges.

In the front row, the ape opened his bag and produced a very large melon.

'Can you see any pears?' said Glod, taking a breath. 'I like pears.'

'I can see a man with a throwing axe!'

'Does it look valuable?' An arrow vibrated in the wall by Lias's head.

It was three in the morning. Sergeant Colon and Corporal Nobbs were reaching the conclusion that anyone who intended to invade Ankh-Morpork probably wasn't going to do so now. And there was a good fire back in the watch house.

'We could leave a note,' said Nobby, blowing on his fingers. 'You know? Come back tomorrow, sort of thing?'

He looked up. A solitary horse was walking under the gate arch. A white horse, with a sombre, black-clad rider.

There was no question of 'Halt, who goes there?' The night watch walked the streets at strange hours and had become accustomed to seeing things not generally seen by mortal men.

Sergeant Colon touched his helmet respectfully.

''Evenin', your lordship,' he said.

'ER . . . GOOD EVENING.'

The guards watched the horse walk out of sight.

'Some poor bugger's in for it, then,' said Sergeant Colon.

'He's dedicated, you got to admit it,' said Nobby. 'Out at all hours. Always got time for people.'

'Yeah.'

The guards stared into the velvety dark. Something not quite right, thought Sergeant Colon.

'What's his first name?' said Nobby.

They stared some more. Then Sergeant Colon, who still hadn't quite been able to put his finger on it, said: 'What do you mean, what's his first name?'

'What's his first name?'

'He's Death,' said the sergeant. '*Death.* That's his whole name. I mean . . . what do you mean? . . . You mean like . . . *Keith* Death?'

'Well, why not?'

'He's just Death, isn't he?'

'No, that's just his *job.* What do his friends call him?'

'What do you mean, *friends*?'

'All right. Please yourself.'

'Let's go and get a hot rum.'

'I think he looks like a Leonard.'

Sergeant Colon remembered the voice. That was it. Just for a moment there . . .

'I must be getting old,' he said. 'For a moment there I thought he sounded like a Susan.'

* * *

'I think they saw me,' whispered Susan, as the horse rounded a corner.

The Death of Rats poked its head out of her pocket.

SQUEAK.

'I think we're going to need that raven,' said Susan. 'I mean, I . . . think I understand you, I just don't know what you're saying . . .'

Binky stopped outside a large house, set back a little from the road. It was a slightly pretentious residence with more gables and mullions than it should rightly have, and this was a clue to its origins: it was the kind of house built for himself by a rich merchant when he goes respectable and needs to do something with the loot.

'I'm not happy about this,' said Susan. 'It can't possibly *work*. I'm human. I have to go to the toilet and things like that. I can't just walk into people's houses and kill them!'

SQUEAK.

'All right, not kill. But it's not good manners, however you look at it.'

A sign on the door said: Tradesmen to rear entrance.

'Do I count as—'

SQUEAK!

Susan normally would never have dreamed of asking. She'd always seen herself as a person who went through the front doors of life.

The Death of Rats scuttled up the path and *through* the door.

'Hang on! *I* can't—'

Susan looked at the wood. She *could.* Of course she could. More memories crystallized in front of her eyes. After all, it was only wood. It'd rot in a few hundred years. By the measure of infinity, it hardly existed at all. On average, considered over the lifetime of the multiverse, most things didn't.

She stepped forward. The heavy oak door offered as much resistance as a shadow.

Grieving relatives were clustered around the bed where, almost lost in the pillows, was a wrinkled old man. At the foot of the bed, paying no attention whatsoever to the keening around it, was a large, very fat, ginger cat.

SQUEAK.

Susan looked at the hourglass. The last few grains tumbled through the pinch.

The Death of Rats, with exaggerated caution, sneaked up behind the sleeping cat and kicked it hard. The animal awoke, turned, flattened its ears in terror, and leapt off the quilt.

The Death of Rats sniggered.

SNH, SNH, SNH.

One of the mourners, a pinch-faced man, looked up. He peered at the sleeper.

'That's it,' he said. 'He's gone.'

'I thought we were going to be here all day,' said the woman next to him, standing up. 'Did you see that wretched old cat move? Animals can tell, you know. They've got this sixth sense.'

SNH, SNH, SNH.

'Well, come on there, I know you're here somewhere,' said the corpse. It sat up.

Susan was familiar with the idea of ghosts. But she hadn't expected it to be like this. She hadn't expected the ghosts to be the living, but they were merely pale sketches in the air compared to the old man sitting up in bed. He looked solid enough, but a blue glow outlined him.

'One hundred and seven years, eh?' he cackled. 'I expect I had you worried for a while there. Where are you?'

'Er, HERE,' said Susan.

'Female, eh?' said the old man. 'Well, well, well.'

He slid off the bed, spectral nightshirt flapping, and was suddenly pulled up short as though he'd reached the end of a chain. This was more or less the case; a thin line of blue light still tethered him to his late habitation.

The Death of Rats jumped up and down on the pillow, making urgent slashing movements with its scythe.

'Oh, sorry,' said Susan, and sliced. The blue line snapped with a high-pitched, crystalline twang.

Around them, sometimes walking through them, were the mourners. Mourning seemed to have stopped, now the old man had died. The pinch-faced man was feeling under the mattress.

'Look at 'em,' said the old man nastily. 'Poor ole Grandad, sob, sob, sorely missed, we won't see his like again, where did the ole bugger leave his will? That's my youngest son, that is. Well, if you can call a card every Hogswatchnight a son. See his wife? Got a smile like a wave on a slop bucket. And she ain't the worst of 'em. Relatives? You can keep 'em. I only stayed alive out of mischief.'

A couple of people were exploring under the bed. There was a humorous porcelain clang. The old man capered behind them, making gestures.

'Not a chance!' he chortled. 'Heh heh! It's in the cat basket! I left all the money to the cat!'

Susan looked around. The cat was watching them anxiously from behind the washstand.

Susan felt some response was called for.

'That was very . . . kind of you . . .' she said.

'Hah! Mangy thing! Thirteen years of sleepin' and crappin' and waiting for the next meal to turn up? Never took half an hour's exercise in his big fat life. Up until they find the will, anyway. Then he's going to be the richest fastest cat in the world—'

The voice faded. So did its owner.

'What a dreadful old man,' said Susan.

She looked down at the Death of Rats, who was trying to make faces at the cat.

'What'll happen to him?'

SQUEAK.

'Oh.' Behind them a former mourner tipped a drawer out on to the floor. The cat was beginning to tremble.

Susan stepped out through the wall.

Clouds curled behind Binky like a wake.

'Well, that wasn't *too* bad. I mean, no blood or anything. And he was very old and not very nice.'

'That's all right, then, is it?' The raven landed on her shoulder.

'What're you doing here?'

'Rat Death here said I could have a lift. I've got an appointment.'

SQUEAK.

The Death of Rats poked its nose out of the saddlebag.

'Are we a cab service?' said Susan coldly.

The rat shrugged and pushed a lifetimer into her hand.

Susan read the name etched on the glass.

'Volf Volfssonssonssonsson? Sounds a bit Hublandish to me.'

SQUEAK.

The Death of Rats clambered up Binky's mane and took up station between the horse's ears, tiny robe flapping in the wind.

Binky cantered low over a battlefield. It wasn't a major war, just an inter-tribal scuffle. Nor were there any obvious armies – the fighters seemed to be two groups of individuals, some on horseback, who happened coincidentally to be on the same side. Everyone was dressed in the same sort of furs and exciting leatherwear, and Susan was at a loss to know how they told friend from foe. People just seemed to shout a lot and swing huge swords and battleaxes at random. On the other hand, anyone you managed to hit instantly *became* your foe, so it probably all came out right in the long run. The point was that people were dying and acts of incredibly stupid heroism were being performed.

SQUEAK.

The Death of Rats pointed urgently downward.

'Gee . . . down.'

Binky settled on a small hillock.

'Er . . . right,' said Susan. She pulled the scythe out of its holster. The blade sprang into life.

It wasn't hard to spot the souls of the dead. They were coming off the battlefield arm in arm, friend and hitherto foe alike, laughing and stumbling, straight towards her.

Susan dismounted. And concentrated.

'Er,' she said, 'ANYONE HERE BEEN KILLED AND CALLED VOLF?'

Behind her, the Death of Rats put its head in its paws.

'Er. HELLO?'

No one took any notice. The warriors trooped past. They were forming a line on the edge of the battlefield, and appeared to be waiting for something.

She didn't have to . . . do . . . all of them. Albert had tried to explain, but a memory had unfolded anyway. She just had to do *some*, determined by timing or historical importance, and that meant all the others happened; all she had to do was keep the momentum going.

'You got to be more assertive,' said the raven, who had alighted on a rock. 'That's the trouble with women in the professions. Not assertive enough.'

'Why'd you want to come here?' she said.

'This is a battlefield, isn't it?' said the raven

patiently. 'You've got to have ravens afterwards.' Its freewheeling eyes swivelled in its head. 'Carrion regardless, as you might say.'

'You mean everyone gets eaten?'

'Part of the miracle of nature,' said the raven.

'That's horrible,' said Susan. Black birds were already circling in the sky.

'Not really,' said the raven. 'Horses for courses, you might say.'

One side, if that's what you could call it, was fleeing the field of battle with the others in pursuit.

The birds started to settle on what was, Susan realized with horror, an early breakfast. Soft bits, sunny side up.

'You'd better go and look for your lad,' said the raven. 'Otherwise he'll miss his ride.'

'What ride?'

The eyes orbited again.

'You ever learn mythology?' it said.

'No. Miss Butts says it's just made-up stories with little literary content.'

'Ah. Deary me. Can't have that, can we? Oh, well. You'll soon see. Must rush.' The raven leapt into the air. 'I generally try to get a seat near the head.'

'What will I—'

And then someone started to sing. The voice swooped out of the sky like a sudden wind. It was a rather good mezzo-soprano—

'Hi-jo-to! Ho! Hi-jo-to! Ho!'

And after it, mounted on a horse almost as fine as Binky, was a woman. Very definitely. A lot of woman. She was as much woman as you could get in one place without getting two women. She was dressed in chain mail, a shiny 46-D-cup breastplate, and a helmet with horns on it.

The assembled dead cheered as the horse cantered in for a landing. There were six other singing horse-women plunging out of the sky behind it.

'Isn't it always the same?' said the raven, flapping away. 'You can wait hours without seeing one and then you get seven all at once.'

Susan watched in astonishment as each rider picked up a dead warrior and galloped up into the sky again. They disappeared abruptly a few hundred yards up and reappeared again almost instantly for a fresh passenger. Soon there was a busy shuttle service operating.

After a minute or two one of the women trotted her horse over to Susan and pulled a scroll of parch-ment out of her breastplate.

'What ho! Says here Volf,' she said, in the brisk voice used by people on horseback when addressing mere pedestrians. 'Volf the Lucky . . . ?'

'Er. I don't know – I MEAN, I DON'T KNOW WHICH ONE HE IS,' said Susan helplessly.

The helmeted woman leaned forward. There was something rather familiar about her.

'Are you new?'

'Yes. I mean, YES.'

'Well, don't stand there like a big girl's blouse. Jolly well go and fetch him, there's a good sport.'

Susan looked around wildly, and saw him at last. He wasn't very far away. A youngish man, outlined in flickering pale blue, was visible among the fallen.

Susan hurried over, scythe at the ready. There was a blue line connecting the warrior to his former body.

SQUEAK! shouted the Death of Rats, jumping up and down and making suggestive motions.

'Left hand thumb up, right hand bent at the wrist, give it some wellie!' shouted the horned woman.

Susan swung the scythe. The line snapped.

'What happened?' said Volf. He looked down. 'That's me down there, isn't it?' he said. He turned slowly. 'And down *there.* And over *there.* And . . .'

He looked at the horned female warrior and brightened up.

'By Io!' he said. 'It's true? Valkyries will carry me off to the hall of Blind Io where there is perpetual feasting and drinking?'

'Don't, I mean DON'T ASK ME,' said Susan.

The Valkyrie reached down and hauled the warrior across her saddle.

'Just keep quiet, there's a good chap,' she said.

She stared thoughtfully at Susan.

'Are you a soprano?' she said.

'Pardon?'

'Can you sing at all, gel? Only we could do with another soprano. Far too many mezzo-sopranos around these days.'

'I'm not very musical, I'm sorry.'

'Oh, well. Just a thought. Must be going.' She threw back her head. The mighty breastplate heaved. 'Hi-jo-to! Ho!'

The horse reared, and galloped into the sky.

Before it reached the clouds it shrank to a gleaming pinpoint, which winked.

'What,' said Susan, 'was all that about?'

There was a flurry of wings. The raven alighted on the head of the recently departed Volf.

'Well, these guys believe that if you die in battle some big fat singing horned women carry you off to a sort of giant feast hall where you gobble yourself silly for the rest of eternity,' said the raven. It belched genteelly. 'Damn stupid idea, really.'

'But it just happened!'

'Still a daft idea.' The raven looked around at the stricken battlefield, empty now except for the fallen and the flocks of his fellow ravens. 'What a waste,' he added. 'I mean, just look at it all. Such a terrible waste.'

'Yes!'

'I mean, I'm near bursting and there's hundreds of 'em untouched. I think I'll see if I can have a doggy bag.'

'They're dead bodies!'

'Right!'

'What are you *eating*?'

'It's all right,' said the raven, backing away. 'There's enough for everyone.'

'That's disgusting!'

'I didn't kill 'em,' it said.

Susan gave up.

'She looked a lot like Iron Lily,' she said, as they walked back to the patient horse. 'Our gym mistress. Sounded like her, too.' She imagined the warbling Valkyries pounding across the sky. *Get some warrior, you bunch of fainting blossoms . . .*

'Convergent evolution,' said the raven. 'Often happens. I read once where apparently the common octopus has an eye almost exactly the same as the human eyeb— caw!'

'You were going to say something like: except for the taste, weren't you?' said Susan.

'Negger grossed by bind,' said the raven indistinctly.

'Sure?'

'Leg go ogg by beak glease?'

Susan released her grip.

'This is dreadful,' she said. 'This is what he used to do? There's no element of choice?'

SQUEAK.

'But what if they don't deserve to die?'

SQUEAK.

The Death of Rats contrived to indicate, quite effectively, that in that case they could apply to the universe and point out that they didn't deserve to die. In which case it was up to the universe to say, oh, didn't you? oh, well, that's all right, then, you can go on living. It was a remarkably succinct gesture.

'So . . . my grandfather was Death, and he just let nature take its course? When he could have done some good? That's *stupid*.'

The Death of Rats shook its skull.

'I mean, was Volf on the right side?' said Susan.

'Hard to say,' said the raven. 'He was a Vasung. The other side were Bergunds. Apparently it all started with a Bergund carrying off a Vasung woman a few hundred years ago. Or it may have been the other way round. Well, the other side invaded their village. There was a bit of a massacre. And then the *other* ones went to the *other* village and there was another massacre. After that, you might say, there was some residual bad feeling.'

'Very well, then,' said Susan. 'Who's next?'

SQUEAK.

The Death of Rats landed on the saddle. It leaned down and, with some effort, hauled another hourglass out of the pack. Susan read the label.

It said: Imp y Celyn.

Susan had a sensation of falling backwards.

'I *know* this name,' she said.

SQUEAK.

'I . . . remember it from somewhere,' said Susan. 'It's important. He's . . . important . . .'

The moon hung over the desert of Klatch like a huge ball of rock.

It wasn't much of a desert to be graced by so impressive a moon.

It was just part of the belt of deserts, growing progressively hotter and drier, that surrounded the Great Nef and the Dehydrated Ocean. And no one would have thought much about it if people very like Mr Clete of the Musicians' Guild hadn't come along and made maps and put across this part of the desert an innocent little dotted line that marked a border between Klatch and Hersheba.

Up until that time the D'regs, a collection of cheerfully warlike nomadic tribes, had roamed the desert quite freely. Now there was a line, they were sometimes Klatchian D'regs and sometimes

Hershebian D'regs, with all the rights due to citizens of both states, particularly the right to pay just as much tax as could be squeezed out of them and be drafted in to fight wars against people they'd never heard of. So as a result of the dotted line Klatch was now incipiently at war with Hersheba and the D'regs, Hersheba was at war with the D'regs and Klatch, and the D'regs were at war with everyone, including one another, and having considerable fun because the D'reg word for 'stranger' was the same as for 'target'.

The fort was one of the legacies of the dotted line.

Now it was a dark rectangle on the hot silver sands. From it came what could very accurately be called the strains of an accordion, since someone seemed to want to play a tune but kept on running into difficulties after a few bars, and starting again.

Someone knocked on the door.

After a while there was a scraping on the other side and a small hatch opened.

'Yes, offendi?'

IS THIS THE KLATCHIAN FOREIGN LEGION?

The face of the little man on the other side of the door went blank.

'Ah,' he said, 'you've got me there. Hang on a moment.' The hatch shut. There was a whispered discussion on the other side of the door. The hatch opened.

'Yes, it appears we are the . . . the . . . what was that again? Right, got it . . . the Klatchian Foreign Legion. Yes. What was it you were wanting?'

I WISH TO JOIN.

'Join? Join what?'

THE KLATCHIAN FOREIGN LEGION.

'Where's that?'

There was some more whispering.

'Oh. Right. Sorry. Yes. That's us.'

The doors swung open. The visitor strode in. A legionary with corporal's stripes on his arm walked up to him.

'You'll have to report to . . .' his eyes glazed a little, '. . . you know . . . big man, three stripes . . . on the tip of my tongue a moment ago . . .'

SERGEANT?

'Right,' said the corporal, with relief. 'What's your name, soldier?'

ER . . .

'You don't have to say, actually. That's what the . . . the . . .'

KLATCHIAN FOREIGN LEGION?

'. . . what it's all about. People join to . . . to . . . with your mind, you know, when you can't . . . things that happened . . .'

FORGET?

'Right. I'm . . .' The man's face went blank. 'Wait a minute, would you?'

He looked down at his sleeve. 'Corporal . . .' he said. He hesitated, looking worried. Then an idea struck him and he pulled at the collar of his vest and twisted his neck until he could squint, with considerable difficulty, at the label thus revealed.

'Corporal . . . Medium? Does that sound right?'

I DON'T THINK SO.

'Corporal . . . Hand Wash Only?'

PROBABLY NOT.

'Corporal . . . Cotton?'

IT'S A POSSIBILITY.

'Right. Well, welcome to the . . . er . . .'

KLATCHIAN FOREIGN LEGION . . .

'Right. The pay is three dollars a week and all the sand you can eat. I hope you like sand.'

I SEE YOU CAN REMEMBER ABOUT SAND.

'Believe me, you won't ever forget sand,' said the corporal bitterly.

I NEVER DO.

'What did you say your name was?'

The stranger remained silent.

'Not that it matters,' said Corporal Cotton. 'In the . . .'

KLATCHIAN FOREIGN LEGION?

'. . . right . . . we give you a *new* name. You start out afresh.'

He beckoned to another man.

'Legionary . . . ?'

'Legionary . . . er . . . ugh . . . er . . . Size 15, sir.'

'Right. Take this . . . man away and get him a . . .' he snapped his fingers irritably, '. . . you know . . . thing . . . clothes, everyone wears them . . . sand-coloured—'

UNIFORM?

The corporal blinked. For some inexplicable reason the word 'bone' kept elbowing its way into the melting, flowing mess that was his consciousness.

'Right,' he said. 'Er. It's a twenty-year tour, legionary. I hope you're man enough for it.'

I LIKE IT ALREADY, said Death.

* * *

'I suppose it's legal for me to go in licensed premises?' said Susan, as Ankh-Morpork appeared on the horizon again.

SQUEAK.

The city slid under them again. Where there were wider streets and squares she could make out individual figures. Huh, she thought . . . if only they knew I was up here! And, despite everything, she couldn't help feeling superior. All the people down there had to think about were, well, ground-level things. Mundane things. It was like looking down at ants.

She'd always known she was different. Much more *aware* of the world, when it was obvious that most people went through it with their eyes shut and their brains set to 'simmer'. It was comforting in a way to know that she *was* different. The feeling wrapped around her like an overcoat.

Binky landed on a greasy jetty. On one side the river sucked at the wooden pilings.

Susan slid off the horse, unshipped the scythe, and stepped inside the Mended Drum.

There was a riot going on. The patrons of the Drum tended to be democratic in their approach to aggressiveness. They liked to see that everyone got some. So, although it was the consensus of the audience that the trio were lousy musicians, and therefore a suitable target, various fights had broken out because people had been hit by badly aimed missiles, or hadn't had a fight all day, or were just trying to reach the door.

Susan had no difficulty in spotting Imp y Celyn.

He was at the front of the stage, his face a mask of terror. Behind him was a troll, with a dwarf trying to hide behind it.

She glanced at the hourglass. Just a few more seconds . . .

He was really rather attractive, in a dark, curly-headed sort of way. He looked a little elvish.

And familiar.

She'd felt sorry for Volf, but at least he was on a battlefield. Imp was on a stage. You didn't expect to die on stage.

I'm standing here with a scythe and an hourglass waiting for someone to die. He's not much older than me and I'm not supposed to do anything about it. That's silly. And I'm sure I've seen him . . . before . . .

No one actually tried to *kill* musicians in the Drum. Axes were thrown and crossbows fired in a good-humoured, easy-going way. No-one really aimed, even if they were capable of doing so. It was more fun watching people dodge.

A big, red-bearded man grinned at Lias, and selected a small throwing axe from his bandolier. It was okay to throw axes at trolls. They tended to bounce off.

Susan could see it all. It'd bounce off, and hit Imp. No one's fault, really. Worse things happened at sea. Worse things happened in Ankh-Morpork all the time, often continuously.

The man doesn't even mean *to kill him. It's so sloppy. That's not how things should go. Someone ought to do something about it.*

She reached over to grab the axe handle.

SQUEAK!

'Shut up!'

Whaaauum.

Imp stood like a discus thrower as the chord filled across the noisy room.

It rang like an iron bar dropped on a library floor at midnight.

Echoes bounced back from the corners of the room. Each one bore its own load of harmonics.

It was an explosion of sound in the same way that a Hogswatchnight rocket explodes, each falling spark exploding again . . .

Imp's fingers caressed the strings, picking out three more chords. The axe-thrower lowered his axe.

This was music that had not only escaped but had robbed a bank on the way out. It was music with its sleeves rolled up and its top button undone, raising its hat and grinning and stealing the silver.

It was music that went down to the feet by way of the pelvis without paying a call on Mr Brain.

The troll picked up his hammers, looked blankly at his stones, and then began to beat out a rhythm.

The dwarf took a deep breath, and extracted from the horn a deep, throbbing sound.

People drummed their fingers on the edge of the tables. The orang was sitting with a huge rapt grin on his face, as though he'd swallowed a banana sideways.

Susan looked down at the hourglass marked Imp y Celyn.

The top bulb was now quite empty of sand, but something blue flickered in there.

She felt tiny pin-like claws scrabble up her back and find purchase on her shoulder.

The Death of Rats looked down at the glass.

SQUEAK, it said, quietly.

Susan still wasn't good on Rat but she thought she knew 'uh-oh' when she heard it.

Imp's fingers danced over the strings, but the sound that came from them was no relative to the tones of harp or lute. The guitar screamed like an angel who had just discovered why it was on the wrong side. Sparks glittered on the strings.

Imp himself had his eyes shut and was holding the instrument close to his chest, like a soldier holding a spear at the port. It was hard to know who was playing what.

And still the music flooded out.

The Librarian's hair was standing on end, all over his body. The ends crackled.

It made you want to kick down walls and ascend the sky on steps of fire. It made you want to pull all the switches and throw all the levers and stick your fingers in the electric socket of the universe to see what happened next. It made you want to paint your bedroom wall black and cover it with posters.

Now various muscles on the Librarian's body were twitching with the beat as the music earthed itself through him.

There was a small party of wizards in the corner. They were watching the performance with their mouths open.

And the beat strode on, and crackled from mind to mind, snapping its fingers and curling its lip.

Live music. Music with rocks in it, running wild . . .

Free at last! It leapt from head to head, crackling in through the ears and heading for the hindbrain. Some were more susceptible than others . . . closer to the beat . . .

It was an hour later.

The Librarian knuckled and swung through the midnight drizzle, head exploding with music.

He landed on the lawns of Unseen University and ran into the Great Hall, hands waving wildly overhead to maintain balance.

He stopped.

Moonlight filtered in through the big windows, illuminating what the Archchancellor always referred to as 'our mighty organ', to the general embarrassment of the rest of the faculty.

Rack upon rack of pipes entirely occupied one wall, looking like pillars in the gloom or possibly resembling the stalagmites of some monstrously ancient cave. Almost lost among them was the player's pulpit, with its three giant keyboards and the hundred knobs for special sound effects.

It wasn't often used, except for the occasional civic affair or Wizards' Excuse Me.*

*Wizards did not have balls. There was a popular song about it. But they did hold their annual Excuse Me, or free-for-all dance, which was one of the highlights of the Ankh-Morpork social calendar. The Librarian in particular always looked forward to it, and used an *amazing* amount of hair cream.

But the Librarian, energetically pumping the bellows and making occasional little 'ooks' of excitement, felt there was a lot more that it could do.

A fully grown male orang-utan may look like an amiable pile of old carpets but he has a strength in him that would make a human of equivalent weight eat lots of rug. The Librarian only stopped pumping when the lever was too hot to hold and the air reservoirs were farting and whistling around the rivets.

Then he swung himself up into the organist's seat.

The whole edifice was humming softly under the enormous pent-up pressure.

The Librarian locked his hands together and cracked his knuckles, which is impressive when you have as many knuckles as an orang-utan.

He raised his hands.

He hesitated.

He lowered his hands again and pulled out the Vox Humana, the Vox Dei and the Vox Diabolica.

The moan of the organ took on a more urgent tone.

He raised his hands.

He hesitated.

He lowered his hands and pulled out all the rest of the stops, including the twelve knobs with '?' on them and the two with faded labels warning in several languages that they were on no account to be touched, ever, in any circumstances.

He raised his hands.

He raised his feet also, positioning them over some of the more perilous pedals.

He shut his eyes.

He sat for a moment in contemplative silence, a test pilot ready to slit the edge of the envelope in the starship Melody.

He let the plangent memory of the music fill his head and flow down his arms and fill his fingers.

His hands dropped.

'What did we *do*? What did we *do*?' said Imp. Excitement ran its barefoot races up and down his spine.

They were sitting in the tiny cramped room behind the bar.

Glod took off his helmet and wiped the inside.

'Would you believe four beats to the bar, two-four time, melody led, with the bass beat forward in the melody?'

'What's all dat?' said Lias. 'What's all dem words mean?'

'You're a musician, ain't you?' said Glod. 'What do you think you do?'

'I hits 'em with de hammers,' said Lias, one of nature's drummers.

'But that bit you did . . .' said Imp, 'you know . . . in the middlle . . . you know, *bam-bah bam-bah bambamBAH* . . . how did you know how to do that bit?'

'It was just de bit dat had to go dere,' said Lias.

Imp looked at the guitar. He'd put it on the table. It was still playing quietly to itself, like a cat purring.

'That's not a normall instrument,' he said, shaking a finger at it. 'I was just standing there and it started pllaying all by itsellf!'

'Probably belonged to a wizard, like I said,' said Glod.

'Nah,' said Lias. 'Never knew any wizard who was musical. Music and magic don't mix.'

They looked at it.

Imp had never heard of an instrument that played itself before, except the legendary harp of Owen Mwnyy, which sang when danger threatened. And that had been back in the days when there were dragons around. Singing harps went well with dragons. They seemed out of place in a city with guilds and everything.

The door swung open.

'That was . . . astonishing, boys,' said Hibiscus Dunelm. 'Never heard anything like it! Can you come back tomorrow night? Here's your five dollars.'

Glod counted the coins.

'We did four encores,' he said darkly.

'I'd complain to the Guild, if I was you,' said Hibiscus.

The trio looked at the money. It looked very impressive to people whose last meal had been twenty-four hours ago. It wasn't Guild rate. On the other hand, it had been a long twenty-four hours.

'If you come back tomorrow,' said Hibiscus, 'I'll make it . . . six dollars, how about that?'

'Oh, wow,' said Glod.

Mustrum Ridcully was jolted upright in bed, because the bed itself was being gently vibrated across the floor.

So it had happened at last!

They were out to get him.

The tradition of promotion in the University by filling dead men's shoes, sometimes by firstly ensuring the death of the man in those shoes, had lately ceased. This was largely because of Ridcully himself, who was big and kept himself in trim and, as three late-night aspirants to the Archchancellorship had found, also had very good hearing. They had been variously hung out of the window by their ankles, knocked unconscious with a shovel, and had their arm broken in two places. Besides, Ridcully was known to sleep with two loaded crossbows by his bed. He was a kind man and probably wouldn't shoot you in *both* ears.

That sort of consideration encouraged a more patient type of wizard. Everyone dies sooner or later. They could wait.

Ridcully took stock and found his first impression was mistaken.

There appeared to be no murderous magic going on. There was just sound, cramming the room to every corner.

Ridcully shuffled into his slippers and went out into the corridor, where other members of the faculty were milling around and blearily asking one another what the hell was happening. Plaster rained down on them from the ceiling in a steady fog.

'Who's causing that din?' shouted Ridcully. There was a mute chorus of unheard replies, and much shrugging of shoulders.

'Well, I will find *out*,' growled the Archchancellor, and set off for the stairs with the others trailing after him.

He walked without his knees or elbows bending very much, a sure sign of a forthright man in a bad temper.

The trio said nothing all the way out of the Drum. They said nothing all the way to Gimlet's delicatessen. They said nothing while they waited in the queue, and then all they said was: 'So . . . right . . . that's one Quatre-rodenti with extra newts, hold the chillis, one Klatchian Hots with double salami and a Four Strata, no pitchblende.'

They sat down to wait. The guitar played a little four-note riff. They tried not to think about it. They tried to think about other things.

'I think I change my name,' said Lias, eventually. 'I mean . . . Lias? Not a good name for the music business.'

'What'll you change it to?' said Glod.

'I thought . . . don't laugh . . . I thought . . . Cliff?' said Lias.

'*Cliff?*'

'Good troll name. Very stony. Very rocky. Nothing wrong with it,' said Cliff *né* Lias, defensively.

'Well . . . yes . . . but, I dunno, I mean . . . well . . . Cliff? Can't see anyone lasting long in *this* business with a name like *Cliff*.'

'Better than Glod, anyway.'

'I'm sticking with Glod,' said Glod. 'And Imp is sticking with Imp, right?'

Imp looked at the guitar. It's not right, he thought. I hardly touched it. I just . . . And I feel so tired . . . I . . .

'Not sure,' he said, wretchedly. 'Not sure if Imp is the right name for . . . this music.' His voice trailed off. He yawned.

'Imp?' said Glod, after a while.

'Hmm?' said Imp. And he'd felt someone was watching him out there. That was daft, of course. He couldn't say to someone 'I was on stage and I thought someone was watching me'. They'd say 'Really? That's really *occult,* that is . . .'

'Imp?' said Glod, 'why're you snapping your fingers like that?'

Imp looked down.

'Was I?'

'Yes.'

'Just thinking. My name . . . it's not right for this music, either.'

'What does it mean in real language?' said Glod.

'Well, allll my familly are *y Celyns*,' said Imp, ignoring the insult to an ancient tongue. 'It means "of the holllly". That's allll that grows in Llamedos, you see. Everything else just rots.'

'I wasn't goin' to say,' said Cliff, 'but *Imp* sounds a bit like *elf* to me.'

'It just means "smallll shoot",' said Imp. 'You know. Like a bud.'

'Bud y Celyn?' said Glod. 'Buddy? Worse than Cliff, in my opinion.'

'I . . . think it sounds right,' said Imp.

Glod shrugged, and pulled a handful of coins out of his pocket.

'We've still got more'n four dollars,' he said. 'I know what we should do with it, too.'

'We should put it towards Guild membership,' said the new Buddy.

Glod stared into the middle distance.

'No,' he said. 'We haven't got the sound right. I mean, it was very good, very . . . *new*,' he stared hard at Imp-cum-Buddy, 'but there's still something missing . . .'

The dwarf gave Buddy *né* Imp another penetrating stare.

'Do you know you're shaking all over?' he said. 'Moving around on your seat like you got a pant full of ant.'

'I can't help it,' said Buddy. He wanted to sleep, but a rhythm was bouncing around inside his head.

'I saw it too,' said Cliff. 'When we was walking here, you were bouncing along.' He looked under the table. 'And you is tapping your feet.'

'And you *keep* snapping your fingers,' said Glod.

'I can't stop thinking about the music,' said Buddy. 'You're right. We need . . .' he drummed his fingers along the table, '. . . a sound like . . . *pang pang pang PANG Pang* . . .'

'You mean a keyboard?' said Glod.

'Do I?'

'They've got one of those new pianofortes just over the river in the Opera House,' said Glod.

'Yah, but dat sort of thing ain't for our kind of music,' said Cliff. 'Dat sort of thing is for big fat guys in powdered wigs.'

'I reckon,' said Glod, giving Buddy another

lopsided stare, 'if we put it anywhere near Im— near Buddy, it'll be for our kind of music soon enough. So go and get it.'

'I heard where it cost four hundred dollars,' said Cliff. 'No-one's got that many teeth.'

'I didn't mean *buy* it,' said Glod. 'Just . . . borrow it for a while.'

'Dat's stealing,' said Cliff.

'No it's not,' said the dwarf. 'We'll let them have it back when we've finished with it.'

'Oh. Dat's all right den.'

Buddy wasn't a drummer or a troll and he could see the technical flaw in Glod's argument. And, a few weeks ago, he'd have said so. But then he'd been a good circle-going boy from the valleys, who didn't drink, didn't swear and played the harp at every druidic sacrifice.

Now he *needed* that piano. The sound had been *nearly* right.

He snapped his fingers in time with his thoughts.

'But we ain't got anyone to play it,' said Cliff.

'You get the piano,' said Glod. 'I'll get the piano player.'

And all the time they kept glancing at the guitar.

The wizards advanced in a body towards the organ. The air around it vibrated as if super-heated.

'What an unholy noise!' shouted the Lecturer in Recent Runes.

'Oh, I don't know!' screamed the Dean. 'It's rather catchy!'

Blue sparks crackled between the organ pipes. The

Librarian could just be seen high in the trembling structure.

'Who's pumping it?' screamed the Senior Wrangler.

Ridcully looked around at the side. The handle seemed to be going up and down by itself.

'I'm not having this,' he muttered, 'not in *my* damn university. It's worse than *students*.'

And he raised his crossbow and fired, right at the main bellows.

There was a long-drawn-out wail in the key of A, and then the organ exploded.

The history of the subsequent seconds was put together during a discussion in the Uncommon Room where the wizards went for a stiff drink or, in the Bursar's case, a warm milk shortly afterwards.

The Lecturer in Recent Runes swore that the 64-foot Gravissima organ pipe went skywards on a pillar of flame.

The Chair of Indefinite Studies and the Senior Wrangler said that when they found the Librarian upside down in one of the fountains in Sator Square, outside the University, he was going 'ook ook' to himself and grinning.

The Bursar said that he'd seen a dozen naked young women bouncing up and down on his bed, but the Bursar occasionally said things like this anyway, especially when he'd been indoors a lot.

The Dean said nothing at all.

His eyes were glazed.

Sparks crackled in his hair.

He was wondering if he'd be allowed to paint his bedroom black.

. . . the beat went on . . .

The lifetimer of Imp stood in the middle of the huge desk. The Death of Rats walked around it, squeaking under his breath.

Susan looked at it, too. There was no doubt that all the sand was in the bottom bulb. But something else had filled the top and was pouring through the pinch. It was pale blue and coiling in frantically on itself, like excited smoke.

'Have you ever seen anything like it?' she said.

SQUEAK.

'Nor me.'

Susan stood up. The shadows around the walls, now that she'd got used to them, seemed to be of *things* – not exactly machinery, but not exactly furniture either. There had been an orrery on the lawn at the college. The distant shapes put her in mind of it, although what stars it measured in what dark courses she really couldn't say. They seemed to be projections of things too strange even for this strange dimension.

She'd wanted to save his life, and that was *right.* She knew it. As soon as she'd seen his name she . . . well, it was important. She'd inherited some of Death's memory. She couldn't have met the boy, but perhaps *he* had. She felt that the name and the face had established themselves so deeply in her mind now that the rest of her thoughts were forced to orbit them.

Something else had saved him first.

She held the lifetimer up to her ear again.

She found herself tapping her foot.

And realized that distant shadows were moving.

She ran across the floor, the real floor, the one outside the boundaries of the carpet.

The shadows looked more like mathematics would be if it was solid. There were vast curves of . . . something. Pointers like clock hands, but longer than a tree, moved slowly through the air.

The Death of Rats climbed on to her shoulder.

'I suppose you don't know what's happening?'

SQUEAK.

Susan nodded. Rats, she supposed, died when they should. They didn't try to cheat, or return from the dead. There were no such things as zombie rats. Rats knew when to give up.

She looked at the glass again. The boy – and she used the term as girls will of young males several years older than them – the boy had played a chord on the guitar or whatever it was, and history had been bent. Or had skipped, or something.

Something besides her didn't want him dead.

It was two o'clock in the morning, and raining.

Constable Detritus, Ankh-Morpork City Watch, was guarding the Opera House. It was an approach to policing that he'd picked up from Sergeant Colon. When you were all by yourself in the middle of a rainy night, go and guard something big with handy overhanging eaves. Colon had pursued this policy for years, as a result of which no major landmark had ever been stolen.*

It had been an uneventful night. About an hour earlier a 64-foot organ pipe had dropped out of the sky. Detritus had wandered over to inspect the crater, but he wasn't quite certain if this was *criminal* activity. Besides, for all he knew this was how you got organ pipes.

For the last five minutes he'd also been hearing muffled thumps and the occasional tinkling noise from inside the Opera House. He'd made a note of it. He did not wish to appear stupid. Detritus had never been inside the Opera House. He didn't know what sound it normally made at 2 a.m.

The front doors opened, and a large oddly shaped flat box came out, hesitantly. It advanced in a curious way – a few steps forward, a couple of steps back. And it was also talking to itself.

Detritus looked down. He could see . . . he paused . . . at least seven legs of various sizes, only four of which had feet.

He shambled across to the box and banged on the side.

'Hello, hello, hello, what is all this . . . then?' he said, concentrating to get the sentence right.

The box stopped.

Then it said, 'We're a piano.'

Detritus gave this due consideration. He wasn't sure what a piano was.

*Well, except for Unseen University once, but that was just a student prank.

'A piano move about, does it?' he said.

'It's . . . we've got legs,' said the piano.

Detritus conceded the point.

'But it are the middle of the night,' he said.

'Even pianos have to have time off,' said the piano.

Detritus scratched his head. This seemed to cover it.

'Well . . . all right,' he said.

He watched the piano jerk and wobble down the marble steps and round the corner.

It carried on talking to itself:

'How long have we got, d'you think?'

'We ought to make it to the bridge. He not clever enough to be a drummer.'

'But he's a policeman.'

'So?'

'Cliff?'

'Yup?'

'We might get caught.'

'He can't stop us. We're on a mission from Glod.'

'Right.'

The piano tottered onward through the puddles for a little while, and then asked itself:

'Buddy?'

'Yup?'

'Why did I just say dat?'

'Say what?'

'About us being on a mission . . . you know . . . from Glod?'

'Weeell . . . the dwarf said to us, go and get the piano, and his name is Glod, so—'

'Yeah. Yeah. Right . . . but . . . he *could've* stopped us, I mean, dere's nothing special about some mission from some dwarf—'

'Maybe you were just a bit tired.'

'Maybe dat's it,' said the piano, gratefully.

'Anyway, we *are* on a mission from Glod.'

'Yup.'

Glod sat in his lodgings, watching the guitar.

It had stopped playing when Buddy had gone out, although if he put his ear close to the strings he was sure that they were still humming very gently.

Now he very carefully reached out and touched the—

To call the sudden snapping sound discordant would be too mild. The sound had a snarl, it had talons.

Glod sat back. Right. Right. It was Buddy's instrument. An instrument played by the same person over the years could become very adapted to them, although not in Glod's experience to the point of biting someone else. Buddy hadn't had it a day yet, but the principle maybe was the same.

There was an old dwarf legend about the famous Horn of Furgle, which sounded itself when danger was near and also in the presence, for some reason, of horseradish.

And there was even an Ankh-Morpork legend, wasn't there, about some old drum in the Palace or somewhere that was supposed to bang itself if an enemy fleet was seen sailing up the Ankh? The legend had died out in recent centuries, partly because this was the Age of Reason and also because no enemy fleet could sail up the Ankh without a gang of men with shovels going in front.

And there was a troll story about some stones that, on frosty nights . . .

The *point* was that magical instruments turned up every so often.

Glod reached out again.

JUD-Adud-adud-duh.

'All right, all right . . .'

The old music shop was right up against the University, after all, and magic did leak out despite what the wizards always said about the talking rats and walking trees just being statistical flukes. But this didn't *feel* like magic. It felt a lot older than that. It felt like music.

Glod wondered whether he should persuade Im— Buddy to take it back to the shop, get a proper guitar . . .

On the other hand, six dollars was six dollars. At least.

Something hammered on the door.

'Who's that?' said Glod, looking up.

The pause outside was long enough to let him guess. He decided to help out.

'Cliff?' he said.

'Yup. Got a piano here.'

'Bring it on in.'

'Had to break off der legs and der lid and a few other bits but it's basically okay.'

'Bring it on in, then.'

'Door's too narrow.'

Buddy, coming up the stairs behind the troll, heard the crunch of woodwork.

'Try it again.'

'Fits perfectly.'

There was a piano-shaped hole around the doorway. Glod was standing next to it, holding his axe. Buddy looked at the wreckage all over the landing.

'What the hell are you doing?' he said. 'That's someone else's wall!'

'Well? It's someone else's piano.'

'Yes, but . . . you can't just hack holes in the wall—'

'What's more important? Some wall or getting the sound right?' said Glod.

Buddy hesitated. Part of him thought: that's ridiculous, it's only *music.* Another part of him thought, rather more sharply: that's ridiculous, it's only a wall. All of him said: 'Oh. Since you put it like that . . . but what about the piano player?'

'I told you, I know just where to find one,' said Glod.

A tiny part of him was amazed: I've hacked a hole in my own wall! It took me *days* to nail that wallpaper on properly.

Albert was in the stable, with a shovel and a wheelbarrow.

'Go well?' he said, when Susan's shadow appeared over the half-door.

'Er . . . yes . . . I suppose . . .'

'Pleased to hear it,' said Albert, without looking up. The shovel thumped on the barrow.

'Only . . . something happened which probably wasn't usual . . .'

'Sorry to hear that.'

Albert picked up the wheelbarrow and trundled it in the direction of the garden.

Susan knew what she was supposed to do. She was supposed to apologize, and then it'd turn out that crusty old Albert had a heart of gold, and they'd be friends after all, and he'd help her and tell her things, and—

And she'd be some stupid girl who couldn't cope.

No.

She went back to the stable, where Binky was investigating the contents of a bucket.

The Quirm College for Young Ladies encouraged self-reliance and logical thought. Her parents had sent her there for that reason.

They'd assumed that insulating her from the fluffy edges of the world was the safest thing to do. In the circumstances, this was like not telling people about self-defence so that no one would ever attack them.

Unseen University was used to eccentricity among the faculty. After all, humans derive their notions of what it means to *be* a normal human being by constant reference to the humans around them, and when those humans are other wizards the spiral can only wiggle downwards. The Librarian was an orang-utan, and no one thought that was at all odd. The Reader in Esoteric Studies spent so much time reading in what the Bursar referred to as 'the smallest room'* that he was generally referred to as the Reader in The Lavatory, even on official documents. The Bursar himself in any normal society would have been considered more unglued than a used stamp in a downpour. The Dean had spent seventeen years writing a treatise on *The Use of the Syllable 'ENK' in Levitation Spells of the Early Confused Period.* The Archchancellor, who regularly used the long gallery above the Great Hall for archery practice and had accidentally shot the Bursar twice, thought the whole faculty was as crazy as loons, whatever a loon was. 'Not enough fresh air,' he'd say. 'Too much sittin' around indoors. Rots the brain.' More often he'd say, 'Duck!'

None of them, apart from Ridcully and the Librarian, were early risers. Breakfast, if it happened at all, happened around mid-morning. Wizards lined the buffet, lifting the big silver lids of the tureens and wincing at every clang. Ridcully liked big greasy breakfasts, especially if they included those slightly translucent sausages with the green flecks that you can only hope is a herb of some sort. Since it was the Archchancellor's prerogative to choose the menu,

*The smallest room in Unseen University is in fact a broom cupboard on the fourth floor. He *really* meant the privy. The Reader had a theory that all the really good books in any building – at least, all the really funny ones† – gravitate to a pile in the privy but no one ever has time to read all of them, *or even knows how they came to be there.* His research was causing extreme constipation and a queue outside the door every morning.

†The ones with cartoons about cows and dogs. And captions like: 'As soon as he saw the duck, Elmer knew it was going to be a bad day'.

many of the more squeamish wizards had stopped eating breakfast altogether, and got through the day just on lunch, tea, dinner and supper and the occasional snack.

So there weren't too many in the Great Hall this morning. Besides, it was a bit draughty. Workmen were busy somewhere up in the roof.

Ridcully put down his fork.

'All right, who's doing it?' he said. 'Own up, that man.'

'Doing what, Archchancellor?' said the Senior Wrangler.

'Somone's tappin' his foot.'

The wizards looked along the table. The Dean was staring happily into space.

'Dean?' said the Senior Wrangler.

The Dean's left hand was held not far from his mouth. The other was making rhythmic stroking motions somewhere in the region of his kidneys.

'I don't know what he thinks he's doin',' said Ridcully, 'but it looks unhygienic to me.'

'I think he's playing an invisible banjo, Archchancellor,' said the Lecturer in Recent Runes.

'Well, it's quiet, at least,' said Ridcully. He looked at the hole in the roof, which was letting unaccustomed daylight into the hall. 'Anyone seen the Librarian?'

The orang-utan was busy.

He had holed up in one of the Library cellars, which he currently used as a general workshop and book hospital. There were various presses and guillotines, a bench full of tins of nasty substances where he made his own binding glue and all the other tedious cosmetics of the Muse of literature.

He'd brought a book down with him. It had taken even him several hours to find it.

The Library didn't only contain magical books, the ones which are chained to their shelves and are very dangerous. It also contained perfectly ordinary books, printed on commonplace paper in mundane ink. It would be a mistake to think that they weren't also dangerous, just because reading them didn't make fireworks go off in the sky. Reading them sometimes did the more dangerous trick of making fireworks go off in the privacy of the reader's brain.

For example, the big volume open in front of him contained some of the collected drawings of Leonard of Quirm, skilled artist and certified genius with a mind that wandered so much it came back with souvenirs.

Leonard's books were full of sketches – of kittens, of the way water flows, of the wives of influential Ankh-Morporkian merchants whose portraits had provided his means of making a living. But Leonard had been a genius and was deeply sensitive to the wonders of the world, so the margins were full of detailed doodles of whatever was on his mind at that moment – vast water-powered engines for bringing down city walls on the heads of the enemy, new types of siege guns for pumping flaming oil over the enemy, gunpowder rockets that showered the enemy with burning phosphorus, and other manufactures of the Age of Reason.

And there had been something else. The Librarian had noticed it in passing once before, and had been slightly puzzled by it. It seemed out of place.*

His hairy hand thumbed through the pages. Ah . . . here it was . . .

Yes. Oh, *YES.*

. . . *It spoke to him in the language of the Beat* . . .

The Archchancellor made himself comfortable at his snooker table.

He'd long ago got rid of the official desk. A snooker table was much to be preferred. Things didn't fall off the edge, there were a number of handy pockets to keep sweets and things in, and when he was bored he could shovel the paperwork off and set up trick shots.† He never bothered to shovel the paperwork back on afterwards. In his experience, anything really important never got written down, because by then people were too busy shouting.

He picked up his pen and started to write.

He was composing his memoirs. He'd got as far as the title: *Along the Ankh with Bow, Rod and Staff with a Knob on the End.*

*And didn't appear to do anything to the enemy *at all.*

†He was a wizard. Trick shots for a wizard aren't the old three-times-round-the-table jobs. His best one was once off the cushion, once off a seagull, once off the back of the head of the Bursar who'd been walking along the corridor outside *last Tuesday* (a bit of temporal spin there) and a tricky rebound off the ceiling. He'd missed sinking the actual shot by a whisker, but it had been pretty tricky, even so.

'Not many people realize,' he wrote, 'that the river Ankh has a large and varied pifcine population—'*

He flung down the pen and stormed along the corridor into the Dean's office.

'What the hell's *that*?' he shouted.

The Dean jumped.

'It's, it's, it's a guitar, Archchancellor,' said the Dean, walking hurriedly backwards as Ridcully approached. 'I just bought it.'

'I can *see* that, I can *hear* that, what was it you were tryin' to *do*?'

'I was practising, er, riffs,' said the Dean. He waved a badly printed woodcut defensively in Ridcully's face.

The Archchancellor grabbed it.

'"Blert Wheedown's Guitar Primer",' he read. '"Play your Way to Succefs in Three Easy Lefsons and Eighteen Hard Lefsons". Well? I've nothin' against guitars, pleasant airs, a-spying young maidens one morning in May and so on, but that wasn't *playin'*. That was just *noise.* I mean, what was it supposed to *be*?'

'A lick based on an E pentatonic scale using the major seventh as a passing tone?' said the Dean.

The Archchancellor peered at the open page.

*And this was true. Nature can adapt to practically anything. There *were* fish evolved to live in the river. They looked like a cross between a soft-shelled crab and an industrial vacuum cleaner, and tended to explode in fresh water, and what you had to use for bait was nobody's business, but they were *fish* and a sportsman like Ridcully never cared about what the quarry tasted like.

'But *this* says "Lesson One: Fairy Footsteps",' he said.

'Um, um, um, I was getting a bit impatient,' said the Dean.

'You've never been musical, Dean,' said Ridcully. 'It's one of your good points. Why the sudden interest – *what* have you got on your feet?'

The Dean looked down.

'I *thought* you were a bit taller,' said Ridcully. 'You standing on a couple of planks?'

'They're just thick soles,' said the Dean. 'Just . . . just something the dwarfs invented, I suppose . . . dunno . . . found them in my closet . . . Modo the gardener says he thinks they're crêpe.'

'That's strong language for Modo, but I'd say he's right enough.'

'No . . . it's a kind of rubbery stuff . . .' said the Dean, dismally.

'Erm . . . excuse me, Archchancellor . . .'

It was the Bursar, standing in the doorway. A large red-faced man was behind him, craning over his shoulder.

'What is it, Bursar?'

'Erm, this gentleman has got a—'

'It's about your monkey,' said the man.

Ridcully brightened up.

'Oh, yes?'

'Apparently, erm, he sto— *removed* some wheels from this gentleman's carriage,' said the Bursar, who was on the depressive side of his mental cycle.

'You sure it was the Librarian?' said the Archchancellor.

'Fat, red hair, says "ook" a lot?'

'That's him. Oh, dear. I wonder why he did that?' said Ridcully. 'Still, you know what they say . . . a five-hundred-pound gorilla can sleep where he likes.'

'But a three-hundred-pound monkey can give me my bloody wheels back,' said the man, unmoved. 'If I don't get my wheels back, there's going to be trouble.'

'Trouble?' said Ridcully.

'Yeah. And don't think you can scare me. Wizards don't scare me. Everyone knows there's a rule that you mustn't use magic against civilians.' The man thrust his face close to Ridcully and raised a fist.

Ridcully snapped his fingers. There was an inrush of air, and a croak.

'I've always thought of it more as a guideline,' he said, mildly. 'Bursar, go and put this frog in the flower-bed and when he becomes his old self give him ten dollars. Ten dollars would be all right, wouldn't it?'

'Croak,' said the frog hastily.

'Good. And *now* will someone tell me what's going on?'

There was a series of crashes from downstairs.

'Why do I think,' said Ridcully to the world in general, 'that this isn't going to be the answer?'

The servants had been laying the tables for lunch. This generally took some time. Since wizards took their meals seriously, and left a lot of mess, the tables were in a permanent state of being laid, cleaned or occupied. Place-settings alone took a lot of time.

Each wizard required nine knives, thirteen forks, twelve spoons and one rammer, quite apart from all the wine-glasses.

Wizards often turned up in ample time for the next meal. In fact they were often there in good time to have second helpings of the last one.

A wizard was sitting there now.

'That's Recent Runes, ain't it?' said Ridcully.

He had a knife in each hand. He also had the salt, pepper and mustard pots in front of him. And the cake-stand. And a couple of tureen covers. All of which he was hitting vigorously with the knives.

'What's he doing that for?' said Ridcully. 'And, Dean, will you stop tapping your feet?'

'Well, it's catchy,' said the Dean.

'It's *catching*,' said Ridcully.

The Lecturer in Recent Runes was frowning in concentration. Forks jangled across the woodwork. A spoon caught a glancing blow, pinwheeled through the air and hit the Bursar on the ear.

'What the hells does he think he's doing?'

'That really hurt!'

The wizards clustered around the Lecturer in Recent Runes. He paid them no attention whatsoever. Sweat poured down his beard.

'He just broke thc cruet,' said Ridcully.

'It's going to smart for *hours.*'

'Ah, yes, he's as hot as mustard,' said the Dean.

'I'd take that with a pinch of salt,' said the Senior Wrangler.

Ridcully straightened up. He raised a hand.

'Now, someone's about to say something like "I

hope the Watch don't *ketchup* with him", aren't you?' he said. 'Or "That's a bit of a *sauce*", or I bet you're all trying to think of somethin' silly to say about pepper. I'd just like to know what's the difference between this faculty and a bunch of pea-brained idiots.'

'Hahaha,' said the Bursar nervously, still rubbing his ear.

'It wasn't a rhetorical question.' Ridcully snatched the knives out of the Lecturer's hands. The man went on beating the air for a moment, and then appeared to wake up.

'Oh, hello, Archchancellor. Is there a problem?'

'What were you doing?'

The Lecturer looked down at the table.

'He was syncopating,' said the Dean.

'I never was!'

Ridcully frowned. He was a thick-skinned, single-minded man with the tact of a sledgehammer and about the same sense of humour, but he was not stupid. And he knew that wizards were like weather-vanes, or the canaries that miners used to detect pockets of gas. They were by their nature tuned to an occult frequency. If there was anything *strange* happening, it tended to happen to wizards. They turned, as it were, to face it. Or dropped off their perch.

'Why's everyone suddenly so musical?' he said. 'Using the term in its loosest sense, of course.' He looked at the assembled wizardry. And then down towards the floor.

'You've *all* got crêpe on your shoes!'

The wizards looked at their feet with some surprise.

'My word, I *thought* I was a bit taller,' said the Senior Wrangler. 'I put it down to the celery diet.'*

'Proper footwear for a wizard is pointy shoes or good stout boots,' said Ridcully. 'When one's footwear turns creepy, something's amiss.'

'It's crêpe,' said the Dean. 'It's got a little pointy thingy over the—'

Ridcully breathed heavily. '*When your boots change by themselves*—' he growled.

'There's magic afoot?'

'Haha, good one, Senior Wrangler,' said the Dean.

'I want to know what's going on,' said Ridcully, in a low and level voice, 'and if you don't all shut up there will be trouble.'

He reached into the pockets of his robe and, after a few false starts, produced a pocket thaumometer. He held it up. There was always a high level of background magic in the University, but the little needle was on the 'Normal' mark. On average, anyway. It was ticking backwards and forwards across it like a metronome.

Ridcully held it up so they could all see.

'What's this?' he said.

'Four-four time?' said the Dean.

'Music ain't magic,' said Ridcully. 'Don't be daft. Music's just twanging and banging and—'

*The Senior Wrangler had a theory that *long* food – beans, celery and rhubarb – made you taller, because of the famous Doctrine of Signatures. It certainly made him lighter.

He stopped.

'Has anyone got anything they should be telling me?'

The wizards shuffled their blue-suede feet nervously.

'Well,' said the Senior Wrangler, 'it *is* a fact that last night, er, I, that is to say, some of us, happened to be passing by the Mended Drum—'

'Bona-Fide Travellers,' said the Lecturer in Recent Runes. 'It's allowable for Bona-Fide Travellers to get a Drink at Licensed Premises at any Hour of Day or Night. City statute, you know.'

'Where were you travelling from, then?' Ridcully demanded.

'The Bunch of Grapes.'

'That's just around the corner.'

'Yes, but we were . . . tired.'

'All right, all right,' said Ridcully, in the voice of a man who knows that pulling at a thread any more will cause the whole vest to unravel. 'The Librarian was with you?'

'Oh, yes.'

'Go on.'

'Well, there was this music—'

'Sort of twangy,' said the Senior Wrangler.

'Melody led,' said the Dean.

'It was . . .'

'. . . sort of . . .'

'. . . in a way it . . .'

'. . . kind of gets under your skin and makes you feel fizzy,' said the Dean. 'Incidentally, has anyone got any black paint? I've looked everywhere.'

'Under your skin,' murmured Ridcully. He scratched his chin. 'Oh, dear. One of *those.* Stuff leakin' into the universe again, eh? Influences coming from Outside, yes? Remember what happened when Mr Hong opened his takeaway fish bar on the site of the old temple in Dagon Street? And then there were those moving pictures. I was against *them* from the start. And those wire things on wheels. This universe has more damn holes in it than a Quirm cheese. Well, at—'

'Lancre cheese,' said the Senior Wrangler helpfully. 'That's the one with the holes. Quirm is the one with the blue veins.'

Ridcully gave him a look.

'Actually, it didn't *feel* magical,' said the Dean. He sighed. He was seventy-two. It *had* made him feel that he was seventeen again. He couldn't remember having been seventeen; it was something that must have happened to him while he was busy. But it made him feel like he imagined it felt like when you were seventeen, which was like having a permanent red-hot vest on under your skin.

He wanted to hear it again.

'I think they're going to have it again tonight,' he ventured. 'We could, er, go along and listen. In order to learn more about it, in case it's a threat to society,' he added virtuously.

'That's right, Dean,' said the Lecturer in Recent Runes. 'It's our civic duty. We're the city's first line of supernatural defence. Supposing ghastly creatures started coming out of the air?'

'What about it?' said the Chair of Indefinite Studies.

'Well, we'd be there.'

'Yes? That's good, is it?'

Ridcully glared at his wizards. Two of them were surreptitiously tapping their feet. And several of them appeared to be twitching, very gently. The Bursar twitched gently all the time, of course, but that was only his way.

Like canaries, he thought. Or lightning conductors.

'All right,' he said reluctantly. 'We'll go. But we won't draw attention to ourselves.'

'Certainly, Archchancellor.'

'And everyone's to buy their own drink.'

'Oh.'

Corporal (possibly) Cotton saluted in front of the fort's sergeant, who was trying to shave.

'It's the new recruit, sir,' he said. 'He won't obey orders.'

The sergeant nodded, and then looked blankly at something in his own hand.

'Razor, sir,' said the corporal helpfully. 'He just keeps on saying things like IT'S NOT HAPPENING YET.'

'Have you tried burying him up to the neck in the sand? That usually works.'

'It's a bit . . . um . . . thing . . . nasty to people . . . had it a moment ago . . .' The corporal snapped his fingers. 'Thing. Cruel. That's it. We don't give people . . . the Pit . . . these days.'

'This *is* the . . .' the sergeant glanced at the palm of his left hand, where there were several lines of writing, 'the Foreign Legion.'

'Yessir. All right, sir. He's weird. He just sits there all the time. We call him Beau Nidle, sir.'

The sergeant peered bemusedly at the mirror.

'It's your face, sir,' said the corporal.

Susan stared at herself critically.

Susan . . . it wasn't a good name, was it? It wasn't a truly *bad* name, it wasn't like poor Iodine in the fourth form, or Nigella, a name which means 'oops, we wanted a boy'. But it was *dull.* Susan. Sue. Good old Sue. It was a name that made sandwiches, kept its head in difficult circumstances and could reliably look after other people's children.

It was a name used by no queens or goddesses anywhere.

And you couldn't do much even with the spelling. You could turn it into Suzi, and it sounded as though you danced on tables for a living. You could put in a Z and a couple of Ns and an E, but it still looked like a name with extensions built on. It was as bad as Sara, a name that cried out for a prosthetic H.

Well, at least she could do something about the way she looked.

It was the robe. It might be traditional but . . . *she* wasn't. The alternative was her school uniform or one of her mother's pink creations. The baggy dress of the Quirm College for Young Ladies was a proud one and, in the mind of Miss Butts at least, proof against all the temptations of the flesh . . . but it lacked a certain panache as costume for the Ultimate Reality. And pink was not even to be thought of.

For the first time in the history of the universe, a Death wondered about what to wear.

'Hold on,' she said, to her reflection. '*Here* . . . I can create things, can't I?'

She held out her hand and thought: cup. A cup appeared. It had a skull-and-bones pattern around the rim.

'Ah,' said Susan. 'I suppose a pattern of roses is out of the question? Probably not right for the ambience, I expect.'

She put the cup on the dressing table and tapped it. It went *plink* in a solid sort of way.

'Well, then,' she said, 'I *don't* want something soppy and posey. No silly black lace or anything worn by idiots who write poetry in their rooms and dress like vampires and are vegetarians really.'

The images of clothes floated across her reflection. It was clear that black was the only option, but she settled on something practical and without frills. She put her head on one side critically.

'Well, maybe a bit of lace,' she said. 'And . . . perhaps a bit more . . . bodice.'

She nodded at her reflection in the mirror. Certainly it was a dress that no Susan would ever wear, although she suspected that there was a basic Susanness about her which would permeate it after a while.

'It's a good job you're here,' she said, 'or I'd go totally mad. Haha.'

Then she went to see her grandf . . . Death.

There was one place he *had* to be.

* * *

Glod wandered quietly into the University Library. Dwarfs respected learning, provided they didn't have to experience it.

He tugged at the robe of a passing young wizard.

'There's a monkey runs this place, right?' he said. 'Big fat hairy monkey, hands a couple of octaves wide?'

The wizard, a pasty-faced post-graduate student, looked down at Glod with the disdainful air a certain type of person always reserves for dwarfs.

It wasn't much fun being a student in Unseen University. You had to find your pleasures where you could. He grinned a big, wide, innocent grin.

'Why, yes,' he said. 'I do believe right at this moment he's in his workroom in the basement. But you have to be very careful how you address him.'

'Is that so?' said Glod.

'Yes, you have to be sure to say, "Do you want a peanut, Mr Monkey?"' said the student wizard. He signalled a couple of his colleagues. 'That's so, isn't it? He has to say *Mister* Monkey.'

'Oh, yes indeedy,' said a student. 'Actually, if you don't want him to get annoyed it's best to be on the safe side and scratch under your arms. That puts him at his ease.'

'And go ugh-ugh-ugh,' said a third student. 'He likes that.'

'Well, thank you very much,' said Glod. 'Which way do I go?'

'We'll show you,' said the first student.

'That's so very kind.'

'Don't mention it. Only too glad to help.'

The three wizards led Glod down a flight of steps and into a tunnel. Light filtered down through the occasional pane of green glass set in the floor above. Every so often Glod heard a snigger behind him.

The Librarian was squatting down on the floor in a long, high cellar. Miscellaneous items had been scattered on the floor in front of him; there was a cartwheel, odd bits of wood and bone, and various pipes, rods and lengths of wire that somehow suggested that, around the city, people were puzzling over broken pumps and fences with holes in. The Librarian was chewing the end of a piece of pipe and looking intently at the heap.

'That's him,' said one of the wizards, giving Glod a push.

The dwarf shuffled forward. There was another outburst of muffled giggling behind him.

He tapped the Librarian on the shoulder.

'Excuse me—'

'Ook?'

'Those guys just called you a monkey,' said Glod, jerking a thumb in the direction of the door. 'I'd make them say sorry, if I was you.'

There was a creaking, metallic noise, followed very closely by a scuffling outside as the wizards trampled one another in their effort to get away.

The Librarian had bent the pipe into a U-shape, apparently without effort.

Glod went to the door and looked out. There was a pointy hat on the flagstones, trampled flat.

'That was fun,' he said. 'If I'd just asked them

where the Librarian was, they'd have said bugger off, you dwarf. You have to know how to deal with people in this game.'

He came back and sat down beside the Librarian. The ape put a smaller bend in the pipe.

'What're you making?' said Glod.

'Oook-oook-OOK!'

'My cousin Modo is the gardener here,' said Glod. 'He says you're a mean keyboard player.' He stared at the hands, busy in the pipe-bending. They were *big*. And of course there were four of them. 'He was certainly *partly* right,' he added.

The ape picked up a length of driftwood and tasted it.

'We thought you might like to play pianoforte with us at the Drum tonight,' said Glod. 'Me and Cliff and Buddy, that is.'

The Librarian rolled a brown eye towards him, then picked up a piece of wood, gripped one end and began to strum.

'Ook?'

'That's right,' said Glod. 'The boy with the guitar.'

'Eeek.'

The Librarian did a back somersault.

'Oook*oook*-ooka-ooka-OOOka-OOK!'

'I can see you're in the swing of it already,' said Glod.

Susan saddled the horse and mounted up.

Beyond Death's garden were fields of corn, their golden sheen the only colour in the landscape. Death might not have been any good at grass (black) and apple trees (gloss black on black), but all the depth of colour he hadn't put elsewhere he'd put in the fields. They rippled as if in the wind, except that there wasn't any wind.

Susan couldn't imagine why he'd done it.

There was a path, though. It led across the fields for half a mile or so, then disappeared abruptly. It looked as though somebody walked out here occasionally and just stood, looking around.

Binky followed the path and stopped at the end. Then he turned, managing not to disturb a single ear.

'I don't know how you do this,' Susan whispered, 'but you must be able to do it, and you *know* where I want to go.'

The horse appeared to nod. Albert had said that Binky was a genuine flesh-and-blood horse, but maybe you couldn't be ridden by Death for hundreds of years without learning something. He looked as though he'd been pretty bright to start with.

Binky began to trot, and then canter, and then gallop. And then the sky flickered, just once.

Susan had expected more than that. Flashing stars, some sort of explosion of rainbow colours . . . not just a flicker. It seemed a rather dismissive way of travelling nearly seventeen years.

The cornfields had gone, but the garden was pretty much the same. There was the strange topiary and the pond with the skeletal fish. There were, pushing jolly wheelbarrows and carrying tiny scythes, what might have been garden gnomes in a mortal garden but here were cheery little skeletons in black robes. Things tended not to change.

The stables were a little different, though. Binky was in them, for a start.

He whinnied quietly as Susan led him into an empty stall next to himself.

'I'm sure you two know each other,' she said. She'd never expected it to work, but it had to, didn't it? Time was something that happened to other people, wasn't it?

She slipped into the house.

NO. I CANNOT BE BIDDEN. I CANNOT BE FORCED. I WILL ONLY DO THAT WHICH I KNOW TO BE RIGHT . . .

Susan crept along behind the shelves of life-timers. No one noticed her. When you are watching Death fight, you don't notice shadows in the back-ground.

They'd never told her about this. Parents never do. Your father could be Death's apprentice and your mother Death's adopted daughter, but that's just fine detail when they become Parents. Parents were never young. They were merely waiting to be-come Parents.

Susan reached the end of the shelves.

Death was standing over her father . . . she corrected herself, the boy who *would be* her father.

Three red marks burned on his cheek where Death had struck him. Susan raised a hand to the pale marks on her own face.

But that's not how heredity works.

At least . . . the normal kind . . .

Her mother . . . the girl who *would become* her mother . . . was pressed against a pillar. She had actually improved with age, Susan thought. Her dress sense certainly had. And she mentally shook herself. Fashion comments? *Now?*

Death stood over Mort, sword in one hand and Mort's own lifetimer in the other.

YOU DON'T KNOW HOW SORRY THIS MAKES ME, he said.

'*I* might,' said Mort.

Death looked up, and looked straight at Susan. His eye sockets flared blue for a moment. Susan tried to press herself into the shadows.

He looked back down at Mort for a moment, and then at Ysabell, and then back at Susan, and then back down at Mort. And laughed.

And turned the hourglass over.

And snapped his fingers.

Mort vanished, with a small 'pop' of imploding air. So did Ysabell and the others.

It was, suddenly, very quiet.

Death put the hourglass down, very carefully, on the table and looked at the ceiling for a while. Then he said:

ALBERT?

Albert appeared from behind a pillar.

WOULD YOU BE SO GOOD AS TO MAKE ME A CUP OF TEA, PLEASE.

'Yes, Master. Hehe, you sorted him out right enough—'

THANK YOU.

Albert scurried off in the direction of the kitchen.

Once again there was the closest thing there could ever be to silence in the room of lifetimers.

YOU'D BETTER COME OUT.

Susan did so, and stood before the Ultimate Reality.

Death was seven feet tall. He looked taller. Susan had vague memories of a figure carrying her on its shoulders through the huge dark rooms, but in memory it had been a human figure – bony, but human in a way she was certain of but couldn't quite define.

This wasn't human. It was tall, and haughty, and terrible. He might unbend enough to bend the Rules, Susan thought, but that doesn't make him human. This is the keeper of the gate of the world. Immortal, by definition. The end of everything.

He is my *grandfather.*

Will be, anyway. Is. Was.

But . . . there was the thing in the apple tree. Her mind kept swinging back to that. You looked up at the figure, and thought about the tree. It was almost impossible to keep both images in one mind.

WELL, WELL, WELL. YOU HAVE A LOT OF YOUR MOTHER ABOUT YOU, said Death. AND YOUR FATHER.

'How did you know who I am?' said Susan.

I HAVE A UNIQUE MEMORY.

'How can you *remember* me? I haven't even been conceived yet!'

I DID SAY UNIQUE. YOUR NAME IS—

'Susan, but . . .'

SUSAN? said Death bitterly, THEY *REALLY* WANTED TO MAKE SURE, DIDN'T THEY?

He sat down in his chair, steepled his fingers and looked at Susan over the top of them.

She looked back, matching stare for stare.

TELL ME, said Death, after a while, WAS I . . . WILL I BE . . . *AM* I A GOOD GRANDFATHER?

Susan bit her lip thoughtfully.

'If I tell you, won't that be a paradox?'

NOT FOR US.

'Well . . . you've got bony knees.'

Death stared at her.

BONY KNEES?

'Sorry.'

YOU CAME HERE TO TELL ME THAT?

'You've gone missing back . . . there. I'm having to do the Duty. Albert is very worried. I came here to . . . find things out. I didn't know my father worked for you.'

HE WAS VERY BAD AT IT.

'What have you done with him?'

THEY'RE SAFE FOR NOW. I'M GLAD IT'S OVER, HAVING PEOPLE AROUND WAS BEGINNING TO AFFECT MY JUDGEMENT. AH, ALBERT . . .

Albert had appeared on the edge of the carpet, bearing a tea-tray.

ANOTHER CUP, IF YOU WOULD BE SO GOOD.

Albert looked around, and totally failed to see Susan. If you could be invisible to Miss Butts, everyone else was easy.

'If you say so, Master.'

SO, said Death, when Albert had shuffled away, I HAVE GONE MISSING. AND YOU BELIEVE YOU HAVE INHERITED THE FAMILY BUSINESS. *YOU*?

'I didn't want to! The horse and the rat just turned up!'

RAT?

'Er . . . I think that's something that's *going* to happen.'

OH, YES. I REMEMBER. HMM. A HUMAN DOING MY JOB? TECHNICALLY POSSIBLE, OF COURSE, BUT WHY?

'I think Albert knows something, but he changes the subject.'

Albert reappeared, carrying another cup and saucer. He plonked it down pointedly on Death's desk, with the air of one who is being put upon.

'That'll be all, will it, Master?' he said.

THANK YOU, ALBERT. YES.

Albert left again, more slowly than normal. He kept looking over his shoulder.

'He doesn't change, does he?' said Susan. 'Of course, that's the point about this place—'

WHAT DO YOU THINK ABOUT CATS?

'Sorry?'

CATS. DO YOU LIKE 'EM?

'They're . . .' Susan hesitated, 'all right. But a cat's just a cat.'

CHOCOLATE, said Death, DO YOU LIKE CHOCOLATE?

'I think it's possible to have too much,' said Susan.

YOU CERTAINLY DON'T TAKE AFTER YSABELL.

Susan nodded. Her mother's favourite dish had been Genocide by Chocolate.

AND YOUR MEMORY? YOU HAVE A GOOD MEMORY?

'Oh, yes. I . . . remember things. About how to be

Death. About how it's all supposed to work. Look, just then you said you *remembered* about the rat, and it hasn't even happ—'

Death stood up and strode across to the model of the Discworld.

MORPHIC RESONANCE, he said, not looking at Susan. DAMN, PEOPLE DON'T *BEGIN* TO UNDERSTAND IT. SOUL HARMONICS. IT'S RESPONSIBLE FOR SO MANY THINGS.

Susan pulled out Imp's lifetimer. Blue smoke was still pouring through the pinch.

'Can you help me with this?' she said.

Death spun around.

I SHOULD NEVER HAVE ADOPTED YOUR MOTHER.

'Why did you?'

Death shrugged.

WHAT'S THAT YOU'VE GOT THERE?

He took Buddy's lifetimer from her and held it up.

AH. INTERESTING.

'Do you know what it means, Grandad?'

I'VE NOT COME ACROSS IT BEFORE, BUT I SUPPOSE IT'S POSSIBLE, IN CERTAIN CIRCUMSTANCES. IT MEANS . . . SOMEHOW . . . THAT HE HAS RHYTHM IN HIS SOUL . . . *GRANDAD*?

'Oh, no. That can't be right. That's just a figure of speech. And what's wrong with grandad?'

GRANDFATHER I CAN LIVE WITH. GRANDAD? ONE STEP AWAY FROM GRAMPS, IN MY OPINION. ANYWAY, I THOUGHT YOU BELIEVED IN LOGIC. CALLING SOMETHING A FIGURE OF SPEECH DOESN'T MEAN IT'S NOT TRUE.

Death waved the hourglass vaguely.

FOR EXAMPLE, he said, *MANY* THINGS ARE BETTER THAN A POKE IN THE EYE WITH A BLUNT STICK. I'VE NEVER UNDERSTOOD THE PHRASE. SURELY A SHARP STICK WOULD BE EVEN WORSE—

Death stopped.

I'M DOING IT AGAIN! WHY SHOULD I CARE WHAT THE WRETCHED PHRASE MEANS? OR WHAT YOU CALL ME? UNIMPORTANT! GETTING ENTANGLED WITH HUMANS CLOUDS THE THINKING. TAKE IT FROM ME. DON'T GET INVOLVED.

'But I *am* a human.'

I DIDN'T SAY IT WAS GOING TO BE EASY, DID I? DON'T THINK ABOUT IT. DON'T *FEEL*.

'You're an expert, are you?' said Susan hotly.

I MAY HAVE ALLOWED MYSELF SOME FLICKER OF EMOTION IN THE RECENT PAST, said Death, BUT I CAN GIVE IT UP ANY TIME I LIKE.

He held up the hourglass again.

IT'S AN INTERESTING FACT THAT MUSIC, BEING OF ITS NATURE IMMORTAL, CAN SOMETIMES PROLONG THE LIFE OF THOSE INTIMATELY ASSOCIATED WITH IT, he said, I'VE NOTICED THAT FAMOUS COMPOSERS IN PARTICULAR HANG ON FOR A LONG TIME. DEAF AS POSTS, MOST OF THEM, WHEN I COME CALLING. I EXPECT SOME GOD SOMEWHERE FINDS THAT VERY AMUSING. Death contrived to look disdainful. IT'S THEIR KIND OF JOKE.*

*And, of course, one that misfires. Deafness doesn't prevent composers hearing the music. It prevents them hearing the distractions.

He set the glass down and twanged it with a bony digit.

It went *whauuummmmeeee-chida-chida-chida.*

HE HAS NO LIFE. HE HAS MUSIC.

'Music's taken him over?'

YOU COULD PUT IT LIKE THAT.

'Making his life longer?'

LIFE IS EXTENSIBLE. IT HAPPENS OCCASIONALLY AMONG HUMANS. NOT OFTEN. USUALLY TRAGICALLY, IN A THEATRICAL KIND OF WAY. BUT THIS ISN'T ANOTHER HUMAN. THIS IS MUSIC.

'He played something, on some sort of stringed instrument like a guitar—'

Death turned.

INDEED? WELL, WELL, WELL . . .

'Is that important?'

IT IS . . . INTERESTING.

'Is it something I should know?'

IT IS NOTHING IMPORTANT. A PIECE OF MYTHOLOGICAL DEBRIS. MATTERS WILL RESOLVE THEMSELVES, YOU MAY DEPEND UPON IT.

'What do you mean, resolve themselves?'

HE WILL PROBABLY BE DEAD IN A MATTER OF DAYS.

Susan stared at the lifetimer.

'But that's dreadful!'

ARE YOU ROMANTICALLY INVOLVED WITH THE YOUNG MAN?

'What? No! I've only ever seen him once!'

YOUR EYES DIDN'T MEET ACROSS A CROWDED ROOM OR ANYTHING OF THAT NATURE?

'No! Of course not.'

WHY SHOULD YOU CARE, THEN?

'Because he matt— because he's a human being, that's why,' said Susan, surprised at herself. 'I don't see why people should be messed around like that,' she added lamely. 'That's all. Oh, I don't know.'

He leaned down again until his skull was on a level with her face.

BUT MOST PEOPLE ARE RATHER STUPID AND WASTE THEIR LIVES. HAVE YOU NOT SEEN THAT? HAVE YOU NOT LOOKED DOWN FROM THE HORSE AT A CITY AND THOUGHT HOW MUCH IT RESEMBLED AN ANT HEAP, FULL OF BLIND CREATURES WHO THINK THEIR MUNDANE LITTLE WORLD IS REAL? YOU SEE THE LIGHTED WINDOWS AND WHAT YOU WANT TO THINK IS THAT THERE MAY BE MANY INTERESTING STORIES BEHIND THEM, BUT WHAT YOU KNOW IS THAT REALLY THERE ARE JUST DULL, DULL SOULS, MERE CONSUMERS OF FOOD, WHO THINK THEIR INSTINCTS ARE EMOTIONS AND THEIR TINY LIVES OF MORE ACCOUNT THAN A WHISPER OF WIND.

The blue glow was bottomless. It seemed to be sucking her own thoughts out of her mind.

'No,' whispered Susan, 'no, I've never thought like that.'

Death stood up abruptly and turned away, YOU MAY FIND THAT IT HELPS, he said.

'But it's all just *chaos,*' said Susan. 'There's no sense to the way people die. There's no justice!'

HAH.

'*You* take a hand,' she persisted. 'You just saved my father.'

I WAS FOOLISH. TO CHANGE THE FATE OF ONE

INDIVIDUAL IS TO CHANGE THE WORLD. I REMEMBER THAT. SO SHOULD YOU.

Death still hadn't turned to face her.

'I don't see why we shouldn't change things if it makes the world better,' said Susan.

HAH.

'Are you too *scared* to change the world?'

Death turned. The very sight of his expression made Susan back away.

He advanced slowly towards her. His voice, when it came, was a hiss.

YOU SAY THAT TO *ME*? YOU STAND THERE IN YOUR PRETTY DRESS AND SAY THAT TO *ME*? YOU? YOU PRATTLE ON ABOUT CHANGING THE WORLD? COULD YOU FIND THE COURAGE TO ACCEPT IT? TO KNOW WHAT *MUST BE DONE* AND DO IT, WHATEVER THE COST? IS THERE ONE HUMAN ANYWHERE IN THE WORLD WHO KNOWS WHAT DUTY *MEANS*?

His hands opened and shut convulsively.

I SAID YOU MUST REMEMBER . . . FOR US, TIME IS ONLY A PLACE. IT'S ALL SPREAD OUT. THERE IS WHAT IS, AND WHAT WILL BE. IF YOU CHANGE THAT, YOU CARRY THE RESPONSIBILITY FOR THE CHANGE. AND THAT IS TOO HEAVY TO BEAR.

'That's just an excuse!'

Susan glared at the tall figure. Then she turned and marched out of the room.

SUSAN?

She stopped halfway across the floor, but didn't turn around. 'Yes?'

REALLY . . . BONY KNEES?

'Yes!'

* * *

It was probably the first piano case that'd ever been made, and made out of a carpet at that. Cliff swung it easily on to his shoulder and picked up his sack of rocks in the other hand.

'Is it heavy?' said Buddy.

Cliff held the piano up on one hand and weighed it reflectively.

'A bit,' he said. The floorboards creaked underneath him. 'Do you think we should've took all dem bits out?'

'It's bound to work,' said Glod. 'It's like . . . a coach. The more bits you take off, the faster it goes. Come on.'

They set out. Buddy tried to look as inconspicuous as a human can look if he is accompanying a dwarf with a big horn, an ape, and a troll carrying a piano in a bag.

'I'd like a coach,' said Cliff, as they headed for the Drum. 'Big black coach with all dat liver on it.'

'Liver?' said Buddy. He was beginning to get accustomed to the name.

'Shields and dat.'

'Oh. Livery.'

'And dat.'

'What'd you get if you had a pile of gold, Glod?' said Buddy. In its bag the guitar twanged gently to the sound of his voice.

Glod hesitated. He wanted to say that for a dwarf the whole point of having a pile of gold was, well, to have a pile of gold. It didn't have to do anything other than be just as oraceous as gold could be.

'Dunno,' he said. 'Never thought I'd have a pile of gold. What about you?'

'I swore I'd be the most famous musician in the world.'

'Dat's dangerous, dat kinda swear,' said Cliff.

'Oook.'

'Isn't it what every artist wants?' said Buddy.

'In my experience,' said Glod, 'what every true artist wants, really *wants,* is to be paid.'

'And famous,' said Buddy.

'Famous I don't know about,' said Glod. 'It's hard to be famous and alive. I just want to play music every day and hear someone say, "Thanks, that was great, here is some money, same time tomorrow OK?"'

'Is that all?'

'It's a lot. I'd like people to say, "We need a good horn man, get Glod Glodsson!"'

'Sounds a bit dull,' said Buddy.

'I like dull. It lasts.'

They reached the side door of the Drum and entered a gloomy room that smelled of rats and second-hand beer. There was a distant murmur of voices from the bar.

'Sounds like there's a lot of people in,' said Glod.

Hibiscus bustled up. 'You boys ready, then?' he said.

'Hold on a minute,' said Cliff. 'We ain't discussed our pay.'

'I said six dollars,' said Hibiscus. 'What d'you expect? You aren't Guild, and the Guild rate is eight dollars.'

'We wouldn't ask you for eight dollars,' said Glod.

'Right!'

'We'll take sixteen.'

'Sixteen? You can't do that! That's almost twice Guild rate!'

'But there's a lot of people out there,' said Glod. 'I bet you're renting a lot of beer. We don't mind going home.'

'Let's talk about this,' said Hibiscus. He put his arm around Glod's head and led him to a corner of the room.

Buddy watched the Librarian examine the piano. He'd never seen a musician begin by trying to eat his instrument. Then the ape lifted the lid and regarded the keyboard. He tried a few notes, apparently for taste.

Glod returned, rubbing his hands.

'That's sorted *him* out,' he said. 'Hah!'

'How much?' said Cliff.

'Six dollars!' said Glod.

There was some silence.

'Sorry,' said Buddy. 'We were waiting for the "-teen".'

'I had to be firm,' said Glod. 'He got down to two dollars at one point.'

Some religions say that the universe was started with a word, a song, a dance, a piece of music. The Listening Monks of the Ramtops have trained their hearing until they can tell the value of a playing card by listening to it, and have made it their task to listen intently to the subtle sounds of the universe to piece together, from the fossil echoes, the very first sounds.

There was certainly, they say, a very strange noise at the beginning of everything.

But the keenest ears (the ones who win most at poker), who listen to the frozen echoes in ammonites and amber, swear they can detect some tiny sounds before that.

It sounded, they say, like someone counting: One, Two, Three, Four.

The very best one, who listened to basalt, said he thought he could make out, very faintly, some numbers that came even earlier.

When they asked him what it was, he said: 'It sounds like One, Two.'

No one ever asked what, if there *was* a sound that called the universe into being, happened to it afterwards. It's mythology. You're not supposed to ask that kind of question.

On the other hand, Ridcully believed that everything had come into being by chance or, in the particular case of the Dean, out of spite.

Senior wizards didn't usually drink in the Mended Drum except when they were off duty. They were aware that they were here tonight in some sort of ill-defined official capacity, and were seated rather primly in front of their drinks.

There was a ring of empty seats around them, but it was not very big because the Drum was unusually crowded.

'Lot of ambience in here,' said Ridcully, looking

around. 'Ah, I see they do Real Ale again. I'll have a pint of Turbot's Really Odd, please.'

The wizards watched him as he drained the mug. Ankh-Morpork beer has a flavour all its own; it's something to do with the water. Some people say it's like consommé, but they are wrong. Consommé is cooler.

Ridcully smacked his lips happily.

'Ah, we certainly know what goes into good beer in Ankh-Morpork,' he said.

The wizards nodded. They certainly did. That's why they were drinking gin and tonic.

Ridcully looked around. Normally at this time of night there was a fight going on somewhere, or at least a mild stabbing. But there was just a buzz of conversation and everyone was watching the small stage at the far end of the room, where nothing was happening in large amounts. There was theoretically a curtain across it; it was only an old sheet, and there was a succession of thuds and thumps from behind it.

The wizards were quite close to the stage. Wizards tend to get good seats. Ridcully thought he could make out some whispering, and see shadows moving behind the sheet.

'He said, what do we call ourselves?'

'Cliff, Buddy, Glod and the Librarian. I thought he knew that.'

'No, we've got to have one name for all of us.'

'Dey rationed, den?'

'Something like The Merry Troubadours, maybe.'

'Oook!'

'Glod and the Glodettes?'

'Oh, yes? How about Cliff and the Cliffettes?'

'Oook ook Oook-ook?'

'No. We need a different type of name. Like the music.'

'How about *Gold?* Good dwarf name.'

'No. Something different from that.'

'*Silver*, then.'

'Ook!'

'I don't think we should name ourselves after any kind of heavy metal, Glod.'

'What's so special? We're a band of people who play music.'

'Names are important.'

'The guitar is special. How about The Band With Buddy's Guitar In It?'

'Oook.'

'Something shorter.'

'Er . . .'

The universe held its breath.

'The Band With Rocks In?'

'I *like* it. Short and slightly dirty, just like me.'

'Oook.'

'We ought to think up a name for the music, too.'

'It's bound to occur to us sooner or later.'

Ridcully looked around the bar.

On the opposite side of the room was Cut-Me-Own-Throat Dibbler, Ankh-Morpork's most spectacularly unsuccessful businessman. He was trying to sell someone a felonious hot dog, a sign that some recent sure-fire business venture had collapsed.

Dibbler sold his hot sausages only when all else failed.*

He gave Ridcully a wave at no charge.

The next table was occupied by Satchelmouth Lemon, one of the Musicians' Guild's recruiting officers, with a couple of associates whose apparent knowledge of music extended only to the amount of percussion available on the human skull. His determined expression suggested that he was not there for his health, although the fact that the Guild officers had a mean look about them rather hinted he was there for other people's health, mostly in order to take it away.

Ridcully brightened up. The evening might just possibly be more interesting than he had expected.

There was another table near the stage. He nearly didn't notice it, and then his gaze swivelled back to it of its own accord.

There was a young woman sitting there, all by herself. Of course, it wasn't unusual to see young women in the Drum. Even unaccompanied young women. They were generally there in order to become accompanied.

The odd thing was that, although people were jammed along the benches, she had space all around her. She was quite attractive in a skinny way,

*It wasn't the taste. Plenty of hot dogs taste bad. But Dibbler had now actually managed to produce sausages that didn't taste of anything. It was weird. No matter how much mustard, ketchup and pickle people put on them, they still didn't taste of *anything*. Not even the midnight dogs they sell to drunks in Helsinki can quite manage that.

Ridcully thought. What was the tomboy word? Gammon, or something. She was wearing a black lace dress of the sort worn by healthy young women who want to look consumptive, and had a raven sitting on her shoulder.

She turned her head, saw Ridcully looking at her, and vanished.

More or less.

He was a wizard, after all. He felt his eyes watering as she flickered in and out of vision.

Ah. Well, he'd heard the Tooth Fairy girls were in the city these days. It'd be one of the night people. They probably had a day off, just like everyone else.

A movement on the table made him look down. The Death of Rats scrittered past, carrying a bowl of peanuts.

He turned back to the wizards. The Dean was still wearing his pointy hat. There was also something slightly shiny about his face.

'You look hot, Dean,' said Ridcully.

'Oh, I'm lovely and cool, Archchancellor, I assure you,' said the Dean. Something runny oozed past his nose.

The Lecturer in Recent Runes sniffed suspiciously.

'Is someone cooking bacon?' he said.

'Take it off, Dean,' said Ridcully. 'You'll feel a lot better.'

'Smells more like Mrs Palm's House of Negotiable Affection to *me,*' said the Senior Wrangler.

They looked at him in surprise.

'I just happened to walk past once,' he said quickly.

'Runes, please take the Dean's hat off for him, will you?' said Ridcully.

'I assure you—'

The hat came off. Something long and greasy and very nearly the same pointy shape flopped forward.

'Dean,' said Ridcully eventually, 'what have you done to your hair? It looks like a spike at the front and a duck's arse, excuse my Klatchian, at the back. And it's all shiny.'

'Lard. That'd be the bacon smell,' said the Lecturer.

'That's true,' said Ridcully, 'but what about the floral smell?'

'*mumblemumblemumblelavendermumble*,' said the Dean sullenly.

'Pardon, Dean?'

'I said it's because I added lavender oil,' said the Dean loudly. 'And some of us happen to think it's a nifty hairstyle, thank you so very much. Your trouble, Archchancellor, is that you don't understand people of our age!'

'What . . . you mean seven months older than me?' said Ridcully.

This time the Dean hesitated.

'What did I just say?' he said.

'Have you been taking dried frog pills, old chap?' said Ridcully.

'Of course not, they're for the mentally unstable!' said the Dean.

'Ah. There's the trouble, then.'

The curtain went up or, rather, was jerkily pulled aside.

The Band With Rocks In blinked in the torchlight.

No one clapped. On the other hand, no one threw anything, either. By Drum standards, this was a hearty welcome.

Ridcully saw a tall, curly-headed young man clutching what looked like an undernourished guitar or possibly a banjo that had been used in a fight. Beside him was a dwarf, holding a battle horn. At the rear was a troll, hammer in each paw, seated behind a pile of rocks. And to one side was the Librarian, standing in front of . . . Ridcully leaned forward . . . what appeared to be the skeleton of a piano, balanced on some beer-kegs.

The boy looked paralysed by the attention.

He said: 'Hello . . . er . . . Ankh-Morpork . . .'

And, this amount of conversation apparently having exhausted him, he started to play.

It was a simple little rhythm, one that you might easily have ignored if you'd met it in the street. It was followed by a sequence of crashing chords and then, Ridcully realized, it *hadn't* been followed by the chords, because the rhythm was there all the time. Which was impossible. No guitar could be played like that.

The dwarf blew a sequence of notes on the horn. The troll picked up the beat. The Librarian brought both hands down upon the piano keyboard, apparently at random.

Ridcully had never heard such a din.

And then . . . and then . . . it wasn't a din any more.

It was like that nonsense about white light that the young wizards in the High Energy Magic Building went on about. They said that all the colours together made up white, which was bloody nonsense as far as Ridcully was concerned, because everyone knew that if you mixed up all the colours you could get your hands on, you got a sort of greeny-brown mess which certainly wasn't any kind of white. But now he had a vague idea what they meant.

All this noise, this mess of music, suddenly came together and there was a new music inside it.

The Dean's quiff was quivering. The whole crowd was moving.

Ridcully realized his foot was tapping. He stamped on it with his other foot.

Then he watched the troll carry the beat and hammer the rocks until the walls shook. The Librarian's fingers swooped along the keyboard. Then his toes did the same. And all the time the guitar hooted and screamed and sang out the melody.

The wizards were bouncing in their seats and twirling their fingers in the air.

Ridcully leaned over to the Bursar and screamed at him.

'What?' shouted the Bursar.

'I said, they've all gone mad except me and you!'

'What?'

'It's the music!'

'Yes! It's great!' said the Bursar, waving his skinny hands in the air.

'And I'm not too certain about you!'

Ridcully sat down again and pulled out the thaumometer. It was vibrating crazily, which was no help at all. It didn't seem to be able to decide if this was magic or not.

He nudged the Bursar sharply.

'This ain't magic! This is something else!'

'You're exactly right!'

Ridcully had the feeling that he suddenly wasn't speaking the right language.

'I mean it's too much!'

'Yes!'

Ridcully sighed.

'Is it time for your dried frog pill?'

Smoke was coming out of the stricken piano. The Librarian's hands were walking through the keys like Casanunda in a nunnery.

Ridcully looked around. He felt all alone.

Someone else hadn't been overcome by the music. Satchelmouth had stood up. So had his two associates.

They had drawn some knobbly clubs. Ridcully knew the Guild laws. Of course, they had to be enforced. You couldn't run a city without them. This certainly wasn't licensed music – if ever there was unlicensed music, this was it. Nevertheless . . . he rolled up his sleeve and prepared a quick fireball, just in case.

One of the men dropped his club and clutched his foot. The other one spun around as if something had slapped his ear. Satchelmouth's hat dented, as if someone had just hit him on the head.

Ridcully, one eye watering terribly, thought he made out the Tooth Fairy girl bringing the handle of a scythe down on Satchelmouth's head.

The Archchancellor was quite a bright man but often had trouble in forcing his train of thought to change tracks. He was having difficulty with the idea of a scythe, after all, grass didn't have teeth – and then the fireball burned his fingers, and *then,* as he sucked frantically at them, he realized that there was something in the sound. Something *extra.*

'Oh, no,' he said, as the fireball floated to the floor and set fire to the Bursar's boot, *'it's alive.'*

He grabbed the beer mug, finished the contents hurriedly, and rammed it upside down on the table-top.

The moon shone over the Klatchian desert, in the vicinity of the dotted line. Both sides of it got exactly the same amount of moonlight, although minds like Mr Clete's deplored this state of affairs.

The sergeant strolled across the packed sand of the parade ground. He stopped, sat down, and produced a cheroot. Then he pulled out a match, reached down and struck it on something sticking out of the sand, which said:

GOOD EVENING.

'I expect you've had enough, eh, soldier?' said the sergeant.

ENOUGH WHAT, SERGEANT?

'Two days in the sun, no food, no water . . . I expect you're delirious with thirst and are just begging to be dug out, eh?'

YES. IT IS CERTAINLY VERY DULL.

'Dull?'

I AM AFRAID SO.

'*Dull?* It's not meant to be dull! It's the Pit! It's meant to be a horrible physical and mental torture! After one day of it you're supposed to be a . . .' The sergeant glanced surreptitiously at some writing on his wrist, '. . . a raving madman! I've been watching you all day! You haven't even groaned! I can't sit in my . . . thing, you sit in it, there's papers and things . . .'

OFFICE.

'. . . working, with you outside like this! I can't bear it!'

Beau Nidle glanced upwards. He felt it was time for a kindly gesture.

HELP, HELP. HELP, HELP, he said.

The sergeant sagged with relief.

THIS ASSISTS PEOPLE TO FORGET, DOES IT?

'Forget? People forget *everything* when they're given . . . er . . .'

THE PIT.

'Yes! That's it!'

AH. DO YOU MIND IF I ASK A QUESTION?

'What?'

DO YOU MIND IF PERHAPS I HAVE ANOTHER DAY?

The sergeant opened his mouth to reply, and the D'regs attacked over the nearest sand-dune.

'Music?' said the Patrician. 'Ah. Tell me more.'

He leaned back in an attitude that suggested attentive listening. He was extremely good at listening. He created a kind of mental suction. People told him things just to avoid the silence.

Besides, Lord Vetinari, the supreme ruler of Ankh-Morpork, rather liked music.

People wondered what sort of music would appeal to such a man.

Highly formalized chamber music, possibly, or thunder-and-lightning opera scores.

In fact the kind of music he really liked was the kind that *never got played.* It ruined music, in his opinion, to torment it by involving it on dried skins, bits of dead cat and lumps of metal hammered into wires and tubes. It ought to stay written down, on the page, in rows of little dots and crotchets, all neatly caught between lines. Only there was it pure. It was when people started doing things with it that the rot set in. Much better to sit quietly in a room and read the sheets, with nothing between yourself and the mind of the composer but a scribble of ink. Having it played by sweaty fat men and people with hair in their ears and spit dribbling out of the end of their oboe . . . well, the idea made him shudder. Although not much, because he never did anything to extremes.

So . . .

'And then what happened?' he said.

'An' then he started singin', yerronner,' said Cumbling Michael, licensed beggar and informal informant. 'A song about Great Fiery Balls.'

The Patrician raised an eyebrow.

'Pardon?'

'Somethin' like that. Couldn't really make out the words, the reason bein', the piano exploded.'

'Ah? I imagine this interrupted the proceedings somewhat.'

'Nah, the monkey went on playin' what was left,' said Cumbling Michael. 'And people got up and started cheerin' and dancin' and stampin' their feet like there was a plague of cockroaches.'

'And you say the men from the Musicians' Guild were hurt?'

'It was dead strange. They were white as a sheet afterwards. At least,' Cumbling Michael thought about the state of his own bedding, 'white as *some* sheets—'

The Patrician glanced at his reports while the beggar talked. It had certainly been a strange evening. A riot at the Drum . . . well, that was normal, although it didn't sound exactly like a typical riot and he'd never heard of wizards *dancing*. He rather felt he recognized the signs . . . There was only one thing that could make it worse.

'Tell me,' he said. 'What was Mr Dibbler's reaction to all this?'

'What, yerronner?'

'A simple enough question, I should have thought.'

Cumbling Michael found the words *'But how did you know ole Dibbler was there? I never said'* arranging themselves for the attention of his larynx, and then had second, third and fourth thoughts about saying them.

'He just sat and stared, yerronner. With his mouth open. And then he rushed right out.'

'I see. Oh, dear. Thank you, Cumbling Michael. Feel free to leave.'

The beggar hesitated.

'Foul Ole Ron said as yerronner sometimes pays for information,' he said.

'Did he? Really? He said that, did he? Well, that *is* interesting.' Vetinari scribbled a note in the margin of a report. 'Thank you.'

'Er—'

'Don't let me detain you.'

'Er. No. Gods bless yerronner,' said Cumbling Michael, and ran for it.

When the sound of the beggar's boots had died away the Patrician strolled over to the window, stood with his hands clasped behind his back, and sighed.

There were probably city states, he reasoned, where the rulers only had to worry about the *little* things . . . barbarian invasions, the balance of payments, assassination, the local volcano erupting. There weren't people busily opening the door of reality and metaphorically saying, 'Hi, come on in, pleased to see you, what a nice axe you have there, incidentally, can I make some money out of you since you're here?'

Sometimes Lord Vetinari wondered what *had* happened to Mr Hong. Everyone knew, of course. In general terms. But not exactly *what.*

What a city. In the spring, the river caught fire. About once a month, the Alchemists' Guild exploded.

He walked back to his desk and made another brief note. He was rather afraid that he was going to have to have someone killed.

Then he picked up the third movement of Fondel's *Prelude in G Major* and settled back to read.

Susan walked back to the alley where she'd left Binky. There were half a dozen men lying around on the cobbles, clutching parts of themselves and moaning. Susan ignored them. Anyone trying to steal Death's horse soon understood the expression 'a world of hurts'. Binky had a good aim. It would be a very small, very private world.

'The music was playing him, not the other way

round,' she said. 'You could see. I'm not sure his fingers even touched the strings.'

SQUEAK.

Susan rubbed her hand. Satchelmouth had turned out to have quite a hard head.

'Can I kill it without killing him?'

SQUEAK.

'Not a hope,' the raven translated. 'It's all that's keeping him alive.'

'But Granda . . . but he said it'll end up killing him anyway!'

'It's a big wide wonderful universe all right,' said the raven.

SQUEAK.

'But . . . look, if it's a . . . a parasite, or something like that,' said Susan, as Binky trotted skywards, 'what's the good of it killing its host?'

SQUEAK.

'He says you've got him there,' said the raven. 'Drop me off over Quirm, will you?'

'What does it *want* him for?' said Susan. 'It's using him, but what *for*?'

'Twenty-seven dollars!' said Ridcully. 'Twenty-seven dollars to get you out! And the sergeant kept *grinning* all the time! Wizards *arrested*!'

He walked along the row of crestfallen figures.

'I mean, how often does the Watch get *called in* to the Drum?' said Ridcully. 'I mean, what did you think you were doing?'

'mumblemumblemumble,' said the Dean, looking at the floor.

'I'm sorry?'

'mumblemumbledancingmumble.'

'Dancing,' said Ridcully levelly, walking back along the row. 'That's dancing, is it? Banging into people? Throwin' one another over yer shoulders? Twirling around all over the place? Not even trolls act like that (not that I've got anything against trolls mind you marvellous people marvellous people) and you're supposed to be *wizards.* People are supposed to look up to you and that's *not* because you're somersaulting over their heads, Runes, don't think I didn't notice that little display, I was frankly disgusted. The poor Bursar has had to have a lie down. Dancing is . . . round in circles, don'tcherknow, Maypoles and suchlike, healthy reels, perhaps a little light ballroom . . . *not* swinging people round like a dwarf with a battleaxe (mind you salt of the earth dwarfs I've always said so). Do I make myself clear?'

'mumblemumblemumbleeveryonewasdoingit-mumble,' said the Dean, still looking at the floor.

'I never thought I'd say this to any wizard over the age of eighteen, but you're all gated until further notice!' shouted Ridcully.

Being confined to the campus was not much of a punishment. The wizards usually distrusted any air that hadn't hung around indoors for a while, and mostly lived in a kind of groove between their rooms and the dining table. But they were feeling strange.

'mumblemumbledon'tseewhymumble,' mumbled the Dean.

He said, much later on, on the day when the music died, that it must have been because he'd never been really young, or at least young while just being old enough to know he was young. Like most wizards, he'd begun his training while still so small that the official pointy hat came down over his ears. And after that he'd just been, well, a wizard.

He had the feeling, once again, that he'd missed out on something somewhere. He'd never really realized it until the last couple of days. He didn't know what it was. He just wanted to *do* things. He didn't know what they were. But he wanted to do them soon. He wanted . . . he felt like a lifelong tundra dweller when he wakes up one morning with a deep urge to go water-skiing. He certainly wasn't going to stay indoors when there was music in the air . . .

'mumblemumblemumblenotgonnastayindoors-mumble.'

Unaccustomed feelings surged through him. He wanted to disobey! Disobey everything! Including the law of gravity. He was definitely not going to fold his clothes before going to bed! Ridcully was going to say, oh, you're a rebel, are you, what are you rebelling against, and he'd say . . . he'd say something pretty damn memorable, that's what he'd do! He was—

But the Archchancellor had stalked off.

'mumblemumblemumble,' said the Dean defiantly, a rebel without a pause.

There was a knock at the door, barely audible above the din. Cliff opened it a cautious fraction.

'It's me, Hibiscus. Here's your beers. Drink 'em up and get out!'

'How can we get out?' said Glod. 'Every time they see us they force us to play some more!'

Hibiscus shrugged. 'I don't care,' he said. 'But you owe me a dollar for the beer and twenty-five dollars for the broken furniture—'

Cliff shut the door.

'I could negotiate with him,' said Glod.

'No, we can't afford it,' said Buddy.

They looked at one another.

'Well, the crowd loved us,' said Buddy. 'I think we were a big success. Er.'

In the silence Cliff bit the end off a beer bottle and poured the contents over his head.*

'What we all want to know is,' said Glod, 'what you thought you were doing out there?'

'Oook.'

'And how come,' said Cliff, crunching up the rest of the bottle, 'we all knew what to play?'

'Oook.'

'And also,' said Glod, 'what you were singing.'

'Er . . .'

' "Don't Tread On My New Blue Boots"?' said Cliff.

'Oook.'

' "Good Gracious Miss Polly"?' said Glod.

'Er . . .'

' "Sto Helit Lace"?' said Cliff.

'Oook?'

'It's a kind of very fine lace they make in the city of Sto Helit,' said Glod.

*Troll beer is ammonium sulphide dissolved in alcohol and tastes like drinking fermented batteries.

Glod gave Buddy a lopsided look.

'That bit where you said "hello, baby",' he said. 'Why'd you do that?'

'Er . . .'

'I mean, it's not as if they even allow small children into the Drum.'

'I don't know. The words were just there,' said Buddy. 'They were sort of part of the music . . .'

'And you were . . . moving about in a funny way. Like you were having trouble with your trousers,' said Glod. 'I'm not expert on humans, of course, but I saw some ladies in the audience looking at you like a dwarf looks at a girl when he knows her father's got a big shaft and several rich seams.'

'Yeah,' said Cliff, 'and like when a troll is thinking: hey, will you look at der strata on dat one . . .'

'You're *certain* you've got no elvish in you, are you?' said Glod. 'Once or twice I thought you were acting a bit . . . elvish.'

'*I don't know what's happening!*' said Buddy.

The guitar whined.

They looked at it.

'What we do is,' said Cliff, 'we take dat and throw it in de river. All those in favour say "Aye". Or "Oook", as the case may be.'

There was another silence. No one rushed to pick up the instrument.

'But the thing is,' said Glod, 'the thing is . . . they *did* love us out there.'

They thought about this.

'It didn't actually feel . . . *bad*,' said Buddy.

'Got to admit . . . I never had an audience like dat in my whole life,' said Cliff.

'Oook.'

'If we're so good,' said Glod, 'why ain't we rich?'

''Cos you do the negotiatin',' said Cliff. 'If we've got to pay for der furniture, I'm soon goin' to have to eat my dinner through a straw.'

'You saying I'm no good?' said Glod, getting angrily to his feet.

'You blow good horn. But you ain't no financial wizard.'

'Hah, I'd just like to see—'

There was a knock on the door.

Cliff sighed. 'Dat'll be Hibiscus again,' he said. 'Pass me dat mirror. I'll try to hit one out on de other side.'

Buddy opened the door. Hibiscus was there, but behind a smaller man wearing a long coat and a wide, friendly grin.

'Ah,' said the grin. 'You'd be Buddy, right?'

'Er, yes.'

And then the man was inside, without actually appearing to have moved, and kicking the door shut in the landlord's face.

'Dibbler's the name,' the grin went on. 'C. M. O. T. Dibbler. I dare say you've heard of me?'

'Oook!'

'I ain't talking to you! I'm talking to you other guys.'

'No,' said Buddy, 'I don't think we have.'

The grin appeared to widen.

'I hear you boys are in a bit of trouble,' said Dibbler. 'Broken furniture and whatnot.'

'We're not even going to get paid,' said Cliff, glaring at Glod.

'Well now,' said Dibbler, 'it could just be that I could help you there. I'm a businessman. I do business. I can see you boys are musicians. You play music. You don't want to worry your heads about money stuff, right? Gets in the way of the creative processes, am I right? How about if you leave that to me?'

'Huh,' said Glod, still smarting from the insult to his financial acumen. 'And what can *you* do?'

'Well,' said Dibbler, 'I can get you paid for to-night, for a start.'

'What about the furniture?' said Buddy.

'Oh, stuff gets busted here every night,' said Dibbler expansively. 'Hibiscus was just having you on. I'll square it with him. Confidentially, you want to watch out for people like him.'

He leaned forward. If his grin had been any wider the top of his head would have fallen off.

'This city, boys,' he said, 'is a jungle.'

'If he can get us paid, I trust him,' said Glod.

'As simple as dat?' said Cliff.

'I trust anyone who gives me money.'

Buddy glanced at the table. He didn't know why, but he had a feeling that if something was wrong the guitar would do something – play a discord, maybe. But it just purred gently to itself.

'Oh, all right. If it means I get to keep my teef, I'm all for it,' said Cliff.

'Okay,' said Buddy.

'Great! Great! We can make beautiful music together! At least – you boys can, eh?'

He pulled out a sheet of paper and a pencil. In Dibbler's eyes, the lion roared.

Somewhere high in the Ramtops, Susan rode Binky over a cloudbank.

'How could he *talk* like that?' she said. 'Play around with people's lives, and then talk about duty?'

All the lights were on in the Musicians' Guild.

A gin bottle played a tattoo on the edge of a glass. Then it rattled briefly on the desktop as Satchelmouth put it down.

'Doesn't anyone know who the hells they are?' Mr Clete said, as Satchelmouth managed to grip the glass on the second try. '*Someone* must know who they are!'

'Dunno about the boy,' said Satchelmouth. 'No one's ever seen him before. An' . . . an' . . . well, you know trolls . . . could've been anyone . . .'

'One of them was definitely the Librarian from the University,' said Herbert 'Mr Harpsichord' Shuffle, the Guild's own librarian.

'We can leave him for now,' said Clete.

The others nodded. No one really wanted to attempt to beat up the Librarian if there was anyone smaller available.

'What about the dwarf?'

'Ah.'

'Someone said they thought he was Glod Glodsson. Lives in Phedre Road somewhere—'

Clete growled. 'Get some of the lads over there right *now.* I want the position of musicians in this city explained to them *right now.* Hat. Hat. Hat.'

The musicians hurried through the night, the din of the Mended Drum behind them.

'Wasn't he nice,' said Glod. 'I mean, we haven't just got our pay, but he was so interested he gave us twenty dollars of his own money!'

'I tink what he said,' said Cliff, 'was dat he'd give us twenty dollars *with* interest.'

'Same thing, isn't it? And he said he could get us more jobs. Did you read the contract?'

'Did you?'

'It was very small writing,' said Glod. He brightened up. 'But there was a lot of it,' he added. 'Bound to be a good contract, with that much writing on it.'

'The Librarian ran away,' said Buddy. 'Oooked a lot, and ran away.'

'Hah! Well, he'll be sorry later on,' said Glod. 'Later on, people'll talk to him and he'll say: I left, you know, before they became famous.'

'He'll say ook.'

'Anyway, that piano's going to need some work.'

'Yeah,' said Cliff. 'Like, I saw once where dis guy made stuff out of matches. *He* could repair it.'

A couple of dollars became two lamb kormas and pitchblende vindaloo at the Curry Gardens, along with a bottle of wine so chemical that even trolls could drink it.

'And after this,' said Glod, as they sat down to wait for the food, 'we'll find somewhere else to stay.'

'What wrong with your place?' said Cliff.

'It's too draughty. It's got a piano-shaped hole in the door.'

'Yes, but you put it there.'

'So what?'

'Won't the landlord object?'

'Of course he'll object. That's what landlords are *for*. Anyway, we're on the up and up, lads. I can feel it in my water.'

'I thought you were just happy to get paid,' said Buddy.

'Right. Right. But I'm even happier to get paid a lot.'

The guitar hummed. Buddy picked it up, and plucked a string.

Glod dropped his knife.

'That sounded like a piano!' he said.

'I think it can sound like anything,' said Buddy. 'And now it knows about pianos.'

'Magic,' said Cliff.

'Of *course* magic,' said Glod. 'That's what I keep *saying*. A strange old thing found in a dusty old shop one stormy night—'

'It wasn't stormy,' said Cliff.

'—it's *bound* to . . . yes, all right, but it was raining a bit . . . it's *bound* to be a bit special. I bet if we was to go back now the shop wouldn't be there. And that'd prove it. Everyone knows things bought from shops which aren't there next day are dead mysterious and items of Fate. Fate's smiling on us, could be.'

'Doing something on us,' said Cliff. 'I hope it's smiling.'

'And Mr Dibbler said he'd find us somewhere really special to play tomorrow.'

'Good,' said Buddy. 'We *must* play.'

'Right,' said Cliff. 'We play all right. It's our job.'

'People should hear our music'

'Sure.' Cliff looked puzzled. 'Right. Of course. Dat's what we want. And some pay, too.'

'Mr Dibbler'll help us,' said Glod, who was too preoccupied to notice the edge in Buddy's voice. 'He must be very successful. He's got an office in Sator Square. Only very posh businesses can afford that.'

A new day dawned.

It had hardly finished doing so before Ridcully hurried through the dewy grass of the University gardens and hammered on the door of the High Energy Magic Building.

Generally he never went near the place. It wasn't that he didn't understand what it was the young wizards in there were actually doing, but because he strongly suspected that they didn't, either. They seemed to positively enjoy becoming less and less certain about everything and would come in to dinner saying things like 'Wow, we've just overturned Marrowleaf's Theory of Thaumic Imponderability! Amazing!' as if it was something to be proud of, instead of gross discourtesy.

And they were always talking about splitting the thaum, the smallest unit of magic. The Archchancellor couldn't see the point. So you had bits all over the place. What good would that do? The universe was bad enough without people poking it.

The door opened.

'Oh, it's you, Archchancellor.'

Ridcully pushed the door open further.

''Morning, Stibbons. Glad to see you're up and about early.'

Ponder Stibbons, the faculty's youngest member, blinked at the sky.

'Is it morning already?' he said.

Ridcully pushed his way past him and into the HEM. It was unfamiliar ground for a traditional wizard. There wasn't a skull or dribbly candle to be seen; this particular room looked like an alchemist's laboratory had suffered the inevitable explosion and landed in a blacksmith's shop.

Nor did he approve of Stibbons's robe. It was the right length but a washed-out greeny-grey, with pockets and toggles and a hood with a bit of rabbit fur around the edge. There weren't any sequins or jewels or mystic symbols *anywhere.* Just a blodgy stain where Stibbons's pen leaked.

'You ain't been out lately?' said Ridcully.

'No, sir. Er. Should I have been? I've been busy working on my Make-It-Bigger device. You know, I showed you—'*

*Not with very good results, however. Stibbons spent weeks grinding lenses and blowing glassware and had finally produced a device which showed the tremendous amount of tiny animals there were in one drop of water from the river Ankh.

The Archchancellor had taken a look and then remarked that anything in which that much life could exist *had* to be healthy.

'Right, right,' said Ridcully, looking around. 'Anyone else been working in here?'

'Well . . . there's me, and Tez the Terrible and Skazz and Big Mad Drongo, I think . . .'

Ridcully blinked.

'What are they?' he said. And then, from the depths of memory, a horrible answer suggested itself. Only a very specific species had names like that.

'*Students?*'

'Er. Yes?' said Ponder, backing away. 'That's all right, isn't it? I mean, this *is* a university . . .'

Ridcully scratched his ear. The man was right, of course. You had to have some of the buggers around, there was no getting away from it. Personally, he avoided them whenever possible, as did the rest of the faculty, occasionally running the other way or hiding behind doors whenever they saw them. The Lecturer in Recent Runes had been known to lock himself in his wardrobe rather than take a tutorial.

'You better fetch 'em,' he said. 'The fact is, I seem to have lost my faculty.'

'For what, Archchancellor?' said Ponder, politely.

'What?'

'Sorry?'

They looked at one another in incomprehension, two minds driving opposite ways up a narrow street and waiting for the other man to reverse first.

'*The* faculty,' said Ridcully, giving up. 'The Dean and whatnot. Gone totally round the corner. Been up all night, playing guitars and whatnot. The Dean's made himself a coat out of leather.'

'Well, leather *is* a very practical and functional material—'

'Not the way he's using it,' said Ridcully darkly . . .

[. . . the Dean stood back. He'd borrowed a dressmaker's dummy from Mrs Whitlow, the housekeeper.

He'd made some changes to the design that had buzzed around his brain. For one thing, a wizard in his very soul is loath to wear any garment that doesn't reach down at least to the ankles, so there was quite a lot of leather. Lots of room for all the studs.

He'd started with: DEAN.

That had hardly begun to fill the space. After a while he'd added: BORN TO, and left a space because he wasn't quite sure *what* he'd been born to. BORN TO EAT BIG DINNERS wouldn't be appropriate.

After some more bemused thought he'd gone on to: LIVE FATS DIE YO GNU. It wasn't quite right, he could see; he'd turned the material over while he was making the holes for the studs and had sort of lost track of which direction he was going.

Of course, it didn't matter *which* direction you went, just so long as you went. That's what music with rocks in it was all about . . .]

. . . 'and Recent Runes is in his room playing drums, and the rest of them have all got guitars, and what the Bursar's done to the bottom of *his* robe is really strange,' said Ridcully. 'And the Librarian's wandering around the place pinchin' stuff and no one listens to a word I say.'

He stared at the students. It was a worrying sight, and not just because of the natural look of students. Here were some people who, while this damn music was making everyone tap their feet, had stayed indoors all night – *working*.

'What are you lot *doing* in here?' he said. 'You . . . what's your name?'

The student wizard pinned by Ridcully's pointing finger squirmed anxiously.

'Er. Um. Big Mad Drongo,' he said, twisting the brim of his hat in his hands.

'Big. Mad. Drongo,' said Ridcully. 'That's your name, is it? That's what you've got sewn on your vest?'

'Um. No, Archchancellor.'

'It is . . . ?'

'Adrian Turnipseed, Archchancellor.'

'So why're you called Big Mad Drongo, Mr Turnipseed?' said Ridcully.

'Um . . . um . . .'

'He once drank a whole pint of shandy,' said Stibbons, who had the decency to look embarrassed.

Ridcully gave him a carefully blank look. Oh, well. They'd have to do.

'All right, you lot,' he said, 'what do you make of this?'

He produced from his robe a Mended Drum beer tankard with a beer mat fastened over the top with a piece of string.

'What have you got in there, Archchancellor?' said Ponder Stibbons.

'A piece of music, lad.'

'Music? But you can't trap music like that.'

'I wish I was a clever bugger like you and knew every damn thing,' said Ridcully. 'That big flask over there . . . You – Big Mad Adrian – take the top off it, and be ready to slam it down again when I say. Ready with that lid, Mad Adrian . . . *right*!'

There was a brief angry chord as Ridcully pulled the beer mat off the mug and upended it quickly into the flask. Mad Drongo Adrian slammed the lid down, in total terror of the Archchancellor.

And then they could hear it . . . a persistent faint beat, rebounding off the inner walls of the glass flask.

The students peered in at it.

There was something in there. A sort of movement in the air . . .

'I trapped it in the Drum last night.'

'That's not possible,' said Ponder. 'You can't trap music.'

'That isn't Klatchian mist, lad.'

'It's been in that mug since last night?' said Ponder.

'Yes.'

'But that's not possible!'

Ponder looked absolutely crestfallen. There are some people born with the instinctive feeling that the universe is solvable.

Ridcully patted him on the shoulder.

'You never thought that being a wizard was going to be easy, did you?'

Ponder stared at the jar, and then his mouth snapped into a thin line of determination.

'Right! We're going to sort this out! It must be something to do with the frequency! That's right! Tez the Terrible, get the crystal ball! Skazz, fetch the roll of steel wire! It must be the frequency!'

The Band With Rocks In slept the night away in a single males' hostel in an alley off Gleam Street, a fact that would have interested the four enforcers of the Musicians' Guild sitting outside a piano-shaped hole in Phedre Road.

Susan strode through the rooms of Death, seething gently with anger and just a touch of fear, which only made the anger worse.

How could anyone even *think* like that? How could anyone be content to just be the personification of a blind force? Well, there were going to be changes . . .

Her father had tried to change things, she knew. But only because he was, well, quite frankly, a bit soppy.

He'd been made a duke by Queen Keli of Sto Lat. Susan knew what the title meant – duke meant 'war leader'. But her father never fought anyone. He seemed to spend all his time travelling from one wretched city state to another, all over the Sto Plains, just talking to people and trying to get them to talk to other people. He'd never killed anyone, as far as Susan knew, although he may have talked a few politicians to death. That didn't seem to be much of a job for a war leader. Admittedly there didn't seem to be all the little wars there used to be, but it was . . . well . . . not a *proud* kind of life.

She walked through the hall of lifetimers. Even those on the highest shelves rattled gently as she passed.

She'd save lives. The good could be spared, and the bad could die young. It would all balance up, too. She'd *show* him. As for responsibility, well . . . humans always made changes. That was what being human was all about.

Susan opened another door and stepped into the library.

It was a room even bigger than the hall of lifetimers. Bookcases rose like cliffs; a haze obscured the ceiling.

But of course it'd be childish, she told herself, to think that she could go in waving the scythe like a magic wand and turn the world into a better place overnight. It might take some time. So she should start in a small way and work up.

She held out a hand.

'I'm not going to do the voice,' she said. 'That's just unnecessary drama and really a bit stupid. I just want the book of Imp y Celyn, thank you very much.'

Around her the busyness of the library went on. Millions of books quietly carried on writing themselves, causing a rustle like that of cockroaches.

She remembered sitting on a knee or, rather, sitting on a cushion on a knee, because the knee itself had been out of the question. Watching a bony finger follow the letters as they formed on the page. She'd learned to read her own life—

'I'm waiting,' said Susan meaningfully.

She clenched her fists.

IMP Y CELYN, she said.

The book appeared in front of her. She just managed to catch it before it fluttered to the floor.

'Thank you,' she said.

She flicked through the pages of his life until she came to the last one, and stared. Then she hastily went back until she found, written neatly down, his death in the Drum. It was all there – all untrue. He hadn't died. The book was lying. Or – and this she knew was a far more accurate way of looking at it – the book was true and reality was lying.

What was more important was that from the moment of his death the book was writing music. Page after page had been covered with neat staves. While Susan watched, a clef drew itself in a series of careful loops.

What did it want? Why should it save his life?

And it was vitally important that she save him instead. She could feel the certainty like a ball-bearing in her mind. It was absolutely imperative. She'd never met him up close, she'd not exchanged a word with him, he was just one person, but it was *him* she had to save.

Grandfather had said she shouldn't do that sort of thing. What did he know about anything? He'd never *lived*.

* * *

Blert Wheedown made guitars. It was quiet, satisfying work. It took him and Gibbsson, the apprentice, about five days to make a decent instrument, if the wood was available and properly seasoned. He was a conscientious man who'd devoted many years to the perfection of one type of musical instrument, on which he himself was no mean performer.

In his experience, guitarists came in three categories. There were the ones he thought of as real musicians, who worked at the Opera House or for one of the small private orchestras. There were the folk singers, who couldn't play but that was all right because most of them couldn't sing either. Then there were the – hemhem – troubadours and other swarthy types who thought a guitar was, like a red rose in the teeth, a box of chocolates and a strategically placed pair of socks, another weapon in the battle of the sexes. They didn't play at all, apart from one or two chords, but they were regular customers. When leaping out of a bedroom window just ahead of an angry husband the one thing a paramour is least concerned about leaving behind is his instrument.

Blert thought he'd seen them all.

Mind you, first thing this morning he'd sold some to some wizards. That was unusual. Some of them had even bought Blert's guitar primer.

The bell rang.

'Yes—' Blert looked at the customer, and made a huge mental effort '—sir?'

It wasn't just the leather jerkin. It wasn't just the wristbands with studs. It wasn't just the broadsword.

It wasn't just the helmet with the spikes. It was the leather *and* the studs *and* the sword *and* the helmet. This customer couldn't possibly be in categories one or two, Blert decided.

The figure stood, looking uncertain, hands gripping convulsively, clearly not at home in a dialogue situation.

'This a guitar shop?' it said.

Blert looked around at the merchandise hanging from walls and ceiling.

'Er. Yes?' he said.

'I wants one.'

As for category three, he didn't look like someone used to bothering with chocolates or roses. Or even 'hello'.

'Er . . .' Blert grabbed one at random and held it out in front of him. 'One like this?'

'I wants one that goes *blam-Blam-blamma-BLAM-blammmm-oooiiieeee.* Y'know?'

Blert looked down at the guitar. 'I'm not sure it does that,' he said.

Two enormous black-nailed hands took it out of his grasp.

'Er, you're holding it wro—'

'Got a mirror?'

'Er, no—'

One hairy hand was raised high in the air, and then plunged towards the strings.

Blert never wanted to repeat the next ten seconds. People shouldn't be allowed to do that sort of thing to a defenceless musical instrument. It was like raising a little pony, feeding it and grooming it properly, plaiting ribbons in its tail, giving it a nice field with bunnies and daisies in it, and then watching the first rider take it out with spurs and a whip.

The thug played as if he were searching for something. He didn't find it, but as the last discords faded away his features twisted into the determined expression of one who intends to go on looking.

'Yer, right. How much?' he said.

It was on sale for fifteen dollars. But Blert's musical soul rebelled. He snapped.

'Twenty-five dollars,' was what he snapped.

'Yer, right. Will this be enough, then?'

A small ruby was produced from somewhere in a pocket.

'I can't change that!'

Blert's musical soul was still protesting, but his business head stepped in and flexed its elbows.

'But, but, but I'll throw in my guitar primer and a strap and a couple of pleckies, yes?' he said. 'It's got pictures of where to put your fingers and everything, yes?'

'Yer, right.'

The barbarian walked out. Blert stared at the ruby in his hand.

The bell rang. He looked up.

This one wasn't quite so bad. There were fewer studs, and the helmet had only two spikes.

Blert's hand shut around the jewel.

'Don't tell me you want a guitar?' he said.

'Yep. One of them that goes *whoweeecooiwweeeeoowwwwngngngng.*'

Blert looked around wildly.

'Well, there's this one,' he said, grabbing the nearest instrument. 'I don't know about *wooeeeoow-weee* but here's my primer as well and a strap and some pleckies, that'll be thirty dollars and I'll tell you what I'll do, I'll throw in the space between the strings for free, okay?'

'Yep. Er. Got a mirror?'

The bell rang.

And rang.

An hour later Blert leaned on the door-frame of his workshop, a manic grin on his face and his hands on his belt to stop the weight of money in his pockets pulling his trousers down.

'Gibbsson?'

'Yes, boss?'

'You know those guitars you made? When you were learning?'

'The ones you said sounded like a cat going to the toilet through a sewn-up bum, boss?'

'Did you throw them away?'

'No, boss. I thought: I'll keep them, so's in five years' time when I can make proper instruments, I'll be able to take 'em out and have a good laugh.'

Blert wiped his forehead. Several small gold coins fell out with his handkerchief.

'Where did you put them, out of interest?'

'Chucked 'em inna shed, boss. Along with that whaney timber you said was about as useful as a mermaid in a chorus line.'

'Just fetch them out again, will you? And that timber.'

'But *you* said—'

'And bring me a saw. And then nip out and get me, oh, a couple of gallons of black paint. And some sequins.'

'Sequins, boss?'

'You can get them up at Mrs Cosmopilite's dress shop. And ask her if she's got any of those glittery ankhstones. And some fancy material for straps. Oh . . . and see if she can lend us her biggest mirror . . .'

Blert hitched up his trousers again.

'And then go down to the docks and hire a troll and tell him to stand in the corner and if anyone else comes in and tries to play . . .' he paused, and then remembered, 'Pathway to Paradise, I think they said it's called . . . he's to pull their head off.'

'Shouldn't he give them a warning?' said Gibbsson.

'That will *be* the warning.'

It was an hour later.

Ridcully had got bored and sent Tez the Terrible over to the kitchens to see about a snack. Ponder and the other two had been busying themselves around the flask, messing around with crystal balls and wire. And now . . .

There was a wire stretched between two nails on the bench. It was a blur as it twanged an interesting beat.

Big curved green lines hung in the air above it.

'What's that?' said Ridcully.

'That's what the sound looks like,' said Ponder.

'Sound *looks* like,' said Ridcully. 'Well, there's a thing. I never saw sound looking like that. This is what you boys used magic for, is it? Looking at sound? Hey, we've got some nice cheese in the kitchen, how about we go and listen to how it smells?'

Ponder sighed.

'It's what sound would be if your ears were eyes,' he said.

'Really?' said Ridcully, brightly. 'Amazing!'

'It looks *very* complicated,' said Ponder. 'Simple when you look at it from a distance and up close, very complex. Almost . . .'

'Alive,' said Ridcully, firmly.

'Er . . .'

It was the one known as Skazz. He looked about seven stone and had the most interesting haircut Ridcully had ever seen, since it consisted of a shoulder-length fringe of hair all round. It was only the tip of his nose poking out which told the world which way he was facing. If he ever developed a boil on the back of his neck, people would think he was walking the wrong way.

'Yes, Mr Skazz?' said Ridcully.

'Er. I read something about this once,' said Skazz.

'Remarkable. How did you manage that?'

'You know the Listening Monks up in the Ramtops? They say that there's a background noise to the universe? A sort of echo of some sound?'

'Sounds sensible to me. The whole universe starting up, bound to make a big bang,' said Ridcully.

'It wouldn't have to be very loud,' said Ponder. 'It'd just have to be everywhere, all at once. I read that book. Old Riktor the Counter wrote it. The Monks are still listening to it, he said. A sound that never fades away.'

'Sounds like loud to me,' said Ridcully. 'Got to be loud to be heard any distance. If the wind's in the wrong direction, you can't even hear the bells on the Assassins' Guild.'

'It wouldn't have to be loud to be heard everywhere,' said Ponder. 'The reason being, at that point *everywhere* was all in one place.'

Ridcully gave him the look people give conjurors who've just removed an egg from their ear.

'Everywhere was all in one place?'

'Yes.'

'So where was everywhere else?'

'That was all in one place, too.'

'The same place?'

'Yes.'

'Crunched up very small?'

Ridcully was beginning to show certain signs. If he had been a volcano, natives living nearby would be looking for a handy virgin.

'Haha, in fact you could say it was crunched up very big,' said Ponder, who always walked into it. 'The reason being, space didn't exist until there was a universe, so anything there was, was everywhere.'

'The same everywhere we had just now?'

'Yes.'

'All right. Go on.'

'Riktor said he thought that the sound came first. One great big complicated chord. The biggest, most complicated sound there ever was. A sound so complex that you couldn't play it *within* a universe, any more than you can open a box with the crowbar that's inside it. One great chord which . . . as it were

. . . *played* everything into being. Started the music, if you like.'

'A sort of *ta-dahhh*?' said Ridcully.

'I suppose so.'

'I thought the universe came into being because some god cut off some other god's wedding tackle and made the universe out of it,' said Ridcully. 'Always seemed straightforward to me. I mean, it's the kind of thing you can imagine happenin'.'

'Well—'

'Now you're telling me someone blew a big hooter and here we are?'

'I don't know about *someone*,' said Ponder.

'Noises don't just make themselves, that I do know,' said Ridcully.

He relaxed a bit, certain in his own mind that reason had prevailed, and patted Ponder on the back.

'It needs some work, lad,' he said. 'Old Riktor was a bit . . . unsound, y'know. He thought everything came down to numbers.'

'Mind you,' said Ponder, 'the universe does have a rhythm. Day and night, light and dark, life and death—'

'Chicken soup and croutons,' said Ridcully.

'Well, not every metaphor bears close examination.'

There was a knock on the door. Tez the Terrible entered, carrying a tray. He was followed by Mrs Whitlow, the housekeeper.

Ridcully's jaw dropped.

Mrs Whitlow curtsied.

'Good morning, hyour grace,' she said.

Her ponytail bobbed. There was a rustle of starched petticoats.

Ridcully's jaw rose again, but only so that he could say: 'What *have* you done to your—'

'Excuse me, Mrs Whitlow,' said Ponder quickly, 'but have you served breakfast to any of the faculty this morning?'

'That's right, Mr Stibbons,' said Mrs Whitlow. Her ample and mysterious bosom shifted under its sweater. 'None of the gentlemen came down, so I got trays taken up to them all. Daddio.'

Ridcully's gaze continued downwards. He'd never thought of Mrs Whitlow as having legs before. Of course, in theory the woman needed something to move around on, but . . . well . . .

But there were two pudgy knees protruding from the huge mushroom of skirts. Further down there were white socks.

'Your hair—' he began, hoarsely.

'Is there something wrong?' said Mrs Whitlow.

'Nothing, nothing,' said Ponder. 'Thank you very much.'

The door closed behind her.

'She was snapping her fingers as she went out, just like you said,' said Ponder.

'Wasn't the only thing that's snapped,' said Ridcully, still shuddering.

'Did you look at her shoes?'

'I think my eyes shut themselves protectively about there.'

'If it's really alive,' said Ponder, 'then it's very contagious.'

* * *

This scene took place in Crash's father's coach-house, but it was an echo of a scene evolving all around the city.

Crash hadn't been christened Crash. He was the son of a rich dealer in hay and feedstuffs, but he despised his father for being dead from the neck up, totally concerned with material things, un-imaginative and also for paying him a ridiculous three dollars a week allowance.

Crash's father had left his horses in the coach-house. At the moment they were both trying to squeeze into one corner, having tried fruitlessly to kick a hole in the walls.

'I reckon I nearly had it that time,' said Crash, as hay dust poured down from the roof and woodworm hurried off to find a better home.

'It isn't— I mean, it ain't like the sound we heard in the Drum,' said Jimbo critically. 'It's a bit like it, but it isn— it ain't it.'

Jimbo was Crash's best friend and wished he was one of the people.

'It's good enough to start with,' said Crash. 'So you and Noddy, you two get guitars. And Scum, you . . . you can play the drums.'

'Dunno how,' said Scum. It was actually his name.

'*No one* knows how to play the drums,' said Crash patiently. 'There's nothing to *know*. You just hit them with the sticks.'

'Yeah, but what if I sort of miss?'

'Sit closer. Right,' said Crash, sitting back. 'Now

. . . the important thing, the *really* important thing is . . . what're we going to call ourselves?'

Cliff looked around.

'Well, I reckon we look at every house and I'm damned if I see der name Dibbler anywhere,' he growled.

Buddy nodded. Most of Sator Square was the frontage of the University, but there was room for a few other buildings. They were the sort that have a dozen brass plates by the door. The sort that hinted that even wiping your feet on the doormat was going to cost you dear.

'Hello, boys.'

They turned. Dibbler beamed at them over a tray of possible sausages and buns. There were a couple of sacks beside him.

'Sorry we're late,' said Glod, 'but we couldn't find your office anywhere.'

Dibbler spread his arms wide.

'This *is* my office,' he said, equally expansively. 'Sator Square! Thousands of square feet of space! Excellent communications! Passing trade! Try these on,' he added, picking up one of the sacks and opening it. 'I had to guess at sizes.'

They were black, and made of cheap cotton. One of them was XXXXL.

'A vest with words on?' said Buddy.

'"The Band With Rocks In",' Cliff read, slowly. 'Hey, dat's us, isn't it?'

'What do we want these for?' said Glod. 'We know who we are.'

'Advertising,' said Dibbler. 'Trust me.' He put a brown cylinder in his mouth and lit the end. 'Wear them tonight. Have I got a gig for you!'

'Have you?' said Buddy.

'That's what I said!'

'No, you asked us,' said Glod. 'How should we know?'

'Has it got dat livery on der side?' said Cliff.

Dibbler started again.

'It's a big place, you'll get a great audience! *And* you'll get . . .' he looked at their trusting, open faces, 'ten dollars over Guild rate, how about that?'

Glod's face split into a big grin. 'What, each?' he said.

Dibbler gave them another appraising look. 'Oh . . . no,' he said. 'Fair do's. Ten dollars between you. I mean, be serious. You need exposure.'

'Dere's dat word again,' said Cliff. 'The Musicians' Guild'll be right on our necks.'

'Not this place,' said Dibbler. 'Guaranteed.'

'Where is it, then?' said Glod.

'Are you ready for this?'

They blinked at him. Dibbler beamed, and blew a cloud of greasy smoke.

'The Cavern!'

The beat went on . . .

Of course, there are bound to be a few mutations . . .

Gortlick and Hammerjug were songwriters, and fully paid-up members of the Guild. They wrote dwarf songs for all occasions.

Some people say this is not hard to do so long as you can remember how to spell 'Gold', but this is a little bit cynical. Many dwarf songs* are on the lines of 'Gold, gold, gold' but it's all in the inflexion; dwarfs have thousands of words for 'gold' but will use any of them in an emergency, such as when they see some gold that doesn't belong to them.

They had a small office in Tin Lid Alley, where they sat either side of an anvil and wrote popular songs to mine along to.

'Gort?'

'What?'

'What do you think of this one?'

Hammerjug cleared his throat.

'I'm mean and turf and I'm mean and turf and
  I'm mean and turf and I'm mean and turf,
'And me an' my friends can walk towards you
  with our hats on backwards in a menacing way,
'Yo!'

Gortlick chewed the end of his composing hammer thoughtfully.

'Good rhythm,' he said, 'but the words need some work.'

'You mean more gold, gold, gold?'

'Ye-es. What're you thinking of calling it?'

'Er . . . r . . . rat . . . music . . .'

'Why rat music?'

Hammerjug looked puzzled.

*All right – *all* dwarf songs. Except the one about Hiho.

'Couldn't really say,' he said. 'It was just an idea I had in my brain.'

Gortlick shook his head. Dwarfs were a burrowing race. He knew what they liked.

'Good music's got to have *hole* in it,' he said. 'You ain't got nothing if you ain't got hole.'

'Now calm down, calm down,' said Dibbler. 'It's the biggest venue in Ankh-Morpork, that's why. I don't see what the problem is . . .'

'The Cavern?' screamed Glod. 'Chrysoprase the troll runs it, that's the problem!'

'Dey say he's a godfather in the Breccia,' said Cliff.

'Now now, that's never been proved . . .'

'Only 'cos it's very hard to prove things when someone's scooped a hole in your head and buried your feet in it!'

'There's no need for this prejudice, just because he's a troll—' said Dibbler.

'*I'm* a troll! So I can be prejudiced against trolls, all right? He's one mean mutherlode! Dey say when dey found the De Bris gang none of 'em had any teef—'

'What *is* the Cavern?' said Buddy.

'Troll place,' said Cliff. 'Dey say—'

'It'll be great! Why worry?' said Dibbler.

'It's a gambling joint, too!'*

*Troll gambling is even simpler than Australian gambling. One of the most popular games is One Up, which consists of throwing a coin in the air and betting on whether it will come down again.

'But the Guild won't go in there,' said Dibbler. 'Not if they know what's good for them.'

'And *I* know what's good for me, too!' shouted Glod. 'I'm good at knowing that! It's good for me not to go into a troll dive!'

'They threw axes at you in the Drum,' said Dibbler, reasonably.

'Yes, but only in fun. It's not as if they were aiming.'

'Anyway,' said Cliff, 'only trolls and damn silly young humans go there who think it clever to drink in a troll bar. You won't get an audience.'

Dibbler tapped the side of his nose.

'You play,' he said. 'You'll get an audience. That's *my* job.'

'The doors aren't big enough for me to go in!' snapped Glod.

'They're *huge* doors,' said Dibbler.

'They ain't big enough for me 'cos if you try to get me in there you'll have to drag the street in too, on account of me holding on to it!'

'No, be sensible—'

'No!' screamed Glod. 'And I'm screaming for all three of us!'

The guitar whined.

Buddy swung it around until he could hold it, and played a couple of chords. That seemed to calm it down.

'I think it . . . er . . . likes the idea,' he said.

'It likes the idea,' said Glod, simmering down a little bit. 'Oh, good. Well, do you know what they do to dwarfs who go into the Cavern?'

'We do need the money, and it's probably not worse than what the Guild'll do to us if we play anywhere else,' said Buddy. 'And we've got to play.'

They stood looking at one another.

'What you boys should do now,' said Dibbler, blowing out a smoke ring, 'is find somewhere nice and quiet to spend the day. Have a bit of a rest.'

'Damn right,' said Cliff. 'I never expected to carry these rocks around the whole time—'

Dibbler raised a finger. 'Ah,' he said, 'I thought of that, too. You don't want to waste your talents lugging stuff around, that's what I told myself. I hired you a helper. Very cheap, only a dollar a day, I'll take it straight out of your wages so's you don't have to bother about it. Meet Asphalt.'

'Who?' said Buddy.

''S me,' said one of the sacks beside Dibbler.

The sack opened up a bit and turned out not to be a sack at all, but a . . . a sort of crumpled . . . a kind of mobile heap of . . .

Buddy felt his eyes watering. It *looked* like a troll, except that it was shorter than a dwarf. It wasn't *smaller* than a dwarf – what Asphalt lacked in height he made up in breadth and, while on the subject, also in smell.

'How come,' said Cliff, 'he's so short?'

''N'elephant sat on me,' said Asphalt, sulkily.

Glod blew his nose.

'Only sat?'

Asphalt was already wearing a 'Band With Rocks In' shirt. It was tight across the chest but reached down to the floor.

'Asphalt'll look after you,' said Dibbler. 'There isn't anything he doesn't know about show business.'

Asphalt gave them a big grin.

'You'll be okay with me,' he said. 'I've worked with 'em all, I have. Been everywhere, done it all.'

'We *could* go to the Fronts,' said Cliff. 'No-one around there when the University's on holiday.'

'Good. Got things to organize,' said Dibbler. 'See you tonight. The Cavern. Seven o'clock.'

He strode off.

'You know the funny thing about him?' said Glod.

'What?'

'The way he was smoking that sausage. Do you think he knew?'

Asphalt grabbed Cliff's bag and slung it easily over his shoulder.

'Let's go, boss,' he said.

'An elephant sat on you?' said Buddy, as they crossed the square.

'Yup. At the circus,' said Asphalt. 'I used to muck 'em arht.'

'That's how you got like that?'

'Nope. Din't get like this 'til elephants had sat on me free, fo' times,' said the small flat troll. 'Dunno why. I'd be cleanin' up after 'em, next minute it'd all be dark.'

'I'd have quit after the first time, me,' said Glod.

'Nah,' said Asphalt, with a contented smile. 'Couldn't do that. Show business is in me soul.'

* * *

Ponder looked down at the thing they had hammered together.

'I don't understand it either,' he said. 'But . . . it looks as though we can trap it in a string, and it makes the string play the music *again.* It's like an iconograph for sound.'

They'd put the wire inside the box, which resonated beautifully. It played the same dozen bars, over and over again.

'A box of music,' said Ridcully. 'My word!'

'What I'd like to try,' said Ponder, 'is getting the musicians to play in front of a lot of strings like this. Perhaps we could trap the music'

'What for?' said Ridcully. 'What on Disc for?'

'Well . . . if you could get music in boxes you wouldn't need musicians any more.'

Ridcully hesitated. There was a lot to be said for the idea. A world without musicians had a certain appeal. They were a scruffy bunch, in his experience. Quite unhygienic.

He shook his head, reluctantly.

'Not this sort of music,' he said. 'We want to stop it, not make more of it.'

'What exactly is wrong with it?' said Ponder.

'It's . . . well, can't you see?' said Ridcully. 'It makes people act funny. Wear funny clothes. Be rude. Not do what they're told. I can't do a thing with them. It's not right. Besides . . . remember Mr Hong.'

'It's certainly very unusual,' said Ponder. 'Can we get some more? For study purposes? Arch-chancellor?'

Ridcully shrugged. 'We follow the Dean,' he said.

'Good grief,' breathed Buddy, in the huge echoing emptiness. 'No wonder they call it the Cavern. It's *huge*.'

'I feel dwarfed,' said Glod.

Asphalt ambled to the front of the stage.

'One two, one two,' he said. 'One. One. One two, one tw—'

'Three,' said Buddy helpfully.

Asphalt stopped and looked embarrassed.

'Just trying the, you know, just trying the . . . trying out the . . .' he muttered. 'Just trying . . . it.'

'We'll never fill this,' said Buddy.

Glod poked in a box by the side of the stage.

He said, 'We might. Look at these.'

He unrolled a poster. The others clustered around.

'Dat's a picture of us,' said Cliff. 'Someone painted a picture of us.'

'Looking mean,' said Glod.

''S a good one of Buddy,' said Asphalt. 'Waving his guitar like that.'

'Why's there all that lightning and stuff?' said Buddy.

'I never look that mean even when I'm mean,' said Glod.

'"The New Sounde Dat's Goin' Arounde",' Cliff read, his forehead wrinkling with the effort.

'"The Bande With Rockes",' said Glod.

'Oh, *no*. It says we're going to be here and *everything*,' moaned Glod. 'We're dead.'

'"Bee There Orr Bee A Rectangular Thyng",' said Cliff. 'I don't understand that.'

'There's dozens of these rolls in here,' said Glod. 'They're *posters.* You know what that means? He's been having them stuck up in places. Talking of which, when the Musicians' Guild get hold of us—'

'Music's free,' said Buddy. 'It has to be free.'

'What?' said Glod. 'Not in *this* dwarf's town!'

'Then it should be,' said Buddy. 'People shouldn't have to pay to play music.'

'Right! That boy's right! That's just what I've always said! Isn't that what I've always said? That's what I've said, right enough.'

Dibbler emerged from the shadows in the wings. There was a troll with him who, Buddy surmised, must have been Chrysoprase. He wasn't particularly big, or even very craggy. In fact he had a smooth and glossy look to him, like a pebble found on a beach. There wasn't a trace of lichen anywhere.

And he was wearing clothes. Clothes, other than uniforms or special work clothes, weren't normally a troll thing. Mostly they wore a loincloth to keep stuff in, and that was that. But Chrysoprase had a suit on. It looked badly tailored. It was in fact very well tailored, but even a troll with no clothes on looks fundamentally badly tailored.

Chrysoprase had been a very quick learner when he arrived in Ankh-Morpork. He began with an important lesson: hitting people was thuggery. Paying other people to do the hitting on your behalf was good business.

'I'd like you lads to meet Chrysoprase,' said

Dibbler. 'An old friend of mine. Me and him go way back. That right, Chrys?'

'Indeed.' Chrysoprase gave Dibbler the warm friendly smile a shark bestows on a haddock with whom it suits it, for now, to swim in the same direction. A certain play of silicon muscles in the corners also suggested that, one day, certain people would regret 'Chrys'.

'Mr Throat tells me youse boys is the best ting since slicing bread,' he said. 'Youse got everyting youse need?'

They nodded, mutely. People tended not to speak to Chrysoprase in case they said something that offended him. They wouldn't know it at the time, of course. They'd know it later, when they were in some dark alley and a voice behind them said: Mr Chrysoprase is *really upset.*

'Youse go and rest up in your dressing room,' he went on. 'Youse wants any food or drink, youse only got to say.'

He'd got diamond rings on his fingers. Cliff couldn't stop staring at them.

The dressing room was next to the privies and half full of beer barrels. Glod leaned on the door.

'I don't need the money,' he said. 'Just let me get out of here with my life, that's all I ask.'

'Oo ownt ave oo orry—' Cliff began.

'You're trying to speak with your mouth shut, Cliff,' said Buddy.

'I *said*, you don't have to worry, you've got der wrong sort of teeth,' said the troll.

There was a knock on the door. Cliff slammed his

hand back over his mouth. But the knock turned out to belong to Asphalt, who was carrying a tray.

There were three types of beer. There were even smoked rat sandwiches with the crusts and tails cut off. And there was a bowl of finest anthracite coke with ash on it.

'Crunch it up good,' moaned Glod, as Cliff took his bowl. 'It may be the last chance you get—'

'Maybe no one'll turn up and we can go home?' said Cliff.

Buddy ran his fingers over the strings. The others stopped eating as the chords filled up the room.

'Magic,' said Cliff, shaking his head.

'Don't you boys worry,' said Asphalt. 'If there are any problems, it's the other guys who'll get it in the teeth.'

Buddy stopped playing.

'What other guys?'

''S funny thing,' said the little troll, 'suddenly everyone's playing music with rocks in it. Mr Dibbler's signed up another band for the concert, too. To kind of warm it up.'

'Who?'

''S called Insanity,' said Asphalt.

'Where are they?' said Cliff.

'Well, put it like this . . . you know how *your* dressing room is *next* to the privy?'

Crash, behind the Cavern's raggedy curtain, tried to tune his guitar. Several things got in the way of this simple procedure. Firstly, Blert had realized what his customers really wanted and, praying forgiveness from his ancestors, had spent more time gluing on bits of glittery stuff than he had on the actual functioning sections of the instrument. To put it another way, he'd knocked in a dozen nails and tied the strings to them. But this wasn't too much of a problem, because Crash himself had the musical talent of a blocked nostril.

He looked at Jimbo, Noddy and Scum. Jimbo, now the bass player (Blert, giggling hysterically, had used a bigger lump of wood and some fence wire), was holding up his hand hesitantly.

'What is it, Jimbo?'

'One of my guitar strings has broke.'

'Well, you've got five more, ain't you?'

'Yur. But I doesn't know how to play them, like.'

'You didn't know how to play six, right? So now you're a bit less ignorant.'

Scum peered around the curtain.

'Crash?'

'Yes?'

'There's hundreds of people out there. Hundreds! A lot of 'em have got guitars, too. They're sort of waving 'em in the air!'

Insanity listened to the roar from the other side of the curtain. Crash did not have too many brain-cells, and they often had to wave to attract one another's attention, but he had a tiny flicker of doubt that the sound that Insanity had achieved, while a *good* sound, was *the* sound that he'd heard last night in the Drum. *The* sound made him want to scream and dance, while the *other* sound made him . . . well

. . . made him want to scream and smash Scum's drum-kit over its owner's head, quite frankly.

Noddy took a peek between the curtains.

'Hey, there's a bunch of wiz . . . I think they're wizards, right in the front row,' he said. 'I'm . . . pretty sure they're wizards, but, I mean . . .'

'You can *tell,* stupid,' said Crash. 'They've got pointy hats.'

'There's one with . . . pointy hair . . .' said Noddy.

The rest of Insanity applied eyes to the gap.

'Looks like . . . a kind of unicorn spike made out of hair . . .'

'What's that he's got on the back of his robe?' said Jimbo.

'It says BORN TO RUNE,' said Crash, who was the fastest reader in the group and didn't need to use his finger at all.

'The skinny one's wearing a flared robe,' said Noddy.

'He *must* be old.'

'And they've all got guitars! Do you reckon they've come to see us?'

'Bound to have,' said Noddy.

'That's a bodacious audience,' said Jimbo.

'Yeah, that's right, bodacious,' said Scum. 'Er. What's bodacious mean?'

'Means . . . means it bodes,' said Jimbo.

'Right. It looks like it's boding all right.'

Crash thrust aside his doubts.

'Let's get out there,' he said, 'and really show them what Music With Rocks In is about!'

* * *

Asphalt, Cliff and Glod sat in one corner of the dressing room. The roar of the crowd could be heard from here.

'Why's he not saying anything?' Asphalt whispered.

'Dunno,' said Glod.

Buddy was staring at nothing, with the guitar cradled in his arms. Occasionally he'd slap the casing, very gently, in time with whatever thoughts were sluicing through his head.

'He goes like that sometimes,' said Cliff. 'Just sits and looks at the air—'

'Hey, they're shouting something out there,' said Glod. 'Listen.'

The roar had a rhythm to it.

'Sounds like "Rocks, Rocks, Rocks",' said Cliff.

The door burst open and Dibbler half-ran, half-fell in.

'You've got to get out there!' he shouted. 'Right now!'

'I thought the Insanitary boys—' Glod began.

'Don't even ask,' said Dibbler. 'Come on! Otherwise they'll wreck the place!'

Asphalt picked up the rocks.

'Okay,' he said.

'No,' said Buddy.

'What dis?' said Dibbler. 'Nerves?'

'No. Music should be free. Free as the air and the sky.'

Glod's head spun around. Buddy's voice had a faint suggestion of harmonics.

'Sure, right, that's what I said,' said Dibbler. 'The Guild—'

Buddy unfolded his legs and stood up.

'I expect people had to pay to get in here, didn't they?' he said.

Glod looked at the others. No one else seemed to have noticed it. But there was a twang on the edge of Buddy's words, a sibilance of strings.

'Oh, *that.* Of course,' said Dibbler. 'Got to cover expenses. There's your wages . . . wear and tear on the floor . . . heating and lighting . . . depreciation . . .'

The roar was louder now. It had a certain foot-stamping component.

Dibbler swallowed. He suddenly had the look of a man prepared to make the supreme sacrifice.

'I could . . . maybe go up . . . maybe . . . a dollar,' he said, each word fighting its way out of the strong-room of his soul.

'If we go on stage now, I want us to do another performance,' said Buddy.

Glod glared suspiciously at the guitar.

'What? *No* problem. I can soon—' Dibbler began.

'Free.'

'Free?' The word got past Dibbler's teeth before they could snap shut. He rallied magnificently. 'You don't want paying? Certainly, if—'

Buddy didn't move.

'I mean, we don't get paid and people don't have to pay to listen. As many people as possible.'

'Free?'

'Yes!'

'Where's the profit in that?'

An empty beer bottle vibrated off the table and smashed on the floor. A troll appeared in the doorway, or at least part of it did. It wouldn't be able to get into the room without ripping the door-frame out, but it looked as though it wouldn't think twice about doing so.

'Mr Chrysoprase says, what's happening?' it growled.

'Er—' Dibbler began.

'Mr Chrysoprase don't like being kept waiting.'

'I know, it—'

'He gets sad if he's kept waiting—'

'All *right*!' shouted Dibbler. 'Free! And that's cutting my own throat. You do know that, don't you?'

Buddy played a chord. It seemed to leave little lights in the air.

'Let's go,' he said softly.

'I know this city,' Dibbler mumbled, as The Band With Rocks In hurried towards the vibrating stage. 'Tell people something's free and you'll get thousands of them turning up—'

Needing to eat, said a voice in his head. It had a twang.

Needing to drink.

Needing to buy Band With Rocks In shirts . . .

Dibbler's face, very slowly, rearranged itself into a grin.

'*A free* festival,' he said. 'Right! It's our public duty. Music *should* be free. And sausages in a bun should be a dollar each, mustard extra. Maybe a dollar-fifty. And that's cutting my own throat.'

* * *

In the wings, the noise of the audience was a solid wall of sound.

'There's *lots* of them,' said Glod. 'I never played for that many in my entire life!'

Asphalt was arranging Cliff's rocks on the stage and getting massive applause and catcalls.

Glod glanced up at Buddy. He hadn't let go of the guitar all this time. Dwarfs weren't given to deep introspection, but Glod was suddenly aware of a desire to be a long way from here, in a cave somewhere.

'Best of luck, you guys,' said a flat little voice behind them.

Jimbo was bandaging Crash's arm.

'Er, thanks,' said Cliff. 'What happened to you?'

'They threw something at us,' said Crash.

'What?'

'Noddy, I think.'

What could be seen of Crash's face broke into a huge and terrible smile.

'We done it, though!' he said. 'We done music with rocks in all right! That bit where Jimbo smashed his guitar, they *loved* that bit!'

'Smashed his guitar?'

'Yeah,' said Jimbo, with the pride of the artist. 'On Scum.'

Buddy had his eyes closed. Cliff thought he could see a very, very faint glow surrounding him, like a thin mist. There were tiny points of light in it.

Sometimes, Buddy looked very elvish.

Asphalt scurried off the stage.

'Okay, all done,' he said.

The others looked at Buddy.

He was still standing with his eyes shut, as if he was asleep on his feet.

'We'll . . . get on out there, then?' said Glod.

'Yes,' said Cliff, 'we'll get on out there, will we? Er. Buddy?'

Buddy's eyes snapped open suddenly.

'Let's rock,' he whispered.

Cliff had thought that the sound was loud before, but it hit him like a club as they trooped out of the wings.

Glod picked up his horn. Cliff sat down and found his hammers.

Buddy walked to the centre of the stage and, to Cliff's amazement, just stood there looking down at his feet.

The cheering began to subside.

And then died away altogether. The huge hall was filled with the hush of hundreds of people holding their breath.

Buddy's fingers moved.

He picked out three simple little chords.

And then he looked up.

'Hello, Ankh-Morpork!'

Cliff felt the music rise up behind him and rush him forward into a tunnel of fire and sparks and excitement. He brought his hammers down. And it was Music With Rocks In.

C. M. O. T. Dibbler stood out in the street so that he didn't have to hear the music. He was smoking a cigar and doing calculations on the back of an overdue bill for stale buns.

Lessee . . . okay, have it outside somewhere, so there's no rent . . . maybe ten thousand people, one sausage-inna-bun each at a dollar-fifty, no, say a dollar-seventy-five, mustard tenpence extra – ten thousand Band With Rocks In shirts at five dollars each, make that ten dollars . . . add stall rental for other traders, because people who like Music With Rocks In could probably be persuaded to buy *anything* . . .

He was aware of a horse coming along the street. He paid it no attention until a female voice said: 'How do I get in here?'

'No chance. Tickets all sold out,' said Dibbler, without turning his head. Even Band With Rocks In posters, people had been offering *three dollars* just for posters, and Chalky the troll could knock out a hundred a—

He looked up. The horse, a magnificent white one, watched him incuriously.

Dibbler looked around. 'Where'd she go?'

There were a couple of trolls lounging just inside the entrance. Susan ignored them. They ignored her.

In the audience, Ponder Stibbons looked both ways and cautiously opened a wooden box.

The stretched string inside began to vibrate.

'This is all wrong!' he shouted in Ridcully's ear. 'This is *not* according to the laws of sound!'

'Maybe they're not laws!' screamed Ridcully.

People a foot away couldn't hear him. 'Maybe they're just guidelines!'

'No! There *have* to be laws!'

Ridcully saw the Dean try to climb on the stage in the excitement. Asphalt's huge troll feet landed heavily on his fingers.

'Oh, I say, good shot,' said the Archchancellor.

A prickling sensation on the back of his neck made him look around.

Although the Cavern was crowded, a space seemed to have formed in the floor. People were pressed together but, somehow, this circle was as inviolate as a wall.

In the middle of it was the girl he'd seen in the Drum. She was walking across the floor, holding her dress daintily.

Ridcully's eyes watered.

He stepped forward, concentrating. You could do almost anything if you concentrated. Anyone could have stepped into the circle if their senses had been prepared to let them know it was there. Inside the circle the sound was slightly muted.

He tapped her on the shoulder. She spun around, startled.

'Good evening,' said Ridcully. He looked her up and down, and then said, 'I'm Mustrum Ridcully, Archchancellor of Unseen University. I can't help wondering who you are.'

'Er . . .' The girl looked panicky for a moment. 'Well, technically . . . I suppose I'm Death.'

'Technically?'

'Yes. But not on duty at the moment.'

'Very glad to hear that.'

There was a shriek from the stage as Asphalt threw the Lecturer in Recent Runes into the audience, which applauded.

'Can't say I've seen that much of Death,' said Ridcully. 'But in so far as I have, he's tended to be . . . well, *he,* to start with. And a good deal thinner . . . ?'

'He's my grandfather.'

'Ah. Ah. Really? I didn't even know he was—' Ridcully stopped. 'Well, well, well, fancy that. Your grandfather? And you're in the family firm?'

'Shut up, you stupid man,' said Susan. 'Don't you dare patronize me. You see him?' She pointed to the stage, where Buddy was in mid-riff. 'He's going to die soon because . . . because of *silliness.* And if you can't do anything about it, go *away*!'

Ridcully glanced at the stage. When he looked back, Susan had vanished. He made a mighty effort and thought he caught a glimpse of her a little way off, but she knew he was looking for her and he had no chance of finding her now.

Asphalt got back into the dressing room first. There is something very sad about an empty dressing room. It's like a discarded pair of underpants, which it resembles in a number of respects. It's seen a lot of activity. It may even have witnessed excitement and a whole gamut of human passions. And now there's nothing much left but a faint smell.

The little troll dumped the bag of rocks on the floor and bit the top off a couple of beer bottles.

Cliff entered. He got halfway across the floor and

then fell over, hitting the boards with every part of his body at once. Glod stepped over him and flopped on to a barrel.

He looked at the beer bottles. He took off his helmet. He poured the beer into the helmet. Then he let his head flop forward.

Buddy entered and sat down in the corner, leaning against the wall.

And Dibbler followed. 'Well, what can I say? What *can* I say?' he said.

'Don't ask us,' said Cliff from his prone position. 'How should we know?'

'That was *magnificent*,' said Dibbler. 'What's up with the dwarf? Is he drowning?'

Glod reached out an arm, without looking, smashed the top off another bottle of beer and poured it over his head.

'Mr Dibbler?' said Cliff.

'Yes?'

'I think we want to talk. Just us, like. The band. If you don't mind.'

Dibbler looked from one to the other. Buddy was staring at the wall. Glod was making bubbling noises. Cliff was still on the floor.

'Okay,' he said, and then added brightly, 'Buddy? The free performance . . . *great* idea. I'll start organizing it right away and you can do it just as soon as you get back from your tour. Right. Well, I'll just—'

He turned to leave and walked into Cliff's arm, which was suddenly blocking the doorway.

'Tour? What tour?'

Dibbler backed off a little. 'Oh, a few places.

Quirm, Pseudopolis, Sto Lat—' He looked around at them. 'Didn't you want that?'

'We'll talk about dat later,' said Cliff.

He pushed Dibbler out of the door and slammed it shut.

Beer dripped off Glod's beard.

'Tour? Three more nights of *this*?'

'What's the problem?' said Asphalt. 'It was great! Everyone was cheering. You did two hours! I had to keep kickin' 'em off the stage! I never felt so—'

He stopped.

'That's it, really,' said Cliff. 'The fing is, I go on dat stage, I sits down not knowing even what we're goin' to do, next minute Buddy plays something on his . . . on that *thing*, next I'm goin' *bam-Bam-chcha-chcha-BAM-bam. I* don't know what I'm playing. It just comes in my head and down my arms.'

'Yes,' said Glod. 'Me, too. Seems to me I'm getting stuff out of that horn I never put in there.'

'And it ain't like proper playing,' said Cliff. 'That's what I'm saying. It's more like being played.'

'You've been in show business a long time, right?' said Glod to Asphalt.

'Yep. Been there, done it. Seem 'em all.'

'You ever seen an audience like that?'

'I've seen 'em throw flowers and cheer at the Opera House—'

'Ha! Just flowers? Some woman threw her . . . clothing at the stage!'

'Dat's right! Landed on my head!'

'And when Miss VaVa Voom did the Feather Dance down at the Skunk Club in Brewer Street, the whole audience rushed the stage when she was down to the last feather—'

'That was like this, was it?'

'No,' the troll admitted. 'I got to say it, I ain't never seen an audience so . . . *hungry.* Not even for Miss VaVa Voom, and they were pretty damn peckish then, I can tell you. Of course, no one threw underwear on to the stage. She used to throw it *off* the stage.'

'Dere's something else,' said Cliff. 'Dere's four people in this room and only three of 'em's talking.'

Buddy looked up.

'The music's important,' he mumbled.

'It ain't music,' said Glod. 'Music don't do *this* to people. It don't make them feel like they've been put through a wringer. I was sweating so much I'm going to have to change my vest any day now.' He rubbed his nose. 'Also, I looked at that audience, and I thought: they paid money to get in here. I bet it came to more than ten dollars.'

Asphalt held up a slip of paper.

'Found this ticket on the floor,' he said.

Glod read it.

'A dollar-fifty?' he said. 'Six hundred people at a dollar-fifty each? That . . . that's four hundred dollars!'

'Nine hundred,' said Buddy, in the same flat tone, 'but the money isn't important.'

'The money's not important? You keep on saying that! What kind of musician *are* you?'

There was still a muted roar from outside.

'You want to go back to playing for half a dozen

people in some cellar somewhere after this?' said Buddy. 'Who's the most famous horn player there ever was, Glod?'

'Brother Charnel,' said the dwarf promptly. 'Everyone knows that. He stole the altar gold from the Temple of Offler and had it made into a horn and played magical music until the gods caught up with him and pulled his—'

'Right,' said Buddy, 'but if you went out there now and asked who the most famous horn player is, would they remember some felonious monk or would they shout for Glod Glodsson?'

'They'd—'

Glod hesitated.

'Right,' said Buddy. 'Think about that. A musician has to be *heard.* You can't stop now. We can't stop now.'

Glod waved a finger at the guitar.

'It's that thing,' he said. 'It's too dangerous.'

'I can handle it!'

'Yes, but where's it going to end?'

'It's not how you finish that matters,' said Buddy. 'It's how you get there.'

'That sounds *elvish* to me—'

The door burst open again.

'Er,' said Dibbler, 'boys, if you don't come back and play something else then we're in the deep brown . . .'

'Can't play,' said Glod. 'I've run out of breath through lack of money.'

'I said ten dollars, didn't I?' said Dibbler.

'Each,' said Cliff.

Dibbler, who hadn't expected to get away with less than a hundred, waved his hands in the air.

'Gratitude, is it?' he said. 'You want me to cut my own throat?'

'We'll help. If you like,' said Cliff.

'All right, all right, thirty dollars,' said Dibbler. 'And I go without my tea.'

Cliff looked at Glod, who was still digesting the thing about the most famous horn player in the world.

'There's a lot of dwarfs and trolls in the audience,' said Cliff.

'"Cavern Deep, Mountain High"?' said Glod.

'No,' said Buddy.

'What, then?'

'I'll think of something.'

The audience spilled out into the street. The wizards gathered around the Dean, snapping their fingers.

'Wella-wella-wella—' sang the Dean happily.

'It's gone midnight!' said the Lecturer in Recent Runes, snapping his fingers, 'and I don't care a bit! What shall we do now?'

'We could have a rumble,' said the Dean.

'That's true,' said the Chair of Indefinite Studies, 'we did miss dinner.'

'We missed dinner?' said the Senior Wrangler. 'Wow! *That's* Music With Rocks In! We just don't *care*!'

'No, I meant . . .' The Dean paused. He wasn't quite sure, now he came to really think about it, what he *had* meant. 'It's a long walk back to the

University,' he conceded. 'I suppose we could at least stop for a coffee or something.'

'Maybe a doughnut or two,' said Recent Runes.

'And perhaps some cake,' said the Chair.

'I could just fancy some apple pie,' said the Senior Wrangler.

'And some cake.'

'Coffee,' said the Dean. 'Ye-ess. A coffee bar. That's right.'

'What's a coffee bar?' said the Senior Wrangler.

'Like a chocolate bar?' said Recent Runes. The missed dinner, hitherto forgotten, was beginning to loom large in everyone's stomachs.

The Dean looked down at his shiny new leather robe. Everyone had said how good it was. They'd admired BORN TO RUNE. His hair was right, too. He was thinking of shaving off his beard but just leaving the side bits because *that* felt right. And coffee . . . yes . . . coffee was in there somewhere. Coffee was all part of It.

And there was the music. That was in there. That was everywhere.

But there was something else, too. Something missing. He wasn't sure what it was, only that he'd know it if he ever saw it.

It was very dark in the alley behind the Cavern, and only the keenest-sighted would have seen several figures pressed against the wall.

The occasional glint of a tarnished sequin would indicate to those who knew about such things that these were the Musicians' Guild's crack enforcers, the Grisham Frord Close Harmony Singers. Unlike most of the people employed by Mr Clete they did, in fact, genuinely have some musical talent.

They'd also been in to see the band.

'Do-wop, uh do-wop, uh do-wop—' said the thin one.

'Bubububuh—' said the tall one. There's always a tall one.

'Clete's right. If they keep pulling in audiences like that, everyone else is out of the show,' said Grisham.

'Oh *yeah*,' said the bass man.

'When they come through that door—' three more knives slipped from their sheaths '—well, just take your time from me.'

They heard the sound of feet on stairs. Grisham nodded.

'A-one, a-two, a-one-two-thr—'

GENTLEMEN?

They pivoted.

A dark figure stood behind them, holding a glowing scythe in its hands. Susan smiled horribly.

TAKE IT FROM THE TOP?

'Oh, *nooo*,' said the bass man.

Asphalt unbolted the door and stepped out into the night.

'Hey, what was that?' he said.

'What was what?' said Dibbler.

'I thought I heard some people running away . . .' The troll stepped forward. There was a *ting*. He reached down and picked up something.

'And whoever it was dropped this . . . .'

'Just some item or other,' said Dibbler loudly. 'Come along, boys. You don't have to go back to any flophouse tonight. It's The Gritz for *you*!'

'That's a troll hotel, isn't it?' said Glod suspiciously.

'Troll*ish*,' said Dibbler, waving a hand irritably.

'Hey, I bin in dere once doing cabarett!' said Cliff. 'Dey got nearly everything! Water out of taps in nearly every room! A speaking tube so's you can holler your meal order right down to the kitchen, and dese guys with actual shoes on who brings it right to you! The works!'

'Treat yourself!' said Dibbler. 'You boys can afford it!'

'And then there's this tour, is there?' said Glod sharply. 'We can afford that too, can we?'

'Oh, I shall help out with that,' said Dibbler expansively. 'Tomorrow you'll go to Pseudopolis, that'll take two days, then you can come back via Sto Lat and Quirm and be back here on Wednesday for the Festival. Great idea that. Giving something to the community, I've always been in favour of giving to the community. It's very good for . . . for . . . for the community. I'll get it all organized while you're away, okay? And then . . .' He put one arm around Buddy's shoulders and another around Glod's head. 'Genua! Klatch! Hersheba! Chimera! Howondaland! Maybe even the Counterweight Continent, they're talking about discovering it again real soon now, great opportunities for the right people! With your music and my unerring business sense, the world is our mollusc! Now, you just go off with Asphalt, the best rooms now, nothing's too much for my boys, and get some sleep without worrying about the bill—'

'Thank you,' said Glod.

'—you can pay it in the morning.'

The Band With Rocks In shambled away in the direction of the best hotel.

Dibbler heard Cliff say, 'What's a mollusc?'

'It's like two plates of precipitated calcium carbonate with a salty slimy fishy thing in the middle.'

'Sounds tasty. You don't have to eat dat bit in the middle, do you?'

When they'd gone, Dibbler looked at the knife he'd taken from Asphalt. It had sequins on it.

Yes. A few days with the lads out of the way was definitely a good move.

On his perch in the gutter above, the Death of Rats gibbered to himself.

Ridcully walked slowly out of the Cavern. Only a light drift of used tickets on the steps bore witness to the hours of music.

He felt like someone watching a game who didn't know the rules. For example, the boy had been singing . . . what was it? *Rave In.* What the hell did that mean? *Raving,* yes, he could understand *that,* and in the Dean's case it was perfectly accurate. Rave In? But everyone else had seemed to know what was meant. And then there had been, as far as he could remember, a song about not stepping on someone's shoes. Fair enough, sensible suggestion, no one wanted their feet trodden on, but why a song asking people to avoid doing so should have such an effect Ridcully was at a loss to understand.

And as for the girl . . .

Ponder bustled up, clutching his box.

'I've got nearly all of it, Archchancellor!' he shouted.

Ridcully glanced past him. There was Dibbler, still bearing a tray of unsold Band With Rocks In shirts.

'Yes, fine, Mr Stibbons (shutupshutupshutup),' he said. 'Jolly good, let's get back home.'

'Good evening, Archchancellor,' said Dibbler.

'Why, hello, Throat,' said Ridcully. 'Didn't see you there.'

'What's in that box?'

'Oh, nothing, nothing at all—'

'It's amazing!' said Ponder, full of the undirected excitement of the true discoverer and idiot. 'We can trap the arragh aargh aargh.'

'My word, clumsy old me,' said Ridcully, as the young wizard clutched at his leg. 'Here, let me take that *totally innocent* device you have there—'

But the box had tumbled out of Ponder's arms. It hit the street before Ridcully could catch it, and the lid flew off.

The music spilled out into the night.

'How did you do that?' said Dibbler. 'It is magic?'

'The music lets itself be trapped so you can hear it again and again,' said Ponder. 'And I think you did that on purpose, sir!'

'You can hear it again and again?' said Dibbler. 'What, by just opening a box?'

'Yes,' said Ponder.

'No,' said Ridcully.

'Yes you can,' said Ponder. 'I showed you, Archchancellor? Don't you remember?'

'No,' said Ridcully.

'Any kind of box?' said Dibbler, in a voice choked with money.

'Oh, yes, but you have to stretch a wire inside it so the music has somewhere to live and ouch ouch ouch.'

'Can't think what's come over me with these sudden muscular spasms,' said Ridcully. 'Come, Mr Stibbons, let us not waste any more of Mr Dibbler's valuable time.'

'Oh, you're not wasting it,' said Dibbler. 'Boxes full of music, eh?'

'*We'll* take this one,' said Ridcully, snatching it up. 'It's an important magical experiment.'

He frogmarched Ponder away, which was a little hard because the youth was bent double and wheezing.

'What did you have to go . . . and do . . . that for?'

'Mr Stibbons, I know you to be a man who seeks to understand the universe. Here's an important rule: never give a monkey the key to the banana plantation. Sometimes you can just see an accident waiting to— oh, no.'

He let Ponder go and waved vaguely up the street.

'Got any theories about *that*, young man?'

Something golden-brown and viscous was oozing out on to the street from what was just possibly, behind the mounds of the stuff, a shop. As the two wizards watched there was a tinkle of glass and the brown substance began to emerge from the second floor.

Ridcully stamped forward and scooped up a handful, leaping back before the wall could reach him. He sniffed at it.

'Is it some ghastly emanation from the Dungeon Dimensions?' said Ponder.

'Shouldn't think so. Smells like coffee,' said Ridcully.

'Coffee?'

'Coffee-flavoured froth, anyway. Now, why is it I have this feeling that there's going to be wizards in there somewhere?'

A figure lurched out of the foam, dripping brown bubbles.

'Who goes there?' said Ridcully.

'Ah, yes! Did anyone get the number of that ox-cart? Another doughnut, if you would be so good!' said the figure brightly, and fell over into the froth.

'That sounded like the Bursar to me,' said Ridcully. 'Come along, lad. It's only bubbles.' He strode into the foam.

After a moment's hesitation Ponder realized that the honour of young wizardry was at stake, and pushed his way in behind him.

Almost immediately he bumped into someone in the fog of bubbles.

'Er, hello?'

'Who's that?'

'It's me, Stibbons. I've come to rescue you.'

'Good. Which way is out?'

'Er—'

There were some explosions somewhere in the coffee cloud and a popping noise. Ponder blinked. The level of bubbles was sinking.

Various pointy hats appeared like drowned logs in a drying lake.

Ridcully waded over, coffee froth dripping from his hat.

'Something bloody stupid's been going on here,' he said, 'and I'm going to wait quite patiently until the Dean owns up.'

'I don't see why you should assume it was me,' muttered a coffee-coloured column.

'Well, who *was* it, then?'

'The Dean said the coffee ought to be frothy,' said a mound of foam of a Senior Wranglish persuasion, 'and he did some simple magic and I rather think we got carried away.'

'Ah, so it *was* you, Dean.'

'Yes, all right, but only by coincidence,' said the Dean testily.

'Out of here, all of you,' said Ridcully. 'Back to the University this minute.'

'I mean, I don't see why you should *assume* it's my fault just because sometimes it might happen to be me who—'

The froth had sunk a bit more, to reveal a pair of eyes under a dwarfish helmet.

''Scuse me,' said a voice still under the bubbles, 'but who's going to pay for all this? That's four dollars, thank you very much.'

'The Bursar's got the money,' said Ridcully quickly.

'Not any more,' said the Senior Wrangler. 'He bought seventeen doughnuts.'

'Sugar?' said Ridcully. 'You let him eat sugar. You *know* that makes him, you know, a bit funny. Mrs Whitlow said she'd give notice if we let him get anywhere near sugar again.' He herded the damp wizards towards the door. 'It's all right, my good man, you can trust us, we're wizards, I shall have some money sent around in the morning.'

'Hah, you expect me to believe that, do you?' said the dwarf.

It had been a long night. Ridcully turned and waved his hand at the wall. There was a crackle of octarine fire and the words 'IOU 4 DOLERS' burned themselves into the stone.

'Right you are, no problem there,' said the dwarf, ducking back into the froth.

'I shouldn't think Mrs Whitlow is going to worry,' said the Lecturer in Recent Runes as they squelched through the night. 'I saw her and some of the maids at the, er, concert. You know, the kitchen girls. Molly, Polly and, er, Dolly. They were, er, screaming.'

'I didn't think the music was *that* bad,' said Ridcully.

'No, er, not in pain, er, I wouldn't say that,' said the Lecturer in Recent Runes, beginning to go red, 'but, er, when the young man was waggling his hips like that—'

'He definitely looks elvish to me,' said Ridcully.

'—er, I think she threw some of her, er, under . . . things on to the stage.'

This silenced even Ridcully, at least for a while. Every wizard was suddenly busy with his own private thoughts.

'What, Mrs Whitlow?' the Chair of Indefinite Studies began.

'Yes.'

'What, her—?'

'I, er, think so.'

Ridcully had once seen Mrs Whitlow's washing line. He'd been impressed. He'd never believed there was so much pink elastic in the world.

'What, really her—?' said the Dean, his voice sounding as though it was coming from a long way away.

'I'm, er, pretty sure.'

'Sounds dangerous to me,' said Ridcully briskly. 'Could do someone a serious injury. Now then, you lot, back to the University right now for cold baths all round.'

'*Really* her—?' said the Chair of Indefinite Studies. Somehow, none of them felt able to leave the idea alone.

'Make yourself useful and find the Bursar,' snapped Ridcully. 'And I'd have you lot up in front of the University authorities first thing in the morning, if it wasn't for the fact that you *are* the University authorities . . .'

* * *

Foul Ole Ron, professional maniac and one of Ankh-Morpork's most industrious beggars, blinked in the gloom. Lord Vetinari had excellent night vision. And, unfortunately, a well-developed sense of smell.

'And then what happened?' he said, trying to keep his face turned away from the beggar. Because the fact was that although in actual size Foul Ole Ron was a small hunched man in a huge grubby overcoat, in smell he filled the world.

In fact Foul Ole Ron was a physical schizophrenic. There was Foul Ole Ron, and there was the *smell* of Foul Ole Ron, which had obviously developed over the years to such an extent that it had a distinct personality. Anyone could have a smell that lingered long after they'd gone somewhere else, but the smell of Foul Ole Ron could actually arrive somewhere several minutes *before* he did, in order to spread out and get comfortable before he arrived. It had evolved into something so striking that it was no longer perceived with the nose, which shut down instantly in self-defence; people could tell that Foul Ole Ron was approaching by the way their ear wax started to melt.

'Buggrit, buggrit, wrong side out, I *told* 'em, buggrem . . .'

The Patrician waited. With Foul Ole Ron you had to allow time for his wandering mind to get into the same vicinity as his tongue.

'. . . spyin' on me with magic, I *told* 'em, bean soup, see here . . . and then everyone was dancing, you see, and then afterwards there were two of the wizards in the street and one of them was going on about catching the music in a box and Mr Dibbler was interested and then the coffee house exploded and they all went back to the University . . . buggrit, buggrit, buggrem, see if I don't.'

'The coffee house exploded, did it?'

'Frothy coffee all over the place, yerronner . . . bugg—'

'Yes, yes, and so on,' said the Patrician, waving a thin hand. 'And that's all you can tell me?'

'Well . . . bug—'

Foul Ole Ron caught the Patrician's eye and got a grip on himself. Even in his own highly individualized sanity he could tell when not to push his threadbare luck. His Smell wandered around the room, reading documents and examining the pictures.

'They say,' he said, 'that he drives all the women mad.' He leaned forward. The Patrician leaned back. 'They say after he moved his hips like that . . . Mrs Whitlow threw her . . . wossnames . . . on to the stage.'

The Patrician raised an eyebrow.

' "Wossnames"?'

'You know.' Foul Ole Ron moved his hands vaguely in the air.

'A pair of pillow cases? Two sacks of flour? Some very baggy trou— oh. I see. My word. Were there any casualties?'

'Dunno, yerronner. But there's something I *do* know.'

'Yes?'

'Uh . . . Cumbling Michael says yerronner sometimes pays for information . . . ?'

'Yes, I know. I can't imagine how these rumours get about,' said the Patrician, getting up and opening a window. 'I shall have to have something done about it.'

Once again, Foul Ole Ron reminded himself that while he was probably insane he definitely wasn't as mad as all that.

'Only I got this, yerronner,' he said, pulling something out of the horrible recesses of his clothing. 'It says writing on it, yerronner.'

It was a poster, in glowing primary colours. It couldn't have been very old, but an hour or two as Foul Ole Ron's chest-warmer had aged it considerably. The Patrician unfolded it with a pair of tweezers.

'Them's the pictures of the music players,' said Foul Ole Ron helpfully, 'and that's writing. And there's more writing there, look. Mr Dibbler had Chalky the troll run 'em off just now, but I nipped in after and threatened to breathe on everyone less'n they gives me one.'

I'm sure that worked famously,' said the Patrician.

He lit a candle and read the poster carefully. In the presence of Foul Ole Ron, all candles burned with a blue edge to the flame.

'"Free Festival of Music with Rocks In It",' he said.

'That's where you don't have to pay to go in,' said Foul Ole Ron helpfully. 'Buggrem, buggrit.'

Lord Vetinari read on.

'In Hide Park. Next Wednesday. Well, well. A public open space, of course. I wonder if there'll be many people there?'

'Lots, yerronner. There was hundreds couldn't get into the Cavern.'

'And the band looks like that, do they?' said Lord Vetinari. 'Scowling like that?'

'Sweating, most of the time I saw 'em,' said Foul Ole Ron.

' "Bee There Orr Bee A Rectangular Thyng",' said the Patrician. 'This is some sort of occult code, do you think?'

'Couldn't say, yerronner,' said Foul Ole Ron. 'My brain goes all slow when I'm thirsty.'

' "They Are Totallye Unable To Bee Seene! And A Longe Way Oute!" ' said Lord Vetinari solemnly. He looked up. 'Oh, I *am* sorry,' he said. 'I'm sure I can find someone to give you a cool refreshing drink . . .'

Foul Ole Ron coughed. It had sounded like a perfectly sincere offer but, somehow, he was suddenly not at all thirsty.

'Don't let me keep you, then. Thank you so very much,' said Lord Vetinari.

'Er . . .'

'Yes?'

'Er . . . nothing . . .'

'Very good.'

When Ron had buggrit, buggrit, buggrem'd down the stairs, the Patrician tapped his pen thoughtfully on the paper and stared at the wall.

The pen kept bouncing on the word *Free.*

Finally he rang a small bell. A young clerk put his head around the door.

'Ah, Drumknott,' said Lord Vetinari, 'just go and tell the head of the Musicians' Guild he wants a word with me, will you?'

'Er . . . Mr Clete is already in the waiting room, your lordship,' said the clerk.

'Does he by any chance have some kind of poster with him?'

'Yes, your lordship.'

'And is he very angry?'

'This is very much the case, your lordship. It's about some festival. He *insists* you have it stopped.'

'Dear me.'

'And he demands that you see him instantly.'

'Ah. Then leave him for, say, twenty minutes, then show him up.'

'Yes, your lordship. He keeps saying that he wants to know what you are doing about it.'

'Good. Then I can ask him the same question.'

The Patrician sat back. *Si non confectus, non reficiat.* That was the motto of the Vetinaris. Everything worked if you just let it happen.

He picked up a stack of sheet-music and began to listen to Salami's *Prelude to a Nocturne on a Theme by Bubbla.*

After a while he looked up.

'Don't hesitate to leave,' he snapped.

The Smell slunk away.

SQUEAK!

'Don't be stupid! All I did was frighten them off.

It's not as though I hurt them. What's the good of having the power if you can't use it?'

The Death of Rats put his nose in his paws. It was a *lot* easier, with rats.*

C. M. O. T. Dibbler often did without sleep, too. He generally had to meet Chalky at night. Chalky was a large troll but tended to dry up and flake in daylight.

Other trolls looked down on him because he came from a sedimentary family and was therefore a very low-class troll indeed. He didn't mind. He was a very amiable character.

He did odd jobs for people who needed something unusual in a hurry and without entanglements and who had clinking money. And this job was pretty odd.

'Just boxes?' he said.

'With lids,' said Dibbler. 'Like this one I've made. And a bit of wire stretched inside.'

Some people would have said 'Why?' or 'What

*Rats had featured largely in the history of Ankh-Morpork. Shortly before the Patrician came to power there was a terrible plague of rats. The city council countered it by offering twenty pence for every rat tail. This did, for a week or two, reduce the number of rats – and then people were suddenly queuing up with tails, the city treasury was being drained, and no-one seemed to be doing much work. And there *still* seemed to be a lot of rats around. Lord Vetinari had listened carefully while the problem was explained, and had solved the thing with one memorable phrase which said a lot about him, about the folly of bounty offers, and about the natural instinct of Ankh-Morporkians in any situation involving money: 'Tax the rat farms.'

for?' but Chalky didn't make his money like that. He picked up the box and turned it this way and that.

'How many?' he said.

'Just ten to start with,' said Dibbler. 'But I think there'll be more later. Lots and lots more.'

'How many's ten?' said the troll.

Dibbler held up both hands, fingers extended.

'I'll do them for two dollar,' said Chalky.

'You want me to cut my own throat?'

'Two dollar.'

'Dollar each for these and a dollar-fifty for the next batch.'

'Two dollar.'

'All right, all right, two dollars each. That's ten dollars the lot, right?'

'Right.'

'And that's cutting my own throat.'

Chalky tossed the box aside. It bounced on the floor and the lid came off.

Some time later a small, greyish-brown mongrel dog, on the prowl for anything edible, limped into the workshop and sat peering into the box for a while.

Then it felt a bit of an idiot and wandered off.

Ridcully hammered on the door of the High Energy Magic Building as the city clocks were striking two. He was supporting Ponder Stibbons, who was asleep on his feet.

Ridcully was not a quick thinker. But he always got there eventually.

The door opened and Skazz's hair appeared.

'Are you facin' me?' said Ridcully.

'Yes, Archchancellor.'

'Let us in, then, the dew's soaking through me boots.'

Ridcully looked around as he helped Ponder in.

'Wish I knew what it was that keeps you lads working all hours,' he said. 'I never found magic that interesting when I was a lad. Go and fetch some coffee for Mr Stibbons here, will you? And then get your friends.'

Skazz bustled off and Ridcully was left alone, except for the slumbering Ponder.

'What *is* it they do?' he said. He never really tried to find out.

Skazz had been working at a long bench by one wall.

At least he recognized the little wooden disc. There were small oblong stones ranged on it in a couple of concentric circles, and a candle lantern positioned on a swivelling arm so that it could be moved anywhere around the circumference.

It was a travelling computer for druids, a sort of portable stone circle, something they called a 'knee-top'. The Bursar had sent off for one once. It had said For the Priest In a Hurry on the box. He'd never been able to make it work properly and now it was used as a doorstop. Ridcully couldn't see what they had to do with magic.

After all, it wasn't much more than a calendar and you could get a perfectly good calendar for 8p.

Rather more puzzling was the huge array of glass tubes behind it. That was where Skazz had been working; there was a litter of bent glassware and jars and bits of cardboard where the student had been sitting.

The tubing seemed to be alive.

Ridcully leaned forward.

It was full of ants.

They scuttled along the tubing and through complex little spirals in their thousands. In the silence of the room, their bodies made a faint, continuous rustling.

There was a slot level with the Archchancellor's eyes. The word 'In' was written on a piece of paper that had been pasted onto the glass.

And on the bench was an oblong of card which looked just the right shape to go in the slot. It had round holes punched in it.

There were two round holes, then a whole pattern of round holes, and then a further two holes. On it, in pencil, someone had scribbled '2 x 2'.

Ridcully was the kind of man who'd push any lever, just to see what it did.

He put the card in the obvious slot . . .

There was an immediate change in the rustling. Ants trailed in their busy way through the tubing. Some of them appeared to be carrying seeds . . .

There was a small dull sound and a card dropped out of the other end of the glass maze.

It had four holes in it.

Ridcully was still staring at it when Ponder came up behind him, rubbing his eyes.

''S our ant counter,' he said.

'Two plus two equals four,' said Ridcully. 'Well, well, I never knew that.'

'It can do other sums as well.'

'You tellin' me ants can count?'

'Oh, no. Not individual ants . . . it's a bit hard to explain . . . the holes in the cards, you see, block up some tubes and let them through others and . . .' Ponder sighed, 'we think it might be able to do other things.'

'Like what?' Ridcully demanded.

'Er, that's what we're trying to find out . . .'

'You're trying to find out? Who built it?'

'Skazz.'

'And *now* you're trying to find out what it does?'

'Well, we think it might be able to do quite complicated maths. If we can get enough bugs in it.'

Ants were still bustling around the enormous crystalline structure.

'Had a rat thingy, a gerbil or something, when I was a lad,' said Ridcully, giving up in the face of the incomprehensible. 'Spent all the time on a treadmill. Round and round, all night long. This is a bit like that, yes?'

'In very broad terms,' said Ponder carefully.

'Had an ant farm, too,' said Ridcully, thinking faraway thoughts. 'The little devils never could plough straight.' He pulled himself together. 'Anyway, get the rest of your chums here right now.'

'What for?'

'A bit of a tutorial,' said Ridcully.

'Aren't we going to examine the music?'

'In good time,' said Ridcully. 'But first, we're going to talk to someone.'

'Who?'

'I'm not sure,' said Ridcully. 'We'll know when he turns up. Or her.'

Glod looked at their suite. The hotel owners had just left, after going through the 'dis is der window, it really opens, dis is der pump, you get water out of it wit der handle here, dis is me waiting for some money' routine.

'Well, that just about does it. That just about puts the iron helmet on it, that does,' he said. 'We play Music With Rocks In all evening, and we've got a room that looks like *this*?'

'It's homely,' said Cliff. 'Look, trolls don't have much to do with de frills of life—'

Glod looked towards his feet.

'It's on the floor and it's soft,' he said. 'Silly me for thinking it was a carpet. Someone fetch me a broom. No, someone fetch me a shovel. *Then* someone fetch me a broom.'

'It'll do,' said Buddy.

He put down his guitar and stretched out on the wooden slab that was apparently one of the beds.

'Cliff,' said Glod, 'can I have a word?'

He jerked a stubby thumb at the door.

They conferred on the landing.

'It's getting bad,' said Glod.

'Yep.'

'He hardly says a word now when he's not on stage.'

'Yep.'

'Ever met a zombie?'

'I know a golem. Mr Dorfl down in Long Hogmeat.'

'Him? He's a genuine zombie?'

'Yep. Got a holy word on his head, I seen it.'

'Yuk. Really? I buy sausages from him.'

'Anyway . . . what *about* zombies?'

'. . . you couldn't tell from the taste, I thought he was a really good sausage-maker . . .'

'What were you saying about zombies?'

'. . . funny how you can know someone for years and then find out they've got feet of clay . . .'

'Zombies . . .' said Cliff patiently.

'What? Oh. Yes. I mean he acts like one.' Glod recalled some of the zombies in Ankh-Morpork. 'At least, like zombies are supposed to act.'

'Yep. I know what you mean.'

'And we both know why.'

'Yep. Er. Why?'

'The guitar.'

'Oh, that. Yeah.'

'When we're on stage, that *thing* is in charge—'

In the silence of the room, the guitar lay in the dark by Buddy's bed and its strings vibrated gently to the sound of the dwarf's voice . . .

'Okay, so what do we do about it?' said Cliff.

'It's made of wood. Ten seconds with an axe, no more problem.'

'I'm not sure. That ain't no ordinary instrument.'

'He was a nice kid when we met him. For a human,' said Glod.

'So what do we do? I don't think we could get it off him.'

'Maybe we could get him to—'

The dwarf paused. He was aware of a fuzzy echo to his voice.

'That damn thing is *listening* to us!' he hissed. 'Let's go outside.'

They ended up out in the road.

'Can't see how it can listen,' said Cliff. 'An instrument's for listening to.'

'The strings listen,' said Glod, flatly. 'That is *not* an ordinary instrument.'

Cliff shrugged. 'Dere's one way we could find out,' he said.

Early morning fog filled the streets. Around the University it was sculpted into curious forms by the slight magical background radiation. Strange-shaped things moved across the damp cobbles.

Two of them were Glod and Cliff.

'Right,' said the dwarf. 'Here we are.'

He looked up at a blank wall.

'I knew it!' he said. 'Didn't I say? Magic! How many times have we heard this story? There's a mysterious shop no one's ever seen before, and someone goes in and buys some rusty old curio, and it turns out to—'

'Glod—'

'—some kind of talisman or a bottle full of genie, and then when there's trouble they go back and the shop—'

'Glod—?'

'—has *mysteriously disappeared* and gone back to whatever dimension it came from— yes, what is it?'

'You're on the wrong side of the road. It's over here.'

Glod glared at the blank wall, and then turned and stomped across the road.

'It was a mistake anyone could have made.'

'Yep.'

'It doesn't invalidate anything I said.'

Glod rattled the door and, to his surprise, found it was unlocked.

'It's gone two in the morning! What kind of music shop is open at two in the morning?' Glod struck a match.

The dusty graveyard of old instruments loomed around them. It looked as though a number of prehistoric animals had been caught in a flash flood and then fossilized.

'What's that one that looks like a serpent?' whispered Cliff.

'It's called a Serpent.'

Glod was uneasy. He'd spent most of his life as a musician. He hated the sight of dead instruments, and these *were* dead. They didn't belong to anyone. No one played them. They were like bodies without life, people without souls. Something they had contained had gone. Every one of them represented a musician down on his luck.

There was a pool of light in a grove of bassoons. The old lady was deeply asleep in a rocking chair, with a tangle of knitting on her lap and a shawl around her shoulders.

'Glod?'

Glod jumped. 'Yes? What?'

'Why are we here? We know the place exists now—'

'*Grab some ceiling, hooligans!*'

Glod blinked at the crossbow bolt pricking the end of his nose, and raised his hands. The old lady had gone from asleep to firing stance without apparently passing through any intermediate stage.

'This is the best I can do,' he said. 'Er . . . the door wasn't locked, you see, and . . .'

'So you thought you could rob a poor defenceless old lady?'

'Not at all, not at all, in fact we—'

'I belongs to the Neighbourhood Witch scheme, I do! One word from me and you'll be hopping around looking for some princess with an amphibian fixation—'

'I think dis has gone far enough,' said Cliff. He reached down and his huge hand closed over the bow. He squeezed. Bits of wood oozed between his fingers.

'We're quite harmless,' he said. 'We've come about the instrument you sold our friend last week.'

'Are you the Watch?'

Glod bowed.

'No, ma'am. We're musicians.'

'That's supposed to make me feel better, is it? What instrument are you talking about?'

'A kind of guitar.'

The old woman put her head on one side. Her eyes narrowed.

'I won't take it back, you know,' she said. 'It was sold fair 'n' square. Good working condition, too.'

'We just want to know where you got it from.'

'Never got it from nowhere,' said the old lady. 'It's always been here. Don't blow that!'

Glod nearly dropped the flute he'd nervously picked up from the debris.

'. . . or we'll be knee deep in rats,' said the old lady. She turned back to Cliff. 'It's always been here,' she repeated.

'It's got a one chalked on it,' said Glod.

'It's always been here,' said the woman. 'Ever since I've had the shop.'

'Who brought it in?'

'How should I know? I never asks them their name. People don't like that. They just gets the number.'

Glod looked at the flute. There was a yellowing tag attached to it, on which the number 431 had been scrawled.

He stared along the shelves behind the makeshift counter. There was a pink conch shell. That had a number on it, too. He moistened his lips and reached out . . .

'If you blow that, you'd just better have a sacrificial virgin and a big cauldron of breadfruit and turtle meat standing by,' said the old lady.

There was a trumpet next to it. It looked amazingly untarnished.

'And this one?' he said. 'It'll make the world end and the sky fall on me if I give it a tootle, will it?'

'Interesting you should say that,' said the old lady.

Glod lowered his hand, and then something else caught his eye.

'Good grief,' he said, 'is that *still* here? I'd forgotten about that . . .'

'What is it?' said Cliff, and then looked where Glod was pointing.

'That?'

'We've got some money. Why not?'

'Yeah. It might help. But you know what Buddy said. We'd never be able to find—'

'It's a big city. If you can't find it in Ankh-Morpork, you can't find it anywhere.'

Glod picked up half a drumstick and looked thoughtfully at a gong half buried in a pile of music-stands.

'I shouldn't,' said the old lady. 'Not if you don't want seven hundred and seventy-seven skeletal warriors springing out of the earth.'

Glod pointed.

'We'll take this.'

'Two dollars.'

'Hey, why should we pay anything? It's not as though it's yours—'

'Pay up,' said Cliff with a sigh. 'Don't negotiate.'

Glod handed over the money with bad grace, snatched the bag the old lady gave him, and strutted out of the shop.

'Fascinating stock you have here,' said Cliff, staring at the gong.

The old lady shrugged.

'My friend's a bit annoyed because he thought you one of dose mysterious shops you hear about in folk tales,' Cliff went on. 'You know, here today and gone tomorrow. He was looking for you on der other side of der road, haha!'

'Sounds daft to me,' said the old lady, in a voice to discourage any further unseemly levity.

Cliff glanced at the gong again, shrugged, and followed Glod.

The woman waited until their footsteps had died away in the fog.

Then she opened the door and peered up and down the street. Apparently satisfied by its abundance of emptiness, she went back to her counter and reached for a curious lever underneath. Her eyes glowed green for a moment.

'Forget my own head next,' she said, and pulled.

There was a grinding of hidden machinery.

The shop vanished. A moment later, it reappeared on the other side of the road.

Buddy lay looking at the ceiling.

How did food taste? It was hard to remember. He'd eaten meals over the last few days, he must have done, but he couldn't remember the taste. He couldn't remember much of anything, except the playing. Glod and the rest of them sounded as if they were talking through a thick gauze.

Asphalt had wandered off somewhere.

He swung himself off the hard bed and padded over to the window.

The Shades of Ankh-Morpork were just visible in

the grey, cheap-rate light before dawn. A breeze blew in through the open window.

When he turned around, there was a young woman standing in the middle of the floor.

She put her finger to her lips.

'Don't go shouting to the little troll,' she said. 'He's downstairs having some supper. Anyway, he wouldn't be able to see me.'

'Are you my muse?'

Susan frowned.

'I think I know what you mean,' she said. 'I've seen pictures. There were eight of them, led by . . . um . . . Cantaloupe. They're supposed to protect people. The Ephebians believe they inspire musicians and artists, but of course they don't exi—' She paused, and made a conscientious correction. 'At least, I've never met them. My name's Susan. I'm here because . . .'

Her voice trailed away.

'Cantaloupe?' said Buddy. 'I'm pretty sure it wasn't Cantaloupe.'

'Whatever.'

'How did you get in here?'

'I'm . . . Look, sit down. Right. Well . . . you know how some things . . . like the Muses, as you said . . . people think that some things are represented by people?'

A look of temporary understanding informed Buddy's perplexed features.

'Like the Hogfather representing the spirit of the midwinter festival?' he said.

'Right. Well . . . I'm sort of in that business,' said Susan. 'It doesn't exactly matter what I do.'

'You mean you're not human?'

'Oh, yes. But I'm . . . doing a job. I suppose thinking of me as a Muse is probably as good as anything. And I'm here to warn you.'

'A Muse for Music With Rocks In?'

'Not really, but *listen* . . . hey, are you all right?'

'Don't know.'

'You looked all washed-out. Listen. The music is dangerous—'

Buddy shrugged. 'Oh, you mean the Guild of Musicians. Mr Dibbler says not to worry about that. We're leaving the city for—'

Susan stamped forward and picked up the guitar. 'I mean this!'

The strings moved and whined under her hand.

'Don't touch that!'

'It's taken you over,' said Susan, throwing it on to the bed. Buddy grabbed it and played a chord.

'I know what you're going to say,' he said. 'Everyone says it. The other two think it's evil. But it's not!'

'It might not be evil, but it's not right! Not here, not now.'

'Yes, but I can handle it.'

'You can't handle it. It handles you.'

'Anyway, who are you to tell me all this? I don't have to take lessons from a tooth fairy!'

'Listen, it'll *kill* you! I'm sure of it!'

'So I'm supposed to stop playing, then?'

Susan hesitated.

'Well, not exactly . . . because then—'

'Well, *I* don't have to listen to mysterious occult

women! You probably don't even exist! So you can just fly back to your magic castle, okay?'

Susan was temporarily speechless. She was reconciled to the irredeemable dumbness of most of mankind, particularly the section of it that stood upright and shaved in the mornings, but she was also affronted. No one had ever talked to Death like this. At least, not for long.

'All right,' she said, reaching out and touching his arm. 'But you'll see me again, and . . . and you won't like it much! Because, let me tell you, I happen to be—'

Her expression changed. She felt the sensation of falling backwards while standing still; the room drifted past her and away into darkness, pinwheeling around Buddy's horrified face.

The darkness exploded, and there was light.

Dribbly candle light.

Buddy waved his hand through the empty space where Susan had been.

'Are you still here? Where did you go? *Who are you?*'

Cliff looked around.

'Thought I heard something,' he muttered. 'Here, you do know, don't you, dat some of dose instruments weren't just ordin—'

'I know,' said Glod. 'I wish I'd had a go on the rat pipe. I'm hungry again.'

'I mean they were mythi—'

'Yes.'

'So how come dey end up in a second-hand music shop?'

'Ain't you ever hocked your stones?'

'Oh, sure,' said Cliff. 'Everyone does, some time or other, you know that. Sometimes it's all you've got if you want to see another meal.'

'There you are, then. You said it. It's something every working musician's going to do, sooner or later.'

'Yeah, but the thing that Buddy . . . I mean, it's got the number *one* on it . . .'

'Yes.'

Glod peered up at a street-sign.

'"Cunning Artificers",' he said. 'Here we are. Look, half the workshops are still open even at this time of night.' He shifted the sack. Something cracked inside it. 'You knock that side, I'll knock this.'

'Yeah, all right . . . but, I mean, number one. Even the conch shell was number fifty-two. Who used to own the guitar?'

'Don't know,' said Glod, knocking on the first door, 'but I hope they never come back for it.'

'And that,' said Ridcully, 'is the Rite of AshkEnte. Quite easily done. You have to use a fresh egg, though.'

Susan blinked.

There was a circle drawn on the floor. Strange unearthly shapes surrounded it, although when she adjusted her mind set she realized that these were perfectly ordinary students.

'Who are you?' she said. 'What's this place? Let me go this instant!'

She strode across the circle and rebounded from an invisible wall.

The students were staring at her in the manner of those who have heard of the species 'female' but have never expected to get this close to one.

'I demand that you let me go!' She glared at Ridcully. 'Aren't you the wizard I saw last night?'

'That's right,' said Ridcully, 'and *this* is the Rite of AshkEnte. It calls Death into the circle and he – or as it may be, in this case, *she* – can't leave until we say so. There's a lot of stuff in this book here spelled with funny long esses and it goes on about abjuring and conjuration, but it's all show, really. Once you're in, you're in. I must say your predecessor – hah, bit of a pun there – was a lot more gracious about it.'

Susan glared. The circle played tricks with her ideas of space. It seemed most unfair.

'Why have you summoned me, then?' she said.

'That's better. That's more according to the script,' said Ridcully. 'We are allowed to ask you questions, you see. And you have to answer them. Truthfully.'

'Well?'

'Would you like to sit down? A glass of something?'

'No.'

'Just as you like. This new music . . . tell us about it.'

'You summoned *Death* to ask that?'

'I'm not sure who we've summoned,' said Ridcully. 'It is really alive?'

'I . . . think so.'

'Does it live anywhere?'

'It seems to have lived in one instrument but I think it's moving around now. Can I go?'

'No. Can it be killed?'

'I don't know.'

'Should it be here?'

'What?'

'Should it be here?' Ridcully repeated patiently. 'Is it something that's supposed to be happening?'

Susan suddenly felt important. Wizards were rumoured to be wise – in fact, that's where the word came from.* But they were asking *her* things. They were *listening* to her. Pride sparkled in her eyes.

'I . . . don't think so. It's turned up here by some kind of accident. This isn't the right world for it.'

Ridcully looked smug. 'That's what I thought. This isn't right, I said. It's making people try and be things they aren't. How can we stop it?'

'I don't think you can. It's not susceptible to magic.'

'Right. Music's not. Any music. But something must be able to make it stop. Show her your box, Ponder.'

'Er . . . yes. Here.'

He lifted the lid. Music, slightly tinny but still recognizable, drifted out into the room.

'Sounds like a spider trapped in a matchbox, don't it?' said Ridcully.

*From the Old *wys-ars,* lit.: one who, at bottom, is very smart.

'You can't reproduce music like that on a piece of wire in a box,' said Susan. 'It's against nature.'

Ponder looked relieved.

'That's what I said,' he said. 'But it does it anyway. It wants to.'

Susan stared at the box.

She began to smile. There was no humour in it.

'It's unsettling people,' said Ridcully. 'And . . . look at this.' He pulled a roll of paper out of his robe and unfolded it. 'Caught some lad trying to paste this on to our gates. Blooming cheek! So I took it off him and told him to hop it, which was,' Ridcully looked smugly at his fingertips, 'quite appropriate as it turned out. It's going on about some festival of Music With Rocks In. It'll all end with monsters from another dimension breaking through, you can rely on that. That's the sort of thing that happens a lot in these parts.'

'Excuse me,' said Big Mad Adrian, his voice cargoed with suspicion, 'I don't want to cause any trouble, right, but is this Death or not? I've seen pictures, and they didn't look like her.'

'We did the Rite stuff,' said Ridcully. 'And this is what we got.'

'Yes, but my father's a herring fisherman and he doesn't just find herring in his herring nets,' said Skazz.

'Yeah. She could be anyone,' said Tez the Terrible. 'I thought Death was taller and bonier.'

'She's just some girl messing about,' said Skazz.

Susan stared at them.

'She hasn't even got a scythe,' said Tez.

Susan concentrated. The scythe appeared in her hands, its blue-edged blade making a noise like a finger dragged around the rim of a glass.

The students straightened up.

'But I've always thought it was time for a change,' said Tez.

'Right. It's about time girls got a chance in the professions,' said Skazz.

'Don't you dare patronize me!'

'That's right,' said Ponder. 'There's no reason why Death has to be male. A woman could be almost as good as a man in the job.'

'You're doing it very well,' said Ridcully.

He gave Susan an encouraging smile.

She rounded on him. I'm Death, she thought – technically, anyway – and this is a fat old man who has no right to give me any kind of orders. I'll glare at him, and he'll soon realize the gravity of his situation. She glared.

'Young lady,' said Ridcully, 'would you care for breakfast?'

The Mended Drum seldom closed. There tended to be a lull around six in the morning, but Hibiscus stayed open so long as someone wanted a drink.

Someone wanted a lot of drinks. Someone indistinct was standing at the bar. Sand seemed to be running out of him and, in so far as Hibiscus could tell, he had a number of arrows of Klatchian manufacture sticking in him.

The barman leaned forward.

'Have I seen you before?'

I'M IN HERE QUITE OFTEN, YES. A WEEK LAST WEDNESDAY, FOR EXAMPLE.

'Ha! That was a bit of a do. That's when poor old Vince got stabbed.'

YES.

'Asking for it, calling yourself Vincent the Invulnerable.'

YES. INACCURATE, TOO.

'The Watch are saying it was suicide.'

Death nodded. Going into the Mended Drum and calling yourself Vincent the Invulnerable *was* clearly suicide by Ankh-Morpork standards.

THIS DRINK'S GOT MAGGOTS IN IT.

The barman squinted at it.

'That's not a maggot, sir,' he said. 'That's a worm.'

OH THAT'S BETTER, IS IT?

'It's supposed to be there, sir. That's mexical, that is. They put the worm in to show how strong it is.'

STRONG ENOUGH TO DROWN WORMS?

The barman scratched his head. He'd never thought of it in those terms.

'It's just something people drink,' he said vaguely.

Death picked up the bottle and held it up to what normally would have been eye level. The worm rotated forlornly.

WHAT'S IT LIKE? he said.

'Well, it's a sort of—'

I WASN'T TALKING TO YOU.

* * *

'Breakfast?' said Susan. 'I mean—' BREAKFAST?

'It must be coming up to that time,' said the Archchancellor. 'It's a long time since I last had breakfast with a charming young woman.'

'Good grief, you're all just as bad as each other,' said Susan.

'Very well, scratch *charming*,' said Ridcully evenly. 'But the sparrows are coughin' in the trees and the sun is peepin' over the wall and I smell cookin', and having a meal with Death is a chance that doesn't happen to everyone. You don't play chess, do you?'

'Extremely well,' said Susan, still bewildered.

'Thought as much. All right, you fellows. You can go back to prodding the universe. Will you step this way, madam?'

'I can't leave the circle!'

'Oh, you can if I invite you. It's all a matter of courtesy. I don't know if you've ever had the concept explained?'

He reached out and took her hand. She hesitated, then stepped across the chalk line. There was a slight tingling feeling.

The students backed away hurriedly.

'Go on, get on with it,' said Ridcully. 'This way, madam.'

Susan had never experienced charm before. Ridcully possessed quite a lot of it, in a twinkly-eyed kind of way.

She followed him across the lawns to the Great Hall.

The breakfast tables had been laid out, but they

were unoccupied. The big sideboard had sprouted copper tureens like autumn fungi. Three rather young maids were waiting patiently behind the array.

'We tend to help ourselves,' said Ridcully conversationally, lifting a cover. 'Waiters and so on make too much nois— this is some sort of a joke, is it?'

He prodded what was under the cover and beckoned the nearest maid.

'Which one are you?' he said. 'Molly, Polly or Dolly?'

'Molly, your lordship,' said the maid, dropping a curtsy and trembling slightly. 'Is there something wrong?'

'A-wrong-wrong-wrong-wrong, a-do-wrong-wrong,' said the other two maids.

'What happened to the kippers? What's this? Looks like a beef patty in a bun,' said Ridcully, staring at the girls.

'Mrs Whitlow gave instructions to the cook,' said Molly nervously. 'It's a—'

'—yay-yay-yay—'

'—it's a burger.'

'You're telling me,' said Ridcully. 'And why've you got a beehive made of hair on your head, pray? Makes you look like a matchstick.'

'Please sir, we—'

'You went to see the Music With Rocks In concert, did you?'

'Yes, sir.'

'Yay, yay.'

'You, er, you didn't throw anything on the stage, did you?'

'No, sir!'

'Where's Mrs Whitlow?'

'In bed with a cold, sir.'

'Not at all surprised.' Ridcully turned to Susan. 'People are playing silly burgers, I'm afraid.'

'I eat only muesli at breakfast,' said Susan.

'There's porridge,' said Ridcully. 'We do it for the Bursar because it's not exciting.' He lifted the lid of a tureen. 'Yes, still here,' he said. 'There's some things Music With Rocks In can't change, and one of them's porridge. Let me help you to a ladleful.'

They sat on either side of the long table.

'Well, isn't this nice?' Ridcully said.

'Are you laughing at me?' said Susan suspiciously.

'Not at all. In my experience, what you mostly get in herring nets is herring. But, speaking as a mortal – a customer, as you might say – I'm interested to know why Death is suddenly a teenage girl instead of the animate natomy we've come to know and . . . know.'

'Natomy?'

'Another word for skeleton. Probably derived from "anatomy".'

'He's my grandfather.'

'Ah. Yes, you said. And that's true, is it?'

'It sounds a bit silly, now I come to tell someone else.'

Ridcully shook his head.

'You should do my job for five minutes. Then tell me about silly,' he said. He took a pencil out of his pocket and cautiously lifted the top half of the bun on his plate.

'There's *cheese* in this,' he said, accusingly.

'But he's gone off somewhere and next thing I know I've inherited the whole thing. I mean, I didn't *ask* for it! Why me? Having to go around with this silly scythe thing . . . that's not what I wanted out of life—'

'It's certainly not something you get careers leaflets about,' said Ridcully.

'Exactly.'

'And I suppose you're stuck with it?' said Ridcully.

'We don't know where he's gone. Albert says he's very depressed about something but he won't say what.'

'Dear me. What could depress Death?'

'Albert seems to think he might do something . . . silly.'

'Oh, dear. Not *too* silly, I hope. Could that be possible? It'd be . . . morticide, I suppose. Or cidicide.'

To Susan's amazement Ridcully patted her hand.

'But I'm sure we'll all sleep safer in our beds knowing that you're in charge,' he said.

'It's all so *untidy*! Good people dying stupidly, bad people living to a ripe old age . . . it's so *disorganized*. There's no sense to it. There's no justice at all. I mean, there's this boy—'

'What boy?'

To Susan's horror and amazement she found that she was blushing. 'Just some boy,' she said. 'He was supposed to have died quite ridiculously, and I was going to save him, and then the *music* saved him, and now it's getting him into all sorts of trouble and I've got to save him anyway and I *don't know why*.'

'Music?' said Ridcully. 'Does he play a sort of guitar?'

'Yes! How did you know?'

Ridcully sighed. 'When you're a wizard you get an instinct for these things.' He prodded his burger some more. 'And lettuce, for some reason. And one very, very thin slice of pickled cucumber.'

He let the bread drop.

'The music *is* alive,' he said.

Something that had been knocking on Susan's attention for the past ten minutes finally used its boots.

'Oh, my god,' she said.

'Which one would that be?' said Ridcully politely.

'It's so *simple*! It strolls into traps! It changes people! They want to play m— I've got to go,' said Susan hurriedly. 'Er. Thank you for the porridge . . .'

'You haven't eaten any of it,' Ridcully pointed out mildly.

'No, but . . . but I had a really good look at it.'

She vanished. After a little while Ridcully leaned forward and waved his hand vaguely in the space where she had been sitting, just in case.

Then he reached into his robe and pulled out the poster about the Free Festival. Great big things with tentacles, that was the problem. Get enough magic in one place and the fabric of the universe gave at the heel just like one of the Dean's socks which, Ridcully noticed, had been in some extremely bright colours the last few days.

He waved a hand at the maids.

'Thank you, Molly, Dolly or Polly,' he said. 'You can clear this stuff away.'

'Yay-yay.'

'Yes, yes, thank you.'

Ridcully felt rather alone. He'd quite enjoyed talking to the girl. She seemed to be the only person in the place who wasn't mildly insane or totally preoccupied with something that he, Ridcully, didn't understand.

He wandered back to his study, but was distracted by the sounds of hammering coming from the Dean's chambers. The door was ajar.

The senior wizards had quite large suites that included study, workshop and bedroom. The Dean was hunched over the furnace in the workshop area, with a smoked-glass mask over his face and a hammer in his hand. He was hard at work. There were sparks.

This was much more cheering, Ridcully thought. Maybe this was an end to all this Music With Rocks In nonsense and a return to some real magic.

'Everythin' all right, Dean?' he said.

The Dean pushed up the glass and nodded.

'Nearly finished, Archchancellor,' he said.

'Heard you bangin' away right down the passage,' said Ridcully, conversationally.

'Ah. I'm working on the pockets,' said the Dean.

Ridcully looked blank. Quite a number of the more difficult spells involved heat and hammering, but pockets was a new one.

The Dean held up a pair of trousers.

They were not, strictly speaking, as trousery as normal trousers; senior wizards developed a distinctive 50″ waist, 25″ leg shape that suggested someone who sat on a wall and required royal assistance to be put together again. They were dark blue.

'You were hammerin' them?' said Ridcully. 'Mrs Whitlow been heavy on the starch again?'

He looked closer.

'You're *rivetin'* them together?'

The Dean beamed.

'These trousers,' he said, 'are where it's at.'

'Are you talkin' Music With Rocks In again?' said Ridcully suspiciously.

'I mean they're cool.'

'Well, better than a thick robe in this weather,' Ridcully conceded, 'but— you're not going to put them on now, are you?'

'Why not?' said the Dean, struggling out of his robe.

'Wizards in trousers? Not in *my* university! It's cissy. People'd laugh,' said Ridcully.

'You always try and stop me doing anything I want!'

'There's no need to take that tone with me—'

'Huh, you never listen to anything I say and I don't see why I shouldn't wear what I like!'

Ridcully glared around the room.

'This room is a total mess!' he bellowed. 'Tidy it up right now!'

'Sharn't!'

'Then it's no more Music With Rocks In for you, young man!'

Ridcully slammed the door behind him.

He slammed it open again and added, 'And I never gave you permission to paint it black!'

He slammed the door shut.

He slammed it open.

'They don't suit you, either!'

The Dean rushed out into the passage, waving his hammer.

'Say what you like,' he shouted, 'when history comes to name these, they certainly won't call them Archchancellors!'

It was eight in the morning, a time when drinkers are trying either to forget who they are or to remember where they live. The other occupants of the Mended Drum were hunched over their drinks around the walls and watching an orang-utan, who was playing Barbarian Invaders and screaming with rage every time he lost a penny.

Hibiscus really wanted to shut. On the other hand, it'd be like blowing up a goldmine. It was all he could do to keep up the supply of clean glasses.

'Have you forgotten yet?' he said.

IT APPEARS I HAVE ONLY FORGOTTEN ONE THING.

'What's that? Hah, silly of me to ask really, seeing as you've forgotten—'

I HAVE FORGOTTEN HOW TO GET DRUNK.

The barman looked at the rows and rows of glasses. There were wine-glasses. There were cocktail glasses. There were beer mugs. There were steins in the shape of jolly fat men. There was a bucket.

'I think you're on the right lines,' he hazarded.

The stranger picked up his most recent glass and wandered over to the Barbarian Invaders machine.

It was made of clockwork of a complex and intricate design. There was a suggestion of many gears and worm drives in the big mahogany cabinet under the game, the whole function of which appeared to be to make rows of rather crudely carved Barbarian Invaders jerk and wobble across a rectangular proscenium. The player, by means of a system of levers and pulleys, operated a small self-loading catapult that moved below the Invaders. This shot small pellets upwards. At the same time the Invaders (by means of a ratchet-and-pawl mechanism) dropped small metal arrows. Periodically a bell rang and an Invader on horseback oscillated hesitantly across the top of the game, dropping spears. The whole assemblage rattled and creaked continuously, partly because of all the machinery and partly because the orang-utan was wrenching both handles, jumping up and down on the Fire pedal, and screaming at the top of his voice.

'I wouldn't have it in the place,' said the barman behind him. 'But it's popular with the customers, you see.'

ONE CUSTOMER, ANYWAY.

'Well, it's better than the fruit machine, at least.'

YES?

'He ate all the fruit.'

There was a screech of rage from the direction of the machine.

The barman sighed. 'You wouldn't think anyone'd make so much fuss over a penny, would you?'

The ape slammed a dollar coin on the counter and went away with two handfuls of change. One penny in a slot allowed a very large lever to be pulled; miraculously, all the Barbarians rose from the dead and began their wobbly invasion again.

'He poured his drink into it,' said the barman. 'It may be my imagination, but I think they're wobbling a bit more now.'

Death watched the game for a while. It was one of the most depressing things he'd ever seen. The things were going to get down to the bottom of the game anyway. Why shoot things at them?

Why . . . ?

He waved his glass at the assembled drinkers.

D'YOU. D'YOU. THING IS, D'YOU KNOW WHAT IT'S LIKE, EH, HAVING A MEMORY SO GOOD, RIGHT, SO GOOD YOU EVEN REMEMBER WHAT HASN'T HAPPENED YET? THAT'S ME. OH, YES. RIGHT ENOUGH. AS THOUGH. AS THOUGH. AS THOUGH THERE'S NO FUTURE . . . ONLY THE PAST THAT HASN'T HAPPENED YET. AND. AND. AND. YOU HAVE TO DO THINGS ANYWAY. YOU KNOW WHAT'S GOING TO HAPPEN AND YOU HAVE TO DO THINGS.

He looked around at the faces. People in the Drum were used to alcoholic lectures, but not ones like this.

YOU SEE. YOU SHEE. YOU SEE STUFF LOOMING UP LIKE ICEBERG THINGS AHEAD BUT YOU MUSTN'T DO ANYTHING ABOUT IT BECAUSE – BECAUSE – BECAUSEITSALAW. CAN'T BREAK THE LAW. 'SGOTABEALAW.

SEE THIS GLASS, RIGHT? SEE IT? 'S LIKE MEMORY.

ONNACOUNTA IF YOU PUT MORE STUFF IN, MORE STUFF FLOWS OUT, RIGHT? 'S' FACT. EVERYONEGOTTA MEMORY LIKE THIS. 'S'WHAT KEEPS HUMANS FROM GOING ISS— ISH— INSH— MAD. 'CEPT ME. POOROLE ME. I REMEMBER EVERYTHING. AS IF IT HAPPENED ONLY TOMORROW. EVERYTHING.

He looked down at his drink.

AH, he said, FUNNY HOW THINGS COME BACK TO YOU, ISN'T IT?

It was the most impressive collapse the bar had ever seen. The tall dark stranger fell backwards slowly, like a tree. There was no cissy sagging of the knees, no cop-out bouncing off a table on the way down. He simply went from vertical to horizontal in one marvellous geometric sweep.

Several people applauded as he hit the floor. Then they searched his pockets, or at least made an effort to search his pockets but couldn't find any. And then they threw him into the river.*

In the giant black study of Death one candle burned, and got no shorter.

Susan leafed frantically through the books.

Life wasn't simple. She knew that; it was *the* Knowledge, which went with the job. There was the simple life of living things but that was, well . . . simple . . .

There were other kinds of life. Cities had life. Anthills and swarms of bees had life, a whole greater than the sum of the parts. Worlds had life.

*Or, at least, on to the river.

Gods had a life made up of the belief of their believers.

The universe danced towards life. Life was a remarkably common commodity. Anything sufficiently complicated seemed to get cut in for some, in the same way that anything massive enough got a generous helping of gravity. The universe had a definite tendency towards awareness. This suggested a certain subtle cruelty woven into the very fabric of space-time.

Perhaps even a music could be alive, if it was old enough. Life is a habit.

People said: I can't get that darn tune out of my head . . .

Not just a beat, but a heartbeat.

And anything alive wants to breed.

C. M. O. T. Dibbler liked to be up at first light, in case there was an opportunity to sell a worm to the early bird.

He had set up a desk in the corner of one of Chalky's workshops. He was, by and large, against the idea of a permanent office. On the positive side it made him easier to find, but on the negative side it made him easier to find. The success of Dibbler's commercial strategy hinged on him being able to find customers, not the other way around.

Quite a large number of people seemed to have found him this morning. Many of them were holding guitars.

'Right,' he said to Asphalt, whose flat head was just visible over the top of the makeshift desk.

'All understood? It'll take you two days to get to Pseudopolis and then you report to Mr Klopstock at the Bull Pit. And I'll want receipts for everything.'

'Yes, Mr Dibbler.'

'It'll be a good idea to get away from the city for a bit.'

'Yes, Mr Dibbler.'

'Did I already say I wanted receipts for everything?'

'Yes, Mr Dibbler,' sighed Asphalt.

'Off you go, then.' Dibbler ignored the troll and beckoned to a group of dwarfs who'd been hanging around patiently. 'Okay, you lot, come over here. So you want to be Music With Rocks In stars, do you?'

'Yes, sir!'

'Then listen here to what I say . . .'

Asphalt looked at the money. It wasn't much to feed four people for several days. Behind him, the interview continued.

'So what do you call yourselves?'

'Er – dwarfs, Mr Dibbler,' said the lead dwarf.

' "Dwarfs"?'

'Yes, sir.'

'Why?'

'Because we are, Mr Dibbler,' said the lead dwarf patiently.

'No, no, no. That won't do. That won't do at all. You gotta have a name with a bit of—' Dibbler waved his hands in the air, '—with a bit of Music With Rocks In . . . uh . . . in. Not just "Dwarfs". You gotta be . . . oh, I don't know . . . something more interesting.'

'But we're *certainly* dwarfs,' said one of the dwarfs.

' "We're Certainly Dwarfs",' said Dibbler. 'Yes, that might work. Okay. I can book you in at the Bunch of Grapes on Thursday. And into the Free Festival, of course. Since it's free you don't get paid, of course.'

'We've written this song,' said the head dwarf, hopefully.

'Good, good,' said Dibbler, scribbling on his notepad.

'It's called "Something's Gotten Into My Beard".'

'Good.'

'Don't you want to hear it?'

Dibbler looked up.

'Hear it? I'd never get anything done if I went around listening to music. Off you go. See you next Wednesday. Next! You all trolls?'

'Dat's right.'

In this case, Dibbler decided not to argue. Trolls were a lot bigger than dwarfs.

'All right. But you've got to spell it with a Z. Trollz. Yep, looks good. Mended Drum, Friday. And the Free Festival. Yes?'

'We've done a song—'

'Good for you. Next!'

'It's us, Mr Dibbler.'

Dibbler looked at Jimbo, Noddy, Crash and Scum.

'You've got a nerve,' he said, 'after last night.'

'We got a bit carried away,' said Crash. 'We was wondering if we could have another chance?'

'You did say the audience loved us,' said Noddy.

'Loathed you. I said the audience *loathed* you,' said Dibbler. 'Two of you kept looking at Blert Wheedown's guitar primer!'

'We've changed our name,' said Jimbo. 'We thought, well, Insanity was a bit daft, it's not a proper name for a serious band that's pushing back the boundaries of musical expression and is definitely going to be big one day.'

'Thursday,' nodded Noddy.

'So now we're Suck,' said Crash.

Dibbler gave them a long, cool look. Bear-baiting, bull-harassing, dog-fighting and sheep-worrying were currently banned in Ankh-Morpork, although the Patrician did permit the unrestricted hurling of rotten fruit at anyone suspected of belonging to a street theatre group. There was perhaps an opening.

'All right,' he said. 'You can play at the Festival. After that . . . we'll see.'

After all, he thought, there was a *possibility* that they'd still be alive.

A figure climbed slowly and unsteadily out of the Ankh on to a jetty by the Misbegot Bridge, and stood for a moment as mud dripped off him and formed a puddle under the planks.

The bridge was quite high. There were buildings on it, lining it on both sides so that the actual roadway was quite cramped. The bridges were quite popular as building sites, because they had a very convenient sewage system and, of course, a source of fresh water.

There was the red eye of a fire in the shadows

under the bridge. The figure staggered towards the light.

The dark shapes around it turned and squinted into the gloom, trying to fathom the nature of the visitor.

'It's a farm cart,' said Glod. 'I know a farm cart when I see one. Even if it *is* painted blue. And it's all battered.'

'It's all you can afford,' said Asphalt. 'Anyway, I put fresh straw in.'

'I thought we were going in the stagecoach,' said Cliff.

'Oh, Mr Dibbler says artistes of your calibre shouldn't travel in a common public vehicle,' said Asphalt. 'Besides, he said you wouldn't want the expense.'

'What do you think, Buddy?' said Glod.

'Don't mind,' said Buddy vaguely.

Glod and Cliff shared a glance.

'I bet if you were to go and see Dibbler and demand something better, you'd get it,' said Glod hopefully.

'It's got wheels,' said Buddy. 'It'll do.'

He climbed aboard and sat down in the straw.

'Mr Dibbler's had some new shirts done,' said Asphalt, aware that there was not a lot of jolliness in the air. 'It's for the tour. Look, it says on the back everywhere you're going, isn't that nice?'

'Yes, when the Musicians' Guild twist our heads round we'll be able to see where we've been,' said Glod.

Asphalt cracked his whip over the horses. They ambled off at a pace that suggested they intended to keep it up all day, and no idiot too soft to really use a whip properly was going to change their minds.

'Buggrit, buggrit! The grawney man, says I. Buggrit. He's a yellow gloak, so he is. Ten thousand years! Buggrit.'

REALLY?

Death relaxed.

There were half a dozen people around the fire. And they were convivial. A bottle was circling the group. Well, actually it was half a tin, and Death hadn't quite worked out what was in it or in the rather larger tin that was bubbling on the fire of old boots and mud.

They hadn't asked him who he was.

None of them had names, as far as he could tell. They had . . . labels, like Stalling Ken and Coffin Henry and Foul Ole Ron, which said something about what they were but nothing about what they had been.

The tin reached him. He passed it on as tactfully as he could, and lay back peacefully.

People without names. People who were as invisible as he was. People for whom Death was always an option. He could stay here awhile.

'*Free* music,' Mr Clete growled. 'Free! What sort of idiot makes music for free? At least you put a hat down, get people to drop the odd copper in. Otherwise what's the point?'

He stared at the paperwork in front of him for so long that Satchelmouth coughed politely.

'I'm thinking,' said Mr Clete. 'That wretched Vetinari. He said it's up to Guilds to enforce guild law—'

'I heard they're leaving the city,' said Satchelmouth. 'On tour. Out in the country, I heard. It's not our law out there.'

'The country,' said Mr Clete. 'Yes. Dangerous place, the country.'

'Right,' said Satchelmouth. 'There's turnips, for a start.'

Mr Clete's eye fell on the Guild's account books. It occurred to him, not for the first time, that far too many people put their trust in iron and steel when gold made some of the best possible weapons.

'Is Mr Downey still head of the Assassins' Guild?' he said.

The other musicians looked suddenly nervous.

'Assassins?' said Herbert 'Mr Harpsichord' Shuffle. 'I don't think anyone's ever called in the Assassins. This is Guild business, isn't it? Can't have another Guild interfering.'

'That's right,' said Satchelmouth. 'What'd happen if people knew we'd used the Assassins?'

'We'd get a lot more members,' said Mr Clete in his reasonable voice, 'and we could probably put the subscriptions up. Hat. Hat. Hat.'

'Now hang on a minute,' said Satchelmouth. 'I don't mind us seeing to people who won't join. That's proper guild behaviour, that is. But Assassins . . . well . . .'

'Well what?' said Mr Clete.

'They *assassinate* people.'

'You want free music, do you?' said Mr Clete.

'Well, of course I don't want—'

'I don't remember you talking like this when you jumped up and down on that street violinist's fingers last month,' said Mr Clete.

'Yeah, well, that wasn't, like, *assassination*,' said Satchelmouth. 'I mean, he was able to walk away. Well, crawl away. And he could still earn a living,' he added. 'Not one that required the use of his hands, sure, but—'

'And that penny whistle lad? That one who plays a chord now every time he hiccups? Hat. Hat. Hat.'

'Yeah, but that's not the sa—'

'Do you know Wheedown the guitar-maker?' said Mr Clete.

Satchelmouth was unbalanced by the change in direction.

'I'm told he's been selling guitars like there was no next Wednesday,' said Mr Clete. 'But I don't see any increase in membership, do you?'

'Well—'

'Once people get the idea that they can listen to music for nothing, where will it end?'

He glared at the other two.

'Dunno, Mr Clete,' said Shuffle obediently.

'Very well. And the Patrician has been ironical at me,' said Mr Clete. 'I'm not having that again. It's the Assassins this time.'

'I don't think we should actually have people *killed*,' said Satchelmouth doggedly.

'I don't want to hear any more from you,' said Mr Clete. 'This is Guild business.'

'Yes, but it's *our* Guild—'

'Exactly! So shut up! Hat! Hat! Hat!'

The cart rattled between the endless cabbage fields that led to Pseudopolis.

'I've been on tour before, you know,' said Glod. 'When I was with Snori Snoriscousin And His Brass Idiots. Every night a different bed. You forget what day of the week it is after a while.'

'What day of the week is it now?' said Cliff.

'See? And we've only been on the road . . . what . . . three hours?' said Glod.

'Where're we stopping tonight?' said Cliff.

'Scrote,' said Asphalt.

'Sounds a really interesting place,' said Cliff.

'Been there before, with the circus,' said Asphalt. 'It's a one-horse town.'

Buddy looked over the side of the cart, but it wasn't worth the effort. The rich silty Sto Plains were the grocery of the continent, but not an awe-inspiring panorama unless you were the kind of person who gets excited about fifty-three types of cabbage and eighty-one types of bean.

Spaced every mile or so on the chequerboard of fields was a village, and spaced rather further apart were the towns. They were called towns because they were bigger than the villages. The cart passed through a couple of them. They had two streets in the form of a cross, one tavern, one seed store, one forge, one livery stable with a name like JOE'S

LIVERY STABLE, a couple of barns, three old men sitting outside the tavern, and three young men lounging outside JOE'S swearing that one day really soon now they were going to leave town and make it big in the world outside. Real soon. Any day now.

'Reminds you of home, eh?' said Cliff, nudging Buddy.

'What? No! Llamedos is all mountains and valleys. And rain. And mist. And evergreens.'

Buddy sighed.

'You had a great house there, I expect?' said the troll.

'Just a shack,' said Buddy. 'Made of earth and wood. Well, mud and wood really.'

He sighed again.

'It's like this on the road,' said Asphalt. 'Melancholy. No one to talk to but each other, I've known people go totally ins—'

'How long has it been now?' said Cliff.

'Three hours and ten minutes,' said Glod.

Buddy sighed.

They were invisible people, Death realized. He was used to invisibility. It went with the job. Humans didn't see him until they had no choice.

On the other hand, he *was* an anthropomorphic personification. Whereas Foul Ole Ron was human, at least technically.

Foul Ole Ron made a small living by following people until they gave him money not to. He'd also got a dog, which added something to Foul Ole Ron's smell. It was a greyish-brown terrier with a torn ear and nasty patches of bare skin; it begged with an old hat in its remaining teeth, and since people will generally give to animals that which they'd withhold from humans it added considerably to the earning power of the group.

Coffin Henry, on the other hand, earned his money by not going anywhere. People organizing important social occasions sent him anti-invitations and little presents of money to ensure he wouldn't turn up. This was because, if they didn't, Henry had a habit of sidling ingratiatingly into the wedding party and inviting people to look at his remarkable collection of skin diseases. He also had a cough which sounded almost solid.

He had a sign on which was chalked 'For sum muny I wunt follo you home. Coff Coff'.

Arnold Sideways had no legs. It was a lack that didn't seem to figure largely among his concerns. He would grab people by their knees and say, 'Have you got change for a penny?', invariably profiting by the ensuing cerebral confusion.

And the one they called the Duck Man had a duck on his head. No one mentioned it. No one drew attention to it. It seemed to be a minor feature of no consequence, like Arnold's leglessness and Foul Ole Ron's independent smell or Henry's volcanic spitting. But it kept nagging at Death's otherwise peaceful mind.

He wondered how to broach the subject.

AFTER ALL, he thought, HE MUST KNOW, MUSTN'T HE? IT'S NOT LIKE LINT ON YOUR JACKET OR SOMETHING . . .

By common agreement they'd called Death Mr Scrub. He didn't know why. On the other hand, he was among people who could hold a lengthy discussion with a door. There may have been a logical reason.

The beggars spent their day wandering invisibly around the streets where people who didn't see them carefully circled out of their way and threw them the occasional coin. Mr Scrub fitted in very well. When he asked for money, people found it hard to say no.

Scrote didn't even have a river. It existed simply because there's only so much land you can have before you have to have something else.

It had two streets in the form of a cross, one tavern, one seed store, one forge, a couple of barns and, in a gesture of originality, one livery stable called SETH'S LIVERY STABLE.

Nothing moved. Even the flies were asleep. Long shadows were the only occupants of the streets.

'I thought you said dis was a one-horse town,' said Cliff, as they pulled up in the rutted, puddled area that was probably glorified by the name of Town Square.

'It must have died,' said Asphalt.

Glod stood up in the cart and spread his arms wide. He yelled: 'Hello, Scrote!'

The name-board over the livery stable parted from its last nail and landed in the dust.

'What I like about this life on the road,' said Glod, 'is the fascinating people and interesting places.'

'I expect it comes alive at night,' said Asphalt.

'Yes,' said Cliff. 'Yes, I can believe dat. Yes. Dis looks like the kind of town dat comes alive at night. Dis looks like the whole town should be buried at the crossroads with a stake through it.'

'Talking of steak . . .' said Glod.

They looked at the tavern. The cracked and peeling sign just managed to convey the words 'The Jolly Cabbage'.

'I doubt it,' said Asphalt.

There were people in the dimly lit tavern, sitting in sullen silence. The travellers were served by the innkeeper, whose manner suggested that he hoped they died horribly just as soon as they left the premises. The beer tasted as if it was happy to connive at this state of affairs.

They huddled at one table, aware of the eyes on them.

'I've heard about places like this,' whispered Glod. 'You go into this little town with a name like Friendly or Amity, and next day you're spare ribs.'

'Not me,' said Cliff. 'I'm too stony.'

'Well, you're in the rockery, then,' said the dwarf.

He looked around at a row of furrowed faces and raised his mug theatrically.

'Cabbages doing well?' he said. 'I see in the fields they're nice and yellow. Ripe, eh? That's good, eh?'

'That's Root Fly, that is,' said someone in the shadows.

'Good, good,' said Glod. He was a dwarf. Dwarfs didn't farm.

'We don't like circuses in Scrote,' said another voice. It was a slow, deep voice.

'We're not a circus,' said Glod brightly. 'We're musicians.'

'We don't like musicians in Scrote,' said another voice.

There seemed to be more and more figures in the gloom.

'Er . . . what *do* you like in Scrote?' said Asphalt.

'Well,' said the barman, now a mere outline in the gathering darkness, 'round about this time of year we generally have a barbecue down by the rockery.'

Buddy sighed.

It was the first time he'd made a sound since they'd arrived in the town.

'I guess we'd better show them what we play,' he said. There was a twang in his voice.

It was some time later.

Glod looked at the door handle. It was a door handle. You got hold of it with your hand. But what was supposed to happen next?

'Door handle,' he said, in case that would help.

'Y'r sposed do s'ning w'vit,' said Cliff, from somewhere near the floor.

Buddy leaned past the dwarf and turned the handle.

'Am'zing,' said Glod, and stumbled forward. He levered himself off the floor and looked around.

'Wh's ths?'

'The tavern keeper said we could stay here for free,' said Buddy.

'S'mess,' said Glod. 'Some'ne fetch me a brm and a scr'bing brsh this min't.'

Asphalt wobbled in, carrying the luggage and with Cliff's sack of rocks in his teeth. He dropped the lot on the floor.

'Well, that was astonishing, sir,' he said. 'The way you just went into that barn and said, and said . . . what was it you said?'

'Let's do the show right here,' said Buddy, lying down on a straw mattress.

'Amazing! They must have been coming in from miles around!'

Buddy stared at the ceiling and played a few chords.

'And that barbecue!' said Asphalt, still radiating enthusiasm. 'The sauce!'

'The be'f!'said Glod.

'The charcoal,' murmured Cliff happily. There was a wide black ring around his mouth.

'And who'davthought,' said Glod, 'that you could brew a beer l'ke that outa cauliflowers?'

'Had a *great* head on it,' said Cliff.

'I thought we were going to be in a bit of trouble there, before you played,' said Asphalt, shaking the beetles out of another mattress. 'I don't know how you got them dancing like that.'

'Yes,' said Buddy.

'And we din't even get paid,' murmured Glod. He slumped back. Shortly there were snores, given a slightly metallic edge by the reverberation in his helmet.

When the others were asleep Buddy put the guitar down on the bed, quietly opened the door and crept downstairs and into the night.

It would have been nice if there had been a full moon. Or even a crescent. A full moon would have been better. But there was just a half-moon, which never appears in romantic or occult paintings despite the fact that it is indeed the most magical phase.

There was a smell of stale beer, dying cabbages, barbecue embers and insufficient sanitation.

He leaned against Seth's livery stable. It shifted slightly.

It was fine when he was on stage or, as it had been tonight, on an old barn door set on a few bricks. Everything was in bright colours. He could feel white-hot images arcing across his mind. His body felt as though it were on fire but also, and this was the important bit, as if it was *meant* to be on fire. He felt alive.

And then, afterwards, he felt dead.

There was still colour in the world. He could recognize it as colour, but it seemed to be wearing Cliff's smoked glasses. Sounds came as if through cotton wool. Apparently the barbecue had been good, he had Glod's word for that; but to Buddy it had been texture and not much else.

A shadow moved across the space between two buildings . . .

On the other hand, he was the best. He knew it, not as some matter of pride or arrogance, but simply as a matter of fact. He could feel the music flowing out of him and into the audience . . .

'This one, sir?' whispered a shadow beside the livery stable, as Buddy wandered along the moonlit street.

'Yes. This one first and then into the tavern for the other two. Even the big troll. There's a spot on the back of the neck.'

'But not Dibbler, sir?'

'Strangely, no. He's not here.'

'Shame. I bought a meat pie off him once.'

'It's an attractive suggestion, but no one's paying us for Dibbler.'

The Assassins drew their knives, the blades blackened to avoid the tell-tale shine.

'I could give you twopence, sir, if that'd help.'

'It's certainly tempting—'

The senior Assassin pressed himself against the wall as Buddy's footsteps grew louder.

He gripped his knife at waist height. No one who knew anything about knives ever used the famous over-arm stabbing motion so beloved of illustrators. It was amateurish and inefficient. A professional would strike upwards; the way to a man's heart was through his stomach.

He drew his hand back and tensed—

An hourglass, glowing faintly blue, was suddenly thrust in front of his eyes.

LORD ROBERT SELACHII? said a voice by his ear. THIS IS *YOUR* LIFE.

He squinted. There was no mistaking the name engraved on the glass. He could see every little grain of sand, pouring into the past . . .

He turned, took one look at the hooded figure, and ran for it.

His apprentice was already a hundred yards away, and still accelerating.

'Sorry? Who's that?'

Susan tucked the hourglass back into her robe and shook out her hair.

Buddy appeared.

'You?'

'Yes. Me,' said Susan.

Buddy took a step nearer.

'Are you going to fade away again?' he said.

'No. I have actually just saved your life, as a matter of fact.'

Buddy looked around at the otherwise empty night.

'From what?'

Susan bent down and picked up a blackened knife.

'This?' she said.

'I know we've had this conversation before, but who are you? Not my fairy godmother, are you?'

'I think you have to be a lot older,' said Susan. She backed away. 'And probably a lot nicer, too. Look, I can't tell you any more. You're not even supposed to see me. I'm not supposed to be here. Neither are you—'

'You're not going to tell me to stop playing again, are you?' said Buddy angrily. 'Because I won't! I'm a musician! If I don't play, what am I then? I might as well be dead! Do you understand? Music is my *life*!'

He took a few steps nearer.

'Why're you following me around? Asphalt said there'd be girls like you!'

'What on Disc do you mean, "girls like me"?'

Buddy subsided a bit, but only a little.

'They follow actors and musicians around,' he said, 'because of, you know, the glamour and everything—'

'*Glamour?* Some smelly cart and a tavern that smells of *cabbages*?'

Buddy held up his hands.

'Listen,' he said urgently. 'I'm doing all right. I'm working, people are listening to me . . . I don't need any more help, all right? I've got enough to worry about, so please keep out of my life—'

There was the sound of running feet and Asphalt appeared, with the other members of the band behind him.

'The guitar was screaming,' said Asphalt. 'Are you all right?'

'You'd better ask her,' muttered Buddy.

All three of them looked directly at Susan.

'Who?' said Cliff.

'She's right in front of you.'

Glod waved a stubby hand in the air, missing Susan by inches.

'It was probably dat cabbage,' said Cliff to Asphalt.

Susan stepped backwards quietly.

'She's right there! But she's going away now, can't you see?'

'That's right, that's right,' said Glod, taking Buddy's arm. 'She's going away now, and good riddance, so just you come on back—'

'Now she's getting on that horse!'

'Yes, yes, a big black horse—'

'It's white, you idiot!'

Hoofprints burned red on the ground for a moment and then faded.

'And it's gone now!'

The Band With Rocks In stared into the night.

'Yes, I can see dat, now you mention it,' said Cliff. 'Dat's a horse dat isn't dere, sure enough.'

'Yes, that's certainly what a horse that's gone looks like,' said Asphalt carefully.

'None of you saw her?' said Buddy, as they manoeuvred him gently back through the pre-dawn greyness.

'I heard where musicians, really *good* musicians, got followed around by these half-naked young women called Muses,' said Glod.

'Like Cantaloupe,' said Cliff.

'We don't call 'em Muses,' said Asphalt, grinning. 'I told you, when I worked for Bertie the Balladeer and His Troubadour Rascals, we used to get any amount of young women hanging arou—'

'Amazing how legends get started, when you come to think about it,' said Glod. 'Just you come along now, my lad.'

'She was there,' Buddy protested. 'She *was* there.'

'Cantaloupe?' said Asphalt. 'You sure, Cliff?'

'Read it in a book once,' said the troll. 'Cantaloupe. I'm pretty sure. Something like that.'

'She was there,' said Buddy.

The raven snored gently on top of his skull, counting dead sheep.

The Death of Rats came through the window in

an arc, bounced off a dribbly candle, and landed on all fours on the table.

The raven opened one eye.

'Oh, it's you—'

Then a claw was round its leg, and the Death of Rats jumped off the skull and into infinite space.

There were more cabbage fields next day, although the landscape did begin to change a bit.

'Hey, that's interesting,' said Glod.

'What is?' said Cliff.

'There's a field of beans over there.'

They watched it until it was out of sight.

'Nice of the people to give us all this food, though,' said Asphalt. 'We shan't be wanting for cabbages, eh?'

'Oh, shut up,' said Glod. He turned to Buddy, who was sitting with his chin resting on his arms.

'Cheer up, we'll be in Pseudopolis in a couple of hours,' he said.

'Good,' said Buddy, distantly.

Glod climbed back into the front of the cart and pulled Cliff towards him.

'Notice the way he goes all quiet?' he whispered.

'Yup. Do you think it'll be . . . you know . . . done by the time we get back?'

'You can get anything done in Ankh-Morpork,' said Glod firmly. 'I must have knocked on every damn door in the Street of Cunning Artificers. Twenty-five dollars!'

'You're complaining? It ain't your tooth dat's paying for it.'

They both turned to look at their guitarist. He was staring out across the endless fields.

'She *was* there,' he muttered.

Feathers spiralled towards the ground.

'You didn't have to go and do that,' said the raven, fluttering upright. 'You could simply ask.'

SQUEAK.

'All right, but *before* would have been better.' The raven ruffled its feathers and looked around at the bright landscape under the dark sky.

'This is the place then, is it?' it said. 'You're *sure* you're not the Death of Ravens too?'

SQUEAK.

'Shape doesn't mean much. Anyway, you've got a pointy snout. What was it you were wanting?'

The Death of Rats grabbed a wing and pulled.

'All right, all right!'

The raven glanced at a garden gnome. It was fishing in an ornamental pond. The fish were skeletal, but this didn't seem to interfere with their enjoyment of life, or whatever it was they were enjoying.

It fluttered and hopped along after the rat.

Cut-Me-Own-Throat Dibbler stood back.

Jimbo, Crash, Noddy and Scum looked at him expectantly.

'What're all the boxes for, Mr Dibbler?' said Crash.

'Yeah,' said Scum.

Dibbler carefully positioned the tenth box on its tripod.

'You boys seen an iconograph?' he said.

'Oh, yes . . . I mean, yeah,' said Jimbo. 'They've got a little demon inside them that paints pictures of things you point it at.'

'This is like that, only for sound,' said Dibbler.

Jimbo squinted past the open lid.

'Can't see any . . . I mean, can't see no demon,' he said.

'That's because there isn't one,' said Dibbler. It was worrying him, too. He'd have been a little bit happier if there'd been a demon or some sort of magic. Something simple and understandable. He didn't like the idea of meddling in science.

'Now then . . . Suck—' he began.

'The Surreptitious Fabric,' said Jimbo.

'What?'

'The Surreptitious Fabric,' Jimbo repeated helpfully. 'It's our new name.'

'Why have you changed it? You haven't been Suck for twenty-four hours.'

'Yeah, but we thought the name was holding us back.'

'How could it be holding you back? You aren't moving.' Dibbler glared at them and shrugged. 'Anyway, whatever you call yourselves . . . I want you to sing your best song, what am I *saying*, in front of these boxes. Not yet . . . not yet . . . wait a moment . . .'

Dibbler retired to the furthest corner of the room and pulled his hat down over his ears.

'All right, you can start,' he said.

He stared in blissful deafness at the group for

several minutes until a general cessation of movement suggested that whatever they had been perpetrating had been committed.

Then he inspected the boxes. The wires were vibrating gently, but there was barely any sound.

The Surreptitious Fabric clustered around.

'Is it working, Mr Dibbler?' said Jimbo.

Dibbler shook his head.

'You boys don't have what it takes,' he said.

'What *does* it take, Mr Dibbler?'

'You've got me there. You've got *something*,' he said, at the sight of their dejected faces, 'but not a lot of it, whatever it is.'

'Er . . . this doesn't mean we're not allowed to play at the Free Festival, does it, Mr Dibbler?' said Crash.

'Maybe,' said Dibbler, smiling benevolently.

'Thanks a lot, Mr Dibbler!'

The Surreptitious Fabric wandered out into the street.

'We need to get it together if we're going to wow them at the Festival,' said Crash.

'What, you mean . . . like . . . learn to play?' said Jimbo.

'No! Music With Rocks In just happens. If you go around *learning* you'll never get anywhere,' said Crash. 'No, I mean . . .' He looked around. 'Better clothes, for one thing. Did you see about them leather coats, Noddy?'

'Sort of,' said Noddy.

'What do you mean, sort of?'

'Sort of leather. I went down the tannery in

Phedre Road and they had some leather all right, but it's a bit . . . whiffy . . .'

'All right, we can get started on them tonight. And how about those leopardskin trousers, Scum? You know we said leopardskin trousers'd be a great idea.'

A look of transcendental worry crossed Scum's face.

'I *kind* of got some,' he said.

'You either got them or you ain't,' said Crash.

'Yeah, but they're *kind* of . . .' said Scum. 'Look, I couldn't find a shop that'd heard of anything like that but, er, you know that circus that was here last week? Only I had a word with the guy in the top hat and, well, it was a kind of a bargain and—'

'Scum,' said Crash quietly, 'what have you bought?'

'Look at it this way,' said Scum with sweating brightness, 'it's sort of leopardskin trousers *and* a leopardskin shirt *and* a leopardskin hat.'

'Scum,' said Crash, his voice low with resigned menace, 'you've bought a leopard, haven't you?'

'Sort of leopardy, yes.'

'Oh, good grief—'

'But sort of a real steal for twenty dollars,' said Scum. 'Nothing important wrong with it, the man said.'

'Why'd he get rid of it, then?' Crash demanded.

'It's sort of deaf. Can't hear the lion-tamer, he said.'

'Well, that's no good to us!'

'Don't see why. Your trousers don't have to listen.'

SPARE A COPPER, YOUNG SIR?

'Push off, grandad,' said Crash easily.

GOOD LUCK TO YOU.

'Too many beggars around these days, my father says,' said Crash, as they pushed past. 'He says the Beggars' Guild ought to do something about it.'

'But the beggars all belong to the Guild,' said Jimbo.

'Well, they shouldn't allow so many people to join.'

'Yes, but it's better than being on the streets.'

Scum, who out of the whole group had the least amount of cerebral activity to get between him and true observation of the world, was trailing behind. He had an uneasy feeling that he'd just walked over someone's grave.

'That one looked a bit sort of thin,' he muttered.

The others weren't paying any attention. They were back to the usual argument.

'I'm fed up with being Surreptitious Fabric,' said Jimbo. 'It's a silly name.'

'Really, really thin,' said Scum. He felt in his pocket.

'Yeah, I liked it best when we were The Whom,' said Noddy.

'But we were only The Whom for half an hour!' said Crash.* 'Yesterday. In between bein' The Blots and Lead Balloon, remember?'

Scum located a tenpenny piece and turned back.

'There's bound to be *some* good name,' said

*A very *grammatical* half an hour, however.

Jimbo. 'I just bet we'll know it's right just as soon as we see it.'

'Oh, yeah. Well, we've got to come up with *some* name we don't start arguing about after five minutes,' said Crash. 'It's not doing our career any good if people don't know who we are.'

'Mr Dibbler says it definitely is,' said Noddy.

'Yes, but a rolling stone gathers no moss, my father says,' said Crash.

'There you go, old man,' said Scum, back down the street.

THANK YOU, said the grateful Death.

Scum hurried to catch up with the others, who were back on the subject of leopards with hearing difficulties.

'Where did you put it, Scum?' said Crash.

'Well, you know your sort of bedroom—'

'How do you kill a leopard?' said Noddy.

'Hey, here's an idea,' said Crash, gloomily. 'We let it choke to death on Scum.'

The raven inspected the hallway clock with the practised eye of one who knows the value of good props.

As Susan had noted, it was not so much small as dimensionally displaced; it looked small, but in the same way that something very big a long way away looks small – that is to say, the mind keeps reminding the eyes that they are wrong. But this was up close as well. It was made of some dark, age-blackened wood. There was a pendulum, which oscillated slowly.

The clock had no hands.

'Impressive,' said the raven. 'That scythe blade on the pendulum. Nice touch. Very Gothic. No one could look at that clock and not think—'

SQUEAK!

'All right, all right, I'm coming.' The raven fluttered across to an ornamental door-frame. There was a skull-and-bones motif on it.

'Excellent taste,' it said.

SQUEAK. SQUEAK.

'Well, *anyone* can do plumbing, I expect,' said the raven. 'Interesting fact. Did you know the lavatory was actually named after Sir Charles Lavatory? Not many people—'

SQUEAK.

The Death of Rats pushed at the big door leading to the kitchen. It swung open with a creak but, here again, there was something not quite right. A listener had the sense that the creak had been added by someone who, feeling that a door like that with a door surround like that *ought* to creak, had inserted one.

Albert was washing up at the stone sink and staring at nothing.

'Oh,' he said, turning, 'it's you. What's this thing?'

'I'm a raven,' said the raven, nervously. 'Incidentally, one of the most intelligent birds. Most people would say it's the mynah bird, but—'

SQUEAK!

The raven ruffled its feathers.

'I'm here as an interpreter,' it said.

'Has he found him?' said Albert.

The Death of Rats squeaked at length.

'Looked everywhere. No sign,' said the raven.

'Then he don't want to be found,' said Albert. He smeared the grease off a plate with a skull pattern on it. 'I don't like that.'

SQUEAK.

'The rat says that's not the worst thing,' said the raven. 'The rat says you ought to know what the granddaughter has been doing . . .'

The rat squeaked. The raven talked.

The plate shattered on the sink.

'I *knew* it!' Albert shouted. '*Saving* him! She hasn't got the faintest idea! Right! *I'm* going to sort this out. The Master thinks he can slope off, eh? Not from old Albert! You two wait here!'

There were already posters up in Pseudopolis. News travels fast, especially when C. M. O. T. Dibbler is paying for the horses . . .

'Hello, Pseudopolis!'

They had to call out the city Watch. They had to organize a bucket chain from the river. Asphalt had to stand outside Buddy's dressing room with a club. With a nail in it.

Albert, in front of a scrap of mirror in his bedroom, brushed his hair furiously. It was white. At least, long ago it was white. Now it was the colour of a tobacco addict's index finger.

'It's my duty, that's what it is,' he muttered. 'Don't know where he'd be without me. Maybe he *does* remember the future, but he always gets it wrong! Oh, he can go on worrying about the eternal verities, but who has to sort it out when all's said and done . . . Muggins, that's who.'

He glared at himself in the mirror.

'Right!' he said.

There was a battered shoe-box under the bed. Albert pulled it out very, very carefully and took the top off. It was half full of cotton wool; nestling in the wool, like a rare egg, was a lifetimer.

Engraved on it was the name: Alberto Malich.

The sand inside was frozen, immobile, in mid-pour. There wasn't much left in the top bulb.

No time passed, here.

It was part of the Arrangement. He worked for Death, and time didn't pass, except when he went into the World.

There was a scrap of paper by the glass. The figures '91' had been written at the top, but lower numbers trailed down the page after it. 73 . . . 68 . . . 37 . . . 19.

Nineteen!

He must have been daft. He'd let his life leak away by hours and minutes, and there had been a lot more of them lately. There'd been all that business with the plumber, of course. And shopping. The Master didn't like to go shopping. It was hard to get served. And Albert had taken a few holidays, because it was nice to see the sun, any sun, and feel wind and rain; the Master did his best, but he could never get them right. And decent vegetables, he couldn't do them properly either. They never tasted *grown.*

Nineteen days left in the world. But more than enough.

Albert slipped the lifetimer into his pocket, put on an overcoat, and stamped back down the stairs.

'You,' he said, pointing to the Death of Rats, 'you can't sense a trace of him? There must be *something*. Concentrate.'

SQUEAK.

'What did he say?'

'He said all he can remember is something about sand.'

'Sand,' said Albert. 'All right. Good start. We search all the sand.'

SQUEAK?

'Wherever the Master is, he'll make an impression.'

Cliff awoke to a swish-swish sound. The shape of Glod was outlined in the light of dawn, wielding a brush.

'What're you doing, dwarf?'

'I got Asphalt to get some paint,' said Glod. 'These rooms are a disgrace.'

Cliff raised himself on his elbows and looked around.

'What do you call the colour on the door?'

'Eau-de-Nil.'

'Nice.'

'Thank you,' said Glod.

'The curtains are good, too.'

The door creaked open. Asphalt came in, with a tray, and kicked the door shut behind him.

'Oh, sorry,' he said.

'I'll paint over the mark,' said Glod.

Asphalt put the tray down, trembling with excitement.

'Everyone's talking about you guys!' he said. 'And they're saying it was about time they built a new theatre anyway. I've got you eggs and bacon, eggs and rat, eggs and coke, and . . . and . . . what was it . . . oh, yes. The Captain of the Watch says if you're still in the city at sunrise he will personally have you buried alive. I've got the cart all ready by the back door. Young women have been writing things on it in lipstick. Nice curtains, by the way.'

All three of them looked at Buddy.

'He hasn't moved,' said Glod. 'Flopped down right after the show and out like a light.'

'He was certainly leaping around last night,' said Cliff.

Buddy continued to snore gently.

'When we get back,' said Glod, 'we ought to have a nice holiday somewhere.'

'Dat's right,' said Cliff. 'If we get out of dis alive, I'm going to put my rock kit on my back and take a long walk, and the first time someone says to me, "What are dem things on your back?" dat's where I'm gonna settle down.'

Asphalt peered down into the street.

'Can you all eat fast?' he said. 'Only there's some men in uniform out there. With shovels.'

Back in Ankh-Morpork, Mr Clete was astonished.

'But we hired you!' he said.

'The term is "retained", not "hired",' said Lord Downey, head of the Assassins' Guild. He looked at Clete with an expression of unconcealed distaste. 'Unfortunately, however, we can no longer entertain your contract.'

'They're *musicians*,' said Mr Clete. 'How hard can they be to kill?'

'My associates are somewhat reluctant to talk about it,' said Lord Downey. 'They seem to feel that the clients are protected in some way. Obviously, we will return the balance of your fee.'

'Protected,' muttered Clete, as they stepped thankfully through the archway of the Assassins' Guild.

'Well, I told you what it was like in the Drum when—' Satchelmouth began.

'That's just superstition,' snapped Clete. He glanced up at a wall, where three Festival posters flaunted their primary colours.

'It was stupid of you to think Assassins would be any good outside the city,' muttered Clete.

'Me? I never—'

'Get them more than five miles from a decent tailor and a mirror, and they go all to pieces,' Clete added.

He stared at the poster.

'*Free*,' he muttered. 'Did you put it about that anyone who plays at this Festival is right out of the Guild?'

'Yes, sir. I don't think they're worrying, sir. I mean, some of 'em have been getting together, sir. See, they say since there's a lot more people want to be musicians than we'll allow in the Guild then we should—'

'It's mob rule!' said Clete. 'Banding together to force unacceptable rules on a defenceless city!'

'Trouble is, sir,' said Satchelmouth, 'if there's a lot of them . . . if they think of talking to the palace . . . well, you know the Patrician, sir . . .'

Clete nodded glumly. Any Guild was powerful just so long as it self-evidently spoke for its constituency. He thought of hundreds of musicians flocking to the palace. Hundreds of *non-Guild* musicians . . .

The Patrician was a pragmatist. He never tried to fix things that worked. Things that didn't work, however, got broken.

The only glimmer of hope was that they'd all be too busy messing around with music to think about the bigger picture. It had certainly worked for Clete.

Then he remembered that the blasted Dibbler man was involved.

Expecting Dibbler not to think about anything concerning money was like expecting rocks not to think about gravity.

'Hello? Albert?'

Susan pushed open the kitchen door. The huge room was empty.

'Albert?'

She tried upstairs. There was her own room, and there was a corridor of doors that didn't open and possibly never could – the doors and frames had an all-in-one, moulded-together look. Presumably

Death had a bedroom, although proverbially Death never slept. Perhaps he just lay in bed reading.

She tried the handles until she found one that turned.

Death *did* have a bedroom.

He'd got many of the details right. Of course. After all, he saw quite a lot of bedrooms. In the middle of the acres of floor was a large four-poster bed, although when Susan gave it an experimental prod it turned out that the sheets were as solid as rock.

There was a full-length mirror, and a wardrobe. She had a look inside, just in case there was a selection of robes, but there was nothing in there except a few old shoes in the bottom.*

A dressing table held a jug-and-basin set with a motif of skulls and omegas, and a variety of bottles and other items.

She picked them up, one by one. After-shave lotion. Pomade. Breath freshener. A pair of silver-backed hairbrushes.

It was all rather sad. Death clearly had picked up an idea of what a gentleman should have on his dressing table, without confronting one or two fundamental questions.

Eventually she found a smaller, narrower staircase.

'Albert?'

There was a door at the top.

*Old shoes always turn up in the bottom of every wardrobe. If a *mermaid* had a wardrobe old shoes would turn up in the bottom of it.

'Albert? Anyone?'

It's not actually barging in if I call out first, she told herself. She pushed open the door.

It was a very small room. *Really* small. It contained a few sticks of bedroom furniture and a small narrow bed. A small bookcase contained a handful of small uninteresting-looking books. There was a piece of ancient paper on the floor which, when Susan picked it up, turned out to be covered with numbers, all crossed out except the last one, which was: 19.

One of the books was *Gardening In Difficult Conditions.*

She went back down to the study. She'd known that there was no-one in the house. There was a dead feeling in the air.

There was the same feeling in the gardens. Death could create most things, except for plumbing. But he couldn't create life itself. That had to be added, like yeast in bread. Without it, everything was beautifully neat and tidy and boring, boring, boring.

This is what it must have been like, she thought. *And then, one day, he adopted my mother. He was curious.*

She took the path through to the orchard again.

And when I was born Mum and Dad were so afraid that I felt at home here they brought me up to be . . . well . . . a Susan. What kind of name is that for Death's granddaughter? A girl like that should have better cheekbones, straight hair and a name with Vs and Xs in it.

And there, once again, was the thing he'd made

for her. All by himself. Working it all out from first principles . . .

A swing. A simple swing.

It was already burning hot in the desert between Klatch and Hersheba.

The air shimmied, and then there was a pop. Albert appeared on a sand-dune. There was a clay-brick fort on the horizon.

'The Klatchian Foreign Legion,' he muttered, as sand began its inexorable progress into his boots.

Albert trudged towards it with the Death of Rats sitting on his shoulder.

He knocked on the door, which had a number of arrows in it. After a while a small hatch slid back.

'What do you want, offendi?' said a voice from somewhere behind it.

Albert held up a card.

'Have you seen someone who didn't look like this?' he demanded.

There was silence.

'Then let's say: have you seen some mysterious stranger who didn't talk about his past?' said Albert.

'This is the Klatchian Foreign Legion, offendi. People don't talk about their past. They join up to . . . to . . .'

It dawned on Albert as the pause lengthened that it was up to him to get the conversation going again.

'Forget?'

'Right. Forget. Yes.'

'So have you had any recent recruits who were a little, shall we say, odd?'

'Might have done,' said the voice slowly. 'Can't remember.'

The hatchway slammed shut.

Albert hammered on it again. The hatchway opened.

'Yes, what is it?'

'Are you sure you can't remember?'

'Remember what?'

Albert took a deep breath.

'I demand to see your commanding officer!'

The hatch shut. The hatch opened.

'Sorry. It appears that I *am* the commanding officer. You're not a D'reg or a Hershebian, are you?'

'Don't you know?'

'I'm . . . pretty sure I must have done. Once. You know how it is . . . head like . . . thing, you know . . . With holes in . . . You drain lettuce in it . . . er . . .'

There was the sound of bolts being pulled back, and a wicket door opened in the gateway.

The possible officer was a sergeant, in so far as Albert was at all familiar with Klatchian ranks. He had the look about him of someone who, among the things he couldn't remember, would include a good night's sleep. If he could remember to.

There were a few other Klatchian soldiers inside the fort, sitting or, just barely, standing. Many were bandaged. And there was a rather greater number of soldiers slumped or lying on the packed sand who'd never need a night's sleep ever again.

'What's been happening here?' said Albert. His tone was so authoritative that the sergeant found himself saluting.

'We were attacked by D'regs, sir,' he said, swaying slightly. 'Hundreds of them! They outnumbered us . . . er . . . what's the number after nine? Got a one in it.'

'Ten.'

'Ten to one, sir.'

'I see you survived, though,' said Albert.

'Ah,' said the sergeant. 'Yes. Er. Yes. That's where it all gets a bit complicated, in fact. Er. Corporal? That's you. No, you just next to him. The one with the two stripes?'

'Me?' said a small fat soldier.

'Yes. Tell him what happened.'

'Oh. Right. Er. Well, the bastards had shot us full of arrows, right? An' it looked like it was all up with us. Then someone suggested sticking bodies up on the battlements with their spears and crossbows and everything so's the bastards'd think we was still up to strength—'

'It's not an original idea, mind you,' said the sergeant. 'Been done dozens of times.'

'Yeah,' said the corporal awkwardly. 'That's what *they* must've thought. And then . . . and then . . . when they was galloping down the sand-dunes . . . when they was almost on us, laughing and everything, saying stuff like "that old trick again" . . . someone shouted "Fire!" *and they did*.'

'The dead men—?'

'I joined the Legion to . . . er . . . you know, with your mind . . .' the corporal began.

'Forget?' said Albert.

'That's right. Forget. And I've been getting good

at it. But I'm not going to forget my old mate Nudger Malik stuck full of arrows and still giving the enemy what for,' said the corporal. 'Not for a long time. I'm going to give it a try, mind you.'

Albert looked up at the battlements. They were empty.

'Someone formed 'em up in formation and they all marched out, afterwards,' said the corporal. 'And I went out to look just now and there was just graves. They must have dug them for one another . . .'

'Tell me,' said Albert, 'who is this "someone" to whom you keep referring?'

The soldiers looked at one another.

'We've just been talking about that,' said the sergeant. 'We've been trying to remember. He was in . . . the Pit . . . when it started . . .'

'Tall, was he?' said Albert.

'Could have been tall, could have been tall,' nodded the corporal. 'He had a tall voice, certainly.' He looked puzzled at the words coming out of his own mouth.

'What did he look like?'

'Well, he had a . . . with . . . and he was about . . . more or less a . . .'

'Did he look . . . loud and deep?' said Albert.

The corporal grinned with relief. 'That's him,' he said. 'Private . . . Private . . . Beau . . . Beau . . . can't quite remember his name . . .'

'I know that when he walked out of the . . .' the sergeant began, and began to snap his fingers irritably, '. . . thing you open and shut. Made of wood. Hinges and bolts on it. Thank you. Gate.

That's right . . . gate. When he went out of the gate he said . . . what was it he said, corporal?'

'He said, "EVERY LAST DETAIL", sir.'

Albert looked around the fort.

'So he's gone.'

'Who?'

'The man you were just telling me about.'

'Oh. Yes. Er. Have you any idea who he was, offendi? I mean, it was amazing . . . talk about morale . . .'

'Esprit de corpse?' said Albert, who could be nasty at times. 'I suppose he didn't say where he was going next?'

'Where who was going next?' said the sergeant, wrinkling his forehead in honest enquiry.

'Forget I asked,' said Albert.

He took a last look round the little fort. It probably didn't matter much in the history of the world whether it survived or not, whether the dotted line on the map went one way or the other. Just like the Master to tinker with things . . .

Sometimes he tries to be human, too, he thought. And he makes a pig's ear out of it.

'Carry on, sergeant,' he said, and wandered back into the desert.

The legionnaires watched him disappear over the dunes, and then got on with the job of tidying up the fort.

'Who d'you think he was?'

'Who?'

'The person you just mentioned.'

'Did I?'

'Did you what?'

Albert crested a dune. From here the dotted line was just visible, winding treacherously across the sand.

SQUEAK.

'You and me both,' said Albert.

He removed an extremely grubby handkerchief from a pocket, knotted it in all four corners, and put it on his head.

'Right,' he said, but there was a trace of uncertainty in his voice. 'Seems to me we're not being logical about this.'

SQUEAK.

'I mean, we could be chasing him all over the place.'

SQUEAK.

'So maybe we ought to think about this.'

SQUEAK.

'Now . . . if you were on the Disc, definitely feeling a bit strange, and could go absolutely anywhere, anywhere at all . . . where would you go?'

SQUEAK?

'Anywhere at all. But somewhere where no one remembers your name.'

The Death of Rats looked around at the endless, featureless and above all *dry* desert.

SQUEAK.

'You know, I think you're right.'

It was in an apple tree.

He built me a swing, Susan remembered.

She sat and stared at the thing.

It was quite complicated. In so far as the thinking

behind it could be inferred from the resulting construction, it had run like this:

Clearly a swing should be hung from the stoutest branch.

In fact – safety being paramount – it would be better to hang it from the *two* stoutest branches, one to each rope.

They had turned out to be on opposite sides of the tree.

Never go back. That was part of the logic. Always press on, step by logical step.

So . . . he'd removed about six feet from the middle of the tree's trunk, thus allowing the swing to, well, swing.

The tree hadn't died. It was still quite healthy.

However, the lack of a major section of trunk had presented a fresh problem. This had been overcome by the addition of two large props under the branches, a little further out from the ropes of the swing, keeping the whole top of the tree at about the right height off the ground.

She remembered how she'd laughed, even then. And he'd stood there, quite unable to see what was wrong.

And then she saw it all, all laid out.

That was how Death worked. He never understood exactly what he was doing. He'd do something, and it would turn out wrong. *Her mother; suddenly he had a grown woman on his hands and didn't know what to do next.* So he did something else to make it right, which made it more wrong. *Her father. Death's apprentice!* And when *that* went wrong, and its potential wrongness was built right into it, he did something else to make it right.

He'd turned over the hourglass.

After that, it was all a matter of maths.

And the Duty.

'Hello . . . hells, Glod, tell me where we are . . . Sto Lat! Yay!'

It was an even bigger audience. There'd been more time for the posters to be up, more time for the word-of-mouth from Ankh-Morpork. And, the band realized, a solid core of people had followed them from Pseudopolis.

In a brief break between numbers, just before the bit where people started leaping around on the furniture, Cliff leaned over to Glod.

'You see dat troll in der front row?' he said. 'The one Asphalt's jumping on the fingers of?'

'The one that looks like a spoil heap?'

'She was in Pseudopolis,' said Cliff, beaming. 'She keeps looking at me!'

'Go for it, lad,' said Glod, emptying the spit from his horn. 'In like Flint, eh?'

'You think she's one of dem gropies Asphalt told us about?'

'Could be.'

Other news had travelled fast, too. Dawn saw another redecorated hotel room, a royal proclamation from Queen Keli that the band was to be out of the city in one hour on pain of pain, and one more rapid exit.

Buddy lay in the cart as it bumped over the cobbles towards Quirm.

She hadn't been there. He'd scanned the audience on both nights, and she hadn't been there. He'd even got up in the middle of the night and walked through the empty streets, in case *she* was looking for him. Now he wondered if she existed. If it came to that, he was only half certain that *he* existed, except for the times when he was on stage.

He half listened to the conversation from the others.

'Asphalt?'

'Yes, Mr Glod?'

'Cliff and me can't help noticing something.'

'Yes, Mr Glod?'

'You've been carrying a heavy leather bag around, Asphalt.'

'Yes, Mr Glod.'

'It was a bit heavier this morning, I think.'

'Yes, Mr Glod.'

'It's got the money in it, yes?'

'Yes, Mr Glod.'

'How much?'

'Er. Mr Dibbler said I wasn't to worry you with money stuff,' said Asphalt.

'We don't mind,' said Cliff.

'That's right,' said Glod. 'We *want* to worry.'

'Er.' Asphalt licked his lips. There was something deliberate in Cliff's manner. 'About two thousand dollars, Mr Glod.'

The cart bounced on for a while. The landscape had changed a little. There were hills, and the farms were smaller.

'Two thousand dollars,' said Glod. '*Two* thousand

dollars. Two *thousand* dollars. Two thousand *dollars.*'

'Whyd' you keep saying two thousand dollars?' said Cliff.

'I've never had a *chance* to say two thousand dollars.'

'Just don't say it so loud.'

'TWO THOUSAND DOLLARS!'

'Ssh!' said Asphalt, desperately, as Glod's shout echoed off the hills. 'This is bandit country!'

Glod eyed the satchel. 'You're telling me,' he said.

'I don't mean Mr Dibbler!'

'We're on the road between Sto Lat and Quirm,' said Glod patiently. 'This isn't the Ramtops road. This is civilization. They don't rob you on the road in civilization.' He glanced darkly at the satchel again. 'They wait until you've got into the cities. That's why it's called civilization. Hah, can you tell me the last time anyone was ever robbed on this road?'

'Friday, I believe,' said a voice from the rocks.

'Oh, bugg—'

The horses reared up and then galloped forward. Asphalt's crack of the whip had been an almost instinctive reaction.

They didn't slow down until they were several miles further along the road.

'Just shut up about money, all right?' hissed Asphalt.

'I'm a professional musician,' said Glod. 'Of *course* I think about money. How far is it to Quirm?'

'A lot less now,' said Asphalt. 'A couple of miles.'

And after the next hill the city lay before them, nestling in its bay.

There was a cluster of people at the town's gates, which were closed. Afternoon sunlight glittered off helmets.

'What do you call them long sticks with axes on the end?' said Asphalt.

'Pikes,' said Buddy.

'There's certainly a lot of them,' said Glod.

'They can't be for us, can dey?' said Cliff. 'We're only musicians.'

'And I can see some men in long robes and gold chains and things,' said Asphalt.

'Burghers,' said Glod.

'You know that horseman that passed us this morning . . .' said Asphalt. 'I'm thinking that maybe news travels.'

'Yes, but *we* didn't break up dat theatre,' said Cliff.

'Well, you only gave them six encores,' said Asphalt.

'We didn't do all dat rioting in the streets.'

'I'm sure the men with the pointy blades will understand that.'

'Maybe dey don't want der hotels redecorated. I *said* it was a mistake, orange curtains with yellow wallpaper.'

The cart came to a halt. A rotund man with a tricorn hat and a fur-trimmed cloak scowled uncomfortably at the band.

'Are you the musicians known as The Band With Rocks In?' he said.

'What seems to be the problem, officer?' said Asphalt.

'I am the mayor of Quirm. According to the laws of Quirm, Music With Rocks In cannot be played in the city. Look, it says so right here . . .'

He flourished a scroll. Glod caught it.

'That ink looks wet to me,' he said.

'Music With Rocks In represents a public nuisance, is proven to be injurious to health and morals and to cause unnatural gyrations of the body,' said the man, pulling the scroll back.

'You mean we can't come into Quirm?' said Glod.

'You can come in if you must,' said the mayor. 'But you're not to play.'

Buddy stood up on the cart.

'But we've *got* to play,' he said. The guitar swung around on its strap. He gripped the neck and raised his strumming hand threateningly.

Glod looked around in desperation. Cliff and Asphalt had put their hands over their ears.

'Ah!' he said. 'I think what we have here is an occasion for negotiation, yes?'

He got down from the cart.

'I expect what your worship hasn't heard of,' he said, 'is the music tax.'

'What music tax?' said Asphalt and the mayor together.

'Oh, it's the latest thing,' said Glod. 'On account of the popularity of Music With Rocks In. Music tax, fifty pence a ticket. Must have amounted to, oh, two hundred and fifty dollars in Sto Lat, I reckon.

More than twice that in Ankh-Morpork, of course. Patrician thought it up.'

'Really? Sounds like Vetinari right enough,' said the mayor. He rubbed his chin. 'Did you say two hundred and fifty dollars in Sto Lat? Really? And that place is hardly any size.'

A watchman with a feather in his helmet saluted nervously.

'Excuse me, your worship, but the note from Sto Lat *did* say—'

'Just a minute,' said the mayor testily. 'I'm thinking . . .'

Cliff leaned down.

'Dis is bribery, is it?' he whispered.

'This is taxation,' said Glod.

The watchman saluted again.

'But really, sir, the guards at—'

'Captain,' snapped the mayor, still staring thoughtfully at Glod, 'this is politics! Please!'

'As well?' said Cliff.

'And to show goodwill,' said Glod, 'it'd be a good idea if we paid the tax *before* the peformance, don't you think?'

The mayor looked at them in astonishment, a man not certain he could get his mind around the idea of musicians with money.

'Your worship, the message said—'

'Two hundred and fifty dollars,' said Glod.

'Your worship—'

'Now, captain,' said the mayor, apparently reaching a decision, 'we know that folk are a bit odd in Sto Lat. It's only music, after all. I *said* I thought it was an odd note. I can't see the harm in music. And these young me— people are clearly very successful,' he added. This obviously carried a lot of weight with the mayor, as it does with many people. No one likes a *poor* thief.

'Yes,' he went on, 'it'd be just like the Lats to try that on us. They think we're simple just because we live out here.'

'Yes, but the Pseudopo—'

'Oh, them. Stuck-up bunch. Nothing wrong with a bit of music, is there? Especially,' the mayor eyed Glod, 'when it's for the civic good. Let 'em in, captain.'

Susan saddled up.

She knew the place. She'd even seen it once. They'd put a new fence along the road now, but it was still dangerous.

She knew the time, too.

Just before they called it Dead Man's Curve.

'Hello, Quirm!'

Buddy struck a chord. And a pose. A faint white glow, like the glitter of cheap sequins, outlined him.

'Uh-huh-*huh*!'

The cheering became the familiar wall of sound.

I thought we were going to get killed by people who didn't like us, Glod thought. *Now I think it's possible to be killed by people who love us . . .*

He looked around carefully. There were guards around the walls; the captain had been no fool. *I just hope Asphalt put the horse and cart outside like I asked him . . .*

He glanced at Buddy, sparkling in the limelight.

A couple of encores and then down the back stairs and away, Glod thought. The big leather satchel had been chained to Cliff's leg. Anyone snatching it would find themselves towing one ton of drummer.

I don't even know what we're going to play, thought Glod. *I never do, I just blow and . . . there it is. You can't tell me that's right.*

Buddy whirled his arm like a discus thrower and a chord sprang away and into the ears of the audience.

Glod raised the horn to his lips. The sound that emerged was like burning black velvet in a windowless room.

Before the Music With Rocks In spell filled his soul, he thought: *I'm going to die. That's part of the music. I'm going to die really soon. I can feel it. Every day. It's getting closer . . .*

He glanced at Buddy again. The boy was scanning the audience, as if he was looking for someone in the screaming throng.

They played 'There's A Great Deal Of Shaking Happening'. They played 'Give Me That Music With Rocks In'. They played 'Pathway To Paradise' (and a hundred people in the audience swore to buy a guitar in the morning).

They played with heart and especially with soul.

They got out after the ninth encore. The crowd was still stamping its feet for more as they climbed through the privy window and dropped into the alley.

Asphalt emptied a sack into the leather satchel.

'Another seven hundred dollars!' he said, helping them onto the cart.

'Right, and we get ten dollars each,' said Glod.

'You tell Mr Dibbler,' said Asphalt, as the horses' hoofs clattered towards the gates.

'I will.'

'It doesn't matter,' said Buddy. 'Sometimes you do it for the money, but sometimes you do it for the show.'

'Hah! That'll be the day.' Glod fumbled under the seat. Asphalt had stashed two crates of beer there.

'There's the Festival tomorrow, lads,' rumbled Cliff. The gate arch passed above them. They could still hear the stamping from here.

'After that we'll have a new contract,' said the dwarf. 'With lots of zeroes in it.'

'We got zeroes now,' said Cliff.

'Yeah, but they ain't got many numbers in *front* of them. Eh, Buddy?'

They looked around. Buddy was asleep, the guitar clutched to his chest.

'Out like a candle,' said Glod.

He turned back again. The road stretched ahead of them, pale in the starlight.

'You said you just wanted to work,' said Cliff. 'You said you didn't want to be famous. How'd you like it, having to worry about all that gold, and having girls throw their chain mail at you?'

'I'd just have to put up with it.'

'I'd like a quarry,' said the troll.

'Yeah?'

'Yeah. Heart-shaped.'

* * *

A dark, stormy night. A coach, horses gone, plunged through the rickety, useless fence and dropped, tumbling, into the gorge below. It didn't even strike an outcrop of rock before it hit the dried river-bed far below and erupted into fragments. Then the oil from the coach-lamps ignited and there was a second explosion, out of which rolled – because there are certain conventions, even in tragedy – a burning wheel.

What was strange to Susan was that she felt nothing. She could *think* sad thoughts, because in the circumstances they had to be sad. She knew who was in the coach. But it had already happened. There was nothing she could do to stop it, because if she'd stopped it, it wouldn't have happened. And she was here watching it happen. So she hadn't. So it had. She felt the logic of the situation dropping into place like a series of huge leaden slabs.

Perhaps there was somewhere where it *hadn't* happened. Perhaps the coach had skidded the other way, perhaps there had been a convenient rock, perhaps it hadn't come this way at all, perhaps the coachman had remembered about the sudden curve. But those possibilities could only exist if there was *this* one.

This wasn't her knowledge. It flowed in from a mind far, far older.

Sometimes the only thing you could do for people was to be there.

She rode Binky into the shadows by the cliff road, and waited. After a minute or two there was a clattering of stones and a horse and rider came up an almost vertical path from the river-bed.

Binky's nostrils flared. Parapsychology has no word for the uneasy feeling you have when you're in the presence of yourself.*

Susan watched Death dismount and stand looking down at the river-bed, leaning on his scythe.

She thought: but he could have done *something*.

Couldn't he?

The figure straightened, but did not turn around.

YES. I COULD HAVE DONE SOMETHING.

'How . . . how did you know I was here . . . ?'

Death waved a hand irritably.

I REMEMBER YOU. AND NOW UNDERSTAND THIS: YOUR PARENTS KNEW THINGS MUST HAPPEN. EVERYTHING MUST HAPPEN *SOMEWHERE*. DO YOU NOT THINK I SPOKE TO THEM OF THIS? BUT I CANNOT GIVE LIFE. I CAN ONLY GRANT . . . EXTENSION. CHANGELESSNESS. ONLY HUMANS CAN GIVE LIFE. AND THEY WANTED TO BE HUMAN, NOT IMMORTAL. IF IT HELPS YOU, THEY DIED INSTANTLY. *INSTANTLY*.

I've got to ask, Susan thought. I've got to say it. Or *I'm* not human.

'I could go back and save them . . . ?' Only the faintest tremor suggested that the statement was a question.

SAVE? *FOR WHAT*? A LIFE THAT HAS RUN OUT? *SOME THINGS END*. I KNOW THIS. SOMETIMES I HAVE THOUGHT OTHERWISE. BUT . . . WITHOUT DUTY, WHAT AM I? THERE HAS TO BE A LAW.

*Although, strictly speaking, humans feel it all the time.

He climbed into the saddle and, still without turning to face her, spurred Binky out and over the gorge.

There was a haystack behind a livery stable in Phedre Road. It bulged for a moment, and there was a muffled swearing.

A fraction of a second later there was a bout of coughing and another, much better, swear-word inside a grain silo down near the cattle market.

Very shortly after that some rotten floorboards in an old feed store in Short Street exploded upwards, followed by a swear-word that bounced off a flour sack.

'Idiot rodent!' bellowed Albert, fingering grain out of his ear.

SQUEAK.

'I should think so! What size do you think I am?'

Albert brushed hay and flour off his coat and walked over to the window.

'Ah,' he said, 'let us repair to the Mended Drum, then.'

In Albert's pocket, sand resumed its interrupted journey from future to past.

Hibiscus Dunelm had decided to close up for an hour. It was a simple process. First he and his staff collected any unbroken mugs and glasses. This didn't take long. Then there was a desultory search for any weapons with a high resale value, and a quick search of any pockets whose owners were unable to object on account of being drunk, dead or both. Then the furniture was moved aside and everything else was swept out of the back door and into the broad brown bosom of the river Ankh, where it piled up and, by degrees, sank.

Finally, Hibiscus locked and bolted the big front door. . .

It wouldn't shut. He looked down. A boot was wedged in it.

'We're shut,' he said.

'No, you ain't.'

The door ground back, and Albert was inside.

'Have you seen this person?' he demanded, thrusting a pasteboard oblong in front of Dunelm's eyes.

This was a gross breach of etiquette. Dunelm wasn't in the kind of job where you survived if you told people you'd seen people. Dunelm could serve drinks all night without seeing anyone.

'Never seen him before in my life,' he said, automatically, without even looking at the card.

'You've got to help me,' said Albert, 'otherwise something dreadful will happen.'

'Push off!'

Albert kicked the door shut behind him.

'Just don't say I didn't warn you,' he said. On his shoulder the Death of Rats sniffed the air suspiciously.

A moment later Hibiscus was having his chin pressed firmly into the boards of one of his tables.

'Now, I know he'd come in here,' said Albert, who wasn't even breathing heavily, 'because everyone does, sooner or later. Have another look.'

'That's a Caroc card,' said Hibiscus indistinctly. 'That's Death!'

'That's right. He's the one on the white horse. You can't miss him. Only he wouldn't look like that in here, I expect.'

'Let me get this straight,' said the landlord, trying desperately to wriggle out of the iron grip. 'You want me to tell you if I've seen someone who *doesn't* look like that?'

'He'd have been odd. Odder than most.' Albert thought for a moment. 'And he'd have drunk a lot, if I know him. He always does.'

'This *is* Ankh-Morpork, you know.'

'Don't be cheeky, or I'll get angry.'

'You mean you're not angry now?'

'I'm just impatient. You can try for angry if you like.'

'There was . . . someone . . . few days ago. Can't remember exactly what he looked like—'

'Ah. That'd be him.'

'Drank me dry, complained about the Barbarian Invaders game, got legless and then . . .'

'What?'

'Can't recall. We just threw him out.'

'Out the back door?'

'Yes.'

'But that's just river out there.'

'Well, most people come round before they sink.'

SQUEAK, said the Death of Rats.

'Did he say anything?' said Albert, too busy to pay attention.

'Something about remembering everything, I

think. He said . . . he said being drunk didn't make him forget. Kept going on about doorknobs and . . . hairy sunlight.'

'Hairy sunlight?'

'Something like that.'

And the pressure on Hibiscus's arm was suddenly released. He waited a second or two and then, very cautiously, turned his head.

There was no one behind him.

Very carefully, Hibiscus bent down to look under the tables.

Albert stepped out into the dawn and, after some fumbling, produced his box. He opened it and glanced at his lifetimer, then snapped the lid shut.

'All right,' he said. 'What next?'

SQUEAK!

'What?'

And someone hit him across the head.

It wasn't a killing stroke. Timo Laziman of the Thieves' Guild knew what happened to thieves who killed people. The Assassins' Guild came and talked briefly to them – in fact, all they said was, 'Goodbye.'

All he'd wanted to do was knock the old man out so that he could rifle his pockets.

He'd not expected the sound as the body hit the ground. It was like the tinkle of broken glass, but with unpleasant overtones that carried on echoing in Timo's ears long after they should have stopped.

Something leapt from the body and whirred into his face. Two skeletal claws grabbed his ears and a bony muzzle jerked forward and hit him hard on the forehead. He screamed and ran for it.

The Death of Rats dropped to the ground again and scurried back to Albert. It patted his face, kicked him frantically a few times and then, in desperation, bit him on the nose.

Then it grabbed Albert's collar and tried to pull him out of the gutter, but there was a warning tinkle of glass.

The eye sockets turned madly towards the Drum's closed front door. Ossified whiskers bristled.

A moment later Hibiscus opened the door, if only to stop the thunderous knocking.

'I *said* we're—'

Something shot between his legs, paused momentarily to bite him on the ankle, and scuttled towards the back door, nose pressed firmly to the floor.

It was called Hide Park not because people could, but because a hide was once a measure of land capable of being ploughed by one man with three-and-one-half oxen on a wet Thursday, and the park was exactly this amount of land, and people in Ankh-Morpork stick to tradition and often to other things as well.

And it had trees, and grass, and a lake with actual fish in it. And, by one of those twists of civic history, it was a fairly safe place. People seldom got mugged in Hide Park. Muggers like somewhere safe to sunbathe, just like everyone else. It was, as it were, neutral territory.

And it was already filling up, even though there was nothing much to see except the workmen still hammering together a large stage by the lake. An area behind it had been walled off with strips of cheap sacking nailed to stakes. Occasionally excited people would try to get in and would be thrown into the lake by Chrysoprase's trolls.

Among the practising musicians Crash and his group were immediately noticeable, partly because Crash had his shirt off so that Jimbo could paint iodine on the wounds.

'I thought you were joking,' he growled.

'I did *say* it was in your bedroom,' said Scum.

'How'm I going to play my guitar like this?' said Crash.

'You can't play your guitar anyway,' said Noddy.

'I mean, look at my hand. Look at it.'

They looked at his hand. Jimbo's mum had put a glove on it after treating the wounds; they hadn't been very deep, because even a stupid leopard won't hang around anyone who wants to take its trousers off.

'A glove,' said Crash, in a terrible voice. 'Whoever heard of a serious musician with a glove? How can I ever play my guitar with a glove on?'

'How can you ever play your guitar anyway?'

'I don't know why I put up with you three,' said Crash. 'You're cramping my artistic development. I'm thinking of leaving and forming my own band.'

'No you won't,' said Jimbo, 'because you won't find anyone even worse than us. Let's face it. We're rubbish.'

He was voicing a hitherto unspoken yet shared thought. The other musicians around them were, it was true, quite bad. But that's all they were. Some of them had some minor musical talent; as for the rest, they merely couldn't play. They didn't have a drummer who missed the drums and a bass guitarist with the same natural rhythm as a traffic accident. And they'd generally settled on their name. They might be unimaginative names, like 'A Big Troll and Some Other Trolls', or 'Dwarfs With Altitude', but at least they knew who they *were.*

'How about "We're A Rubbish Band"?' said Noddy, sticking his hands in his pockets.

'We may be rubbish,' snarled Crash, 'but we're Music With Rocks In rubbish.'

'Well, well, and how's it all going, then?' said Dibbler, pushing his way through the sacking. 'It won't be long now – what're *you* doing here?'

'We're in the programme, Mr Dibbler,' said Crash meekly.

'How can you be in the programme when I don't know what you're called?' said Dibbler, waving a hand irritably at one of the posters. 'Your name up there, is it?'

'We're probably where it says *Ande Supporting Bandes,*' said Noddy.

'What happened to your hand?' said Dibbler.

'My trousers bit it,' said Crash, glowering at Scum. 'Honest, Mr Dibbler, can't you give us one more chance?'

'We'll see,' said Dibbler, and strode away.

He was feeling too cheerful to argue much. The

sausages-in-a-bun were selling very fast, but they were just covering minor expenses. There were ways of making money out of Music With Rocks In that he'd never thought of . . . and C. M. O. T. Dibbler thought of money all the time.

For example, there were the shirts. They were of cotton so cheap and thin that it was practically invisible in a good light and tended to dissolve in the wash. He'd sold six hundred already! At five dollars each! All he had to do was buy them at ten for a dollar from Klatchian Wholesale Trading and pay Chalky half a dollar each to print them.

And Chalky, with un-troll-like initiative, had even printed off his own shirts. They said:

ChalKies,
12 The Scours
Thyngs Done.

And people were *buying* them, *paying* money to advertise Chalky's workshop. Dibbler had never dreamed that the world could work like this. It was like watching sheep shear themselves. Whatever was causing this reversal of the laws of commercial practice he wanted in big lumps.

He'd already sold the idea to Plugger the shoemaker in New Cobblers* and a hundred shirts had just walked out of the shop, which was more than

* PLUGGERS
They've Got Soles
FEEL THE NALES!

Plugger's merchandise usually did. People wanted clothes just because they had writing on!

He was making money. Thousands of dollars in a day! And a hundred music traps were lined up in front of the stage, ready to capture Buddy's voice. If it went on at this rate, in several billion years he'd be rich beyond his wildest dreams!

Long Live Music With Rocks In!

There was only one small cloud in this silver lining.

The Festival was due to start at noon. Dibbler had planned to put on a lot of the small, bad groups first – that is to say, all of them – and finish with The Band. So there was no reason to worry if they weren't here right now.

But they weren't here right now. Dibbler was worried.

A tiny dark figure quartered the shores of the Ankh, moving so fast as to be a blur. It zigzagged desperately back and forth, snuffling.

People didn't see it. But they saw the rats. Black, brown and grey, they were leaving the godowns and wharfs by the river, running over one another's backs in a determined attempt to get as far away as possible.

A haystack heaved, and gave birth to a Glod.

He rolled out on to the ground, and groaned. Fine rain was drifting over the landscape. Then he staggered upright, looked around at the rolling fields, and disappeared behind a hedge for the moment.

He trotted back a few seconds later, explored the haystack for a while until he found a part that was lumpier than normal, and kicked it repeatedly with his metal-topped boot.

'Ow!'

'C flat,' said Glod. 'Good morning, Cliff. Hello, world! I don't think I can stand life in the fast leyline, you know – the cabbages, the bad beer, all those rats pestering you all the time—'

Cliff crawled out.

'I must have had some bad ammonium chloride last night,' he said. 'Is the top of my head still on?'

'Yes.'

'Pity.'

They hauled Asphalt out by his boots and brought him round by pounding him repeatedly.

'You're our road manager,' said Glod. 'You're supposed to see no harm comes to us.'

'Well, I'm doing that, ain't I?' Asphalt muttered. 'I'm not hitting you, Mr Glod. Where's Buddy?'

The three circled the haystack, prodding at bulges which turned out to be damp hay.

They found him on a small rise in the ground, not very far away. A few holly bushes grew there, carved into curves by the wind. He was sitting under one, guitar on his knees, rain plastering his hair to his face.

He was asleep, and soaking wet.

On his lap, the guitar played raindrops.

'He's weird,' said Asphalt.

'No,' said Glod. 'He's wound up by some strange compulsion which leads him through dark pathways.'

'Yeah. Weird.'

The rain was slackening off. Cliff glanced at the sky.

'Sun's high,' he said.

'Oh, no!' said Asphalt. 'How long were you asleep?'

'Same as I am awake,' said Cliff.

'It's almost noon. Where did I leave the horses? Has anyone seen the cart? Someone wake him up!'

A few minutes later they were back on the road.

'An' you know what?' said Cliff. 'We left so quick last night I never did know if she turned up.'

'What was her name?' said Glod.

'Dunno,' said the troll.

'Oh, that's *real* love, that is,' said Glod.

'Ain't you got any romance in your soul?' said Cliff.

'Eyes crossed in a crowded room?' said Glod. 'No, not really—'

They were pushed aside as Buddy leaned forward.

'Shut up,' he said. The voice was low and contained no trace whatsoever of humour.

'We were only joking,' said Glod.

'Don't.'

Asphalt concentrated on the road, aware of the general lack of amiability.

'I expect you're looking forward to the Festival, eh?' he said, after a while.

No one replied.

'I expect there'll be big crowds,' he said.

There was silence, except for the clatter of the hoofs and the rattle of the cart. They were in the hills now, where the road wound alongside a gorge. There wasn't even a river down there, except in the wettest season. It was a gloomy area. Asphalt felt that it was getting gloomier.

'I expect you'll really have fun,' he said, eventually.

'Asphalt?' said Glod.

'Yes, Mr Glod?'

'Watch the road, will you?'

The Archchancellor polished his staff as he walked along. It was a particularly good one, six feet long and quite magical. Not that he used magic very much. In his experience, anything that couldn't be disposed of with a couple of whacks from six feet of oak was probably immune to magic as well.

'Don't you think we should have brought the senior wizards, sir?' said Ponder, struggling to keep up.

'I'm afraid that taking them along in their present frame of mind would only make whatever happens—' Ridcully sought for a useful phrase, and settled for '—happen worse. I've insisted they stay in college.'

'How about Drongo and the others?' said Ponder hopefully.

'Would they be any good in the event of a thaumaturgical dimension rip of enormous proportions?' said Ridcully. 'I remember poor old Mr Hong. One minute he was dishing up an order of double cod and mushy peas, the next . . .'

'Kaboom?' said Ponder.

'"Kaboom"?' said Ridcully, forcing his way up

the crowded street. 'Not that I heard tell. More like "Aaaaerrrrscream-gristle-gristle-gristle-crack" and a shower of fried food. Big Mad Adrian and his friends any good when the chips are down?'

'Um. Probably not, Archchancellor.'

'Correct. People shout and run about. That never did any good. A pocket full of decent spells and a well-charged staff will get you out of trouble nine times out of ten.'

'Nine times out of ten?'

'Correct.'

'How many times have you had to rely on them, sir?'

'Well . . . there was Mr Hong . . . that business with the Thing in the Bursar's wardrobe . . . that dragon, you remember . . .' Ridcully's lips moved silently as he counted on his fingers. 'Nine times, so far.'

'It worked every time, sir?'

'Absolutely! So there's no need to worry. Gangway! Wizard comin' through.'

The city gates were open. Glod leaned forward as the cart rumbled in.

'Don't go straight to the park,' he said.

'But we're late,' said Asphalt.

'This won't take long. Go to the Street of Cunning Artificers first.'

'That's right on the other side of the river!'

'It's important. We've got to pick up something.'

People flocked the streets. This wasn't unusual,

except that this time most of them were moving the same way.

'And you get down in the back of the cart,' said Glod to Buddy. 'We don't want young women trying to rip your clothes off, eh, Buddy . . . ?'

He turned. Buddy had gone to sleep again.

'Speaking for myself—' Cliff began.

'You've only got a loincloth,' said Glod.

'Well, they could grab it, couldn't they?'

The cart threaded its way through the streets until it turned into Cunning Artificers.

It was a street of tiny shops. In this street you could have anything made, repaired, crafted, rebuilt, copied or forged. Furnaces glowed in every doorway; smelters smoked in every backyard. Makers of intricate clockwork eggs worked alongside armourers. Carpenters worked next door to men who carved ivory into tiny shapes so delicate that they used grasshoppers' legs, cast in bronze, for saws. At least one in every four craftsmen was making tools to be used by the other three. Shops didn't just abut, they overlapped; if a carpenter had a big table to make he relied on the goodwill of his neighbours to make space, so that he'd be working at one end of it while two jewellers and a potter were using the other end as a bench. There were shops where you could drop in to be measured in the morning and pick up a complete suit of chain mail with an extra pair of pants in the afternoon.

The cart stopped outside one small shop and Glod leapt down and went inside.

Asphalt heard the conversation:

'Have you done it?'

'Here you are, mister. Right as rain.'

'Will it play? You know I said where you have to have spent a fortnight wrapped in a bullock hide behind a waterfall before you should touch one of these things.'

'Listen, mister, for this kind of money it had me in the shower for five minutes with a chamois leather on me head. Don't tell me that's not good enough for folk music.'

There was a pleasant sound, which hung in the air for a moment before being lost in the busy din of the street.

'We said twenty dollars, right?'

'No, you said twenty dollars. *I* said twenty-five dollars.'

'Just a minute, then.'

Glod came out, and nodded at Cliff.

'All right,' he said. 'Cough up.'

Cliff growled, but fumbled for a moment somewhere at the back of his mouth.

They heard the cunning artificer say, 'What the hell's that?'

'A molar. Got to be worth at least—'

'It'll do.'

Glod came out again with a sack, which he tucked under the seat.

'Okay,' he said. 'Head for the park.'

They went in through one of the back gates. Or, at least, tried to. Two trolls barred their way. They had the glossy marble patina of Chrysoprase's basic gang thugs. He didn't have henchmen. Most trolls weren't clever enough to hench.

'Dis is for der bands,' one said.

'Dat's right,' said the other one.

'We *are* The Band,' said Asphalt.

'Which one?' said the first troll. 'I got a list here.'

'Dat's right.'

'We're The Band With Rocks In,' said Glod.

'Hah, you ain't *them.* I've seen *them.* Dere's a guy with this glow round him, and when he plays der guitar it goes—'

Whauauauaummmmm-eeeee-gngngn.

'Dat's *right*—'

The chord curled around the cart.

Buddy was standing up, guitar at the ready.

'Oh, wow,' said the first troll. 'This are *amazing*!' He fumbled in his loincloth and produced a dog-eared piece of paper. 'You couldn't write your name down, could you? My boy Clay, he won't *believe* I met—'

'Yes, yes,' said Buddy wearily. 'Pass it up.'

'Only it not for me, it for my boy Clay—' said the troll, jumping from one foot to the other in excitement.

'How d'you spell it?'

'It don't matter, he can't read anyway.'

'Listen,' said Glod, as the cart trundled into the backstage area, 'someone's already playing. I *said* we—'

Dibbler hurried up.

'What kept you?' he said. 'You'll be on soon!

Right after . . . Boyz From The Wood. How did it go? Asphalt, come here.'

He pulled the small troll into the shadows at the back of the stage.

'You brought me some money?' he said.

'About three thousand—'

'Not so loud!'

'I'm only whispering it, Mr Dibbler.'

Dibbler looked around carefully. There was no such thing as a whisper in Ankh-Morpork when the sum involved had the word 'thousand' in it somewhere; people could hear you *think* that kind of money in Ankh-Morpork.

'You be sure and keep an eye on it, right? There's going to be more before this day's out. I'll give Chrysoprase his seven hundred dollars and the rest is all prof—' He caught Asphalt's little beady eye and remembered himself. 'Of course, there's depreciation . . . overheads . . . advertising . . . market research . . . buns . . . mustard . . . basically, I'll be lucky if I break even. I'm practically cutting me own throat in this deal.'

'Yes, Mr Dibbler.'

Asphalt peered around the edge of the stage.

'Who's that playing now, Mr Dibbler?'

' "And you".'

'Sorry, Mr Dibbler?'

'Only they write it &U,' said Dibbler. He relaxed a little and pulled out a cigar. 'Don't ask me why. The right kind of name for musicians ought to be something like Blondie and his Merry Troubadours. Are they any good?'

'Don't you know, Mr Dibbler?'

'It's not what *I* call music,' said Dibbler. 'When I was a lad we had proper music with real words . . . "Summer is icumen in, lewdly sing cuckoo", that sort of thing.'

Asphalt looked at &U again.

'Well, it's got a beat and you can dance to it,' he said, 'but they're not very good. I mean, people are just watching them. They don't just watch when The Band are playing, Mr Dibbler.'

'You're right,' said Dibbler. He looked at the front of the stage. In between the candles was a row of music traps.

'You'd better go and tell them to get ready. I think this lot are running out of ideas.'

'Um. Buddy?'

He looked up from his guitar. Some of the other musicians were tuning theirs, but he'd found he never had to. He couldn't, anyway. The pegs didn't move.

'What is it?'

'Um,' said Glod. He waved vaguely at Cliff, who grinned sheepishly and produced the sack from behind his back.

'This is . . . well, we thought . . . that is, all of us,' said Glod, 'that . . . well, we saw it, you see, and I know you said it couldn't be repaired but there's people in this city that can do just about *anything* so we asked around, and we knew how much it meant to you, and there's this man in the Street of Cunning Artificers and he said he thought he could do it and it cost Cliff another tooth but here you are anyway because you're right, we're on top of the music business right enough and it's because of you and we know how much this meant to you so it's a sort of thank-you present, well, go on then, *give* it to him.'

Cliff, who'd lowered his arm again as the sentence began to extend, pushed the sack towards the puzzled Buddy.

Asphalt poked his head through the sacking.

'We guys better get on the stage,' he said. 'Come on!'

Buddy put down the guitar. He opened the sack, and began to pull at the linen wrappings inside.

'It's been tuned and everything,' said Cliff helpfully.

The harp gleamed in the sun as the last wrapping came off.

'They can do amazing things with glue and stuff,' said Glod. 'I mean, I know you said there wasn't anyone left in Llamedos that could repair it. But this is Ankh-Morpork. We can fix nearly everything.'

'Please!' said Asphalt, as his head reappeared. 'Mr Dibbler says you've got to come, they've started to throw things!'

'I don't know much about strings,' said Glod, 'but I had a go. Sounds . . . kind of nice.'

'I . . . er . . . don't know what to say,' said Buddy.

The chanting was like a hammer.

'I . . . won this,' said Buddy, in a small, distant world of his own. 'With a song. *Sioni Bod Da,* it was. I worked on it allll winter. Allll about . . . home, you know. And going away, see? And trees and things.

The judges were . . . very plleased. They said that in fifty years I might realllly understand music.'

He pulled the harp towards him.

Dibbler pushed his way through the rabble of musicians backstage until he found Asphalt.

'Well?' he said. 'Where are they?'

'They're just sitting around talking, Mr Dibbler.'

'Listen,' said Dibbler. 'You hear the crowd? It's Music With Rocks In they want! If they don't get it . . . they'd just better get it, all right? Letting the anticipation build up is all very well but . . . *I want them on stage right now!*'

Buddy stared at his fingers. Then he looked up, white-faced, at the other bands milling around.

'You . . . with the guitar . . .' he said hoarsely.

'Me, sir?'

'Give it to me!'

Every nascent group in Ankh-Morpork was in awe of The Band With Rocks In. The guitarist handed his instrument over with the expression of one passing over a holy item to be blessed.

Buddy stared at it. It was one of Mr Wheedown's best.

He struck a chord.

The sound sounded like lead would sound if you could make guitar strings out of it.

'Okay, boys, what's the problem?' said Dibbler, hurrying towards them. 'There's six thousand ears out there waiting to be filled up with music and you're still sitting around?'

Buddy handed the guitar back to the musician and swung his own instrument around on its strap. He played a few notes that seemed to twinkle in the air.

'But I can play *this*,' he said. 'Oh, yes.'

'Right, good, now get up there and play it,' said Dibbler.

'Someone else give me a guitar!'

Musicians fell over themselves to hand them to him. He strummed frantically at a couple. But the notes weren't simply flat. Flat would have been an improvement.

The Musicians' Guild contingent had managed to secure an area close to the stage by the simple expedient of hitting any encroachers very hard.

Mr Clete scowled at the stage.

'I don't understand,' he said. 'It's rubbish. It's all the same. It's just noise. What's so good about it?'

Satchelmouth, who had twice had to stop himself tapping his feet, said, 'We haven't had the main band yet. Er. Are you sure you want to—'

'We're within our rights,' said Clete. He looked around at the shouting people. 'There's a hot dog seller over there. Anyone else fancy a hot dog? Hot dog?' The Guild men nodded. 'Hot dog? Right. That's three hot d—'

The audience cheered. It wasn't the way that an audience normally applauds, with it starting at one point and rippling outwards, but all at once, every single mouth opening at the same time.

Cliff had knuckled on to the stage. He sat down

behind his rocks and looked desperately back towards the wings.

Glod trailed on, blinking in the lights.

And that seemed to be it. The dwarf turned and said something which was lost in the noise, and then stood looking awkward while the cheers gradually subsided.

Buddy came on, staggering slightly as if he'd been pushed.

Up until then Mr Clete had thought the crowd was yelling. And then he realized that it had been a mere murmur of approval compared to what was happening now.

It went on and on while the boy stood there, head bowed.

'But he's not *doing* anything,' Clete shouted into Satchelmouth's ear. 'Why're they all cheering him for not doing anything?'

'Can't say, sir,' said Satchelmouth. He looked around at the glistening, staring, *hungry* faces, feeling like an atheist who has wandered into Holy Communion.

The applause went on. It redoubled again when Buddy slowly raised his hands to the guitar.

'He's not doing *anything*!' screamed Clete.

'He's got us bang to rights, sir,' Satchelmouth bellowed. 'He's not guilty of playing without belonging to the Guild if he doesn't play!'

Buddy looked up.

He stared at the audience so intently that Clete craned to see what it was the wretched boy was staring at.

It was nothing. There was a patch of it right in front of the stage.

People were packed tight everywhere else but there, right in front of the stage, was a little area of cleared grass. It seemed to rivet Buddy's attention.

'Uh-huh-huh . . .'

Clete rammed his hands over his ears but the force of the cheering made his head echo.

And then, very gradually, layer by layer, it died away. It yielded to the sound of thousands of people being very quiet, which was somehow, Satchelmouth thought, a lot more dangerous.

Glod glanced at Cliff, who made a face.

Buddy was still standing, staring at the audience.

If he doesn't play, Glod thought, *then we've had it.*

He hissed at Asphalt, who sidled over.

'Is the cart ready?'

'Yes, Mr Glod.'

'You filled up the horses with oats?'

'Just like you said, Mr Glod.'

'Okay.'

The silence was velvet. And it had that quality of suction found in the Patrician's study and in holy places and deep canyons, engendering in people a terrible desire to shout or sing or yell their name. It was a silence that demanded: fill me up.

Somewhere in the darkness, someone coughed.

Asphalt heard his name hissed from the side of the stage. With extreme reluctance he sidled over to the darkness, where Dibbler was frantically beckoning him.

'You know that bag?' said Dibbler.

'Yes, Mr Dibbler. I put it—'

Dibbler held up two small but very heavy sacks.

'Tip these in and be ready to leave in a big hurry.'

'Yes, that's right, Mr Dibbler, because Glod said—'

'Do it now!'

Glod looked around. *If I throw away the horn and helmet and this chain mail shirt*, he thought, *I might just get out of here alive. What's he* doing?

Buddy put down the guitar and walked into the wings. He returned before the audience had realized what was happening. He was carrying the harp.

He stood facing the audience.

Glod, who was closest to him, heard him murmur: 'Just once? Cwm on? Just one more time? And then I'llll do whatefer you want, see? I'llll pay for it.'

There were a few faint chords from the guitar.

Buddy said, 'I mean it, see.'

There was another chord.

'Just once.'

Buddy smiled at an empty space in the audience, and began to play.

Every note was sharp as a bell and as simple as sunlight – so that in the prism of the brain it broke up and flashed into a million colours.

Glod's mouth hung open. And then the music

unfolded in his head. It wasn't Music With Rocks In, although it used the same doors. The fall of the notes conjured up memories of the mine where he'd been born, and dwarf bread just like Mum used to hammer out on her anvil, and the moment when he'd first realized that he'd fallen in love.* He remembered life in the caves under Copperhead, before the city had called him, and more than anything else he wanted to be home. He'd never realized that humans could sing *hole.*

Cliff laid aside his hammers. The same notes crept into his corroded ears, but in his mind they became quarries and moorlands. He told himself, as emotion filled his head with its smoke, that right after this he was going to go back and see how his old mum was, and never leave ever again.

Mr Dibbler found his own mind spawning strange and disturbing thoughts. They involved things you couldn't sell and shouldn't pay for . . .

The Lecturer in Recent Runes thumped the crystal ball.

'The sound is a bit tinny,' he said.

'Get out of the way, I can't see,' said the Dean.

Recent Runes sat down again.

They stared at the little image.

'This doesn't sound like Music With Rocks In,' said the Bursar.

'Shut up,' said the Dean. He blew his nose.

It was sad music. But it waved the sadness like a

*He'd still got the nugget somewhere.

battle flag. It said the universe had done all it could but you were still alive.

The Dean, who was as impressionable as a dollop of warm wax, wondered if he could learn to play the harmonica.

The last note faded.

There was no applause. The audience sagged a little, as each individual came down from whatever reflective corner they'd been occupying. One or two of them murmured things like 'Yeah, that's how it is', or 'You an' me both, brother'. A lot of people blew their noses, sometimes on other people.

And then reality snuck back in, as it always does.

Glod heard Buddy say, very quietly, 'Thank you.'

The dwarf leaned sideways and said, out of the corner of his mouth: 'What was that?'

Buddy seemed to shake himself awake.

'What? Oh. It's called *Sioni Bod Da.* What do you think?'

'It's got . . . hole,' said Glod. 'It's definitely got hole.'

Cliff nodded. When you're a long way from the old familiar mine or mountain, when you're lost among strangers, when you're just a great big aching nothingness inside . . . only then can you really sing *hole.*

'She's watching us,' whispered Buddy.

'The invisible girl?' said Glod, staring at the empty grass.

'Yes.'

'Ah, yes. I can definitely not see her. Good. And now, if you don't play Music With Rocks In this time, we're dead.'

Buddy picked up the guitar. The strings trembled under his fingers. He felt elated. He'd been allowed to play *it* in front of them. Everything else was unimportant now. Whatever happened next didn't matter.

'You ain't heard *nothing* yet,' he said.

He stamped his foot.

'One, two, one two three four—'

Glod had time to recognize the tune before the music took him. He'd heard it only a few seconds before. But now it *swung*.

Ponder peered into his box.

'I think we're trapping this, Archchancellor,' he said, 'but I don't know what it is.'

Ridcully nodded, and scanned the audience. They were listening with their mouths open. The harp had scoured their souls, and now the guitar was hotwiring their spines.

And there was an empty patch near the stage.

Ridcully put a hand over one eye and focused until the other eye watered. Then he smiled.

He turned to look at the Musicians' Guild and saw, to his horror, that Satchelmouth was raising a crossbow. He seemed to be doing it with reluctance; Mr Clete was prodding him.

Ridcully raised a finger and appeared to scratch his nose.

Even above the sound of the playing he heard the

twang as the crossbow's string broke and, to his secret delight, a yelp from Mr Clete as a loose end caught his ear. He hadn't even thought of that.

'I'm just an old softy, that's my trouble,' Ridcully said to himself. 'Hat. Hat. Hat.'

'You know, this was an extremely good idea,' said the Bursar, as the tiny images moved in the crystal ball. 'What an excellent way to see things. Could we perhaps have a look at the Opera House?'

'How about the Skunk Club in Brewer Street?' said the Senior Wrangler.

'Why?' said the Bursar.

'Just a thought,' said the Senior Wrangler quickly. 'I've never been in there at all in any way, you understand.'

'We really shouldn't be doing this,' said the Lecturer in Recent Runes. 'It's really not a proper use of a magic crystal—'

'I can't think of a better use of a magic crystal,' said the Dean, 'than to see people playing Music With Rocks In.'

The Duck Man, Coffin Henry, Arnold Sideways, Foul Ole Ron and Foul Ole Ron's Smell and Foul Ole Ron's dog ambled around the edges of the crowd. Pickings had been particularly good. They always were when Dibbler's hot dogs were on sale. There were some things people wouldn't eat even under the influence of Music With Rocks In. There were some things even mustard couldn't disguise.

Arnold gathered up the scraps and put them in a

basket on his trolley. There was going to be the prince of a primal soup under the bridge tonight.

The music had poured over them. They ignored it. Music With Rocks In was the stuff of dreams, and there were no dreams under the bridge.

Then they'd stopped and listened, as new music poured out over the park and took every man and woman and thing by the hand and showed him or her or it the way home.

The beggars stood and listened, mouths open. Someone looking from face to face, if anyone *did* look at the invisible beggars, would have had to turn away . . .

Except from Mr Scrub. You couldn't turn away there.

When the band were playing Music With Rocks In again, the beggars got back down to earth.

Except for Mr Scrub. He just stood and stared.

The last note rang out.

Then, as the tsunami of applause began to roll, The Band ran off into the darkness.

Dibbler watched happily from the wings at the other side of the stage. He'd been a bit worried for a while there, but it all seemed back on course now.

Someone tugged at his sleeve.

'What're they doing, Mr Dibbler?'

Dibbler turned.

'Scum, isn't it?' he said.

'It's Crash, Mr Dibbler.'

'What they're doing, Scum, is not giving the audience what they want,' said Dibbler. 'Superb business practice. Wait till they're screaming for it, and then take it away. You wait. By the time the crowd is stamping its feet they'll come prancing back on again. Superb timing. When you learn that sort of trick, Scum—'

'It's Crash, Mr Dibbler.'

'—*then* maybe you'll know how to play Music With Rocks In. Music With Rocks In, Scum—'

'—Crash—'

'. . . isn't *just* music,' said Dibbler, pulling some cotton wool out of his ears. 'It's lots of things. Don't ask me how.'

Dibbler lit a cigar. The din made the match flame flicker.

'Any minute now,' he said. 'You'll see.'

There was a fire that had been made of old boots and mud. A grey shape circled it, snuffling excitedly.

'Get on, get on, get *on*!'

'Mr Dibbler's not going to like this,' moaned Asphalt.

'Tough one for Mr Dibbler,' said Glod, as they hauled Buddy into the cart. 'Now I want to see those hoofs spark, know what I mean?'

'Head for Quirm,' said Buddy, as the cart jerked into motion. He didn't know why. It just seemed the *right* destination.

'Not a good idea,' said Glod. 'People'll probably want to ask questions about that cart I pulled out of the swimming pool.'

'Head towards Quirm!'

'Mr Dibbler's really not going to *like* this,' said Asphalt, as the cart swung out on to the road.

'Any . . . moment . . . now,' said Dibbler.

'I expect so,' said Crash, 'because they're stamping their feet, I think.'

There was indeed a certain thumping under the cheers.

'You wait,' said Dibbler. 'They'll judge it *just right.* No problem. Akk!'

'You're supposed to put your cigar in your mouth the other way round, Mr Dibbler,' said Crash meekly.

The waxing moon lit the landscape as the cart bounced out of the gates and along the Quirm road.

'How did you know I'd got the cart made ready?' said Glod, as they landed after a brief flight.

'I didn't,' said Buddy.

'But you ran out!'

'Yes.'

'Why?'

'It was . . . just . . . time.'

'Why'd you want to go to Quirm?' said Cliff.

'I . . . I can get a boat home, can't I?' said Buddy. 'That's right. A boat home.'

Glod glanced at the guitar. This felt wrong. It couldn't just end . . . and then they'd just walk away . . .

He shook his head. What could go wrong now?

'Mr Dibbler's *really* not going to like this,' moaned Asphalt.

'Oh, shut up,' said Glod. 'I don't know what *he's* got not to like.'

'Well, for a start,' said Asphalt, 'the *main* thing, the thing he won't like most, is . . . um . . . we've got the money . . .'

Cliff reached down under the seat. There was a dull, clinking noise, of the sort made by a lot of gold keeping nice and quiet.

The stage was trembling with the vibration of the stamping. There was some shouting now.

Dibbler turned to Crash and grinned horribly.

'Hey, I've just had a *great* idea,' he said.

A tiny shape swarmed up the road from the river. Ahead of it, the lights of the stage glowed in the dusk.

The Archchancellor nudged Ponder, and flourished his staff.

'Now,' he said, 'if there's a sudden rip in reality and horrible screaming Things come through, our job is to—' He scratched his head. 'What is it the Dean says? Kick a righteous donkey?'

'Some righteous ass, sir,' said Ponder. 'He says kick some righteous ass.'

Ridcully peered at the empty stage.

'I don't see one,' he said.

The four members of The Band sat up and stared straight ahead, over the moonlit plain.

Finally Cliff broke the silence.

'How much?'

'Best part of five thousand dollars—'

'FIVE THOUSAND *DOL*—?'

Cliff clamped his huge hand over Glod's mouth.

'Why?' said Cliff, as the dwarf squirmed.

'MMF MMFMMF *MMFMMFS?*'

'I got a bit confused,' said Asphalt. 'Sorry.'

'We'll never get far enough,' said Cliff. 'You know dat? Not even if we die.'

'I tried to tell you all!' Asphalt moaned. 'Maybe . . . maybe we could take it back?'

'MMF MMF *MMF?*'

'How can we do dat?'

'MMF MMF *MMF?*'

'Glod,' said Cliff, in a reasonable tone of voice, 'I'm going to take my hand away. And you're not to shout. Right?'

'Mmf.'

'Okay.'

'TAKE IT *BACK?* FIVE THOUSAND *DOL*—mmfmmfmmf—'

'I suppose some of dat is ours,' said Cliff, tightening his grip.

'Mmf!'

'I know *I* haven't had any wages,' said Asphalt.

'Let's get to Quirm,' said Buddy urgently. 'We can take out what's . . . ours and send the rest back to him.'

Cliff scratched his chin with his free hand.

'Some of it belongs to Chrysoprase,' said Asphalt. 'Mr Dibbler borrowed some money off'f him to set up the Festival.'

'We won't get away from *him*,' said Cliff, 'except if we drive all the way to the Rim and chuck ourselves over. And even den, only maybe.'

'We could explain . . . couldn't . . . we?' said Asphalt.

A vision of Chrysoprase's gleaming marble head formed in their vision.

'Mmf.'

'No.'

'Quirm, then,' said Buddy.

Cliff's diamond teeth glittered in the moonlight.

'I thought . . .' he said, 'I thought . . . I heard something on the road back there. Sounded like harness—'

The invisible beggars began to wander away from the park. Foul Ole Ron's Smell had stayed on for a while, because it was enjoying the music. And Mr Scrub still hadn't moved.

'We got nearly twenty sausages,' said Arnold Sideways.

Coffin Henry coughed a cough with bones in it.

'Buggrem?' said Foul Ole Ron. 'I told 'em, spyin' on me with rays!'

Something bounded across the trodden turf towards Mr Scrub, ran up his robe and grabbed either side of his hood with both paws.

There was the hollow sound of two skulls meeting.

Mr Scrub staggered backwards.

SQUEAK!

Mr Scrub blinked and sat down suddenly.

The beggars stared down at the little figure jumping up and down on the cobbles. Being of an invisible nature themselves, they were naturally good at seeing things unseen by other men or, in the case of Foul Ole Ron, by any known eyeball.

'That's a rat,' said the Duck Man.

'Buggrit,' said Foul Ole Ron.

The rat pranced in circles on its hind legs, squeaking loudly. Mr Scrub blinked again . . . And Death stood up.

I HAVE TO GO, he said.

SQUEAK!

Death strode away, stopped, and came back. He pointed a skeletal finger at the Duck Man.

WHY, he said, ARE YOU WALKING AROUND WITH THAT DUCK?

'What duck?'

AH. SORRY.

'Listen, how can it go wrong?' said Crash, waving his hands frantically. 'It's *got* to work. Everyone *knows* that when you get your big chance because the star is ill or something, then the audience'll go mad for you. It happens every time, right?'

Jimbo, Noddy and Scum peered around the curtain at the pandemonium. They nodded uncertainly.

Of *course* things always went well when you had your big chance . . .

'We *could* do "Anarchy in Ankh-Morpork",' said Jimbo doubtfully.

'We haven't got that right,' said Noddy.

'Yeah, but there's nothing new about that.'

'I suppose we could give it a try . . .'

'Excellent!' said Crash. He raised his guitar defiantly. 'We *can* do it! For the sake of sex and drugs and Music With Rocks In!'

He was aware of their disbelieving stares.

'You never said you'd had any drugs,' said Jimbo accusingly.

'If it comes to that,' said Noddy, 'I don't reckon you've ever had—'

'One out of three ain't bad!' shouted Crash.

'Yes it is, it's only thirty-three per—'

'Shut up!'

People were stamping their feet and clapping their hands derisively.

Ridcully squinted along his staff.

'There was the Holy St Bobby,' he said. 'I suppose *he* was a righteous ass, come to think about it.'

'Sorry?' said Ponder.

'He was a donkey,' said Ridcully. 'Hundreds of years ago. Got made a bishop in the Omnian church for carrying some holy man, I believe. Can't get more righteous than that.'

'No . . . no . . . no . . . Archchancellor,' said Ponder. 'It's just a sort of military saying. It means . . . the . . . you know, sir . . . backside.'

'I wonder how we tell which bit that is,' Ridcully said. 'The creatures from the Dungeon Dimensions have legs and things all over the place.'

'I don't know, sir,' said Ponder wearily.

'Perhaps we'd just better kick everything, to be on the safe side.'

* * *

Death caught up with the rat near the Brass Bridge.

No one had disturbed Albert. Since he was in the gutter, he'd become nearly as invisible as Coffin Henry.

Death rolled his sleeve up. His hand moved through the fabric of Albert's coat as if it was mist.

DAFT OLD FOOL ALWAYS TOOK IT WITH HIM, he muttered, I CAN'T IMAGINE WHAT HE THOUGHT I'D DO WITH IT . . .

The hand came out, cupping a fragment of curved glass. A pinch of sand glittered on it.

THIRTY-FOUR SECONDS, said Death. He handed the glass to the rat. FIND SOMETHING TO PUT THIS IN. AND DON'T DROP IT.

He stood up and surveyed the world.

There was the *glong-glong-glong* noise of an empty beer bottle bouncing on the stones as the Death of Rats trotted back out of the Mended Drum.

Thirty-four seconds of sand orbited slightly erratically inside it.

Death hauled his servant to his feet. No time was passing for Albert. His eyes were glazed, his body-clock idled. He hung from his master's arm like a cheap suit.

Death snatched the bottle from the rat and tilted it gently. A bit of life began to flow.

WHERE IS MY GRANDDAUGHTER? he said. YOU HAVE TO TELL ME. OTHERWISE I CAN'T KNOW.

Albert's eyes clicked open.

'She's trying to save the boy, Master!' he said. 'She doesn't know the meaning of the word Duty—'

Death tipped the bottle back. Albert froze in mid-sentence.

BUT WE DO, DON'T WE? said Death bitterly, YOU AND ME.

He nodded to the Death of Rats.

LOOK AFTER HIM, he said.

Death snapped his fingers.

Nothing happened, apart from the click.

ER. THIS IS VERY EMBARRASSING. SHE HAS SOME OF MY POWER. I DO SEEM MOMENTARILY UNABLE TO . . . ER . . .

The Death of Rats squeaked helpfully.

NO. YOU LOOK AFTER HIM. I KNOW WHERE THEY'RE GOING. HISTORY LIKES CYCLES.

Death looked at the towers of Unseen University, rising over the rooftops.

AND SOMEWHERE IN THIS TOWN IS A HORSE I CAN RIDE.

'Hold on. Something's coming . . .' Ridcully glared at the stage. 'What are *they*?'

Ponder stared.

'I think . . . they *may* be human, sir.'

The crowd had stopped stamping its collective feet and was watching in a sullen 'this had better be good' silence.

Crash stepped forward with a big mad glossy grin on his face.

'Yes, but any minute they'll split down the middle and gharstely creatures will come out,' said Ridcully hopefully.

Crash hefted his guitar and played a chord.

'My word!' said Ridcully.

'Sir?'

'That sounded *exactly* like a cat trying to go to the lavatory through a sewn-up bum.'

Ponder looked aghast. 'Sir, you're not telling me you ever—'

'No, but that's what it'd sound like, sure enough. Exactly like that.'

The crowd hovered, uncertain of this new development.

'Hello, Ankh-Morpork!' said Crash. He nodded at Scum, who hit his drums at the second attempt.

Ande Supporting Bandes launched into its first and, in the event, last number. Three last numbers, in fact. Crash was trying for 'Anarchy in Ankh-Morpork', Jimbo had frozen because he couldn't see himself in a mirror and was playing the only page he could remember from Blert Wheedown's book, which was the index, and Noddy had got his fingers caught in the strings.

As far as Scum was concerned, tunes' names were things that happened to other people. He was concentrating on the rhythm. Most people don't have to. But for Scum, even clapping his hands was an exercise in concentration. So he played in a small contented world of his own, and didn't even notice the audience rise like a bad meal and hit the stage.

Sergeant Colon and Corporal Nobbs were on duty at the Deosil Gate, sharing a comradely cigarette and listening to the distant roar of the Festival.

'Sounds like a big night,' said Sergeant Colon.

'Right enough, sarge.'

'Sounds like some trouble.'

'Good job we're out of it, sarge.'

A horse came clattering up the street, its rider struggling to keep on. As it got closer they made out the contorted features of C. M. O. T. Dibbler, riding with the ease of a sack of potatoes.

'Did a cart just go through here?' he demanded.

'Which one, Throat?' said Sergeant Colon.

'What do you mean, which one?'

'Well, there was two,' said the sergeant. 'One with a couple of trolls in, and one with Mr Clete just after that. You know, the Musicians' Guild—'

'Oh, no!'

Dibbler pummelled the horse into action again and bounced off into the night.

'What was that about?' said Nobby.

'Someone probably owes him a penny,' said Sergeant Colon, leaning on his spear.

There was the sound of another horse approaching. The watchmen flattened themselves against the wall as it thundered past.

It was big, and white. The rider's black cloak streamed in the air, as did her hair. There was a rush of wind and then they were gone, out on to the plains. Nobby stared after it.

'That was *her*,' he said.

'Who?'

'Susan Death.'

The light in the crystal faded to a dot and winked out.

'That's three days' worth of magic I won't see again,' the Senior Wrangler complained.

'Worth every thaum,' said the Chair of Indefinite Studies.

'Not as good as seeing them live, though,' said the Lecturer in Recent Runes. 'There's something about the way the sweat drips on you.'

'*I* thought it ended just as it was getting good,' said the Chair. 'I thought—'

The wizards went rigid as the howl rang through the building. It was slightly animal but also mineral, metallic, edged like a saw.

Eventually the Lecturer in Recent Runes said, 'Of course, just because we've heard a spine-chilling bloodcurdling scream of the sort to make your very marrow freeze in your bones doesn't automatically mean there's anything wrong.'

The wizards looked out into the corridor.

'It came from downstairs somewhere,' said the Chair of Indefinite Studies, heading for the staircase.

'So why are you going *upstairs*?'

'Because I'm not daft!'

'But it might be some terrible emanation!'

'You don't say?' said the Chair, still accelerating.

'All right, please yourself. That's the students' floor up there.'

'Ah. Er—'

The Chair came down slowly, occasionally glancing fearfully up the stairs.

'Look, nothing can get in,' said the Senior Wrangler. 'This place is protected by very powerful spells.'

'That's right,' said Recent Runes.

'And I'm sure we've all been strengthening them periodically, as is our duty,' said the Senior Wrangler.

'Er. Yes. Yes. Of course,' said Recent Runes.

The sound came again. There was a slow pulsating rhythm in the roar.

'The Library, I think,' said the Senior Wrangler.

'Anyone seen the Librarian lately?'

'He always seems to be carrying something when I see him. You don't think he's up to something occult, do you?'

'This *is* a magical university.'

'Yes, but *more* occult is what I mean.'

'Keep together, will you?'

'*I am* together.'

'For if we are united, what can possibly harm us?'

'Well, (1), a great big—'

'Shut up!'

The Dean opened the library door. It was warm, and velvety quiet. Occasionally, a book would rustle its pages or clank its chains restlessly.

A silvery light was coming from the stairway to the basement. There was also the occasional 'ook'.

'He doesn't sound very upset,' said the Bursar.

The wizards crept down the steps. There was no mistaking the door – the light streamed from it.

The wizards stepped into the cellar.

They stopped breathing.

It was on a raised dais in the centre of the floor, with candles all around it.

It *was* Music With Rocks In.

* * *

A tall dark figure skidded around the corner into Sator Square and, accelerating, pounded through the gateway of Unseen University.

It was seen only by Modo the dwarf gardener, as he happily wheeled his manure barrow through the twilight. It had been a good day. Most days were, in his experience.

He hadn't heard about the Festival. He hadn't heard about Music With Rocks In. Modo didn't hear about most things, because he wasn't listening. He liked compost. Next to compost he liked roses, because they were something to compost the compost for.

He was by nature a contented dwarf, who took in his short stride all the additional problems of gardening in a high magical environment, such as greenfly, whitefly *and* lurching things with tentacles. Proper lawn maintenance could be a real problem when things from another dimension were allowed to slither over it.

Someone pounded across it and disappeared through the doorway of the library.

Modo looked at the marks and said, 'Oh, dear.'

The wizards started breathing again.

'Oh, my,' said the Lecturer in Recent Runes.

'Rave In . . .' said the Senior Wrangler.

'Now *that*'s what I call Music With Rocks In,' sighed the Dean. He stepped forward with the rapt expression of a miser in a goldmine.

The candlelight glittered off black and silver. There was a lot of both.

'Oh, my,' said the Lecturer in Recent Runes. It was like some kind of incantation.

'I say, isn't that my nose-hair mirror?' said the Bursar, breaking the spell. 'That's my nose-hair mirror, I'm sure—'

Except that while the black was black the silver wasn't really silver. It was whatever mirrors and bits of shiny tin and tinsel and wire the Librarian had been able to scrounge and bend into shape . . .

'—it's got the little silver frame . . . why's it on that two-wheeled cart? Two wheels, one after the other? Ridiculous. It'll fall over, depend upon it. And where's the horse going to go, may I ask?'

The Senior Wrangler tapped him gently on the shoulder.

'Bursar? Word to the wizard, old chap.'

'Yes? What is it?'

'I think if you don't stop talking *this minute* the Dean will kill you.'

There were two small cart-wheels, one behind the other, with a saddle in between them. In front of the saddle was a pipe with a complicated double curve in it, so that someone sitting in the saddle would be able to get a grip.

The rest was junk. Bones and tree branches and a jackdaw's banquet of gewgaws. A horse's skull was strapped over the front wheel, and feathers and beads hung from every point.

It was junk, but as it stood in the flickering glow it had a dark, organic quality – not exactly life, but something dynamic and disquieting and coiled and potent that was making the Dean vibrate on his feet.

It radiated something that suggested that, just by existing and looking like it did, it was breaking at least nine laws and twenty-three guidelines.

'Is he in love?' said the Bursar.

'Make it go!' said the Dean. 'It's got to go! It's *meant* to go!'

'Yes, but what *is* it?' said the Chair of Indefinite Studies.

'It's a masterpiece,' said the Dean. 'A triumph!'

'Oook?'

'Perhaps you have to push it along with your feet?' whispered the Senior Wrangler.

The Dean shook his head in a preoccupied way.

'We're wizards, aren't we?' he said. 'I expect we could make it go.'

He walked around the circle. The draught from his studded leather robe made the candle-flames waver and the shadows of the thing danced on the wall.

The Senior Wrangler bit his lip. 'Not too certain about that,' he said. 'Looks like it's got more than enough magic in it as it is. Is it . . . er . . . is it breathing or is that just my imagination?'

The Senior Wrangler spun around and waved a finger at the Librarian.

'You built it?' he barked.

The orang-utan shook his head.

'Oook.'

'What'd he say?'

'He said he didn't build it, he just put it together,' said the Dean, without turning his head.

'Ook.'

'I'm going to sit on it,' said the Dean.

The other wizards felt something draining out of their souls and sudden uncertainty sloshing into its place.

'I wouldn't do that if I were you, old chap,' said the Senior Wrangler. 'You don't know where it might take you.'

'Don't care,' said the Dean. He still didn't take his eyes off the thing.

'I mean, it's not of this world,' said the Senior Wrangler.

'I've been of this world for more than seventy years,' said the Dean, 'and it is extremely boring.'

He stepped into the circle and put his hand on the thing's saddle.

It trembled.

EXCUSE ME.

The tall dark figure was suddenly there, in the doorway, and then in a few strides was in the circle.

A skeletal hand dropped on to the Dean's shoulder and propelled him gently but unstoppably aside.

THANK YOU.

The figure vaulted into the saddle and reached out for the handlebars. It looked down at the thing it bestrode.

Some situations you had to get exactly right . . .

A finger pointed at the Dean.

I NEED YOUR CLOTHES.

The Dean backed away.

'What?'

GIVE ME YOUR COAT.

The Dean, with great reluctance, shrugged off his leather robe and handed it over.

Death put it on. That was *better* . . .

NOW, LET ME SEE . . .

A blue glow flickered under his fingers and spread in jagged blue lines, forming a corona at the tip of every feather and bead.

'We're in a cellar!' said the Dean. 'Doesn't that matter?'

Death gave him a look.

NO.

Modo straightened up, and paused to admire his rose-bed, which contained the finest display of pure black roses he'd ever managed to produce. A high magical environment could be useful, sometimes. Their scent hung on the evening air like an encouraging word.

The flower-bed erupted.

Modo had a brief vision of flames and something arcing into the sky before his vision was blotted out by a rain of beads, feathers and soft black petals.

He shook his head, and ambled off to fetch his shovel.

'Sarge?'

'Yes, Nobby?'

'You know your teeth . . .'

'What teeth?'

'The teeth like in your mouth?'

'Oh, right. Yep. What about 'em?'

'How come they fit together at the back?'

There was a pause while Sergeant Colon prodded the recesses of his mouth with his tongue.

'It uh ah—' he began, and untangled himself. 'Interesting observation, Nobby.'

Nobby finished rolling a cigarette.

'Reckon we should shut the gates, sarge?'

'Might as well.'

With the exact minimum amount of effort they swung the huge gates together. It wasn't much of a precaution. The keys had been lost a long time ago. Even the sign 'Thank you for Nott Invading Our City' was barely readable now.

'I reckon we should—' Colon began, and then peered down the street.

'What's that light?' he said. 'And what's making that noise?'

Blue light glittered on the buildings at the end of the long street.

'Sounds like some kind of wild animal,' said Corporal Nobbs.

The light resolved itself into two actinic blue lances.

Colon shaded his eyes.

'Looks like some kind of . . . horse or something.'

'It's coming straight for the gates!'

The tortured roar bounced off the houses.

'Nobby, I don't think it's gonna stop!'

Corporal Nobbs threw himself flat against the wall. Colon, slightly more aware of the responsibilities of rank, waved his hands vaguely at the approaching light.

'Don't do it! Don't do it!'

And then picked himself up out of the mud.

Rose-petals, feathers and sparks fell softly around him.

In front of him, a hole in the gates sparkled blue around the edges.

'That's old oak, that is,' he said vaguely. 'I just hope they don't make us pay for it out of our own money. Did you see who it was, Nobby? Nobby?'

Nobby edged carefully along the wall.

'He . . . he had a rose in his teeth, sarge.'

'Yes, but would you recognize him if you saw him again?'

Nobby swallowed.

'If I didn't, sarge,' he said, 'it'd have to be one hell of an identity parade.'

'I don't like this, Mr Glod! I don't like this!'

'Shut up and steer!'

'But this isn't the kind of road you're supposed to go fast on!'

'That's all right! You can't see where you're going anyway!'

The cart went around a corner on two wheels. It was starting to snow, a weak, wet snow that melted as soon as it hit the ground.

'But we're back in the hills! That's a drop down there! We'll go over the side!'

'You want Chrysoprase to catch us?'

'Giddyup, yah!'

Buddy and Cliff clung to the sides of the cart as it rocked from side to side into the darkness.

'Are they still behind us?' Glod yelled.

'Can't see anything!' shouted Cliff. 'If you stopped the cart, maybe we could hear something?'

'Yeah, but suppose we heard something *really up close*?'

'Giddyup hiyah!'

'Okay, so how about if we throw the money out?'

'FIVE THOUSAND DOLLARS?'

Buddy looked over the edge of the cart. Darkness with a certain gulch-like quality, a certain suggestion of depth, was a few feet from the side of the road.

The guitar twanged gently to the rhythm of the wheels. He picked it up in one hand. Strange how it was never silent. You couldn't silence it even by pressing on the strings heavily with both hands; he'd tried.

There was the harp beside it. The strings were absolutely silent.

'This is daft!' shouted Glod, from the front. 'Slow down! You nearly had us over the side that time!'

Asphalt hauled on the reins. The cart slowed, eventually, to walking pace.

'That's better—'

The guitar screamed. The note was so high that it hit the ears like a needle. The horses jerked nervously in the shafts and then shot forward again.

'Hold them!'

'I am!'

Glod turned around, gripping the back of the seat.

'Throw that thing out!'

Buddy gripped the guitar and stood up, moving his arm back to hurl the thing into the gorge.

He hesitated.

'Throw it out!'

Cliff got to his feet and tried to take the guitar.

'No!'

Buddy whirled it around his head and caught the troll on the chin, knocking him backwards.

'No!'

'*Glod, slow down—*'

And a white horse was overtaking them. A hooded shape leaned over and grabbed the reins.

The cart hit a stone and was airborne for a moment before crashing back down on the road. Asphalt heard the splintering of posts as the wheels smashed into the fence, saw the traces snap, felt the cart swing around . . .

. . . and stop.

So much happened later that Glod never did tell anyone about the sensation he had, that although the cart had definitely wedged itself uncertainly on the edge of the cliff it had *also* plunged on, tumbling over and over, towards the rocks . . .

Glod opened his eyes. The image tugged at him like a bad dream. But he'd been thrown across the cart as it skewed around, and his head was lying on the backboard.

He was looking straight into the gorge. Behind him, wood creaked.

Someone was holding on to his leg.

'Who's that?' he whispered, in case heavier words would send the cart over.

'It's me. Asphalt. Who's that holding on to my foot?'

'Me,' said Cliff. 'What're you holding on to, Glod?'

'Just . . . something my flailing hand happened to snatch at,' said Glod.

The cart creaked again.

'It's the gold, isn't it?' said Asphalt. 'Admit it. You're holding on to the gold.'

'Idiot dwarf!' shouted Cliff. 'Let it go or we're going to die!'

'Letting go of five thousand dollars *is* dying,' said Glod.

'Fool! You can't take it with you!'

Asphalt scrambled for purchase on the wood. The cart shifted.

'It's going to be the other way around in a minute,' he muttered.

'So who,' said Cliff, as the cart sagged another inch, 'is holding Buddy?'

There was a pause while the three counted their extremities and attachments thereto.

'I . . . er . . . think he might have gone over,' said Glod.

Four chords rang out.

Buddy hung from a rear wheel, feet over the drop, and jerked as the music played an eight-note riff on his soul.

Never age. Never die. Live for ever in that one last white-hot moment, when the crowd screamed. When every note was a heartbeat. Burn across the sky.

You will never grow old. They will never say you died.

That's the deal. You will be the greatest musician in the world.

Live fast. Die young.

The music tugged at his soul.

Buddy's legs swung up slowly and touched the rocks of the cliff. He braced himself, eyes shut, and pulled at the wheel.

A hand touched his shoulder.

'No!'

Buddy's eyes snapped open.

He turned his head and looked into Susan's face, and then up at the cart.

'What . . . ?' he said, his voice slurred with shock.

He let go with one hand and fumbled clumsily for the guitar strap, slipping it off his shoulder. The strings howled as he gripped the guitar's neck and flung it into the darkness.

His other hand slipped on the freezing wheel, and he dropped into the gorge.

There was a white blur. He landed heavily on something velvety and smelling of horse sweat.

Susan steadied him with her free hand as she urged Binky upwards through the sleet.

The horse alighted on the road, and Buddy slipped off into the mud. He raised himself on his elbows.

'*You?*'

'Me,' said Susan.

Susan pulled the scythe out of its holster. The blade sprang out; snowflakes that fell on it split gently into two halves without a pause in their descent.

'Let's get your friends, shall we?'

* * *

There was a friction in the air, as if the attention of the world were being focused. Death stared into the future.

OH, BLAST.

Things were coming apart. The Librarian had done his best, but mere bone and wood couldn't take this sort of strain. Feathers and beads whirled away and landed, smoking, in the road. A wheel parted company from its axle and bounced away, shedding spokes, as the machine took a curve almost horizontally.

It made no real difference. Something like a soul flickered in the air where the missing pieces had been.

If you took a shining machine, and shone a light on it so that there were gleams and highlights, and then *took away the machine but left the light* . . .

Only the horse's skull remained. That and the rear wheel, which spun in forks now only of flickering light, and was smouldering.

The thing whirred past Dibbler, causing his horse to throw him into the ditch and bolt.

Death was used to travelling fast. In theory he was already everywhere, waiting for almost anything else. The fastest way to travel is to be there already.

But he'd never been this fast while going this slow. The landscape had often been a blur, but never while it was only four inches from his knee on the bends.

* * *

The cart shifted again. Now even Cliff was looking down into the darkness.

Something touched his shoulder.

HANG ON TO THIS. BUT DON'T TOUCH THE BLADE.

Buddy leaned past.

'Glod, if you let go of the bag I can—'

'Don't even think about it.'

'There's no pockets in a shroud, Glod.'

'You got the wrong tailor, then.'

In the end Buddy grabbed a spare leg and hauled. One at a time, clambering over one another, the Band eased themselves back on to the road. And turned to look at Susan.

'White horse,' said Asphalt. 'Black cloak. Scythe. Um.'

'You can see her too?' said Buddy.

'I hope we're not going to wish we couldn't,' said Cliff.

Susan held up a lifetimer and peered at it critically.

'I suppose it's too late to cut some sort of deal?' said Glod.

'I'm just looking to see if you're dead or not,' said Susan.

'I *think* I'm alive,' said Glod.

'Hold on to that thought.'

They turned at a creaking sound. The cart slid forward and dropped into the gorge. There was a crash as it hit an outcrop halfway to the bottom, and then a more distant thud as it smashed into the rocks. There was a 'whoomph' and orange flames blossomed as the oil in the lamps exploded.

Out of the debris, trailing flame, rolled a burning wheel.

'We would have been in dat,' said Cliff.

'You think maybe we're better off now?' said Glod.

'Yep,' said Cliff. ''cos we're not dyin' in the wreckage of a burning cart.'

'Yes, but she looks a bit . . . occult.'

'Fine by me. I'll take occult over deep-fried any day.'

Behind them, Buddy turned to Susan.

'I . . . think I've worked it out,' she said. 'The music . . . twisted up history, I think. It's not supposed to be in *our* history. Can you remember where you got it from?'

Buddy just stared. When you've been saved from certain death by an attractive girl on a white horse, you don't expect a shopping quiz.

'A shop in Ankh-Morpork,' said Cliff.

'A mysterious old shop?'

'Mysterious as anything. There—'

'Did you go back? Was it still there? Was it in the same place?'

'Yes,' said Cliff.

'No,' said Glod.

'Lots of interesting merchandise that you wanted to pick up and learn more about?'

'Yes!' said Glod and Cliff together.

'Oh,' said Susan, '*that* kind of shop.'

'I knew it didn't belong here,' said Glod. 'Didn't I say it didn't belong here? I *said* it didn't belong here. I *said* it was eldritch.'

'I thought that meant oblong,' said Asphalt.

Cliff held out his hand.

'It's stopped snowing,' he said.

'I dropped the thing into the gorge,' said Buddy. 'I . . . didn't need it any more. It must have smashed.'

'No,' said Susan, 'it's not as—'

'The clouds . . . now *they* look eldritch,' said Glod, looking up.

'What? Oblong?' said Asphalt.

They all felt it . . . a sensation that the walls had been removed from around the world. The air buzzed.

'What's this now?' said Asphalt, as they instinctively huddled together.

'You ought to know,' said Glod. 'I thought you'd been everywhere and seen everything?'

White light crackled in the air.

And then the air became light, white as moonlight but as strong as sunlight. There was also a sound, like the roar of millions of voices.

It said: *Let me show you who I am. I am the music.*

Satchelmouth lit the coach-lamps.

'Hurry up, man!' shouted Clete. 'We want to *catch* them, you know! Hat. Hat. Hat.'

'I don't see that it matters much if they get away,' Satchelmouth grumbled, climbing onto the coach as Clete lashed the horses into motion. 'I mean, they're *away*. That's all that matters, isn't it?'

'No! You saw them. They're the . . . the *soul* of all this trouble,' said Clete. 'We can't let this sort of thing go on!'

Satchelmouth glanced sideways. The thought was

flooding into his mind, and not for the first time, that Mr Clete was not playing with a full orchestra, that he was one of those people who built their own hot madness out of sane and chilly parts. Satchelmouth was by no means averse to the finger foxtrot and the skull fandango, but he'd never murdered anyone, at least on purpose. Satchelmouth had been made aware that he had a soul and, though it had a few holes in it and was a little ragged around the edges, he cherished the hope that some day the god Reg would find him a place in a celestial combo. You didn't get the best gigs if you were a murderer. You probably had to play the viola.

'How about if we leave it right now?' he said. 'They won't be back—'

'Shut up!'

'But there's no point—'

The horses reared. The coach rocked. Something went past in a blur and vanished in the darkness, leaving a line of blue flames that flickered for a little while, then went out.

Death was aware that at some point he would have to stop. But it was creeping up on him that, in whatever dark vocabulary the ghost machine had been envisaged, the words 'slow down' were as inconceivable as 'drive safely'.

It was not in its very nature to reduce speed in any circumstances other than the dramatically calamitous at the end of the third verse.

That was the trouble with Music With Rocks In. It liked to do things its own way.

Very slowly, still spinning, the front wheel rose off the ground.

Absolute darkness filled the universe.

A voice spake: 'Is that you, Cliff?'

'Yup.'

'Okay. Is this me: Glod?'

'Yup. Sounds like you.'

'Asphalt?'

''Sme.'

'Buddy?'

'Glod?'

'And . . . er . . . the lady in black?'

'Yes?'

'Do you know where we are, miss?'

There was no ground under them. But Susan didn't feel that she was floating. She was simply standing. The fact that it was on nothing was a minor point. She wasn't falling because there was nowhere to fall to, or from.

She'd never been interested in geography. But she had a very strong feeling that this place was not locatable on any atlas.

'I don't know where our *bodies* are,' she said, carefully.

'Oh, good,' said the voice of Glod. 'Really? I'm here, but we don't know where my body is? How about my money?'

There was the sound of faint footsteps far away in the darkness. They approached, slowly and deliberately. And stopped.

A voice said: One. One. One, two. One, two.

Then the footsteps went back into the distance.

After a while, another voice said: One, two, three, four—

And the universe came into being.

It was wrong to call it a big bang. That would just be noise, and all that noise could create is more noise and a cosmos full of random particles.

Matter exploded into being, apparently as chaos, but in fact as a chord. The ultimate power chord. Everything, all together, streaming out in one huge rush that contained within itself, like reverse fossils, everything that it was going to be.

And, zigzagging through the expanding cloud, alive, that first wild live music.

This had shape. It had spin. It had rhythm. It had a beat, and you could dance to it.

Everything did.

A voice right inside Susan's head said: *And I will never die.*

She said, aloud: 'There's a bit of you in everything that lives.'

Yes. I am the heart beat. The back beat.

She still couldn't see the others. The light was streaming past her.

'But he threw away the guitar.'

I wanted him to live for me.

'You wanted him to *die* for you! In the wreckage of the cart!'

What is the difference? He would be dead anyway. But to die in music . . . People will always remember the songs he never had the chance to sing. And they will be the greatest songs of all.

Live your life in a moment.

And then live for ever. Don't fade away.

'Send us back!'

You never left.

She blinked. They were still on the road. The air flickered and crackled, and was full of wet snow.

She looked around into Buddy's horrified face.

'We've got to get away—'

He held up a hand. It was transparent.

Cliff had almost vanished. Glod was trying to grip the handle of the money bag, but his fingers were slipping through it. His face was full of the terror of death or, possibly, of poverty.

Susan shouted: 'He threw you away! That's not *fair*!'

A piercing blue light was heading up the road. No cart could move that fast. There was a roar like the scream of a camel who has just seen two bricks.

The light reached the bend, skidded, hit a rock and leapt into space over the gorge.

There was just time for a hollow voice to say OH B—

. . . before it hit the far wall in one great, spreading circle of flame.

Bones bounced and rolled down to the river-bed, and were still.

Susan spun around, scythe ready to swing. But the music was in the air. It had no soul to aim for.

You could say to the universe, this is not *fair*. And the universe would say: Oh, isn't it? Sorry.

You could save people. You could get there in the nick of time. And something could snap its fingers and say, no, it has to *be* this way. Let me tell you how it has to be. This is how the legend has to go.

She reached out and tried to take Buddy's hand. She could feel it, but only as a coldness.

'Can you hear me?' she shouted, above the triumphant chords.

He nodded.

'It's . . . it's like a legend! It *has* to happen! And I can't stop it – how can I kill something like music?'

She ran to the edge of the gorge. The cart was well on fire. They wouldn't appear in it. They would have *been* in it.

'I can't stop it! It's not *fair*!'

She pounded at the air with her fists.

'*Grandfather!*'

Blue flames flickered fitfully on the rocks of the dry river-bed.

A small fingerbone rolled across the stones until it came up against another, slightly larger bone.

A third bone tumbled off a rock and joined them.

In the semi-darkness there was a rattling among the stones and a handful of little white shapes bounced and tumbled between the rocks until a hand, index-finger reaching for the sky, rose into the night.

Then there was a series of deeper, more hollow noises as longer, larger things skipped end on end through the gloom.

* * *

'I was going to make it better!' shouted Susan. 'What's the good of being Death if you have to obey idiot rules all the time?'

BRING THEM BACK.

As Susan turned, a toe-bone hopped across the mud and scuttled into place somewhere under Death's robe.

He strode forward, snatched the scythe from Susan and, in one movement, whirled it over his head and brought it down on the stone. The blade shattered.

He reached down and picked up a fragment. It glittered in his fingers like a tiny star of blue ice.

IT WAS NOT A REQUEST.

When the music spoke, the falling snow danced.

You can't kill me.

Death reached into his robe, and brought out the guitar. Bits of it had broken off, but this didn't matter; the shape flickered in the air. The strings glowed.

Death took a stance that Crash would have died to achieve, and raised one hand. In his fingers the sliver glinted. If light could have made a noise, it would have flashed *ting*.

He wanted to be the greatest musician in the world. There has to be a law. Destiny runs its course.

For once, Death appeared not to smile.

He brought his hand down on the strings.

There was no sound.

There was, instead, a cessation of sound, the end of a noise which Susan realized she'd been hearing all along. All the time. All her life. A kind of sound you never notice until it stops . . .

The strings were still.

There are millions of chords. There are millions of numbers. And everyone forgets the one that is a zero. But without the zero, numbers are just arithmetic. Without the empty chord, music is just noise.

Death played the empty chord.

The beat slowed. And began to weaken. The universe spun on, every atom of it. But soon the whirling would end and the dancers would look around and wonder what to do next.

It's not time for THAT! Play something else!

I CANNOT.

Death nodded towards Buddy.

BUT *HE* CAN.

He threw the guitar towards Buddy. It passed right through him.

Susan ran and snatched it up, holding it out.

'You've got to take it! You've got to play! You've got to start the music again!'

She strummed frantically at the strings. Buddy winced.

'Please!' she shouted. 'Don't fade away!'

The music screamed in her head.

Buddy managed to grasp the guitar, but stood looking at it as if he'd never seen it before.

'What'll happen if he doesn't play it?' said Glod.

'You'll all die in the wreckage!'

AND THEN, said Death, THE MUSIC WILL DIE. AND THE DANCE WILL END. THE WHOLE DANCE.

The ghostly dwarf gave a cough.

'We're getting paid for this number, right?' he said.

YOU'LL GET THE UNIVERSE.

'And free beer?'

Buddy held the guitar to him. His eyes met Susan's.

He raised his hand, and played.

The single chord rang out across the gorge, and echoed back with strange harmonics.

THANK YOU, said Death. He stepped forward and took the guitar.

He moved suddenly, and smashed the thing against a rock. The strings parted, and *something* accelerated away, towards the snow and the stars.

Death looked at the wreckage with some satisfaction.

NOW *THAT'S* MUSIC WITH ROCKS IN.

He snapped his fingers.

The moon rose over Ankh-Morpork.

The park was deserted. The silver light flowed over the wreckage of the stage, and the mud and half-consumed sausages that marked the spot where the audience had been. Here and there it glinted off broken sound traps.

After a while some of the mud sat up and spat out some more mud.

'Crash? Jimbo? Scum?' it said.

'Is that you, Noddy?' said a sad shape hanging from one of the stage's few remaining beams.

The mud pulled some more mud out of its ears. 'Right! Where's Scum?'

'I think they threw him into the lake.'

'Is Crash alive?'

There was a groan from under a heap of wreckage.

'Pity,' said Noddy, with feeling.

A figure emerged out of the shadows, squelching.

Crash half crawled, half fell out of the rubble.

'You'fe got to admit,' he mumbled, because at some stage in the performance a guitar had hit him in the teeth, 'that waf Music Wif Rocks In . . .'

'All right,' said Jimbo, and slithered off his beam. 'But next time, thanks all the same, I'd rather try sex 'n' drugs.'

'My dad said he'd kill me if I took drugs,' said Noddy.

'This is your brain on drugs . . .' said Jimbo.

'No, this is your brain, Scum, on this lump here.'

'Oh, cheers. Thanks.'

'A painkiller'd be favourite right now,' said Jimbo.

A little closer to the lake a heap of sacking slid sideways.

'Archchancellor?'

'Yes, Mr Stibbons?'

'I think someone trod on my hat.'

'So what?'

'It's still on my head.'

Ridcully sat up, easing the ache in his bones.

'Come on, lad,' he said. 'Let's go home. I'm not sure I'm that interested in music any more. It's a world of hertz.'

A coach rattled along the winding mountain road. Mr Clete was standing on the box, whipping the horses.

Satchelmouth got unsteadily to his feet. The cliff edge was so close he could see right down into the darkness.

'I've had just about altogether too much of this by half,' he shouted, and tried to snatch at the whip.

'Stop that! We'll never catch up with them!' shouted Clete.

'So what? Who cares? I *liked* their music!'

Clete turned. His expression was terrible.

'Traitor!'

The butt-end of the whip caught Satchelmouth in the stomach. He staggered back, clutched at the edge of the coach, and dropped.

His outflung arm caught hold of what felt like a thin branch in the darkness. He swung wildly over the drop until his boots got a purchase on the rock, and his other hand gripped a broken fence-post.

He was just in time to see the cart rumble straight on. The road, on the other hand, curved sharply.

Satchelmouth shut his eyes and held on tight until the last scream and crackle and splinter had died away. When he opened them, it was just in time to see a burning wheel bounce down the canyon.

'Blimey,' he said, 'it was lucky there . . . was . . . some . . . thing . . .'

His gaze went up. And up.

YES. IT WAS, WASN'T IT?

Mr Clete sat up in the ruins of the cart. It was clearly very much on fire. He was lucky, he told himself, to have survived that.

A black-robed figure walked through the flames.

Mr Clete looked at it. He'd never believed in this sort of thing. He never believed in *anything*. But if he *had* believed, he would have believed in someone . . . bigger.

He looked down at what he'd thought was his body, and realized that he could see through it, and that it was fading away.

'Oh, dear,' he said. 'Hat. Hat. Hat.'

The figure grinned, and swung its tiny scythe.

SNH, SNH, SNH.

Much later on, people went down into the canyon and sorted out the remains of Mr Clete from the remains of everything else. There wasn't very much.

There were some suggestions that he was some musician . . . some musician had fled the city or something . . . hadn't he? Or was that something else? Anyway, he was dead now. Wasn't he?

No one took any notice of the other things. Stuff tended to congregate in the dry river-bed. There was a horse's skull, and some feathers and beads. And a few pieces of guitar, smashed open like an eggshell. Although it would be hard to say what had flown.

Susan opened her eyes. She felt wind on her face. There were arms on either side of her. They were supporting her while, at the same time, grasping the reins of a white horse.

She leaned forward. Clouds were scudding by, far below.

'All right,' she said. 'And now what happens?'

Death was silent for a moment.

HISTORY TENDS TO SWING BACK INTO LINE. THEY ARE ALWAYS PATCHING IT UP. THERE ARE ALWAYS SOME MINOR LOOSE ENDS . . . I DARE SAY SOME PEOPLE WILL HAVE SOME CONFUSED MEMORIES ABOUT A CONCERT OF SORTS IN THE PARK. BUT WHAT OF IT? THEY WILL REMEMBER THINGS THAT DID NOT HAPPEN.

'But they *did* happen!'

AS WELL.

Susan stared down at the dark landscape. Here and there were the lights of homesteads and small villages, where people were getting on with their lives without a thought of what was passing by, high over their heads. She envied them.

'So,' she said, 'just for an example, you understand . . . what would happen to the Band?'

OH, THEY MIGHT BE ANYWHERE. Death glanced at the back of Susan's head. TAKE THE BOY, FOR EXAMPLE. PERHAPS HE LEFT THE BIG CITY. PERHAPS HE WENT SOMEWHERE ELSE. GOT A JOB JUST TO MAKE ENDS MEET. BIDED HIS TIME. DID IT HIS WAY.

'But he was due in the Drum that night!'

NOT IF HE DIDN'T GO THERE.

'Can you do that? His life was due to end! You said you can't give life!'

NOT ME. YOU MIGHT.

'What do you mean?'

LIFE CAN BE SHARED.

'But he's . . . gone. It's not as though I'm ever likely to see him again.'

YOU KNOW YOU WILL.

'How do you know that?'

YOU'VE ALWAYS KNOWN. YOU REMEMBER EVERYTHING. SO DO I. BUT YOU ARE HUMAN AND YOUR MIND REBELS FOR YOUR OWN SAKE. SOMETHING GOES ACROSS, THOUGH. DREAMS, PERHAPS. PREMONITIONS. FEELINGS. SOME SHADOWS ARE SO LONG THEY ARRIVE BEFORE THE LIGHT.

'I don't think I understood *any* of that.'

WELL, IT HAS BEEN A LONG DAY.

More clouds passed underneath.

'Grandfather?'

YES.

'You're back?'

IT SEEMS SO. BUSY, BUSY, BUSY.

'So I can stop? I don't think I was very good at it.'

YES.

'But . . . you've just broken a lot of laws . . .'

PERHAPS THEY'RE SOMETIMES ONLY GUIDELINES.

'But my parents still died.'

I COULDN'T HAVE GIVEN THEM MORE LIFE. I COULD ONLY HAVE GIVEN THEM IMMORTALITY. THEY DIDN'T THINK IT WAS WORTH THE PRICE.

'I . . . think I know what they mean.'

YOU'RE WELCOME TO COME AND VISIT, OF COURSE.

'Thank you.'

YOU WILL ALWAYS HAVE A HOME THERE. IF YOU WANT IT.

'Really?'

I SHALL KEEP YOUR ROOM EXACTLY AS YOU LEFT IT.

'Thank you.'

A MESS.

'Sorry.'

I CAN HARDLY SEE THE FLOOR. YOU COULD HAVE TIDIED IT UP A BIT.

'Sorry.'

The lights of Quirm glittered below. Binky touched down smoothly.

Susan looked around at the dark school buildings.

'So I've . . . also . . . been here all the time?' she said.

YES. THE HISTORY OF THE LAST FEW DAYS HAS BEEN . . . DIFFERENT. YOU DID QUITE WELL IN YOUR EXAMS.

'Did I? Who sat them?'

YOU DID.

'Oh.' Susan shrugged. 'What grade did I get in Logic?'

YOU GOT AN A.

'Oh, come *on*. I always get A-plus!'

YOU SHOULD HAVE REVISED MORE.

Death swung up into the saddle.

'Just a minute,' said Susan, quickly. She knew she had to say it.

YES?

'What happened to . . . you know . . . changing the fate of one individual means changing the world?'

SOMETIMES THE WORLD NEEDS CHANGING.

'Oh. Er. Grandfather?'

YES?

'Er . . . the swing . . .' said Susan. 'The one down in the orchard. I mean . . . it was pretty good. A good swing.'

REALLY?

'I was just too young to appreciate it.'

YOU REALLY LIKED IT?

'It had . . . style. I shouldn't think anyone else ever had one like it.'

THANK YOU.

'But . . . all this doesn't alter anything, you know. The world is still full of stupid people. They don't use their brains. They don't seem to want to think straight.'

UNLIKE YOU?

'At least I make an effort. For example . . . if I've been here for the last few days, who's in my bed now?'

I THINK YOU JUST WENT OUT FOR A MOONLIGHT STROLL.

'Oh. That's all right, then.'

Death coughed.

I SUPPOSE . . . ?

'Sorry?'

I KNOW IT'S RIDICULOUS, REALLY . . .

'What is?'

I SUPPOSE . . . YOU HAVEN'T GOT A KISS FOR YOUR OLD GRANDAD?

Susan stared at him.

The blue glow in Death's eyes gradually faded, and as the light died it sucked at her gaze so that it was dragged into the eye sockets and the darkness beyond . . .

. . . which went on and on, for ever. There was no word for it. Even *eternity* was a human idea. Giving it a name gave it a length; admittedly, a very long one. But this darkness was what was left when eternity had given up. It was where Death lived. Alone.

She reached up and pulled his head down and kissed the top of his skull. It was smooth and ivory white, like a billiard ball.

She turned and stared at the shadowy buildings in an attempt to hide her embarrassment.

'I just hope I remembered to leave a window open.' Oh, well, nothing for it. She had to know, even if she felt angry with herself for asking. 'Look, the . . . er, the people I met . . . do you know if I ever see—'

When she turned back, there was nothing there. There were only a couple of hoofprints, fading on the cobbles.

There was no open window. She went around to the door and climbed the stairs in the darkness.

'Susan!'

Susan felt herself fading protectively, out of habit. She stopped it. There was no need for that. There had *never* been a need for that.

A figure stood at the end of the passage, in a circle of lamplight.

'Yes, Miss Butts?'

The headmistress peered at her, as if waiting for her to do something.

'Are you all right, Miss Butts?'

The teacher rallied. 'Do you know it's gone mid-night? For shame! And you're out of bed! And that is *certainly* not the school uniform!'

Susan looked down. It was always hard to get every little detail right. She was still wearing the black dress with the lace.

'Yes,' she said, 'that's right.' She gave Miss Butts a bright friendly smile.

'Well, there *are* school rules, you know,' said Miss Butts, but her tone was hesitant.

Susan patted her on the arm. 'I think they're probably more like guidelines, don't you? Eulalie?'

Miss Butts's mouth opened and shut. And Susan realized that the woman was actually quite short. She had a tall bearing and a tall voice and a tall manner, and was tall in every respect except height. Amazingly, she'd apparently been able to keep this a secret from people.

'But I'd better be off to bed,' said Susan, her mind dancing on adrenalin. 'And you, too. It's far too late to be wandering around draughty corridors at your age, don't you think? Last day tomorrow, too. You don't want to look tired when the parents arrive.'

'Er . . . yes. Yes. Thank you, Susan.'

Susan gave the forlorn teacher another warm smile and headed for the dormitory, where she undressed in the dark and got between the sheets.

The room was silent except for the sound of nine girls breathing quietly and the rhythmic muffled avalanche that was Princess Jade asleep.

And, after a while, the sound of someone sobbing and trying not to be heard. It went on for a long time. There was a lot of catching up to do.

Far above the world, Death nodded. You could choose immortality, or you could choose humanity.

You had to do it for yourself.

It was the last day of the term, and therefore chaotic. Some girls were leaving early, there was a stream of parents of various races, and there was no question of there being any teaching. It was generally accepted all round that the rules were relaxed.

Susan, Gloria and Princess Jade wandered down to the floral clock. It was a quarter to Daisy.

Susan felt empty, but also stretched like a string. She was surprised sparks weren't coming from her fingertips.

Gloria had bought a bag of fried fish from the shop in Three Roses. The smell of hot vinegar and solid cholesterol rose from the paper, without the taint of fried rot that normally gave the shop's produce its familiar edge.

'My father says I've got to go home and marry some troll,' said Jade. 'Hey, if there's any good fish bones in there I'll have them.'

'Have you met him?' said Susan.

'No. But my father says he's got a great big mountain.'

'I wouldn't put up with that, if I was you,' said Gloria, through a mouthful of fish. 'This *is* the Century of the Fruitbat, after all. I'd put my foot down right now and say no. Eh, Susan?'

'What?' said Susan, who'd been thinking of something else; then, when everything had been repeated, she said, 'No. I'd see what he was like first. Perhaps he's quite nice. And then the mountain is a bonus.'

'Yes. That's logical. Didn't your dad send you a picture?' said Gloria.

'Oh, yes,' said Jade.

'Well . . . ?'

'Um . . . it had some nice crevasses,' said Jade thoughtfully. 'And a glacier that my father says is permanent even at midsummer.'

Gloria nodded approvingly.

'He sounds a nice boy.'

'But I've always liked Crag from the next valley. Father hates him. But he's working very hard and saving up and he's nearly got enough for his own bridge.'

Gloria sighed. 'Sometimes it's hard to be a woman,' she said. She nudged Susan. 'Want some fish?'

'I'm not hungry, thanks.'

'It's really good. Not stale old stuff like it used to be.'

'No, thanks.'

Gloria gave her another nudge.

'Want to go and get your own, then?' she said, leering behind her beard.

'Why should I do that?'

'Oh, quite a few girls have gone down there today,' said the dwarf. She leaned closer. 'It's the new boy working there,' she said. 'I'd *swear* he's elvish.'

Something inside Susan was plucked and went twang.

She stood up.

'So *that's* what he meant! Things that *haven't happened yet*.'

'What? Who?' said Gloria.

'The shop in Three Roses Alley?'

'That's right.'

The door to the wizard's house was open. The wizard had put a rocking chair in the doorway and was asleep in the sun.

A raven was perched on his hat. Susan stopped and glared at it.

'And have you got any comment to make?'

'Croak croak,' said the raven, and ruffled its feathers.

'Good,' said Susan.

She walked on, aware that she was blushing. Behind her a voice said, 'Hah!' She ignored it.

There was a blur of movement among the debris in the gutter.

Something hidden by a fish wrapper went:

SNH, SNH, SNH.

'Oh yes, very funny,' said Susan.

She walked on.

And then broke into a run.

Death smiled and pushed aside the magnifying lens and turned away from the Discworld to find Albert watching him.

JUST CHECKING, he said.

'That's right, Master,' said Albert. 'I've saddled up Binky.'

YOU UNDERSTAND I WAS JUST CHECKING?

'Right you are, Master.'

HOW ARE YOU FEELING NOW?

'Fine, Master.'

STILL GOT YOUR BOTTLE?

'Yes, Master.' It was on the shelf in Albert's bedroom.

He followed Death out into the stable-yard, helped him into the saddle, and passed up the scythe.

AND NOW I MUST BE GOING OUT, said Death.

'That's the ticket, Master.'

SO STOP GRINNING LIKE THAT.

'Yes, Master.'

Death rode out, but found himself guiding the white horse down the track to the orchard.

He stopped in front of one particular tree, and stared at it for some time. Eventually he said:

LOOKS PERFECTLY LOGICAL TO *ME*.

Binky turned obediently away and trotted into the world.

The lands and cities of it lay before him. Blue light flamed along the blade of the scythe.

Death felt attention on him. He looked up at the universe, which was watching him with puzzled interest.

A voice which only he heard said: So you're a rebel, little Death? Against what?

Death thought about it. If there was a snappy answer, he couldn't think of one.

So he ignored it, and rode towards the lives of humanity.

They *needed* him.

Somewhere, in some other world far away from the Discworld, someone tentatively picked up a musical instrument that echoed to the rhythm in their soul.

It will never die.

It's here to stay.

THE END

THE DISCWORLD NOVELS

The Discworld novels can be read in any order,
but here they are in the order they were published

1. The Colour of Magic ★
2. The Light Fantastic ★
3. Equal Rites 🧙
4. Mort ⧗
5. Sourcery ★
6. Wyrd Sisters 🧙
7. Pyramids ●
8. Guards! Guards! †
9. Eric ★
10. Moving Pictures ●
11. Reaper Man ⧗
12. Witches Abroad 🧙
13. Small Gods ●
14. Lords and Ladies 🧙
15. Men at Arms †
16. Soul Music ⧗
17. Interesting Times ★
18. Maskerade 🧙
19. Feet of Clay †
20. Hogfather ⧗
21. Jingo †
22. The Last Continent ★
23. Carpe Jugulum 🧙
24. The Fifth Elephant †
25. The Truth ●
26. Thief of Time ⧗
27. The Last Hero ●
28. Night Watch †
29. Monstrous Regiment ●
30. Going Postal ⚙
31. Thud! †
32. Making Money ⚙
33. Unseen Academicals ★
34. Snuff †
35. Raising Steam ⚙

Key:
🧙 Witches
† City Watch
★ Wizards
⧗ Death
⚙ Industrial Revolution
● Standalones

Discworld Books for Younger Readers

The Amazing Maurice and His Educated Rodents

Tiffany Aching & the Nac Mac Feegles:
The Wee Free Men
A Hat Full of Sky
Wintersmith
I Shall Wear Midnight
The Shepherd's Crown

Other Books for Younger Readers

The Carpet People
Only You Can Save Mankind
Johnny and the Dead
Johnny and the Bomb
Nation
Dodger

The Bromeliad Trilogy:
Truckers
Diggers
Wings

Other Terry Pratchett Novels

Good Omens (with Neil Gaiman)
The Dark Side of the Sun
Strata

The Long Earth Series (with Stephen Baxter):
The Long Earth
The Long War
The Long Mars
The Long Utopia
The Long Cosmos

A complete list of Terry Pratchett books – including shorter writing, children's books, illustrated titles, graphic novels, comics and plays – can be found at terrypratchettbooks.com